Disgusting
Beautiful
Immoral

by
Guy New York

Disgusting, Beautiful, Immoral

Copyright © 2014 by Guy New York

All rights reserved. This book or any portion thereof may not be reproduced or used in any manner whatsoever without the express written permission of the publisher except for the use of brief quotations in a book review.

2014
ISBN 978-1495274565

QNY
907 Broadway
New York, NY 10010
www.quickienewyork.com

Chapter One

It was a hot May afternoon, and my air conditioner had broken hours ago. But, with the windows open and the music blasting none of it mattered. Nothing mattered at all. I smiled at every pretty girl I passed, and I sang along at the top of my lungs. A few times I even thought about jerking off, but somehow, I never bothered. My mind drifted back to Talia over and over again, and I got hard at least ten times as I pictured her in my bed the night before we left. In spite of my memories, my jeans stayed buttoned as I flew down the winding highway.

Talia and I had a largely chaste relationship, which I'm sure didn't help. If we had gotten around to fucking I would most likely have moved on, but as it stood, I couldn't get the memories out of my head. She climbed into bed with me after our graduation party and we kissed instantly without saying a word. My hands moved up and down her body with all the skill of a drunk, but somehow she forgave me for everything.

"I don't think we should have sex," she finally whispered, as I kissed her neck and slipped my hand beneath her shirt to cup one of her breasts. I nodded and moaned my understanding, thinking that possibly she knew better than I did. Later that night, when we had mostly stopped kissing, I slid my hand inside her boxers and touched her pussy for the first time. She was softer, wetter, and smoother than anyone I had ever felt, and I gasped in spite of myself.

When I woke up she was gone, but there was a sweet note telling me she loved me, and hoped I had a good trip home. She was going back to the west coast, and besides we had only ever just been friends. She had been the one I turned to after my breakup with Claire, and she had been the one to reaffirm my humanity. I had been so lost, stuck in something that wasn't healthy for anyone, and by the time I got out it was almost too late. But, Talia was there, laughing and smiling with a joy that seemed to never leave her. She was smarter than me, prettier than me, and gentler by far. Yet, somewhere in the core of her being she was a solid as an oak, and I was blowing in the wind without a single ounce of control.

Still, it was all fine. The fields were a blur as I sped through Pennsylvania, pushing the old car to eighty. I cut up across the state, through the strangely named Jersey Shore, PA, and finally crossed over into Jersey herself. There were no oil refineries or airports on that side of the state, and, in fact, not much changed except for the traffic. As I drove down Route 80 the cars grew thicker even as the highway grew wider. The horns started long before Patterson, but as I approached the city I didn't care anymore. I looked north as I drove over the George Washington Bridge, and wondered if I should stop home. I instantly decided against it. I hadn't had a home in five years, and there was no point going back now.

Home meant my father, the memory of my childhood dog, and a house so full of newspapers and old copies of National Geographic that I would be hard pressed to find somewhere to sit down. The bridge, on the other hand, was something else. Back in highschool, I ran over it during track practice. We jogged the three miles to Fort Lee and then ran across to 178th Street. We made a U-turn at the bus depot, jogged across the northern side of the bridge, through the woods of the Palisades, and back to our preppy nirvana on the hill. It was the most daring thing I did back then, and I bragged about it to no end.

Looking down the river, I saw the great buildings of Manhattan reaching up to the sky. The Empire State Building in the middle of the island marked Midtown, and all the way south stood the Twin Towers, looming up into the sky like they had burst from the bedrock a century ago. I pulled off the first exit to the West Side Highway and made my way downtown. I had only one destination in mind, although I doubt she knew I was coming. When I looked back across the river, I shuddered with regret, as unable as ever to admit that Jersey had ever been my home.

I pulled off in the West Village, made my way over to Seventh Avenue and found a place to park. The small car could fit most places, and as luck would have it there was a spot on Cornelia Street right around the corner from Jane's apartment. I left all of my earthly belongings in the car except for my backpack, and I stretched when I finally stood on the broken street. My neck was sore, my legs were tight, and my hands exhausted from gripping the wheel. But, I was done.

I locked the car, mostly for show, and walked up to Jane's stoop. I rang her bell and when she answered I simply said, "It's me." A second later she buzzed me in, and I was suddenly so alive with anticipation that I almost couldn't stand it. There is little in the world I love more than seeing old friends after a long absence, and Jane was no exception. In fact, she was one of the old friends I was looking forward to seeing most, and I was practically jumping by the time I reached the fifth floor of her walk-up.

"What the fuck are you doing here?" she asked as soon as the door was open. I grabbed her up in a hug and we stumbled into her place, my backpack falling to the floor at the entrance. It was a tiny studio, with a kitchen almost on top of her bed, but it didn't matter. It could have been smaller than my dorm room and still have been a perfect NYC apartment.

"I just got here," I said, finally putting her down.

"No shit," she said.

"I mean I just got to New York. I drove all fucking day long with the worst hangover ever."

I kicked my shoes off and lay down on her bed with a sigh and she tossed me a box of Marlboro Lights. I opened it and pulled two cigarettes out. I lit them both before handing her one, and she lay down next to me.

"Did you actually graduate?" she asked.

"Of course. I even did fairly well. Not that anyone is ever going to ask to see a college transcript, but it wouldn't be the end of the world. I'm done, I'm never going back, and I couldn't be happier."

She sat on the bed smoking and staring at me with a grin I found joyfully familiar. I took another few drags off my cigarette before crushing it out on the ashtray, and I instantly moved closer to her on the bed with just one thing on my mind. She grinned again and I put my hand on her leg, feeling her strong muscles through her skin-tight jeans as I leaned in closer.

"Your thigh trick won't work on me," she whispered, without making any effort to move my hand as it slid its way up her leg.

"Does it have to?" I asked.

"You're impossible," she said, before I leaned in and kissed her. She tasted like smoke and curry, and everything about her was so damn familiar I almost couldn't handle it. I pulled her closer to me, and she took a final drag off her cigarette before smothering it out as well. She wrapped her legs around me as we kissed, and I reached up under her shirt and undid her bra.

"What am I going to do with you?" she asked.

"Fuck me?"

A second later, her shirt was gone and we were done talking. I kissed her familiar chin and then her familiar neck. Her familiar hands undid my jeans, and her familiar breasts crashed against my bare skin in a moment of joyful reunion. We tore at the rest of our clothes, kicking our jeans off onto the floor until we were entangled in each other's naked bodies for the first time in over a year. I made my way down her body until her legs opened around my neck, and she cried out when my mouth found her.

"Oh fuck, I forgot how good you are at that."

She was wet and delicious, and I ate her pussy until she finally pulled me back to a kiss and shoved a condom into my hand. My fingers replaced my tongue as we rolled over on the bed, and she thrust down against me as my mind slowly shut off. With her help I got the condom on, and then she was on top of me and everything else was gone. The drive vanished, college was a distant memory, and my break-up might never as well have happened. Jane's pussy was the only thing in the world that mattered, and it wasn't until I was close to coming that I realized there were tears in my eyes.

She bit my shoulder and pulled me to her as we fucked, and it was all I could do to hold off the inevitable. I moved my hands over her body until they slid down, not wanting to leave her behind. She knew as well as I did what I was about to do, and her whole body tightened. I pulled her onto me, looking up at her heaving breasts, and her eyes were closed in ecstasy. She pushed down around me as I grabbed her ass in one hand, and when my finger found her tight hole she screamed out. I worked it into her ass as we fucked, and she bit her lip so hard I thought she might bleed.

It only took a few minutes of me fingering her ass for her to start coming, and I was right behind her. I threw her onto her back, her body still trembling, and I pistoned in and out of her for all I was worth.

"Fuck me," she moaned. "Make me come, Thomas. Do it."

And then I was gone, exploding into the condom as she stared into my eyes and tightened her legs around my body. I kissed her mouth between gasps, and my own ass tightened as I came over and over again. She brushed my hair from my face, and I kissed her chin as we stared into each other's eyes. I touched her cheek as I reached down and squeezed the condom around the base of my cock before finally pulling out.

I got up and walked to the bathroom where I dropped the condom in the toilet and pulled a wash cloth off the shelf. I ran some warm water, wet the rag, and made my way back to the bed. She had another cigarette lit, and I gently wiped the sweat off her body. She shook her head at me as I did it, but she didn't stop me. I finally tossed the rag onto the floor and she reached a hand out so I could take a drag off her smoke.

"I forgot that you know that thing about my ass," she said.

"Jane, everyone knows that thing about your ass."

"Fuck you."

"I am so happy to be here," I said, leaning back and staring at the smoke as it left my mouth. "And not just so I can sit here naked in bed after fucking your brains out. I just had to get the hell out of Indiana. I don't know. I needed old friends again, you know? I needed some city and something other than politically-correct wannabe lesbians arguing with me about semantics. Fuck, it's good to see you again."

"You so did not fuck my brains out. It was nice, but brains are definitely still here. Why do I always say yes to you?"

I lit another cigarette and she nestled in under my arm as we shared it. The wind through the window was warm and our bodies were too. I kissed her hair and she ran her fingers up my leg, both of us lost in our own thoughts. My few minutes of blissful forgetting were gone though, and I was back to thinking full time no matter how hard I tried. But, it was fine. Everything was going to be okay. I was back in the city and Jane was naked and smoking;

the world was as it should be.

"My boyfriend will be here in an hour."

"I didn't know you had a boyfriend!" I said in real surprise. "Is he a good one?"

"I don't know. He's cute and smart and has more money than god. Which is sort of a problem, but so far it's been good. He's a doctor. Like a real doctor. I like him and he likes me, and he's even good to me. He buys me flowers for no reason and helps me study. I don't know. It might last a few more months."

"Sounds terrible, Jane. How can you live with it?"

"I'm sure I'll fuck it up sooner or later."

"Whatever. Anyone lucky enough to have you even for a night is a lucky man."

"Oh, 'cause you've always wanted to be with me."

I looked at her, but she was staring out the window again. Neither of us moved, and there was nothing to say. We had been friends forever and fucking for years, but it had never crossed my mind to ask her out. What we had was something else. It was beautiful and perfect, and anything we said about it would just make it bad. So, I kissed her head and smoked as we looked out onto the brick wall of the next apartment; I smelled the warm smells of spring from the garden far below.

"Do you have somewhere to stay?" she finally asked.

I just shook my head, because it had never occurred to me that I wouldn't stay there.

"I could go home, I guess."

"Yeah, that's what you'll do. Why don't you give me a few hours with the boy, then come back. He never sleeps here because he say there's not enough room for two people to breathe. He'll be here till one or two, but then you can come back. Okay?"

"That would be awesome," I said. "Jane, it's so good to see you, you know that?"

"Yeah, yeah. You're just lucky I let you fuck me this time. You show up after a goddamn year without even an e-mail in between, and I let you in and…"

She trailed off as she lit another smoke, and I finally stood up and gathered my clothes. I pulled on my jeans and t-shirt along with my socks and belt. I finally found my shoes and jacket and walked back to the bed. She was still sitting there naked, and I instantly wanted her again. I wanted to hold her and kiss her, and most of all I wanted to see if she was interested in having something other than a finger up her perfect ass. Fuck, it was time to go.

"Get out of here and don't come back until at least two, okay?"

She stood up and walked to the edge of the bed. Standing on the mattress she was taller than me, and I looked up into her eyes. I kissed her, stole a drag, and then kissed her again. I ran my hand down her back and squeezed her ass, marveling again at her naked body.

"God you are so fucking perfect," I whispered.

She slapped me playfully and pushed me away.

"Get out of here before I throw you out, you little pervert."

She laughed as she walked me to the door, but I was smart enough not to push it. I kissed her one last time in the hallway.

"See you around two."

"Go!" she said.

Chapter Two

The city changes slowly enough that sometimes I don't notice. As I walked from Cornelia Street over to West 4th and then towards the south end of Washington Square Park, I looked at every bar, restaurant, and shop to see what I remembered. That one was there last time, and that one, too, but wasn't there another bar here before? I could hardly remember a drunk night in high school, but I was almost positive. Maybe they shut it down after letting in too many kids like me.

The park on the other hand was changing even slower. Smoke, smoke, smoke, the guys said as they passed me by, and I smiled and shook my head every time. Out of all the places to buy weed in NYC, Washington Square Park was not high on my list. The only time we smoked anything someone bought there it was a disaster. No one got high and two of us got sick. Maybe we just didn't know the right guy to talk to.

The fountain was flowing when I walked passed, and a bunch of college students sat around the rim staring at the water while a drum circle went on behind them. For a moment, I wondered if it was the same drum circle as the last time I was there. Then I wondered if possibly the drum circle never stopped. Could it be that the park has a never ending drum circle that's been going on for years? It was a terrifying thought. After all that time at a liberal arts college, the number of drum circles I needed to hear again was exactly zero.

I walked quickly through the park, past University Place, Broadway, and Cooper Union where I cut south a block to Seventh Street. I was in the mood for a bar, and I was done with my years at divey Indiana saloons, even if pitchers of beer there were only four dollars. I was done with rednecks, football players, and country boys, and I needed some rock and roll and a few shots of something nasty. I passed McSorley's and Burp Castle before finally reaching Blue and Gold. It was quiet, being a Monday night and all, but it didn't matter. By 10 p.m. the bar would be full of other kids my age all looking to get wasted, play pool, and most likely hook up with a friend of a friend. I had more than six hours to kill, and all of that was right up my alley.

I grabbed a beer and a shot from the bar and found an empty booth towards the back by the pool table. I put my feet up on the bench and looked out as the bar slowly began to fill up. When the Lucky Strike girl came around the second time I finally waved to her and filled out her damn form. She smiled and handed me a pack of cigarettes and a black plastic lighter with their logo on it. I packed it hard against my open palm then tore open the top. I don't normally smoke unless I'm with someone like Jane, but fuck it. I was sitting at a bar by myself and a hot girl was handing out free packs of smokes. You only live once.

"Dude! When did you get back?"

I looked up from my beer to see a couple sliding into the seat across from me. They each had a can of PBR in hand and it took me a few seconds before I recognized them.

"Martin?" I asked. "What the hell are you guys doing here?"

"Us? We live like three blocks away. Are you done? I mean, graduated, grown up, adult, all that bullshit?"

"Yeah, I just got here today. I mean, I drove all fucking day and went over to Jane's for a bit. I'm just killing time until I crash. Hey Katie, how's it going?" I said to the girl sitting next to him.

She was staring at the table and waving her hands over the scarred wood very slowly. Her eyes were glazed over, but her smile was as pretty as ever. She finally looked up at me and grinned.

"Hey, you." Her voice was slow and the syllables dragged out. "Welcome home…"

"She's totally high," Martin said.

"Yeah, I'm super high," she said. "I didn't know the brownies were pot brownies."

"She's fucked up," he said again.

"I ate four of them. They were so good."

"You two just out burning off her buzz then?" I asked.

"Yeah man, we're having a fucking party at our place though.

It's sweet. We moved in last month and it's totally killer. We have three bedrooms and a huge living room on the second floor over on 10th Street. I had to pick up some smokes and more beer before it got too late, so I dragged this one along to see if the walk might help her sober up. You wanna come back with us?"

Five minutes later, Martin and I were walking up First Avenue with a swaying girl in between us, and my night was looking up all around. I hadn't seen Martin in at least a year, but he used to hang out with one of my high school friends who went to NYU. We partied whenever I was in town, and he always had something going on. There was always a bar, a show, or a party somewhere, and Martin could tell you in three minutes if it was worthwhile.

Their place was, in fact, awesome. We walked up the stairs and into a full-blown party of people I half remembered, and there was nothing collegiate about it. The apartment was full of real furniture, real art on the walls, and beds in actual frames. It made a full circle around the staircase in the middle of the building, with a huge open room in the front with a bar, a giant television, and four windows looking out onto 10th Street. People were lounging around with drinks in their hands, and music was blasting from speakers hanging high on the walls above the TV.

I lost the two of them almost as soon as I arrived, but I recognized a few other faces, so I made the rounds until I could get a drink. There was a bar in one corner of the living room, and a cute girl in cargo pants and a tank top handed me a gin and tonic. These kids were fucking fancy, and that was just fine with me. After cheap beer, country music, and Arby's, I was perfectly happy with a party that had real glasses and a table with more than three legs.

I mingled my way through the bedrooms until I found the back room where Martin told me Rachel lived. I knew her only slightly better than anyone else at the party, but she gave me a big hug and sat me down in the circle on her floor. She was sitting with two other girls and a dude with long hair and a tattoo of a spider on one arm. All three girls were in short dresses, sitting cross legged on the floor, but other than Rachel I didn't know either of them. They handed me a huge bong, and I took a small hit before passing it back around.

"This is Thomas," Rachel said, pointing the pipe in my direction with a cough. I waved and they smiled at me as I settled into my spot on the floor.

"Have you ever been tied up?" the red-headed girl next to me asked. They all looked at me expectantly, and I realized I had sat down in the middle of a conversation.

"Is this Never-Have-I-Ever?" I asked.

"No, we're just curious. She's been asking dumb questions all night," Rachel said.

"I used to tie up my ex-girlfriend, but she never tied me up," I told them.

They all stopped and stared at me, the smoke thick in the air, and I wasn't sure if it was out of disbelief or something else. The look on the guy's face was especially skeptical.

"What did you tie her up with?" he asked.

"It wasn't professional or anything. I mean we usually used a scarf or a tie or something. Occasionally my belt, I guess. How did this come up?" I asked.

"Wait, you tied your girlfriend up with a belt? Then what did you do?" The redhead leaned in as she asked, and I wasn't sure if I was going to get a lecture or a kiss. I had spent most of my drive trying not to think about Claire, but if there was one thing worth remembering it was the sex.

"You know..." I said, nodding my head.

"What does that mean?" She asked. "'You know?' I don't know! You tied her up, and then what?"

"Then we fucked. I mean sometimes we wrestled a bit or she kicked me and struggled, but in the end we always just fucked until her arms got tired and I untied her."

"I used to sit on this guy's face."

We all looked over to the girl next to Rachel. She was the smallest of the three with big eyes, cute bangs, and and a smile that was half surprise. She had blurted it out so quickly I almost wasn't sure I heard it, and when we all looked at her as she turned so bright red it was almost shocking.

"He begged me for it. I didn't tie him up or anything, but he would lie on the bed and I'd just sit on him. Sometime we did it for like an hour." She looked down at the floor, her fingers tugging on the hem of her dress.

"And he would…" The redhead began, making a gesture with two fingers and her tongue.

She just nodded and her expression seemed to move into something closer to fond reminiscing.

"Was this before or after actual sex?" Rachel asked. "I mean, was he like, going to town after you two already did it?"

"No! There was no sex," she said. "I mean, that was kind of sex, but he didn't want anything else. It was weird actually, but that was all that we ever did. I'd go over to his place and he'd just lie down on the bed or the floor. Sometimes I wouldn't even take my clothes off. I went to Vassar so it's not like I wear panties anyway. I'd just lift up my skirt and kneel over him. He would start to whimper when I got close, and then he'd just lick me until I came or got bored."

"He was never the one to stop either. Once I wanted to see how long he would go, and it lasted for nearly two hours. I came like six times, but I got fucking tired! I finally rolled over and lay there next to him. I even asked him if he wanted to fuck me that time, but he just smiled and said as long as he was making me happy, he was happy. It was sweet even if it was super weird."

"And you broke up with him?" The spider dude was laughing after a long bong hit, but I was thinking the same thing.

"Pussy eating is all nice and shit, but it's not enough for a good relationship. Sometimes a girl needs some dick." Her blush was back again, but Rachel and the redhead nodded their heads in affirmation.

"I totally need to get laid," she said, finally letting go of the fabric between her fingers. "Seriously. I haven't had sex in like a month."

"It's been weeks for me," Rachel added.

"I'm celibate by choice," Spider said. "I mean, Zen and I have been doing this intense meditation recently, and we're not supposed to have sex for a few months. I'm channeling all of my energy into my practice, and it's been really awesome. I can, like, totally feel the chi moving through my body."

"How 'bout you, Thomas? When was the last time you got laid?" Rachel was always direct.

I looked around the room and suddenly felt like the asshole. There was nothing to say other than the truth, but I still felt dumb. I hadn't gotten much since my breakup with Claire, other than one night of making out with Talia, but none of that mattered.

"A few hours ago," I whispered.

"What?" The redhead stared at me in disbelief. "Fuck you. That's so not fair. I'm going into the other room to see if any cute guys have showed up. This is bullshit."

She got up and left as Spider packed another bowl, and the rest of us moved in closer with drinks in hand. We talked for a long time, smoking, drinking, and laughing about nothing in particular, and the party got louder, quieter, drunker, higher, and more desperate. When I got up to piss a few hours later, I saw the redhead making out with a guy in the kitchen. I sat back down just as Spider and Rachel got up to go smoke on the fire escape, and it was just me and Kelly the face-sitter left.

I leaned back against the bed and she moved over next to me and stole a sip of my drink. The bartender was still making gin and tonics and they were absolutely delicious. It took me a few moments to realize she was staring at me, and I wondered what she was thinking. Her face didn't tell me much, but I couldn't look away. Finally, she leaned in and whispered:

"Did you really tie that girl up?"

"Yeah," I nodded.

"And she struggled and kicked as you tore off her clothes?"

"Basically," I said.

"And then you fucked her? You held her down, her hands tied above her head, and you fucked her. Did she stop fighting then?"

"Sometimes. I guess it depended on her mood," I said. "I think it turned her on most to never stop fighting. She would swear at me and scratch as we fucked, and if I moved to untie her she would try to escape."

She stared at me, but the look in her eyes was much clearer. Her short dress had ridden up as she tucked her knees under her arms, and I had to resist trying to confirm her status as a Vassar girl. She was shorter than Rachel by at least a foot, and her feet were smaller than I thought possible. I pictured her kneeling over my face as I opened my mouth between her legs, and in spite of all the drinking I had done, I found myself getting hard in my jeans.

"That is so fucking hot," she said. Kelly was so close to me by then that we were touching, but neither of us moved a hand. She leaned her head down onto my shoulder for a brief moment before turning around and pulling a small blanket off the bed behind us. She covered both our legs, and I stared at her, unsure of what she was doing. Even when her hands vanished beneath the blanket I was still unsure of what was happening.

"Tell me more," she whispered, her breathing faster and her voice deeper. "Tell me about fucking her all tied up. Tell me what you did to her."

My hand brushed her bare leg, but rather than move it away she pressed against me. Her other foot was pulled up beneath her, but this one was almost on my lap, which meant that just beneath the blanket she was practically naked. She placed my hand on the inside of her thigh, still looking into my eyes, and I finally started talking.

"One time she told me to grab her in the hallway. She said she didn't even want to know it was me when I pulled her into my room. I was scared someone would see us, but it didn't matter at that point. I always did whatever she asked, and there was no way I was going to back out. I waited until she was almost at my door before I grabbed her."

Kelly moved my hand further up her thigh until my fingers were just where she wanted them. I looked at her in surprise when she pressed my hand against her wet pussy, but she blushed again and closed her legs around me, holding me in place.

"Keep going," she whispered.

"I threw her on the bed, and locked the door behind me, but she was up by the time I turned around. She screamed at me and asked me what the fuck I wanted with her, but I had her back on the bed a second later with my belt around her wrists. I tied it to the headboard and knelt over her, holding her legs still as I tore her shirt off. She struggled and tried to kick, but I pulled off her jeans, and then finally ripped her panties off with my bare hands."

Kelly's breathing grew faster and faster, and she was so wet I didn't know what to do. I wanted to fuck her or kiss her, but I couldn't stop. She moaned into my ear, but her entire body tensed up whenever I stopped for even a second.

"I was so fucking hard," I whispered, my fingers moving in

and out of her as she circled her clit with her own. "As soon as I saw her lying there naked on the bed, struggling and spitting, I was as hard as rock."

"And then you fucked her?" She was right in my ear, her lips against my skin. "Then you just slid your big cock inside her even as she told you no, right? Please tell me that's what you did. Please?"

I quickly moved her so she was between my legs with her back to me, and I opened her thighs again and brought my hand right back to her pussy. I pushed her hair away from her ear as I reached both arms around her, and opened her as widely as I could.

"I leaned down over her, my clothes still on, but my cock hard in my hand. I told her I was going to fuck her as I rubbed against the lips of her pussy, and she tried to bite me. I kissed her mouth, as I opened her legs wider—just like this—and then I finally did it. She screamed again, but she clenched around me all the same. And then I just fucked her as hard as I could. I slapped her face and slammed into her without stopping."

"And she never stopped, right?" The small woman between my legs was breathing so quickly I thought she might pass out. My fingers were still inside her and she was drenching my hand and the carpet beneath us. She lifted her ass off the floor, pushing harder against me even as she leaned back and kissed the side of my face. "She didn't stop, and you kept fucking her. You fucked her so hard, and…"

"And she kept trying to get away," I said. "She fought until suddenly she was coming so much she couldn't hide it any more. I didn't stop as she shook around me, but I kissed her mouth and pulled her to me until I was as deep inside her as I could go."

"Oh fuck, I'm coming," she moaned, my fingers now a blur as she started to shake in my lap, clenching and bucking her hips as I wrapped my arms around her. "Tell me you came inside her.

Tell me you came in her slutty, little cunt."

"So much," I said, my lips on her ear and neck. I pulled her to me, my cock hard against her back as she came. "I filled her over and over again, and I've never come so hard in my life."

Kelly finally collapsed in my arms, her legs going slack and her shoulder slumping down against me. I was still throbbing, and it was all I could not to jerk myself off against her ass. It had been months since I wanted anyone that badly, but her breathing slowed down and she moved my hands to her legs as she returned to the world. She ran her fingers up and down my arm, and I continued to kiss her hair and hold her tightly.

Eventually, she turned just enough to look me in the eye. She leaned in and kissed me on the lips, and it was a long, slow kiss with just enough of her mouth for me to know she tasted divine.

"Thanks for the story," she whispered. She folded the blanket, flattened her dress, and stood up. She stared at me for a moment longer, then walked out of the room and into the kitchen as I sat there alone, adjusting my hard on on through my tight jeans.

Chapter Three

When we woke up the next morning I was hard against Jane's ass. I had my arms wrapped around her and her hair was a mess in my face. She had closed the window before I got back to her apartment, but it was still chilly inside and her thick blankets were down at the foot of the bed.

"Get your cock away from my ass," she mumbled, as she rolled away from me. She slowly sat up in the bed before kicking her feet over the edge and standing. Jane stumbled to the bathroom, not bothering to close the door as she peed, and then came back to bed. Her t-shirt came just to mid-thigh, and she tugged it down as she climbed back in next to me, this time facing me.

"You came home at 3:30," she said.

"I didn't want to bother you and your fancy doctor boyfriend."

"He left at 12," she said.

"How was I supposed to know that? Besides, I was at a party in the East Village trying to make out with a half-sized girl in a short skirt. I lost track of time."

"I've been on the other end of you trying to make out with someone. Did she survive?"

"She was fine. I'm the one who sat there with a raging hard-on while she got off. But, whatever. It was a fun party. Martin has this huge apartment now on 10th Street and it was good to see people. Rachel was there."

"I think he wants to marry me."

She was leaning on one arm looking at me, and I didn't know what to say. Jane could say the most insane thing with a completely calm voice, and I had no idea if she was serious or not. She kept looking at me though, and all I could do was nod. He wanted to marry her. Jane, who never had a boyfriend for longer than a few weeks had a guy ready to get down on one knee. This was a girl who's longest relationship had been with a guy she met on IRC who lived somewhere in Florida, and now she was getting ready to marry some rich doctor from Columbia?

"What are you going to say?" I asked.

"I don't know. I need coffee."

She got up and walked the few feet to the kitchen, and I couldn't help staring at her ass. Every time she took a step - or bent over - her shirt rode up, and her round cheeks looked back at me. It was crazy that fewer than fifteen hours ago I was inside her and she was kissing me, but now she suddenly felt like a world away. She pulled the coffee down from the shelf, scooped it into the filter, and poured the water into the basin. Her arms moved slowly, and the entire time I watched her in silence.

Finally, it was too much.

"What if he wants a big wedding with a white dress and girls in pink and all that shit? I mean, what if he wants to get married in a church and watch you throw flowers? Jane, this is crazy."

"All I said was I think he wants to marry me. He didn't propose or anything last night, and he certainly didn't bring it up. It's just a feeling."

She didn't move from the counter as the coffee started to bubble, and I finally sat up and opened the window. The room smelled like sex and cigarettes, and the added smell of coffee was starting to wake me up, too. I pulled out a Lucky Strike and lit one as I leaned out the window enough to smell the morning air.

"Since when do you have your own pack?" she asked.

"The girl was giving them away at Blue and Gold."

"I hate that bar. They are so fucking cheap. I've bought like six rounds there without them once buying me one back - it's bullshit."

"Yeah, well that's where I bumped into Martin."

She poured me a cup of coffee when it was done and brought it to me on the bed. She lit her own cigarette and we sat there smoking in silence for a long while. I was still thinking about the girl between my legs the night before and how soft her pussy was when suddenly I was reminded of Talia. Was one softer than the other? Wetter? Smoother? The girl last night had a completely shaved cunt, which totally reminded me of my ex, but Talia's hair had been as soft as her skin. I had run my fingers through it, tugging ever so gently, but last night was a different thing. Kelly, I reminded myself. The girl's name was Kelly.

"I just had a shitty break up, so I suppose I may not be the best person to give marriage advice. I didn't mean to be a dick," I said, hoping it sounded sincere.

"How long ago?" she asked. I hadn't seen Jane since long

before Claire and I even started dating, so the breakup wasn't really on the horizon.

"Six weeks or so. Maybe two months, I don't know. It ended less with a bang and more with a fizzle, but it still sucked. I guess it was the relationship that sucked more than anything, although I'm still totally in love with her. Or lust. Or something, I don't know. My head is messed up, but whatever. It's fine, and I have no right to be complaining."

"Why was it so messed up?" she asked.

"I don't know. I mean, I do know, but I don't want to talk about it. At least the sex was really good. I mean, like amazingly good. It was everything else that didn't work." I looked down into my coffee and stared at the dark liquid for a long time. It was hard to even think about Claire, but after last night some memories would be difficult to get out of my head. Kelly had totally used me and then left me without hardly saying a word. And I let her go, just like I always do. I got her off and she walked away. What a fucking brilliant girl.

"I didn't tell him," Jane said, pulling me back to the present. "I thought about it, but there was no point. How would I explain you anyway?"

"Tell him what?"

"About yesterday. About you. I didn't tell my boyfriend that I fucked you an hour before he came over to cook me dinner. What the hell is wrong with me? I don't even feel guilty. It's like you don't count or something. Maybe I've known you for too long, but it doesn't feel like cheating to me."

"Thanks, Jane."

"I'm serious. I did think about telling him, but he was so sweet all night. He cooked and brought wine and talked about taking me to Italy over the summer for a few weeks. Even the sex was nice. And I don't mean that in a bad way. It was good."

"The sex was nice. And good? Jane that sounds like a mediocre review at best."

"It's not always about the sex, Thomas" she said. "He's different. He's nice and handsome and he's a fucking amazing cook. I like being with him. It feels easy. I don't have to worry about what I say or think about what not to say. I don't have to second guess myself or do much of anything. He takes care of me, and you know what? If he asks me, I'm totally saying yes. Why the hell not? I could do a hell of lot worse than a handsome doctor who pampers the shit out me."

Jane stood up and finished her coffee in one gulp. I lay back down on the bed and watched as she walked to the bathroom. A few seconds later, I heard the shower start, and I pictured her standing naked under the hot water. I reached into my boxers and smiled. There was no way I was going to pass that up.

Once again she hadn't bothered to close the door, and I pulled back the curtain and climbed into the shower behind her without a word. She shook her head but didn't say anything as I started to soap up her back. The water was nearly scalding, but it felt amazingly good, especially after being in the car for so long the day before. I rubbed soap into her skin, massaging her shoulders, but my eyes never left her ass. I kissed the top of her head and pulled her closer to me as I reached my hands down to the backs of her thighs. Still covered in soap, I slid them up until I cupped her ass in both hands. I was painfully hard, and my whole body was trembling.

"I'm not going to fuck you again, Thomas."

"I want this," I said squeezing her harder. She didn't move away, but she didn't lean back either. I pulled her to me, my cock between the cheeks of her ass and my arms around her. "I've wanted this ass since the day I met you, Jane. Please?"

"If I'm not letting you fuck me, I'm definitely not letting you fuck my ass. Come on, don't be a dick."

"Jane, I can't help it. I dream about this ass. I'd write poetry about it if I could, and you're driving me crazy. You came so hard with my finger inside it yesterday, imagine what you would do with my cock inside you? God, I want you."

"Yeah, and I want a million dollars and a fucking pony, now piss off." She turned around and flicked shampoo in my face. She was smiling and laughing, but she was deadly serious. I leaned back against the cold wall, my hand on my dick as she stared at me, and I slowly started to jerk off.

"It's perfect," I whispered.

"And you don't get it."

She leaned back, her hair under the faucet and her breasts pulled back with her arms stretched over her head. She had trimmed her pussy since we fucked the day before, but it didn't matter. All I wanted was for her to turn around. My hand moved faster as she washed her hair, and I didn't think it would take me very long. After last night I was so close to coming I was surprised I was still standing.

"Enjoy," she said, pulling back the curtain and stepping out of the tub. My hand didn't stop as she grabbed a towel and wrapped it around her head. I pushed the curtain open just enough for me to see her, and when she bent over the sink I was done. I pictured myself deep inside her ass and suddenly I was blowing my load all over the shower, my legs trembling beneath me. A second later Jane pulled the curtain back, the towel now wrapped around her body, and stared at me. I was still hard.

"You are such a fucking pervert. And you know what?" She reached a hand in and raised one finger. I watched as she brought it down to my cock and swiped a little bit of my come onto it. She raised it to my lips and without even thinking, I opened my mouth.

"You will never fuck this ass," she said.

And then she was gone, and I was standing there like a douchebag with my mouth open and my dick growing soft. I really should have asked her out three years ago. I'm a fucking idiot. I finally got out, dried myself off and wrapped the towel around my waist. I took a deep breath, adjusted my cock, and walked back into the apartment.

We spent another hour getting dressed, drinking more coffee, and smoking in bed, but true to her word we did not fuck again. I tried to apologize, but she laughed at me and told me I was being dumb. If she didn't know what I was like after six years then she was the stupid one.

"Besides," she said. "I like the fact that you want something from me that you can't have. It's about time the tables were turned on you."

"Jane, I…"

"Yeah, exactly. You can stare at this ass all you want, but you will never get it."

"Now you're just teasing me."

"I'm always teasing you. Anyway, what are you doing today? Do you have somewhere to live or am I supposed to put you up in my tiny apartment until you get a job? Because I don't think I want to explain that to the boyfriend any time soon. It's bad enough I sent him home last night."

"I thought he didn't like to stay here," I said.

"Yeah, well I lied. It's not like it's his favorite, but he would have stayed if I hadn't thrown him out to make room for your sorry face."

Just when I opened my mouth to answer her, the phone rang. She stared at me for a moment longer before walking over to the counter and picking it up.

"It's for you," she said, handing it to me.

"What?"

"I don't know, but it is."

I took the phone from her and said hello.

"Dude, it's Martin. Good to see you last night, but listen I got a question. You just got back, right? Do you have a place to stay yet?"

"Jane was just asking me the same thing. How did you know I was here?"

"You told me you were crashing at Jane's, but listen, that's good. Did you meet Diana last night? The redhead that was making out with Jose in the kitchen? She's moving out. Her mom called this morning and she needs to go home for some emergency thing, and she's just leaving. She already has half her shit in garbage bags, and I thought if you need a place to stay it might work out. We can't really do this place with only two of us."

"You want me to move in with you and Rachel?" Jane just shook her head as I talked, and I could tell she was trying not to laugh.

"Yeah, dude. I mean, if you want. It's five hundred a month. Plus utilities."

"Are you serious? How did you find that place? I mean, yeah, I can do that. I don't have a fucking job yet, but I can get one. For five hundred a month I can definitely get a job. When can I move in?"

"Whenever you want. She'll be gone in like an hour or two. Seriously, it's a hurricane in there right now. But, Thomas, there's one other thing."

"What's that?" I asked.

"Rent is due today. Is that cool?"

"I'll see you in a couple hours. With cash."

Chapter Four

It didn't take long for me to move into Diana's old room. She had packed everything she owned into a 1974 Volvo, which meant that she left a desk, a garbage can, and a four-poster canopy bed with a mattress and boxspring. I drove my car across town, and within a couple of hours the entire contents of my old room were in the new apartment. I stacked my clothes in boxes until I could get a dresser, and hung a few things on the walls. I didn't have a lot of art, but I had a few prints I bought in Japan during my semester abroad, and some paintings that my mother did years ago. It wasn't a big room, but that was just as well.

I cashed my graduation checks, paid Martin, and it was done. I had a room and two roommates, if you didn't count Katie who apparently lived there ninety percent of the time. I was back in New York, and if I didn't have to drive through Indiana again, I was going to be a happy boy. The four of us sat in the living room for a few hours after the craziness of moving was done, and it was a strange feeling. I don't know what I expected when I left school the day before, but this was not it. We talked and chatted, mostly catching up on the more mundane details of our lives.

Martin was still promoting parties and clubs, but he had a day job at an internet company that was supposed to revolutionize payment processing. He was gone most of the time, except when he was throwing a party at the apartment, which apparently was a regular thing. Rachel had just been hired as the personal assistant to the art director of a new magazine called *Lucky*, and she was terrified and excited all at the same time. She started in one week. Katie was still in school for another two years, which meant she was at the apartment a lot during the day, and, of course, at all of the parties. It was unclear to me if she and Martin were dating, but whatever they called it, she was in his room most of the time.

I spent the first week looking for jobs, trying to find old friends, and visiting my favorite bars and restaurants. I talked to Jane on the phone a couple of times, but she was working twelve-hour shifts at the coffee shop, and we didn't get around to meeting up again. Rachel tagged along for many of my outings, and she showed me where the best bodega was along with the pizza place, the laundromat, and the liquor store. I dragged her into Decibel for some fancy sake one night, and she took me to the Holiday Cocktail Lounge where we got so drunk with the bartender we almost didn't make it home.

My new room fit me fine, although, since I hadn't bothered to take down the canopy, my roommates had taken to calling me Princess when I wasn't listening. I didn't have any windows, since it was in the middle of the apartment, and you had to walk through my room to get to the kitchen, but it didn't matter. For five hundred bucks I was willing to take what I could get, and besides, I found that I liked the company. My solo drive had nearly killed all my brain cells and more time alone meant the more time I had to think about Claire. More time to remember her taunting me and teasing me. I moved from being hard to being in tears without much notice.

I finally found a bartending job a few days a week only four blocks from the apartment. It was a little bar called Saints, and they were getting in on the craft beer craze. They had eight taps which they changed out all the time, and while they served a few select whiskeys, most of the patrons just drank beer. I was willing to work whenever they needed me, and because I was so close, the owners liked that I could be there in five minutes if someone bailed on them. It was a friendly place, and while my bosses were bigger beer snobs than I thought possible, it didn't take me long to feel like I fit in.

The second afternoon I was there, Rachel walked in and sat

down at the bar with Kelly in tow.

"Give us two of those fancy fucking IPAs, barkeep," she said.

I poured the beers and set them down, unable to keep my eyes off Kelly. I hadn't seen her since the party, but she was the star of at least half of my masturbation fantasies. Well, maybe a third, if I admitted to the times I thought about Jane's ass. She smiled at me, and I realized her eyes were blue like the fucking summer sky. They were blue like shallow water in the ocean, and they were blue like lapis.

"What's up, face-sitter? Good to see you again," I said.

"Not much, rapey-guy. How are you doing?" She smiled aggressively as she climbed up onto the barstool.

"Hey, that was…"

"I'm fucking with you. Good to see you, too."

Rachel looked back and forth between us both with a raised eyebrow.

"Am I missing something here? Because those are not nicknames that I'm familiar with. Well, the face-sitter I get - sorry, Kell - but, you know what I mean."

"It's nothing," Kelly said. "I just got Thomas to tell me a story after you went out for a smoke last week." She grinned at me and I smiled back as Rachel just shook her head.

"Are you off today?" I asked, sitting on the counter behind the bar. There was only two or three people there besides the girls, and they were sitting in the corner quietly nursing a few Russian Imperial Stouts.

"Yeah, Rach said you were working, so we figured we'd stop by and say hello. I have to go in at seven, and she doesn't start until Monday. Where are you working again? *Spanky Magazine*?"

"*Lucky*, you bitch. And don't get me thinking about it. I'm already worried I'm going to fuck up on my first day."

"Wait, what do you do, Kelly?" I asked. The only thing I

knew about her was that she used to sit on a guy's face, she had a pussy like heaven, and she could fit in my pocket.

"I'm a singer and a journalist."

"She works at a karaoke bar," Rachel said.

"Yeah, but I sing there. I work the karaoke machine. Singing and stuff. You should come visit sometime - you'll like it. Do you sing?"

"I try not to," I said, standing up again so I could at least pretend like I was working. I walked down to the end of the bar while the girls continued talking and drinking their fancy IPAs. The other patrons were still content with their 11.9% black stuff, so I wiped down the bar, washed a few glasses, and then made my way back to my friends. They had finished their beers, but before I could offer to pour them new ones they were up and getting ready to go.

"What do we owe you?" Kelly asked.

"What's the point of bartending if I can't give free beer to hot girls?"

Rachel threw a five on the bar anyway, noting that if I got fired, I wouldn't be able to pay the rent. Kelly just smiled and said thank you as she pulled on her coat.

"Oh, not sure if Martin told you, he's throwing a party tonight." Rachel said, standing at the door with one foot outside.

"Where is it?"

"It's at our place…" she called as she walked out onto the street, the door shutting quickly behind her. Well, at least I had some warning. There had been a few nights when I walked in to find six or seven people drunk on the couch in the living room. I generally joined in, but it's nice to have an idea if there are going to be people partying on your bed before you get home.

I had a fairly slow afternoon, and by eight, when the owners came in to take over the night shift, I had only made fifty bucks.

Still, that was what I made in a week of work-study back in school, and it was definitely better than nothing. I talked with them for a while before heading out the door to see how insane things were at the apartment. I was bummed that Kelly had to work because as exciting as my first night home was, I hadn't been laid again. Jane was complicated, I didn't know what Katie's deal was, and Rachel was just Rachel. We were friends and roommates, but it wasn't going to get dirty anytime soon. Kelly, on the other hand, was just what I needed.

There were only a few people at the party when I arrived, but it was getting busier by the minute. I threw my stuff down in my room, opened a beer from the fridge, and sat down on the couch next to a white girl with a shaved head. It looked like it might have been pink once, but now it was just a smooth batch of blonde fuzz that was begging to be rubbed. She had a tattoo of a pyramid on one shoulder and a giant turtle on the other, and she was drinking a martini with Katie and Martin.

"Oh, hey, this is our new roommate Thomas. He moved in last week when Diana had to peace out. He's cool, although he might try to have sex with you," Martin said.

She turned and looked me up and down before making a faint effort at a toast with her glass. I put out a hand, and she looked at me like I was crazy for a moment before taking it.

"Nice to meet you. I'm Zen."

"Like, as in meditation? Are you Spider's girlfriend?" I asked. She nodded and turned instantly back to the conversation. I swear that sometimes I don't exist. There are days when every person I pass smiles at me and then this. She might as well have told me to fuck off.

I left them without another word and made the loop through the apartment to see if anything else was going on. A few people were in Martin's room and same with Rachel's, but I didn't know any of them, so I went to the kitchen and called Jane.

"What are you doing tonight?" I asked when she picked up.

"The boy is taking me to dinner. Why?"

"Martin's having a party here, and I don't fucking know anyone. And I miss you."

"It's been a week and a half. You just want to get laid," she said.

"I always want to get laid, Jane, but seriously. Come over here instead. You'll make the party better."

"Thomas, I hate parties. I'm anti-social, I don't like strangers, and you're just going to paw at me all night whining about my perfect little ass. Why don't you go hit on that girl from the last party?"

"She's not here," I mumbled.

"Oh, I see. The cutie you want isn't there so you call me up to see if I'll do? What the fuck, man? You only think of me when there's no one else around. I hate being a second choice. Have a good time."

And then she hung up, and I was standing in the kitchen with the phone in my hand like a moron. She was right, of course, but there was nothing to be done about it. I did think of her when no one else was around, but to me that just meant I liked her. It meant she was on my mind and she was safe and stable. Jane was someone I could count on, and not have to deal with the bullshit flirting and everything else that comes with trying to get laid. Besides, I loved her. It was in my own way, but it was love all the same.

"Did you really fingerbang Kelly in my bedroom?"

"Oh, hey, Rachel," I said, startled by her entrance. "I guess so. She asked me to tell her more about tying up my ex, and she got super turned on. Honestly, it didn't feel like I did much of anything. She just kind of took my hand and told me what to say, and I did it. Is she upset?"

"No, it's just that she didn't say anything until it came up at the bar, and even when I pushed her for the story it took her a while to admit it. I don't know, it just felt weird. She's like my best friend, and I think she's awesome, and I don't want to see her get hurt. If you want to, go for it, I'm not trying to stop you. I'm just saying don't fuck it up."

"I'm not an asshole, Rachel. I like her. It was weird that night, but I haven't been able to stop thinking about her. You think she'd be interested?"

"Maybe. She'll be here later after she's done with work. Just don't be a dick."

I went back into the party suddenly more cheerful. I downed a few beers, and mingled for nearly two hours before Jane walked into the room. She was wearing a black dress that was way shorter than normal and high heels. I had never seen Jane in anything other than combat boots, but there she was looking like she had just walked off a runway. She walked up to me slowly and took me by the hand.

"Where's your room?" she asked in a growl. Without another word she dragged me in the direction I pointed, closed the door behind me, and then closed the door to the kitchen as well.

"Do you want to fuck me?" she asked, turning around and facing me.

"Jane, what the hell is going on? I thought you weren't coming. What happened to the boyfriend?"

"Thomas, just answer the question. It's yes or no." She was perfectly still, but her expression was tight and intense. It was one I knew well, and it always made me worried. For a brief moment, I just wanted to hold her in my arms and tell her everything would be okay. But, that's not what she was asking for, and it probably wasn't what she needed.

"Yes," I said after waiting too long. "God yes. You look so

fucking hot."

She took a few steps towards me as she undid her dress, and then she was just wearing heels and pearls, and I swear I had never really seen her before. She was tall and freckled, and her walk had purpose. I tore off my shirt as she approached me, and I had my pants off a few seconds later. By the time she was in front of me, I was completely naked and hard as bone. She grabbed me by the head and pulled me to her until her lips were against my ear.

"Don't be nice. Just fuck," she whispered, and I had to push away flashbacks of Claire. I had made the mistake once of asking her how she wanted to fuck: sweet or rough. She smiled at me like I was a child and shook her head. Do I ever want it sweet? she asked.

I kissed Jane and pulled her to me with as much force as I could, hoping the images in my head might leave me alone. Her hand was on my cock almost instantly, and for the first time since I'd known her she knelt on the floor and took me into her mouth. She always said that blow jobs weren't her thing, and I never stopped to question it. If I was lucky enough to even kiss her, I wasn't going to complain about not getting head.

But she licked me up and down, her hand never once stopping, and I had to hold onto the bed post. Her lips were warm and wet, and she sucked my cock like she was starving. I know it's a cliché, but in this case it was true. There was nothing graceful or elegant about what she did. It was messy, quick, and desperate, and I couldn't stop staring at her. This was a completely new Jane.

"Fuck me," she moaned as she stood up again. "Now."

I had her on her back an instant later, and somehow I knew she didn't mean with my mouth. I pulled open the drawer to my bedside table and scrounged for a condom, throwing papers onto the floor.

"What is it?" she asked, her hands moving between her legs as she looked back at me.

"I can't find a fucking condom," I said.

"Come here." Jane grabbed me by the arm and pulled me back to the bed, her legs opening around me. She kissed my mouth as her hand moved between my legs to grab my cock. Her grasp was tight, on the edge of painful, and she rubbed me against the lips of her pussy. A growl escaped her as she looked down at us, and for a second I didn't recognize her at all.

"I don't care," she finally said thrusting up to me. "I don't fucking care, just do it. I want you in me now."

And then for the first time ever, I slid my bare cock inside her and it was something completely new. I know everyone says it doesn't make a big difference, and the truth is I don't mind wearing condoms. I get paranoid about safety, and my dick isn't so sensitive that I can really tell the difference. Hell, I've had them break on occasion without even knowing it.

But, this was something else, and I didn't know what to do with it. Jane's pussy was amazing, and I wanted to cry right then. I pushed into her, fucking her harder and faster, but there was no way I was going to last. She kept moaning and growling into my ear even as she clenched around me, and she lifted her hips off the bed with a strength I adored.

"Oh, god you feel so good. It feels so much fucking better. Don't stop fucking me," she said.

"Jane I'm gonna come if you keep talking like that. You feel too good. You feel too fucking good."

She stopped moving the second I said it, and I followed her lead. I held still as I looked down into her eyes, and I felt my cock pulsing within her. She was tight and wet, and even looking at us without a condom on was doing things to me. With a grin I had never seen before she moved up, both of us sighing when I slipped out of her. She pulled me in for a kiss and then suddenly rolled over.

I was back inside her a second later, pulling her hips to me on the bed, but her ass was in full view and she knew it. She wiggled and squirmed as I fucked her from behind, and her breathing grew louder and shorter with each second.

"Thomas?" she moaned.

"What is it?" I asked, moving so slowly it hurt.

"Do you still want it? Do you still want to fuck my ass?"

I almost couldn't breathe. There was no way she said that. There was no way she was offering me that. Unless? Fuck, something must have happened with the boyfriend. This wasn't just horny Jane. This was payback Jane, and I knew it the instant the thought hit my brain. But there she was, ass up on the bed with my cock inside her, asking me the one question she knew I couldn't say no to.

"Yes," I said, falling down against her body. I kissed her neck, lifting her hair up as I pushed as deeply inside her as I could go. "Yes Jane, you know I want that ass. Are you serious?"

"Uh-huh," she moaned, still pushing back onto me. "Do it. But, let me hear you beg. Let me hear you beg for it, and then just do it, okay? Then just fuck my ass until you come."

My vision was blurry and I couldn't focus. The music was blasting in the other room, but as far as I was concerned we were the only two people in New York City. I had my hands on her as I pulled out and spread her cheeks. My heart was in my stomach, and even though I knew it was wrong, there was no way I could stop. After all these years, I was going to fuck Jane in the ass.

"Please," I said quietly, then growing louder. "Please, Jane, let me fuck you. Let me fuck this perfect, amazing, magical ass. I want to feel you around me, and I want to hear you come as I fuck you. Please, Jane. Give me your ass"

And then the door opened and light poured in. Kelly stood in the entrance with a bottle of Jack Daniels in her hand.

"Thomas! I made it…" and she stopped right there. I was kneeling on the bed with Jane's ass in front of me, my hard, bare cock positioned right at the entrance to her tight, little hole. Jane turned her head just as Rachel burst into the room behind Kelly. I fell over and sat down on the bed, my dick still standing up straight as Jane rolled onto her side.

"Have you ever heard of fucking knocking?" Jane screamed at them.

"Fuck, oh fuck. Um, sorry about that. I didn't know you had someone here."

And then Kelly backed out of the room pushing Rachel in front of her as she mumbled something I couldn't understand. They closed the door behind them, but it didn't matter. My cock was limp in seconds, and Jane was now shaking her head as if coming out of a dream. I stared at her, my want still lingering for a moment longer, before looking down into my lap as if I had just gotten caught with my hand in her panty drawer.

"Who was that?" she asked, pulling the blanket up over herself.

"That was Kelly."

"The tiny one? That was the girl you were fingering last week? Oh fuck, what the hell were we thinking? Why the fuck did you listen to me?"

"Jane, what the hell? You show up after saying you wouldn't come and just demand that I fuck you. No explanation, no 'Hi' or 'Hello,' just 'Thomas, come fuck me without a condom on. I don't care, I just need to get fucked because something happened, and I can't talk about it.'"

"Don't throw this on me!" she screamed. "Like you're not capable of saying no? Come on, you loved it as much as I did, and if they hadn't walked in you'd be shooting your load up my ass right now without so much as a fucking ounce of guilt. So, don't talk to me about whose goddamn fault it is."

I leaned back against the wall, and didn't know what to say. She was right, of course. I would have done it, no matter how bad an idea it was. It was dumb enough that I fucked her without a condom on, but I was about to try and force my cock up her ass without latex or lube. That was more than idiotic. It was insane.

"Jane, what the hell happened? And yes, it felt amazing. I'm not blaming you for that, because christ it was worth anything. I don't even know how to describe it. I've had sex without one before, but with you..."

"It was different. Thomas, it was..."

And then she was crying and wrapping her arms around me. There was nothing to do but hold her and kiss her tears. It started in her throat, deep pangs of sorrow, and then spread throughout her body. She trembled and shook as her sobbing grew louder and louder. I wiped her eyes with my sheet, and held her there, my arm wrapped tightly around her. I didn't say one word.

"He asked me," she said, minutes later. "Tonight at dinner, he got down on one knee and asked me."

I wanted to ask her what she said, and instinct alone kept my mouth shut. I ran my fingers through her hair as she sat up and rubbed her eyes. I kissed her forehead, unsure of anything, and before I knew what was happening she was standing up and getting dressed. She zipped herself up, put her heels back on, and stared at herself in the mirror as she adjusted her hair.

I pulled my jeans on and held her hands in the dimly lit room.

"Do you want to go eat something? Maybe get a drink somewhere quiet?"

"No, I need to go home. He'll be there soon. I don't know, I'm sorry I dragged you into this. I didn't know what else to do."

"Jane, I..."

She put a finger to my lips and then kissed me.

"I'll call you later," she said before walking out the door.

Chapter Five

"What the fuck? You talk about wanting to hit on Kelly all day and then when she finally shows up you're balls deep in Jane on your bed. What is wrong with you?" Rachel was waiting for me outside my room, standing in the kitchen with her hands on her hips like my mother.

"Do you mind not screaming this out to the whole party?"

She looked down at me, which she does easily since she's two inches taller than I am, and I shifted from foot to foot. I didn't know what to say, but it didn't make any difference. Jane was impossible to explain.

"I think the whole party knows, Thomas. In fact, everyone in the kitchen saw it as well," she said.

"Did Kelly leave?"

"Of course not, she's in my room getting high with Zen and Spider. Don't bother her."

I made my way out the other door and into the living room where possibly word had not yet reached. The party was in full tilt and the room was so packed I could barely make my way to the bar. The same girl as last time was behind it, and she poured me a gin and tonic without even asking. I nodded, trying to say thank you above the noise of the music blasting all around me. Before I could so much as take a sip there was a hand on my shoulder.

"Dude, did I just hear Jane beg you to give it to her up the ass?"

"Martin," I said, grabbing him and pulling him close. "Please don't say that out loud. She has a fucking boyfriend, and I don't need it to get around that she was here at all. Fuck, this is so screwed up."

"Yeah," he said, now in a stage whisper, "but is it true? I mean, did you tap that?"

"I wish. I've wanted it since forever, but no. I mean yes, you heard her correctly, but no I didn't do it. Kelly and Rachel walked in about a second and a half too soon."

He looked at me with something akin to admiration then shook his head. "Bro, they caught you like that? I don't know man, that's kinda fucked up. They should be apologizing or something, because that is not right at all."

"I'm gonna go grab a smoke downstairs, okay? I need some fresh air. And please don't say anything to anyone."

"My lips are sealed, man."

I had to push my way to the door, but by the time I got down to the street I could breath again. Perfect timing for me to light up and inhale that delicious cocktail of New York City air and Lucky Strikes. I leaned against the side of the building and stared at the clouds of smoke as they left my mouth. It was like paint in water or possibly come in a swimming pool. Whatever it was, it was mesmerizing, and I couldn't stop watching it rise up into the warm night until it vanished in the darkness above the street lamp. When I finally closed my eyes, all I could picture was Jane on her hands and knees in front of telling me I could do it. I could still practically feel her around me, and that alone was enough to give me chills. What the hell were we thinking?

"You got an extra?"

Kelly stood next to me, and I hadn't even noticed her come out of the building. I pulled out my pack and lit a new one off the cigarette in my mouth. I handed it to her and she leaned against the wall and took a deep drag.

"Was she the ex-girlfriend? The same one you told me about in the story?"

"God no. I mean, we sort of dated, but not really. She's more of a best friend, but that wasn't super normal for us. We have sex maybe once or twice a year, but she just showed up, and I don't know what the hell is wrong with her. Or me, for that matter. Anyway, I'm sorry about that. I didn't mean for you to have to see it."

"Have to? Are you serious? That was so fucking hot. What, did you think that fingering me meant I was going to turn into a jealous bitch all of a sudden?"

"No, I just didn't…. I don't know. It was awkward."

"Did we interrupt before you could do it?" She asked.

"Do you really want to know?"

"Thomas, you got me off telling me about fucking the shit out of some girl I don't know. What makes you think I don't want to actually watch you do the same thing? Seriously, after walking in on that I almost needed a change of panties. If I wore them."

I dropped my Lucky to the sidewalk and crushed it out with my foot. I had met women who weren't especially jealous, but this was a whole new game. Maybe she just liked to watch. Maybe she didn't like me at all. Or maybe she was just being polite so I didn't feel bad about what happened. Whatever it was, I wasn't used to it.

"We fucked for a few minutes before you came in. But then…" Okay, I probably didn't need to tell her what was about to happen.

"So you were fucking her, but just took a break?"

"No, she moved to her knees…"

"So, you were changing position?" She asked.

"Yeah, but it was because…"

"You can say it," Kelly whispered. She looked up at me with her big blue eyes, and suddenly I realized it might actually turn her on. She took one step closer, and I reached an arm out without thinking, my hand resting on her hip.

"We stopped for a second because she wanted me to do something else." I was almost whispering.

"What did she want you to do?" Kelly leaned against me, her hand on my thigh, far higher than it might have been, and it was moving quickly. I leaned back and closed my eyes for a second, taking a deep drag until I felt her touch my cock. "Come on. Tell me."

"She wanted me to fuck her up the ass," I finally said.

"Holy shit. Now I do feel bad! I mean, interrupting you was one thing, but you were about to do anal? Wow. I don't know what to say."

"What the hell is with you, Kelly? Does it turn you on to hear this shit, or is it something else? I loved having you in my lap last week even though I was just talking, but it still felt like something. I mean, it felt like we were making a connection. I don't fucking know."

"Thomas, are you trying to tell me something? Maybe something about having a little, tiny crush on little, tiny me?"

"Did Rachel tell you?"

She stood directly in front of me and put her hand back on my cock. I was mostly hard, and her fingers kneaded me like she was making bread. I looked into her eyes and her smile was more mischievous than I knew was possible.

"You do have a crush on me, but you also want to fuck me. You want to fuck me hard, don't you, Thomas? You want to just break me in half. You want to see if your big, mean cock can fit in this tiny, little body, and then you want to split me open!"

I stepped back, pushing her hand away from my dick, and there was actual horror on my face.

"What the hell are you talking about?"

"I'm just fucking with you. Relax." She shrugged and took a final drag off her cigarette.

"That's not just fucking with me. Who talks like that? I do have a crush on you, but it's not like that. I don't want to hurt you or anything."

"Can I have another?"

I tossed her another smoke, but didn't move any closer. She was hot. And tiny. But, all that stuff about splitting her open was just completely fucked up. I hadn't once thought about what it would be like to be in that tight, little cunt, or what it would feel like to be able to carry her around the room as we fucked, or how small her ass must be beneath her skirt. I didn't want to hold her down and see just how hard I could fuck her tiny body.

Fuck. Maybe I had thought all of it. Maybe she was right. I started pacing and smoking faster, but I didn't have to like it. The girl had my fucking number.

"I was just kidding with you, Thomas. Do you know how many guys I have to deal with who have that fantasy, though? Seriously. I can tell within thirty seconds if the guy just thinks his dick will look bigger in my hand. I'm a walking fetish, and I forget that not everyone is super creepy."

"Oh believe me, I'm totally creepy. I also happen to have a crush on you, and it's not just because you're so small."

"Only partially."

I shrugged this time, and tried to smile in a charming way, but I was as confused as ever. Was she hitting on me or just trying to tease me? I had enough teasing with Claire, but then again she still turned me on. And she was right, I did like how small she was. I didn't want it to be a turn on, but there was no way around it. I had thought every one of those things even if it was only a half formed thought in the middle of a frantic jerk-off session.

"Do you want to go back up?" I finally asked.

"I was going see if you wanted to come to my place. It's quieter. Also empty."

"Are you serious?"

"You ask that a lot. Is it because you don't believe people in general or just that you don't believe me?"

"I don't believe me. Or my luck, or whatever the hell it is. But seriously, even after what you saw?"

"Why can't you get it through your head? I want to take you home *because* of what I saw. Besides, you didn't finish, you must be ready to explode any minute now. And that I'd like to see."

She started walking without me answering the question at all. I slipped her hand into mine as we made our way up First Avenue, and we walked six blocks without saying a word. I tried not to think about Jane, but I'd be lying if I said it wasn't difficult. We had been friends for so long, and tonight was more complicated than I wanted to admit. Our sex was usually just fun. It's not to say it wasn't good, but it wasn't powerful. It wasn't compelling or even all that meaningful. We had sex like we drank coffee or smoked in the window. But tonight, we did something else.

"It's right here," she said, stopping outside her building. She unlocked the front door and we walked up the small staircase as a single light flickered overhead. The wallpaper was peeling and the stairs were uneven, but it smelled like real wood and for a moment I was somewhere else. I was on Lake George or Star Island. I was anywhere with old buildings and sunsets that never ended.

Her apartment was on the third floor in the back of the building. It was small, but at least twice the size of Jane's. She walked right into her bedroom without a word and shut the door behind us. She lit two red candles and a long stick of incense that smelled like an old temple I visited in Japan. I stood for a moment, adjusting to the dark before she turned, stood up on her tip-toes, and kissed me on the mouth. It hit me instantly that while we had spent a lovely thirty minutes on the floor of Rachel's bedroom, we had never really kissed.

It was sweet and it was slow. It was long and wet. We both tasted like cigarettes, but there was something beneath it as well.

I could taste her, and I don't know how to describe it. I lifted her off the ground, and she wrapped her legs easily around me. She kissed my lips and my chin as I moved to her neck and ear without pause. She held my head between her hands as she bit me gently, and I stared into her perfect blue eyes for way too long.

"What do you want?" she whispered between kisses.

"I want to watch you undress," I said, sure of my desire for the first time all evening. I set her down and sat on her bed, which was really just a thick mattress on the floor. I hardly noticed the rest of the room as she pulled off her light jacket. She was wearing a tank top and jeans beneath it, and her body swayed as if there was music. When she pulled off her top – with her back to me – I suddenly realized she was naked beneath it. She turned to face me, her hands covering her breasts, and I stared at her with open awe.

The buttons of her jeans went slower, and she walked to me until she was only inches away. She pulled down the zipper and I could see nothing but smooth skin beneath the denim.

"I fucking love Vassar," I whispered.

She leaned forward and kissed me as her jeans came off, and when she stood up again she was completely naked in front of me. If I thought she was tiny with clothes on, this was something else. I had a moment of doubt, wondering how old she actually was, before she was on my lap pulling off my shirt, and I stopped caring about anything.

Kelly and I spent hours in bed that night. We licked, sucked, and fucked each other until the sun came up, and even then we had to tell ourselves that we needed to sleep. Each time one of us bit a little harder or kissed more gently, the other was right there. If I held her arms above her head she moaned into my ear, and when she sank her teeth into my inner thigh with one hand wrapped around the base of my cock, I nearly screamed. When I was inside her the world vanished, and even when we waited for me to grow hard once more our bodies felt perfect.

We were far safer than Jane and I had been, and by the time morning came we had a garbage can full of used condoms, a beer bottle full of cigarette butts, and more than a few bruises covering our bodies. In spite of our scratching and pushing though, the sex was incredibly sweet. It was tender, powerful, and slow, and I fell in love over and over again.

When we finally fell asleep it was only after she managed to make me come one last time.

"You do like how tiny I am, don't you?" she whispered, as she tried to get me hard.

"Of course," I said, pushing her back and staring at her body.

"Do you want me to be your little girl?" she purred as she threw a leg over mine. Her cunt pressed into my thigh and somehow my cock twitched back awake. "You like that, don't you? You want to fuck your little girl, I can feel it. How old do you want me to be?"

"I don't even know how old you are," I moaned as I rolled on top of her, my cock now hard against her stomach.

"I'll be anything for you," she whispered as she rolled our last condom down over me. "I'll be as little as you like."

And then I was inside her and she was kissing me. My eyes were open, amazed at the sight of her, and she wrapped her arms around me and pulled me into her with everything she had.

"Fuck me," she whispered, mumbling something else that I couldn't understand.

"What did you say?" I asked, thrusting faster and harder.

"Fuck your little girl," she moaned, and seconds later I was coming and so was she, bucking her hips off the ground. Her face was against my neck and her breathing so loud it was musical. I kissed her everywhere as my body exploded, and I never wanted anything else ever again. I wanted to stay there, coming inside her, in spite of my utter exhaustion, but most of all I wanted it to always be perfect: sweet, hot, joyous, and easy.

We slept for a long time, even as the sun came up outside her window. Sometimes I held her, the big spoon to her little one, and sometimes we rolled away and hardly touched at all. No matter how we lay, each time I woke up it still felt perfect. It was nearly two in the afternoon when we finally got dressed and left the apartment to find something to eat.

Chapter Six

I didn't talk to Jane for three days. I picked up the phone at least six times, but I never dialed her number. I asked my roommates constantly if anyone had called, but even then I was careful. As carefree as Kelly appeared to be, I didn't want to test that by asking about Jane in front of her. At one point, when I was alone for a change, I pulled out an old photo album and sorted through the photos with far more scrutiny than I had in a long time. There were pictures of Jane from the time she was fifteen until just last year, and I stared at each of them hoping to feel closer to her. In one, she had a shaved head and a short skirt on with ripped fishnet stockings. In another, she was dressed to kick ass with tight jeans and boots. The cigarette hanging out of her mouth in almost all of the photos was always the same, and I swear I could still smell her on my sheets.

Each time I thought about calling, or stopping by her apartment, I remembered her standing in my room saying she'd call me. I knew it was true, but I didn't like it. Waiting was not something I was especially good at, but with this it was worse. I desperately needed to know what the hell had happened, but there was something else as well.

Claire was the first women I ever dated who I didn't use condoms with. Sure we stuck to them for the first few months, but after a few breaks, and too many close calls in the shower it just didn't seem important anymore. We didn't bother to get tested for anything, but who cared? We were fucking every day, sometimes two or three times, and it's not like condoms would have made all that much difference. We had licked, sucked, and swallowed each other often enough that if one of us had something, we both did.

And then it got bad and still we didn't stop. I had a suspicion that she was cheating on me, but I couldn't do anything about it. If she came home drunk with her lipstick a little smudged I got angry and she got horny. She'd push and prod, calling me a jealous asshole, until I finally pushed her down and fucked her. Each time I gave in, and I always gave in, she would smile like she had won a bet. She laughed as we fucked and whispered in my ear that I could never say no to her. No matter what happened, or who happened, I would never say no.

When I finally got up the nerve to end things, mostly thanks to Talia convincing me I was worth something, it was less explosive than I might have thought. She showed no surprise at all when I told her it was over, and there was something in her eyes that made me think she had expected it all along. Neither of us cried, and we had the first honest conversation in a very long time. Just before I left, she pulled me in and kissed me on the cheek.

"You were the first one I never cheated on," she whispered. And then, just to make sure I would require therapy for years to come she added, "I love you." It was the one and only time she said the words, and even then I wasn't sure if I believed her.

But that was two months ago, and still I never went to the doctor or the clinic to have my blood work done. I woke up in the middle of the night in a cold sweat convinced I was dying of something no one had ever heard of, and still I didn't go. I waited and waited, convincing myself that if something was wrong I would know about it.

And now Jane. My neurosis only affected me until suddenly someone else was a part of it, too. I told myself that we hadn't fucked for very long, and I didn't come inside her, but it was an excuse and I knew it. I imagined the conversation in my head over and over again, telling Jane we should go to Chelsea and get tested, but I never made the call. I didn't make an appointment for myself either, always insisting to myself we should go together. After three days of worrying, pacing, and trying to keep myself busy, I was turning into a wreck.

And Kelly was noticing. She was busy, and I was picking up more shifts at the bar, but we spent another night together and it was hard to stay focused. The first night had been a blur of drunken lust that just kept getting bigger and more powerful. The second was a definite sequel in every sense of the word. It was shorter and less interesting than the first. The sex wasn't bad, but I wasn't really there. When she left the following morning, I was convinced she wouldn't be back.

"Hey, dude, the phone is for you." Martin stood in the kitchen with a cup of coffee in one hand and the receiver in the other.

I was lying on my bed pretending to read a book and thinking about Jane. I sat up straight and nearly ran to the kitchen.

"Hey," came the soft deep voice on the other end.

"Jane, are you okay?"

"Of course I'm okay. Want to get a drink?"

"Docs?" I asked. Doc Holidays was a country bar around the corner from my apartment that she had introduced me to a few years ago. It was divey, but occasionally quiet in spite of the country music blaring out of the juke box.

"I'll be there in twenty minutes."

And that was the end of our phone call. I pulled my clothes

on, paced back and forth in my room, and then finally headed to the living room to tell anyone home that I was going out. Katie was lying on the couch in a t-shirt and panties watching TV, but Martin had returned to his room. She just nodded when I told her, and I was out the door and onto the street in no time at all. I walked the three blocks to Docs, grabbed a beer and sat down at a booth. I lit a cigarette nervously as I waited, and I was unsure of everything. It's all going to be fine, I said, hoping that if I repeated it enough it would be true.

"Hey, dude," she said, walking in and waving at me from the bar. She ordered a Jack and Coke and came over to where I was sitting. She crawled into the booth, turned so her back was to the wall, and put her boots on the chair next to us. "What's up?"

"Just drinking a beer at this shit hole of a bar. And listening to Kenny Rogers. What's up with you?"

I can pretend to be casual. Hell, maybe I am casual. Maybe it's all fine and dandy, and I don't need to talk about anything at all. Maybe it's all just fucking fine.

"I'm getting married."

And then I spit out my beer, because what the fuck, Jane? I wiped my mouth with my hand as I sat up straight on the bench. Did she really just say that?

"You're serious?"

"Yeah, I told you he asked, right? And I said yes."

"This was all just a few minutes before you came over to my place and fucked me on my bed, right?"

She fumbled with her jacked, pulling a cigarette out and lighting it without once looking at me. Her hand was trembling, and it was only then that I noticed her eyes were red. She alternated between the drink and the smoke before getting up without a word. I watched as the bartender put down two shots and a couple of beers. Jane paid for it and sat down again placing the drinks in front of me.

"To my wedding," she said, raising the glass. I picked up the shot, toasted hers, banged it on the table before knocking it back. She always made me drink Jameson, and damn if I didn't need that. I opened the second beer and sat there staring at her.

"Congrats," I finally said. "That's what I'm supposed to say, right?"

She pounded half her beer before looking at me, and she tossed me a smoke as she lit herself another one. I put it in my mouth, stole her Zippo, and lit it.

"Look, it happened, okay? He asked me and then he had to run out for an emergency. He got a call and had to be at the hospital instantly. I had already said yes, and he kissed me and said he loved me, and then he was out the door. I was alone at the restaurant trying to comprehend the fact that I just said yes. My mind started going, I got an asthma attack, and then I just got up. I left the place with my inhaler stuck in my mouth and a ring on my finger that I still couldn't believe.

"I was just going to walk for a while, but we were only six blocks from your place. I didn't even know I was going there until I saw your apartment and heard the noise. Then I didn't think. I walked in, found you, and you know the rest."

"Yeah, you undressed and begged me to fuck you. Why are you marrying this guy?"

"I love him. I completely and utterly love him." She looked totally sincere.

"And that whole thing on my bed was just…"

"It was me saying goodbye, Thomas. It was nothing." She put her feet back up on the chair and leaned back as she smoked. This was fucking crazy.

"Really, it was nothing? I've been freaking out for the last three days, and you say it's nothing? Jane, I've been going crazy, and now you sit there and tell me it was just goodbye. Are you trying to make me nuts?"

"Come on, you loved it. What's the big deal? I wanted sex and you wanted sex and we did it. And now I'm getting married and that's the end of it. I still love you and want you to be there."

"You want me to be at the wedding?" Now it was my turn to roll my eyes and shake my head.

"Why do you think I called? I want you to read something. Or walk mom down the aisle. I don't know, I want you to do something. You're important. Why have you been freaking out?"

This time it was me who went to the bar just as the juke box starting playing Loretta Lynn. I tried not to sing along to all the words I had somehow learned in Indiana, but it was futile. I will come home a' drinkin with lovin on my mind, Loretta. You're not my mom. I replaced the shots and the beers and carried them back to the table. We toasted again, swallowed the Jameson, and I started on my third beer in less than half an hour. This was going to be a great afternoon.

"So, you're not worried?" I almost asked her about Chelsea and the clinic, but if she wasn't concerned, maybe I was just being crazy. Jane, after all, is much smarter than I am.

"Of course not. I mean, look, I love you and we've been friends for a long time. If I worried about shit with you this would have ended a long time ago. We definitely wouldn't still sleep together when I'm in the mood to make bad decisions. I didn't mean it was goodbye in a bad way, just that I wanted one last time with you. And it was hot. I mean, it was good, you know?"

"It was definitely good, I just didn't expect it, I guess. But I know what you mean. If we can't get through shit like this, we never would have made it that far."

And then suddenly we were talking and laughing like everything was back to normal, and I hardly had time to feel the relief filling me up. Jane was getting married to someone she liked, we had great sex one last time, and I had a new girl who was hot, exciting, and probably waiting for me in my bed as we spoke. The third beer completely hit the spot, and every dumb, little concern I had was gone by the time we moved to the bar and ordered another round of shots.

When we finally said our goodbyes, it was with a kiss that only lasted seconds. It was sweet and friendly. Just like us. Just like me and Jane.

I stumbled into my room, my head spinning, and crashed down on the bed without a thought. I could still taste Jane on my lips, and the bed was so soft. It was so fucking soft I almost didn't bother to take off my clothes. Almost. I pulled the blankets up over my naked body though, and decided that a little nap wouldn't hurt. It was only late afternoon on a warm spring day. There was no hurry for anything at all.

"Hi, Daddy," came a voice in a dream. There was something warm and wet around my cock and the bed felt so good. Everything felt good, and oh my god, what was happening? When I opened my eyes, there was a suspiciously Kelly-shaped lump beneath my blanket and her mouth was very clearly on my dick. I threw the covers off and stared at her tiny naked body as she sucked me. She looked up with her hand wrapped around me and winked before taking me all the way down her throat.

"Do you like that, Daddy?" she asked again, and I realized none of it had been a dream. I grew harder - if that was possible - and moaned out my answer. Relief and lust filled her eyes at the same time, and she went back to my cock with a vengeance I could only be grateful for. After just a few minutes I couldn't handle it any longer, and I pulled her up to me, kissing her wet lips and wrapping my arms around her.

"Did I do it good?" she asked in a little voice I almost

didn't recognize.

"It was perfect, Babygirl," I said without even thinking. My hands went to her ass and she was grinding against me, our kissing growing more intense by the second. This was not something I had done before. Claire and I did all sorts of things that were messed up and kinky, but this was a new thing, and it shot like a bolt of lightning from my ears to my cock. It was a fetish I didn't know I had, but suddenly I needed to know more.

I rolled her off me until she was on her back next to me, and I ran my fingers up her body, watching her chest rise and fall as I looked at her. I kissed her forehead and then her chin. I slid my hand between her legs, feeling how warm and wet she was without entering her at all.

"You are so pretty," I whispered. "You are the prettiest little girl in the whole wide world, do you know that?"

"Do you really think so?"

"Daddy doesn't lie, Babygirl," I said without thinking. She moaned and kissed me again, her mouth crushing into mine and her tongue exploring every inch of me. "Daddy will never lie to you," I said again as I crawled between her legs.

I kissed her lips and her neck. I kissed her breasts, sucking each nipple gently between my teeth, and then I moved to her stomach, trying to hide my impatience. She moaned and writhed beneath me; each sound that she made turned me on more than the last. Her tiny whispers of "yes, Daddy" made my cock twitch, and by the time I opened her legs and stared at her pussy I was shaking with want. I held myself there, overwhelmed by how badly I wanted to taste her, but I relished the feeling of holding back almost as much.

"Please, Daddy," she whispered. "Please."

"Do you want me to taste you?" I asked. "Is that what you want? You want Daddy to taste this little pussy?"

"Yes!" she moaned, lifting her hips off the bed towards my open mouth.

"Have you been a good girl?" I asked. "Have you been a good little girl for Daddy?"

"Yes, I promise. I promise I've been good, Daddy. Please…"

And then I couldn't stop myself. I opened her with my tongue first, sliding up wet skin before pushing as far inside her as I could go. I slid one arm between her legs and beneath her ass, before pulling her closer to me as I fucked her with my tongue like I was trying to climb inside her. Her hips wiggled and thrashed as I ate her, and her screams grew so loud I almost worried about my roommates. But then I was back tasting her briny cunt as I worked two fingers inside her. She started to come almost instantly, and I didn't once stop. I kissed her, licked her, and sucked her as she bucked her hips; she soaked my chin along with the sheets beneath us.

When she finally slowed down I moved up her body, her hands pulling me up to her mouth, and I kissed her with more love than I thought possible. I knew I liked her, and I definitely knew I wanted her, but this was something else. There was a tenderness mixed in with everything that didn't make sense. I wanted to hold her and kiss her, and I wanted to love her. I wanted to make sure everything would always be alright, and I wanted her to know it.

I pulled a condom off the bedside table and rolled it on as she stared at me wide-eyed. Even though we had fucked a million times just a few days before, this was suddenly the first time. She held her breath as I positioned myself against her and neither of us made a sound. I rubbed against her slowly, pushing just the head of my cock inside her, before looking into her big blue eyes one more time.

"Daddy loves you," I whispered. "You know that, don't you?"

"I know, Daddy," she whispered, and then I was inside her and she was around me, and we shared one body so full of lust and love I was ready to burst. I kissed her over and over again, and I wiped the tears away from her eyes with my lips. I brushed her hair as we moved slowly on the bed, and she threw her head back as I pushed deeper inside her. When we stopped kissing it was only to watch our bodies connect and feel everything else.

"I love you, too, Daddy," she moaned, looking back at my face once more. Our kiss was sweeter than anything I had known. My hands clutched her face like she was a precious thing, and I kissed her over and over again as I felt myself getting close to the edge.

"Fuck me," she whispered. "Fuck your little girl and then come for me. Please, come for me, Daddy."

I'd like to say I lasted a second longer than that, but the truth is I was lost at "I love you." I closed my eyes as I thrust into her, and suddenly she was coming again. We both made enough noise to wake up the neighborhood. We cried and screamed as we filled one another, and it felt like we wouldn't ever need to stop.

When I finally pulled out of her, she let out a long sigh that sounded like protest. I kissed her as I dropped the condom on the floor next to the bed and pulled the blanket up around us. She snuggled against me as we kissed, and neither of us spoke for a long time.

"Do you know I called you Daddy the first time at my place?" she said.

"Really? I didn't hear you."

"I think I mumbled it. I was scared you would freak out."

"I've never done that before," I said. "But I don't think freak out is the word I would use. I actually don't know what words to use. Maybe there aren't any."

"I liked it."

"Yeah, me too." I kissed her again, unsure of what was next. It suddenly occurred to me that maybe she did this with every guy she went out with. "Have you done that before? I mean the whole Daddy thing?"

She shook her head and hid it in the pillows with a giggle.

"I've wanted to, but it never felt right. Plus, I never had the nerve. It's funny, but I think I would have been creeped out if some guy suggested it, but with you it felt like it made sense. I don't know why. Are you sure it didn't freak you out?"

"I'm the one who told you I loved you after two dates."

"I said it back. Besides, you said that Daddy loved me. It's different."

"Is it?"

We lay there for a long time without saying anything. I was still drunk from my afternoon with Jane, but my heart was pounding and my cock was still twitching beneath the blankets. Kelly looked lost in thought, with her head on my chest as she ran her hand up my body. She toyed with my limp penis, flopping it back and forth with a giggle, but then simply ran her fingers through my chest hair and sighed.

"Are you getting hungry?" I asked finally.

"I'm starving."

"Let's see if anyone wants a pizza."

Chapter Seven

The next night Jason and Brent returned. Crazy, beautiful, brilliant Brent and funny, awkward, nervous Jason came back. For the first time in over a year, I went out with the boys. It sounds like the start to a bad movie about fraternities, but the truth is that while I mostly had female friends, the couple of guys in my life were my salvation. They moved into an apartment on the Upper West Side right across the street from Jake's Dilemma. They got my number from Jane, called that afternoon, and by 6 p.m. we were eating burgers at St. Mark's Ale House marveling at all the college girls in for free drinks on a Friday night.

"When was the last time the three of us got together like this?" Jason was always the first to move into nostalgia, but it was hard to blame him.

"Dude, are you wasted already? I haven't even heard what Thomas has been up to and you're ready to sing the moose song and drink port in the park. Ease up, brother." Brent was on his second scotch.

I had known Brent since second grade, and it's hard to describe a friendship like that. We took solace in each other's families when ours were driving us crazy, and we got in more trouble than anyone has a right to survive. If someone was breaking into the country club to go skinny dipping in the pool, it was Brent and I. If someone was stealing traffic cones and closing off our high school parking lot, it was probably us. And if two people were whispering in the same girl's ear at a party, chances are good we were there.

"Well, I graduated college, broke up with Claire, fucked Jane, and moved in with that Martin bastard. Not in the order."

"What happened with Claire?" Brent asked. "The one time I came to visit she was fucking awesome. I mean, not to bring that up, but dude, it was epic."

It was Jason's turn to look at us with a raised eyebrow and all we could do was grin. It's not that we left him out of the fun on purpose, but Brent and I tended to get into trouble that he just wasn't around for, and in this case the trouble was Claire. One whirlwind weekend, a bottle of vodka, and two condoms later, the three of us hardly remembered what happened. For my part, it was best to forget it all, but there was no reason to go digging through the past. Not this early in the night.

"I always miss the crazy things," Jason said. "Although from what I've heard, I think this one is for the better. Seriously, I know you loved that girl, but that wasn't healthy at all. She was like a vampire or something. She sucked the life out of you."

"That's not what she sucked out of me," Brent said, followed by his deep throaty laugh that filled the bar in spite of the blasting music. I looked at Jason and smiled, nodding my head the whole time, and he knew there was nothing to be said. He was right, and we didn't have to talk about it.

"You guys want to get out of here? Maybe Blue and Gold or something? I'm tired of hitting on NYU girls." Mostly I was tired of the noise and the baseball game on the television. Yeah, the girls were hot, but I was out with the guys and while it might have been a tradition, the bar was getting old.

"I fucking hate Blue and Gold," Brent said. "Let's go somewhere else. Somewhere we can get in trouble. They always throw us out of there before anything fun happens."

"We could go to Niagara and get picked up by Rachel," I offered. The last couple nights she had gone out with the express purpose of getting laid, and that bar was her hunting ground. It almost wasn't fair. She would leave the apartment and come back twenty minutes later with some big goon on her arm. She'd vanish into her room, make a lot of noise, and an hour later he'd be gone, she'd be smoking on the couch, and asking us what else there was to do.

"Also, lame. Not that I wouldn't bang Rachel. Wait, have I banged Rachel?" Jason raised an eyebrow at us and wiggled his nose. He was the least likely of the three of us to get laid on any given night, but when he did it was always mysterious. It was Elena the Catholic girl who only took it up the ass until her wedding, or Francesca the girl from camp who used to blow him during capture the flag. His stories were always bizarre and if they were told by anyone else we would have laughed and called him a liar. But Jason was honest to a fault, and if his life just happened to be weirder than ours, so be it.

"Let's do Holiday Cocktail Lounge, then Docs," I finally said.

"Those are the two shittiest bars in New York. Other than The International and Mars Bar," Jason said. "We may as well go over to Billy's Topless and stick dollar bills into my grandma's garter."

"Is she still working there?" Brent asked. "I thought she moved to the brothel across the street. Damn, that was a nice piece of ass."

"Listen, you fuckers," I said, "let's get out of here and figure it out on the way. This place is starting to drive me crazy. I don't care if it's Decibel, Docs, or your mom, but I gotta get out of here."

I let them follow me out the door, as I pulled out another free pack of Luckies and threw one into my mouth. Jason handed me a lighter and stole one for himself while Brent made faces at both of us.

"Why are you so pissed about NYU girls?" He asked. "Didn't you just say you banged Jane?"

I took off down the street without a word. They followed close behind with Brent rambling on about not meaning to piss me off. He hadn't, but that wasn't the point. There was no way I could talk about Jane without talking about everything, and we were far too sober to talk about everything yet. We needed a few hours to drink beer, talk about nothing at all, and then, possibly, if the timing was right, we could get to something important. That was just how it went and I wasn't going to break with tradition.

Holiday Cocktail Lounge is not your normal dive bar. At least not in the sense that it's full of college kids and hipsters looking to get drunk off cheap beer. The bartender is not a young woman in spandex, and the decour is not retro-chic. It is simply an old, shitty bar with a half working pool table, a bunch of neon signs and a juke box right in the middle. The bar itself curves around in an almost pleasing arch, and if you looked past the posters and signs, you might notice the dark wood paneling covering everything. The bartender was older than the bar, and he grew more and more unstable until he finally closed the place down, usually around 1 a.m.

We sat down in a booth towards the back and Brent bought the first round of drinks: straight whisky and a beer chaser. Jason bummed another smoke and for a few moments we just sat there staring at each other, feeling the joy of being with old friends again.

"So, I'm dating this girl who calls me El Macho for some reason."

I looked at Brent before putting my feet up and leaning back. I just nodded and he continued. It had been far too long since I heard a Brent Story.

"Maybe I should say was dating, because I left her in Georgia and came home with only a goodbye kiss and some promise that maybe she'd come visit me in New York. Anyway, she's like my height – with the biggest teeters you've ever seen in your life – and the first time we slept together she made me put on this Mexican wrestling mask and tittie fuck her until I came on her face. I shit you not, this was our first night together and we were only half drunk.

"Most of the shit we did was fairly normal, and we started hanging out more and more until she practically lived with me and my roommates. She didn't give me the nickname until after the second time we used the mask, but then she fucking said it in front of everyone and it was over. For the last six months almost everyone I know has called me El Macho, and it's been driving me fucking crazy."

"Thanks for the round El Macho," I said, toasting him with my beer.

"I can't believe I'm living with the famous El Macho. My dad is going to freak out."

"Shut the fuck up, guys. I didn't tell you this story so you could call me that, too. There's a point okay? So, Teeters and I are dating, fucking, or whatever you call it…"

"Wait, you call her Teeters? Your fucking girlfriend? Are you serious? You're like the worst feminist in the history of the world." Jason was laughing, but shaking his head in disbelief.

"That is pretty fucked up, man," I said. "I think you've got me beat, too. Definitely the worst feminist ever."

"I loved Teeters!" Brent screamed, slamming his can of beer onto the table and earning a yell from the bartender to sit the fuck down and don't break anything. "And she loved me and likes her nickname a whole lot more than I like mine so don't even get me started. But that's totally not the point of this story. The point of the story is that one morning when she was still sleeping I happened to pick up the mask and look at it. I usually just put it on and we went to town, but for some reason I looked on the inside."

"And it was full of rats?" Jason offered.

"Bees?" I added helpfully.

"Neither of those make any sense, you morons. No, I looked inside the mask, and written on the tag was her father's name. I was wearing her father's fucking wrestling mask and screwing her! How fucked up is that? What the hell was she thinking? I mean, I almost threw up right then, but instead I kicked it under the bed and when she left for the day I threw it out. I freaked, man, and didn't know what else to do. I brought it to campus and found a dumpster behind the goddamned student center, rolled it up in a paper bag, and stuck it under some boxes.

"At first she didn't say anything. We had sex like normal people, but I could tell she was getting nervous. Finally a few nights later she was like, 'Come on El Macho, let's put the mask on again, I want you to come in my mouth.' I pretended to help her look for it, but I knew. And the more frantic she got, the more creeped out I got. Finally, she was screaming and crying and I didn't know what the fuck to do."

"Did you tell her?" I asked.

"Of course not! What am I stupid?"

"You know some people might like that. The whole Daddy thing," I said. It was quieter than I meant, but my two best friends just stared at me.

"Dude, it was creepy, okay? I bet El Macho was his fucking name in the ring, and she was totally using me to get back at him. Or something. I don't know what was going on. The last few weeks were weird, but I tried to pretend they weren't. We still hung out, but she kept asking about it, and when I offered to get her a new one she said it wouldn't be the same. She didn't even stay over after graduation, and when we left it was with a fucking hug and a lame promise to call sometime."

"Brent, how the hell do these things happen to you? My life is never that weird," Jason said.

"Dude, how about Tina, the girl who dressed up as Slave Princess Leia? Or that chick from camp, or Elena who only took it up the ass? You are by far stranger than any of us. Even El Macho Papi over here."

"Fuck you both," Brent said getting up and going back to the bar for another round. Hell, if he wanted to keep buying us drinks then who was I to complain? Jason and I laughed about his crazy wrestling girl, but by the time he came back we had moved on to something else. We stayed for at least a few hours, drinking more than was possibly good for any of us and by the time we left to go find Doc Holidays – we decided we were only going to bars with holiday in the title – we were solidly smashed.

We stumbled into Docs only to find Kelly and Rachel in a booth by the pool table. They waved at us when we walked in, and before I knew what was happening Kelly was on my lap, Brent and Rachel were flirting in the corner, and Jason had quarters on the pool table. Lyle Lovett was blasting out of the Jukebox and each time Kelly leaned in and kissed my face I felt my cock twitch beneath the table.

"Did we interrupt your boys night, Daddy?" she whispered into my ear.

"Don't call me that here," I mumbled, adjusting my cock in my jeans.

"Why, does it make you nervous? You don't want your friends to hear?"

"Hey, Brent," I said, interrupting his catch up session with Rachel. They had only met a few times before, but they always got along. "Why don't you tell the girls here your El Macho story."

"And why don't you suck my enormous penis and keep your mouth shut," he said. "Or I'll go and start telling your little girlfriend about the time I came to visit you in college."

Kelly was on it in a second. She slid off my lap, grabbed Brent's hand and looked into his eyes. He smiled at her and stared right back, and I was jealous in a fucking second. What the hell?

"I want to hear that story."

"She wants to hear the story, Thomas. I mean, I wasn't going to say anything, but she wants to hear the story."

"I bet she wants to hear about El Macho as well," I said with a grin. He looked at Kelly then back at me. Finally, he picked up his beer and chugged the rest of it before crushing the can in his hand.

"I'll tell you sometime when he's not here, Pookie."

"Your friends are weird, Thomas," Rachel said. She lit a cigarette and stared at us as if we had all come from another planet. She was generally the normal one, although in my crowd that was hard to work out. She was tall and pretty and she liked football. On Saturday nights she wanted to go dancing, possibly blow some coke, and hook up with an insanely hot guy with a big dick. Rachel liked brunch, the Met, and champagne. During the summer she went to the beach and in the winter she went skiing. As normal as chocolate milk.

"Don't lump me in with those guys," Brent said to her. "I'm totally normal. Also I'm Jewish, which I'm sure your mom would like."

"Is that a pick-up line? 'I'm Jewish.' Does that work for you?"

"Normally I have to say I'm Jewish, but I have a big dick. That usually does the trick."

Rachel looked at him like it was the first time, and I wondered what the hell was going on in her brain. She looked him up and down before staring him right in the eyes.

"How big?" she asked.

"Nine inches and thick as a coke can." He didn't miss a beat. As long as I had known Brent he was insecure about some things on occasion, but his dick wasn't one of them. He was a little short, strange in an abnormal way, and louder than a bullhorn. But when it came to his dick, he was solid as the rock of ages.

"Huh," she said, leaning back. "I might have to see that to believe it."

Kelly and I got up to get more beer, and left the two of them on the bench, staring into each other's eyes wondering how far they would go. We passed Jason shooting pool, his face locked in concentration as he lined up his next shot.

"Does he really have a big dick?" she asked. "I don't like huge dicks."

"I guess that's a compliment," I said.

"Thomas, look at me. What the hell would I do with a nine

inch cock? Where would I put it?"

"I have a feeling you'd know just what to do with it."

"And why is that?" she asked, sneaking in under my arm until I had it wrapped around her. I leaned down and whispered in her ear.

"Because you are a very dirty girl, and you've never had enough cock in your life."

She actually blushed, and she looked down at her shoes like a shy little girl. Just then the bartender came over and I screamed out my order over the music: five more Rolling Rocks, which came to a whopping ten dollars. I left her fifteen, and we turned to head back to the table. Before we got two steps though, she paused and looked up at me.

"Are you mad at me, Daddy?" she asked in her smallest voice.

"Because you're such a bad girl and call me Daddy in public?" I asked. She just nodded her head and bit her lip. Christ, I was going to bust a nut in the middle of the bar if this kept going. Of course, I didn't stop though.

"I'm not mad at you, Babygirl," I said, kissing the top of her head. And then more quietly, "but I might have to punish you."

And then I dragged her back to the table and put the beers down for our friends. Kelly's cheeks were bright red and her breathing was quick and short as we sat down. Brent had his hand on Rachel's leg, but they both looked up and turned back to us with drunken smiles.

"Do you remember the first time we got drunk together?" Brent asked. "We were like fifteen and we stole a bottle of my dad's Canadian Club. It was nasty, but we drank half the bottle and ended up walking naked around the block singing They Might Be Giants." He was nearly as drunk as I was.

"Yeah, and we were lucky we didn't end up in jail," I said. "It was almost as bad as when we took that girl skinny dipping up at

Sunrise Pond and didn't find out she was only fourteen until after she had sucked your cock."

"How long have you two known each other?" Kelly asked me.

"Since we were, what, eight?" I asked him, trying not to slur my words too badly.

"I think I was eight and you were seven. We met in second grade and you were a dick. Of course, I was a dick too, but still. Maybe that's why we got along."

"I don't have any friends I've known that long," Rachel said. "Kelly and I have known each other since high school, but I think that's it. I think we were fifteen when we started hanging out."

"I have one friend from fifth grade, but she's a Mormon now and doesn't talk to me." Kelly snuggled up against my arm, but her hand was beneath the table moving quickly up my leg. "She was fun for a while, but I guess she found religion in college. It's too bad, you guys would have liked her." Just as she said it she squeezed my cock through my jeans and smiled at me.

"Do you want to go back to our place?" Rachel asked. " I could used a couch and a bathroom that doesn't smell like desperation and heroin."

Brent gave her a look that was far more lecherous than anything else, and we all got up, pounded the rest of our beers and went to pick up Jason. He was just finishing losing his second game of pool, and I handed him a cigarette as we headed to the front door.

Avenue A was fairly quiet at two in the morning, and the park across the street was dark. We walked up a block to 10th Street and then headed west towards our apartment. It wasn't until we were halfway down the block that the three of us started singing. The girls walked ahead of us, so with our arms around each other we started to sway and walk in time as our voices cracked in the night sky.

When I was a young man, I used to like girls
I'd play with their bodies and fondle their curls.
My girlfriend ran off with a sailor named Bruce,
But I've never been treated like that by a moose.

At the chorus we broke out singing louder than the verse, and I didn't care for one second that it was two a.m. and the street was quiet. For the first time since I had been home, everything felt normal again, and with Jason and Brent back in town, all would be well. No matter what crazy shit happened to us, everything would be just fine.

We swayed and we sang, and by the final chorus the girls were singing along, too.

So it's moose, moose, I want a moose
I have never had anything quite like a moose.
I've had many women, my life had been loose,
But I've never had anything quite like a moose.

Chapter Eight

By the time we got home, we were messy. There is no other way to describe it. We tried to keep quiet, but we quickly realized that Martin and Katie were not in fact sleeping in his room. I didn't know where they were, but it didn't really matter. We turned the lights on, put on some music and fell down onto the couch in the living room without much rhyme or reason.

Kelly lay down on my lap, and I rubbed her shoulders absentmindedly while Jason lay down on the floor. He pulled a pillow off the couch and closed his eyes. He wouldn't wake up for hours if he passed out, but none of us were together enough to do anything about it. Rachel dropped a blanket over him before whispering something in Brent's ear. I watched them cautiously, but a few moments later they disappeared together into her room and shut the door. I pulled Kelly up with me and we found our way to my bed. I undressed her sloppily and we climbed in, completely naked once again. The room was spinning, but I found that looking into her big blue eyes was enough to keep me from getting sick.

"Are you going to punish me now?" she asked, her knee sliding up over my cock.

"If I tried to punish you right now I'd probably break something, and it would most likely be you. I'm too drunk to play games." I wrapped my arms around her and kissed her, but it was especially difficult to focus, even with her soft leg rubbing against me beneath the blanket.

"I don't want to play games, Daddy," she whispered. "I just want you to hold me and tell me I'm a good girl."

"You are so good, Babygirl," I whispered. My cock actually twitched beneath her touch and as she ran her hands up and down my chest it slowly grew harder. I tried not to think of all the things I wanted to do with her, but I kept hearing her voice in my head over and over again and soon I was aching to fuck her.

She climbed on top of me, my cock nestled between the lips of her pussy, and I stared at her sitting there. Her hair hung down over her shoulders covering her small breasts. Her nipples were dark brown and hard as erasers. She moved her hips ever so slowly, both of us staring at the head of my cock where it poked out from between her thighs.

Just then the door opened and Rachel stumbled in, trying – and failing – to keep quiet. She fell to her knees and closed the door behind her, crawling her way slowly towards the bed.

"Are you guys awake?" she asked too loudly, her eyes adjusting to the dim room. She was on the floor in just a pair of panties. Her breasts were three times the size of Kelly's, and I found myself suddenly staring at her. When she reached the bed she finally saw what we were doing and she stopped short.

"Brent passed out," she whispered. "He undressed me, pulled off his shirt, and then started snoring."

"Did you get his pants off?" Kelly asked, raising an eyebrow.

"I might have peeked, but it just made it worse. I'm so fucking horny, can I join you guys?"

"Are you serious?" I was staring at her, my eyes glued to her tits, and for some reason I wondered if Brent would try to call her Teeters Two or something. I had to catch myself from laughing, but she looked completely sincere.

"We were just going to sleep," Kelly said, lying down next to me. My cock was still mostly hard, and she wrapped her hand around it as Rachel watched us from the floor.

"Can't I just watch? Maybe I can get myself off or something. I'm going crazy. Please?"

I turned to face Kelly, but I didn't know what to say. I liked Rachel, but I wasn't ready to just dive into a drunken threesome. Not only was she Kelly's best friend, but I lived with her. Besides, there was no way I was going to share our new fetish with her. No matter what else I felt about it, it was between us, and I didn't want to give that up.

"You can sit at the foot of the bed," Kelly finally said. Rachel climbed up without a word and leaned against one of the tall pillars looking at us. She instantly slid one hand inside her panties as she watched, and I felt more sober than I had in hours.

"These things are useful, Princess," she said, leaning back and pushing her fingers further inside herself. "Are you two gonna fuck? Come on. Let me watch at least."

I kissed Kelly and she kissed me back, but it was a different game, and I wasn't sure what to do. My cock wasn't quite as hard as it had been a few minutes before and even watching Rachel wasn't doing much for me.

"We're really tired, Rach," Kelly said, touching my softening cock gently. "I mean we've been drinking for hours, and I don't know if we're up for it."

"Just suck his cock then," she whispered. "Or let me do it."

Without warning Rachel reached down and slid her panties off her hips and left them wrapped around one ankle as she opened her legs wider. This time both Kelly and I stared, our eyes trying to make out Rachel's pussy in the darkness. Before I could say anything, Kelly's hand grew much firmer even as she slid the other one between her own legs. I wrapped my hand around my cock as well, and for a while the three of us sat there quietly jerking off on the bed. My eyes moved between Kelly's fingers and Rachel's, and I found myself growing hard again the faster my hand moved.

"Do it," Rachel moaned. "Come on, suck him for me."

Kelly didn't need much more than that, and a second later she was between my legs with her lips clamped around me and her throat full of my cock. I moaned her name as she sucked, but I tried to peer over her tiny body to watch Rachel. Her eyes were glued to Kelly's ass, and I finally leaned back and closed my eyes, trying to focus on the amazing sensations running through me. Just as I started to think I might actually come, Kelly stopped for a second and screamed like nothing I had ever heard.

I looked down and saw that Rachel had pulled her legs open and had her mouth buried in Kelly's cunt. I could hear licking and fingering sounds, but there was no longer anything on my dick.

"Holy shit, that's hot," I groaned as I reached down and started to stroke myself again. Kelly sat up so Rachel could get a better angle, and she finally went back to sucking me as her best friend ate her with more and more urgency. I moved back and forth between watching the two girls to watching my own cock, and I couldn't hold back any more.

"Kelly, I'm gonna come," I said, my fingers in her hair.

Rachel didn't slow down, and I could see she had at least three fingers inside her friend's pussy now. Kelly moaned around me and sucked me faster and faster as her own body started to shake. Within seconds I unloaded into her mouth, and she did the best she could to swallow as her own orgasm spread through her body like a heatwave. She shook and trembled, her hand now on her own pussy, as she licked my come from her lips.

Rachel rolled onto her back instantly, her hand clenched tightly between her thighs. She moaned and groaned as she pinched her nipples with her other hand, and Kelly moved up to me as we both watched. Her eyes were closed and her body was slick with sweat. Her fingers moved in her cunt in frantic jerking motions, and she grew louder with each passing second. We stared in awe as she arched her back, her huge breasts flat against her chest, and brought herself closer and closer to her finish.

When she finally came, she rolled into a ball with her legs clenched so firmly around her hand that I thought she might hurt herself. She was panting and whining as she shook at the foot of the bed, and neither of us looked away. When she finally unrolled her body, she let out long sighs of relief that turned into spastic giggles that didn't seem to stop.

"Holy fuck, that was so good. I needed to come so badly," Rachel gasped between breaths.

"I feel funny," Kelly said looking down at her friend.

Rachel was still lying on her back, her long blonde hair falling off the edge of the bed, and her chest rising and falling with her breath. She nodded her head.

"I ate your pussy." Rachel was still giggling with joy and it was fucking adorable.

"You did," Kelly said.

"It was amazing."

"I'll second that, although I think the girl with the pussy

probably has a better idea than I do," I said.

"It was awesome, but I didn't know you did that. I mean, Rach, we've been friends for years but you've never done that before."

"I've never done it with anyone before. I liked it."

I looked at Kelly lying on the bed: her legs partly open and her thighs wet with her own fluids and Rachel's saliva. I stared at Rachel on her back, her tightly trimmed pussy glistening and her eyes glassed over. And I watched my cock, still twitching and still wet from Kelly's mouth. My life was so fucking perfect I didn't know what to do with it.

Rachel left once she recovered from her orgasm, and Kelly and I curled up around each other and passed out within minutes. That night, I dreamed of blonde hair and soft lips.

****

It's hard to notice morning in my room because there are no windows, but a little light creeps in under the doors, and the noise from the neighbors – not to mention my roommates – usually wakes me up. It was around noon when we finally awoke in almost exactly the same position as we had fallen asleep.

"It's smells like sex in here," Kelly said, rolling over and sitting up against her pillow.

"It smells like Rachel's pussy," I said before catching myself. Kelly frowned at me, but nodded her head. It was the truth and we both knew it, but it meant that as soon as we woke up we were back to thinking about the night before.

"Are you okay?" I asked. "I mean, was that weird for you?"

"A little, I guess. I've never thought about doing anything with her before, but it was fun. I was just surprised. I've seen her like that, when she really needs to get laid, but it was still a surprise when she just started eating me. I was totally distracted from sucking Daddy's cock."

She instantly stuck her thumb into her mouth and blushed at me. I pulled her on top of me and kissed her. Just like that I went from sleepy and hungover to hard and awake. I ran my hand down her back to her ass and groaned as I pulled her cheeks, spreading her ass and thighs until I could feel her hot against me.

"You were distracted last night, Babygirl. You know I can't allow that, don't you? If you're going to suck Daddy's cock you're going to need to concentrate much harder." I don't know where it came from, but I was instantly in control in a way that still felt new. I adored her and loved her, and I wanted so many contradictory things at the same time that it hardly made sense. I wanted to punish her, comfort her, fuck her, and watch her get fucked. I wanted to take her over my knee and spank her until she cried, and then I wanted to hold her and wipe away her tears. I wanted to slide inside her and slap her face as we fucked. I wanted everything at once.

"I promise I'll do better," she whispered. "I promise, Daddy."

"Did you like having your little friend lick you?" I asked her, my mind moving quickly in one direction.

"It felt funny," she said.

"Have you ever done that before, baby? Have you ever had a friend do that to you?"

She nodded – looking down – and I pushed her off me and rolled her onto her back. With more force than I intended to I opened her legs and covered her cunt with one hand. She was breathing quickly, and she was so hot I could feel it against my skin.

"How many times, Little One?" I asked. "How many girls have done that to you?"

"Three or four," she whispered. I slipped my fingers inside

her and she moaned even as she tried to cover her mouth with the back of her hand. I pushed deep inside her, my thumb moving to her clit as she wiggled next to me, little cries of pleasure leaking out of her mouth.

"And how many boys?" I finally asked, unsure if this was a game or not. Had she really hooked up with four girls? And did I want to know the answer to this question too?

"What do you mean, Daddy?" she asked, biting her lip.

"How many boys have you been with? How many cocks have you sucked and how many boys have fucked you?" My voice was louder and more demanding, but my fingers never left her and she pushed down onto them even as she tried to look the other way. "Don't lie to me, Babygirl. Don't you dare lie to me."

"Please, don't make me say," she moaned. I stood up without a word and she nearly cried out when I removed my fingers. I stretched my arms above my head before opening the drawer and pulling out a condom. I stared at her face as I rolled it down over my cock, and then I grabbed one ankle and pulled her until she was facing me on the bed. Her legs were open wide and her cunt was red and wet. It was crimson and honey, and for a moment I wanted to take her and damn the game. Patience was not my strong suit.

Instead, I crawled between her legs, my cock positioned right at her entrance, and I pinned her arms above her head. Her breathing quickened even more as I rubbed against her, and she moaned and whined, turning her head this way and that.

"How. Many. Boys. Have you fucked?" I asked, my voice hard and controlled. "I won't ask you again." I held her easily with one hand, and I raised the other in an open palm. She shuddered as if she was afraid, and I leaned down and smacked her cheek gently, before kissing her mouth. I whispered into her ear.

"It's okay, Babygirl. Just tell me, and I'll fuck you. That's what you want, isn't it? Just tell me how many boys, and I'll fuck you no matter what. Everything will be okay. I promise it will all be okay."

"Twenty-two," she finally whispered, turning her face away from me. "I've fucked twenty-two boys."

And then I was inside her, and I felt every second of it. The head of my cock pushed between her lips, and she closed around me as I slid further and further into her. She clenched as I filled her, and I didn't want to be anywhere else.

"It's okay," I whispered as I fucked her faster and faster. "It's okay if you're a little whore. It's okay that my little girl is a slut."

"No, Daddy," she moaned. "I'm a good girl, I promise. I promise I'll be a good girl from now on, just please don't stop."

"I won't," I said, as I opened her legs wider and thrust into her harder. I lifted one of her knees up until it was pressed against her breast, and for a long while all I did was fuck her. My cock pistoned in and out of her, and she cried quietly even as she moaned out "Daddy" with each thrust. She begged me not to stop, she begged me to let her come, and when I kissed her it was with nothing but love and adoration.

"You'll be a good girl," I said, getting closer and closer to coming. "You'll be good for me?"

"Yes, Daddy," she screamed. "Please let me come, please let me."

I stopped for one long painful moment and pulled my cock from within her. The look on her face was ashen, and I realized that she was actually unsure what I was going to do. I reached my hand down to her pussy and touched her with just my fingertips. She moaned and shivered at my touch, but she held her breath tightly inside her body as she struggled.

And then I was inside her again telling her to come for me – telling her to come for Daddy. She screamed out as I filled her, my own body exploding as well. She clenched and screamed. She bit her hand and my mouth. She bucked and twisted as we came there on my bed, and I wrapped my hand in her hair as we shook and trembled. I told her everything was okay over and over again, and I could feel myself filling the condom with more come than I thought possible.

By the time I pulled out of her, we were covered in sweat and there were tears on her face. I rolled onto my back, my hands in my hair as I looked up at the stupid, fucking canopy covering the bed.

"Holy shit, that was insane," I said.

"Oh my god. Thomas, when did we do learn to do that?"

"I'm Thomas again?" I asked, still staring up at the canopy.

"I think I need a break from Daddy or I'll start crying or coming again. Hell, I don't know. I'll start something."

"How about a shower?" I asked, sitting up. She nodded and together we wrapped towels around our waists and walked out into the kitchen. The bathroom was between the kitchen and Rachel's room, and as we opened the door we could hear noises coming from next door. I put a finger to my lips as we leaned in closer, and I could hear Rachel with perfect clarity.

"Oh God, fuck me, Brent. Fuck me harder."

We turned on the hot water, closed the curtain behind us, and stood beneath the showerhead for a very long time without saying anything at all. Next door we could hear grunts and moans, with the occasional sound of skin slapping the wall.

Chapter Nine

Two days later I took Kelly on a real date.

I don't know if it's my generation or just a sign of the times, but dating isn't what it used to be. Hell, it probably was never what it used to be, but these days it's something else entirely. In fact, I can't remember the last time I asked someone out at all, let alone on a date, and I definitely can't remember the last time I got into a relationship with someone I hadn't already slept with. It's strange when I think about it, but part of me wonders if I've simply grown afraid of risk. Maybe it's the unknown, maybe it's rejection, or maybe it's simply a worry that someone might like me or I might like them. Because what could possibly be worse than discovering that you actually like another human being? What could be more terrifying than to realize that someone else might have the ability to crush you with a smile and pound your heart into little pieces with just a few words?

Claire and I met at a party in the woods, and we got drunk off cheep beer and adrenaline. We stumbled back to my room as drunk as we could possibly be and ended up fucking on the floor while still wearing most of our dirty clothes. Before her I dated a woman name Mariko whom I met while living in Japan. We hooked up at a party, spent the night together, and even then it was only when she told me I was her boyfriend that I realized we were in a relationship. In high school, dates were more likely to happen at someone's house or on a school trip than out for coffee, and it was still far more likely that I'd hook up with someone before we ever had a talk about relationships.

But, I asked Kelly to dinner on a Tuesday and she said yes. She was off that night, and I only had to be at the bar until seven, so we were going to dinner and it was going to be a fucking proper date. I didn't have time to change after work, so I dressed up nicely in the morning with a silk tie and a wool herringbone vest. I made more money that day than ever before, and I was forced to admit that my clothing might somehow affect my employment. It was a shocking thing to realize at twenty-three, and I hated myself for it as much as I did the situation.

"Irashaimase!" the waiters screamed as we walked into Go on St.

Marks, and I held up two fingers. They found us a table in the back and we washed our hands with the hot towels they provided. It's not the quietest place in town, but it's especially good for the prices, and I had a plan that required sushi, and more importantly, sake.

"Sumimasen," I said as our waiter walked by. "Nihonshu, wa futatsu onegaishimasu. Sake Hitotsuji Daiginjo kudasai."

He nodded and smiled, and hopefully I was the only who noticed the slight cringe in his bow. I hadn't been to Japan in over a year, but I could still slaughter the language with the best of them. A minute later he brought over two glasses of sake, and I thanked him again in my best Kanto Dialect.

"Are you trying to impress me with your crazy Japanese skills?" Kelly asked as she raised her glass in a toast.

"Yes," I replied firmly. "I surely am."

"Well, it worked."

I grinned as we raised our glasses and managed a reasonable kampai. The sake itself was delicious, and while the sushi wasn't expensive, it would more than break my bank if she wanted another glass of the Daiginjo. The things we do for love. The things we do for lust, too, I suppose, but right then our sweaty nights in the sheets were far less important that the thumping in my chest every time I thought about how lucky I was to have a new girlfriend. I was practically giddy as we ordered, and Kelly was as sweet as can be. The food was delicious, the sake was followed by a giant bottle of Sapporo, and all was right with the world.

"It's nice finally having a real date," I said when the waiter put steaming mugs of hot green tea in front of us. Kelly had a large bowl of red bean ice cream in front of her, but she stopped eating and raised an eyebrow.

"You better be careful there. Pretty soon you'll be calling me your girlfriend or something."

"Heaven forbid," I said with a laugh.

"No, I'm serious. I mean, a date is nice, but…"

"But what? We've been together for like a week now. You've spent four nights in my bed, and we're fucking practically every day. What else would I call you?"

"Well, yeah, but I didn't think you'd stop banging that Jane chick just because you were fucking me too. I know I certainly haven't stopped…"

"Stopped what?" This was not how the conversation was supposed to go. We had been more intimate in the last week than I had ever been with anyone. The things we did were intense and they were real. If this wasn't a relationship, then I sure as hell didn't know what one was.

"Thomas, I just didn't think it meant anything to you. I'm having fun, and I like sex with you, but you've never once asked me if I wanted a relationship. Yeah, I come over a lot, and I like calling you Daddy, but we've never talked about it. Why would I assume you weren't still sleeping with other people?"

"Well, I'm not sleeping with other people! Are you?" It had never occurred to me that Kelly might be fucking someone else. Maybe I'm stupid, or just egotistical, but at the end of the day I couldn't even fathom the logistics. Who had the time? We spend most every day together when we weren't working, and even the few nights apart we usually talked on the phone at least once.

She looked down at her ice cream and took a very dainty bite.

"Kelly, come on. Are you?"

"I'm not gonna answer if you're yelling at me. You never even asked me! This is the first fucking time you've said anything about it, and the first time we did anything normal at all. I don't like being interrogated."

"Fine, I'm just curious. So, Kel, you getting anything on the side?"

She scrunched up her nose, and stuck out her tongue at me. I tried to smile, but my heart was racing and I didn't know what to do with it. For some reason the thought of her with another guy was enough to nearly drive me insane.

"Just once," she finally said.

"Who was he? Was it someone I know?"

"This is not an attractive side of you. It's one thing when we're playing in bed, and then I don't care, although it would be nice to know if it's a game or it's real, but whatever. I don't have to answer this shit if I don't want to."

I ordered another beer even though I could barely afford it, but by then I didn't care any more. My sweet romantic date was going to hell in a chicken basket, and I didn't know what to do about it. I leaned back and took a sip of my beer before pulling a Lucky out of my pocket. The waiter dropped an ashtray on the table before I could get it lit, and we sat in silence for a long time as I smoked. Kelly didn't even ask for one.

"I'm sorry," I finally said. "You're right. I never said anything because I didn't think about it. It didn't occur to me that you might assume I was sleeping with anyone but you, and I made a whole lot of guesses without asking you. I'm not sleeping with anyone else. And I don't want to be sleeping with anyone."

"Even Rachel?" She stuck her tongue out again, but it was a serious question. We had talked about that night a few times since then, and it led to us getting naked almost instantly.

"Even Rachel. If you want to let her eat your pussy again, I don't mind watching though." It was my turn to stick out my tongue and this time she did reach over and steal my cigarette right out of the ash tray. She took a long drag before looking right at me.

"That was so fucking hot," she said. "But look, if you want a real relationship then you have to ask me, honey. Or at least tell me what you want. Or talk to me. Something other than just fucking my brains out and making me come harder that I ever have."

"I do that?" I asked. She nodded and her smile finally returned. "So, about the guy…"

"You really want to know? I thought that was my fetish, not yours. You think you can handle it?"

"You know what?" I asked. "Why don't you tell me about it later. Like maybe when you're lying in my bed with your hands above your head as I kiss your belly and call you pretty names."

"Does that make it easier? If it's a game? I don't mind, and it might be hot, but it's not like the other night when I told you I've only slept with twenty-two guys. This would be real."

I felt two things at the same time right then, and I quickly realized it was becoming a habit with this girl. The first was a kick to the gut. If she lied about the number, what was it really? How many guys had she been with before me, and why the fuck did it destroy my stomach just to think about? The second is that my dick got hard. I can't explain it, and I'm not sure I want to, but right then I was as hard as the sushi boat in front of me. Some combination of her lying to me and having slept with more men turned me on something fierce, and I wanted to take her right there on the table.

"I know," I finally said. "And yes. it makes it a little easier. If it's home, in bed, while you call me certain names, it feels like us. I know it's not just a game, and that makes it hotter, but I don't feel as out of control then. I don't know. Maybe it's a bad idea, but I definitely don't want to hear about it now."

We finished our tea in silence, and I finally paid the bill. It cost almost everything I had made at the bar, but I didn't care. I'd manage rent somehow, but this was important. The waiters bowed as we walked out and I shouted out "Gochisosamadeshita" as best I could. Kelly took my hand and leaned on my shoulder as we merged onto St. Marks, and the night was so warm it nearly took my breath away.

"So, does this mean we're actually going out now?" I asked as we made our way towards Second Avenue.

"That depends. Thomas, would you like to date me? Exclusively, other than Rachel eating my pussy? Do you want me to be your girlfriend?"

I picked her up and swung her around twice. She wrapped her legs around me and smiled as I kissed her again. When I finally put her down, my head was spinning and I was laughing.

"Yes," I said. "Yes I do. Do you want me to be your boyfriend? And your Daddy?"

She stopped and put a hand to her chest. I looked at her, worried for a moment, before I realized she was giving me her shy look. I leaned in and kissed her forehead as she bit her lip and it was all the answer I needed. Of course, I made her say it anyway.

"Yes," she whispered in her little girl voice. "Yes, Daddy."

We did climb into bed when we got home, but it wasn't to wet and hard body parts. At least, not instantly. I kept on my boxers and she stripped down to a tank top and the rare pair of panties as we cuddled beneath the covers with two gin and tonics I mixed at the bar. It was only nine-thirty in the evening, the apartment was empty, and Kelly and I were actually dating.

"Can I ask you something?" I realized I was about to jump into our little game again, but there was so little I knew. Playing was one thing, but I wanted her, and I wanted to know what made her tick.

"You better ask me stuff," she said.

"What's your favorite part? I mean, about the whole Daddy thing. What turns you on about it?"

"Like, do I want to fuck my actual dad? Cause the answer to that is definitely no."

"No, I just mean do you like being told what to do? Do you want to be a good girl more than a bad girl? Do you want me to punish you by teasing or by slapping you? Stuff like that."

She cuddled up closer to me and both of us looked up at the pink canopy above the bed. I was definitely going to have to do something about that soon.

"I like feeling small and safe. I like that you go from being angry to protective, although I'm not sure which one turns me on more. Does that make sense?" I nodded and she kept going. "As for being punished, I don't know. When I asked if I could come, I realized that was huge for me. Like if you said no, I didn't know what I would do, but I knew I would try not to come no matter how hard I needed to. And that was hot.

"And what about you? Why do you like being called Daddy?"

"I have no idea."

"I bet that's not true," she said.

"I liked being in control, but without it feeling scary. With Claire everything was always about power, and it was my job to take it. This feels different. I can never tell when I ask if I want you to be bad or good, but whichever answer you give turns me on. If you're good, then I picture you as my sweet little girl whom I'm sort of corrupting. If you're bad, I get jealous and turned on at the same time. Sometimes I want you to be a little virgin, and sometimes I want you to be a huge slut so I can spank your ass until you cry."

"You want to spank me?" she asked. She sat up in bed and looked down at me, her perfect breasts completely distracting me.

"Would you like that?"

"Like over your knee? Maybe in a little skirt?" she asked.

"I was thinking with your panties around your ankles as you squirm on my lap and promise that it will never happen again. That'll you be good, even though we both know you probably won't."

"Okay, I'm getting wet again. I love what you do to me."

I kissed her and pulled her to me until she was once again

on top. Her lips were warm and soft, and her skin felt amazing against my own. I was as hard as the poster bed, and each time she wiggled it sent shivers through my whole body.

"Do you want to tell Daddy about being a bad girl earlier this week?" I asked, feeling the knot in my stomach tighten up again. I wasn't sure what I wanted to hear, but the combination of our game and the truth was almost too much to handle.

"I don't want to say, Daddy. I don't want you to get mad."

She was giving me an out and I knew it. I could go in either direction, and it was a moment of choice that I wouldn't be able to take back. Did we keep it all just a game, or did it go somewhere else? If we opened the door, could we ever go back?

I rolled her off me and stood her up next to the bed. I kicked my feet off the edge so I was sitting on the side of the mattress and looked up at her. Even standing she was only a few inches taller than me. She looked down at her feet, her nipples so hard they were visible through her tank top.

"You promised to be good, didn't you, Babygirl?" I asked, my voice as strong and stern as I could make it.

"Yes, Daddy," she whispered, shifting her weight back and forth.

"But you weren't good, were you?"

She shook her head, but didn't say a word.

"Answer me when I ask you a question," I said, pulling her to me. She stumbled for a moment and without another thought I laid her down over my knees with her ass up in the air. A loud sigh escaped her lips as I held her there and her whole body quivered.

"No, Daddy," she said.

"Tell me what happened," I said, rubbing my hand over her ass like I was looking for the perfect place to strike first.

"I'm scared, Daddy," she whispered. "I'm scared you'll be angry."

"I'm already angry, and if you make me wait, or don't answer loud enough, I'm going to get more angry. But, I'm not doing this to hurt you, Babygirl. I'm doing this because I love you. Do you understand?"

She nodded her head as I opened her legs just enough to feel the soft flesh on the inside of her thighs. "Now tell me what happened. I won't ask again."

"I met them the other night," she began.

"Them?" I asked, my hand coming down gently against her. I slapped her twice more. "You said it was just once."

"It was, Daddy," she said, flinching each time my hand came down. "It was just once, but there were two of them. I'm sorry, I'm so dirty. I'm sorry."

"Keep going."

"They were so nice to me and they kept telling me how pretty I am. We talked for an hour or two and when they asked if they could walk me home, I just said yes. I didn't think anything would happen, I promise. I didn't know."

My hand came down harder now, and she moaned at each slap. I could feel her getting warmer and her skin turned red at my touch.

"They came into my room and suddenly they were kissing me and kissing each other, and it just felt so good, Daddy. They pressed me between them as they undressed me, and I couldn't stop them. It felt so good."

I slid her panties down a second later and my slaps moved down to her thighs, eliciting screams from my wiggling victim. I opened her legs even wider and slipped my hand between them, feeling how hot her pussy was. When I touched her, she was soaking wet.

"Keep going," I said, my erection now clearly pressing into her stomach as she tried not to move.

"When they had all my clothes off, one of them pushed me

to the floor and suddenly they were both there in my hands. They were so hard and big, and I just...I couldn't help it."

"Did you suck their cocks? Is that what you did, you little slut?"

My hand came down over and over again now, sometime getting so close to the lips of her cunt that she cried out. Her ass was red and her thighs crimson, but still she continued.

"Yes, Daddy. I know I shouldn't have, but I sucked both of them. They were so hard and I couldn't help myself. I feel so dirty, but I couldn't help it."

"And did they fuck you?" I asked, throwing her down onto her back. I couldn't handle the concentration to keep spanking her and it was all feeling too real. Had she really done this? Did she really bring two strange men home just the other day? After everything we had done?

I pulled her shirt apart, tearing it off her body with both hands, and she tried to cover herself. I forced her legs open, slapping her thighs as she struggled, and my blows came down against her breasts as well.

"Tell me, did you fuck them both?"

"Yes, Daddy," she said, looking up at me with tears in her eyes. "I fucked both of them. I was blowing one and the other just started fucking me from behind. I'm so sorry, Daddy, I'm so sorry."

I had her on her stomach a second later and there was a condom on my dick in a heartbeat. Her breathing was quick and short as she lay there, her pretty ass still marked by my hand as I crushed her with my weight. I pulled her head back with one hand in her hair as I pushed up a leg and positioned my cock against her pussy.

"Both of them?" I asked, sliding into her. "You let them both fuck this little pussy? You let them fuck Daddy's little pussy?"

"Yes," she cried between sobs, and I was so far inside her I wasn't sure where I ended and she began. I pulled harder on her hair as I thrust into her and she screamed and struggled, pushing back onto my cock as we fucked. Her face was pressed into the pillow, and I fucked her harder than I ever had before.

"Did you come, Babygirl?" I finally asked, completely unsure if I wanted to know the answer. "Did they make you come? Did you come when those two men fucked you, you whore?"

Her orgasm began at her answer and mine wasn't long behind it. I pulled her to me, my hand now around her throat and my voice nearly as loud as hers. She begged me to forgive her, but I called her terrible names as she shook beneath me, her cunt spasming around me as she came. I squeezed just hard enough that her breathing became ragged, and each time I released her, she gasped for air and promised she'd try harder.

When I came inside her my vision went black. I closed my eyes and was then nearly blinded by bright light, and I thrust into her as I exploded. I finally released her throat and kissed her neck and cheek as I continued to come, her body shaking harder than mine. By the time I collapsed, she had come at least six times, and I felt like I had been run over.

She cried when I pulled out of her, but it turned to a quiet sob when I wrapped my arms around her and pulled her tightly against me. I kissed her hair, and gently touched her shoulder as I whispered in her ear.

'It's okay, Babygirl, everything is okay. I promise, it will all be okay."

I didn't want to let her go, but I didn't know what else to do. I was shocked by what I had done, but equally by what she had said. I couldn't help picturing her between them, letting them fuck her like I had just done, and the combination of jealousy and excitement was nearly too much. Deep down a part of me wanted to be there and see it, no matter what it might do to me. I wanted to watch, I wanted to join, and I wanted to see her come on someone else's cock.

But right then, with her body next to mine, what I wanted most was to keep her safe for the rest of my life. I wanted her never to be afraid, and I wanted to make everything okay again.

We lay there for a long time. At least a half hour passed before either of us said anything of substance. When she turned to face me, I wiped away her tears and kissed her nose, her lips, and her forehead. I ran my fingers through her hair as she stared into my eyes.

"Do you still love me?" she asked.

"Always," I said. "I love you so much."

"Even if I was bad?"

"You can never be bad," I said, kissing her again. She snuggled down against my chest, and I finally reached down and pulled the blanket up over us. We kissed and kissed, holding each other in the warm bed, until eventually we slept.

Chapter Ten

The next two weeks were spent working the bar (I finally picked up a few more shifts,) fucking Kelly, and going out with Jason and Brent. El Macho was sort of dating Rachel, although neither one of them was especially forthcoming. If he was out drinking with me he often crashed in her room, but there were enough nights she made a run to Niagara for me to wonder what was going on. He said I should mind my own business whenever I asked, and I was so happy to have him around that I generally took his advice.

I talked to Jane a few times on the phone, but they were always cut short by something or another. Her wedding plans were moving ahead, but they weren't getting married for at least six months. Apparently he had always dreamed of a Christmas wedding, and since a year and a half was too long, it was going to be this one. I tried to pay attention, but frankly it was difficult for me. I occasionally had flashbacks to that night in my room, and in spite of all the hot kinky sex I was having with Kelly, I made myself come thinking about Jane's ass more times than I care to mention.

The bar was becoming more and more familiar, and when the owners realized I really would show up, they warmed up to me. I occasionally worked with one of them, and I learned more about craft beer that first month than I had picked up in the previous twenty-three years. Brent and Jason came by as often as not, and while I was able to sneak them a few beers, they both had better paying jobs than I did and were happy to support me as much as the bar. Kelly came by on occasion as well, but I got so distracted by her presence that I finally asked her to only come in with friends so I wouldn't be tempted to drag her into the bathroom and fuck her against the wall.

She picked me up one evening from work, and she had a serious look on her face that meant she wanted to talk. Our relationship was going well, and each time we had sex we moved into kinkier and kinkier territory. I spanked her often, and she discovered that she loved to choke on my cock between me slapping her face and calling her names. On occasion I made her wait or beg for nearly an hour before I'd touch her, and she liked me to blindfold her and pretend I was a stranger. We fantasized about Rachel and often came back to her threesome with the two strange men. My desire to watch her get fucked grew stronger each time it came up, and she told me about it in lurid detail. She finally confessed to me that they had been a couple she met at the karaoke bar. They had flirted with her mercilessly all evening, telling her they had never been with a girl before. Watching them kiss and touch each other had been almost as big a turn on as anything else, and she told me about it out of bed as well as in it.

Her statement still took my by surprise as we walked down Third Avenue on our way back to my apartment.

"I want you to come inside me," she said.

"Like without a condom?" I asked. The truth is we had come close at least a few times. I often rubbed against her, and while we always went for latex before it was too late, we waited longer and longer each time. I often would try to slip the condom on while she wasn't looking, and she had trouble telling if I was wearing one at all. It was a fun game, but it felt like a dangerous one.

"Yeah, like inside me."

"Um, I don't know. I mean, it's a little risky, don't you think?"

"Thomas, I want to go get tested with you. I'm on the pill so I'm not worried about getting pregnant. But, we're not fucking anyone else, and it's been almost a month. Besides, one of these days we're going to get so drunk we'll forget about the condom anyway. We can go to the clinic and we'll know in like a week if we're going to die of some horrible disease."

It was a good idea. It was a smart idea. It was an idea that scared the shit out of me, and I had to keep myself walking or else she'd realize how freaked out I was. Jane never once mentioned what had happened, or expressed any worry at all. But, since Claire back in college, I had been a nervous wreck, and I was now dragging Kelly into it as well. I took a deep breath as we walked, and I finally fumbled for a cigarette.

"That sounds awesome," I said. "It's a good idea."

"Are you nervous?" she asked, bumming a smoke from me as we walked.

"A little. I'm not worried about anything in particular, I just haven't been tested in a few years, and I don't know. It freaks me out."

"Me, too. I mean, I'm pretty safe, but it's been a while. But, think on the bright side," she said stopping on the sidewalk and looking up into my eyes. "In seven days you'll be able to fuck me and come in me, and then you get to sleep on the wet spot. Won't that be nice?"

I laughed as we continued on our way, but the lump in my stomach didn't want to go away. She called the following morning though, and before I knew what was happening I was in a clinic in Chelsea with Kelly having blood drawn. The doctor was dry and matter-of-fact, and she seemed almost irritated that we were wasting her time.

"Is there anything wrong with you?" she asked, as I stood there in my underwear in her office. They had already taken blood for HIV and syphilis. She did a swab test for chlamydia, which wasn't the most joyous things in the world, but now all that was left was to look, touch, and pinch.

"I have a little thing on my scrotum," I finally said.

"Drop your boxers," she said with a sigh. She had a flashlight on her head and latex gloves on. She lifted up my balls, rolled them around for a second, until I pointed out the small flap of skin that had worried me since I was twenty.

"It's a skin tag. If it bothers you, talk to your doctor or go see a dermatologist. It's not an STI."

"It's not dangerous?" I asked.

"I don't think so. It doesn't look worrying. Is that it?"

I nodded and she showed me out and back into the waiting room. Kelly came out a few minutes later and we left the building hand in hand, both of us trying not to make the other one nervous. I didn't tell her about my tag, and she didn't say anything about her visit, other than it all seemed fine. We had an appointment the following week to get our results and that was it. We were done and I felt the first bit of relief, even if it was slight. I was still scared about the results, and I didn't like having to wait, but I had done it, and no matter what the doctor said, I could deal with it. We could deal with it together.

The week went by slowly, and I was distracted all the time. I mixed up a few beers at work, broke three pint glasses, and was late once. I didn't tell Jason or Brent, and they both looked at me like I was going crazy each time they saw me. Kelly didn't seem bothered at all, but our sex was slower and less intense. I tried to get into the mood, but I ended up blaming it on the late night shifts I was finally given. Getting home at four in the morning was a valid excuse as far as I was concerned, but I could tell she wasn't happy about it.

Finally, we walked back to the clinic together on a ridiculously hot Saturday afternoon. It was the first week of June and the city was sweltering for the first time. People walked around in as little as possible, and we sweat constantly. I had to keep the door to my room open to get any air, and even then it was hard to sleep.

We had an hour wait before they called our names, and I went in first. They sat me down and handed me a piece of paper with my results on them. I stared at it, but it was a blur of lines, numbers, and words I didn't understand. Couldn't they understand that I was freaked out?

"So, the syphilis came back negative," the nurse said. He was handsome and only a few years older than me. "And here are the HIV results." I stared again, but couldn't figure it out.

"So keep safe and you'll be fine," he said. "You're healthy and nothing looks abnormal. Do you have more than one partner?"

"Wait, it's negative? Is that what you're saying," I asked, relief flooding my voice.

"Yes. The test came back negative, although they're not always one hundred percent."

"Just one right now," I said, finally answering his previous question.

"Well, keep practicing safe sex and come back and get tested again in six months. It's always a good idea to keep up on it."

And then I was back in the waiting room watching a baseball game surrounded by nervous looking people. Kelly was nowhere to be seen and I sat for fifteen minutes, shifting nervously in my seat, before she walked out of the exam room with no discernable expression on her face.

"You all done?" she asked.

"Yeah, how about you?"

"Yup, let's get out of here."

"Wait, what happened? I'm fine, I mean, everything looked normal. How about you?"

"All good," she said looking up at me. "What did you expect? Of course we're fine."

The relief that flooded my body was shocking. I knew I had been nervous, but up until that moment I had no idea how wound up I had been. Ever since Jane, hell ever since Claire, I was a bloody mess, and for the first time in months I felt my body begin to relax in places I didn't know were tight. She took my hand as we headed back across town, and even the heat didn't bother me.

"Want to celebrate?" I asked.

"Docs?" she said.

"I mean I want to fuck you, but Docs sounds good too. I feel like a completely new person."

"You were really worried," she said, stopping me on the street again. "I mean, like freaked out. Did something happen?"

"I don't know, maybe I'm just neurotic. I grew up with so many high school assemblies on AIDS that I was convinced everyone I knew was going to be dead by the time they were this age. And then in college I was insane about safety. Until Claire, the crazy one. Somewhere in the middle we just stopped using condoms, and we hardly ever talked about it."

"And you didn't get tested then?"

"She told me she had been tested already," I said, shaking my head. "And I hadn't ever had sex without a condom, so after a while I just convinced myself I didn't need to. But then I freaked and got too scared anyway, so it didn't matter."

"Much easier to just go, wasn't it?" Her smile was warm and comforting, and I felt like an idiot for having been so worried. Even more, I felt like an idiot for not having done something about it.

"Thank you," I said, wrapping my arm around her as we walked. "Thank you for asking, and for going with me, and just for being amazing."

"I was just being selfish. I hate condoms."

We went back to my place first and had some lunch. We made sandwiches with whatever was left in the fridge, and we talked about nothing at all. Part of me wondered why we didn't jump into bed the second we walked in the door, but the truth was my stomach was still in a knot, and all that tension was taking a long time to leave my body. Kelly was completely relaxed as we ate, and it helped to no end.

We called Jason and Brent who had just woken up, and invited them down to Docs that evening, and we left a note for Rachel telling her the same. It was a night to celebrate. It was still only late afternoon when we were done eating, and we leaned against the counters in the kitchen talking for over an hour. She made a pot of tea, and the longer we stood there sipping it the more relaxed I became. In fact, the more I stared at her sweating beneath her t-shirt, the more I began to wonder if there was any reason to wait much longer. Her shorts were so tiny they almost didn't count, and I had lost my shirt the second we got into the house.

"Fuck, it's hot," I said picking up a catalog and fanning my face with it.

"Want to take a shower?" she asked. "A nice cool shower? We can get cleaned up before Docs, and then go down early to celebrate. I could use a very cold beer soon."

We left our clothes on my bed and walked naked to the bathroom, my eyes glued to her tiny ass the entire time. I was soft when we turned on the water, but by the time she began to soap me up, I was as hard as could be. We kissed beneath the shower, and I could feel the heat leaving my body. I washed her as well, spending extra time on her recently shaved pussy, letting my fingers slide inside her. She was breathing quickly by the time I stood up again; the look in her eyes was as clear as day.

"Here or on the bed?" I asked.

"Now, just for a second. Then you can carry me to the bed and fuck me there, too. I just want to feel you. Now."

"Are you sure?" I asked, bending her over against the wall. "You want me inside you? Just like this? Bare?"

I pressed against her ass, my cock nestling in between her cheeks, as she moaned and arched her back. I teased the lips of her pussy like I had done so many times before, but this was different because I was going to fuck her right there without one goddamned ounce of worry for the first time in my life.

"Just fuck me, Daddy," she moaned, reaching a hand between her legs and rubbing her clit frantically. I teased her for a few moments longer, marveling at how soft she felt against me, but there was no way I could wait. I needed it as much as she did.

Without thinking at all I slid inside her, feeling her around me and revelling in it. She felt amazing, and I wrapped my arms around her as I pushed all the way in. We were both practically holding our breath as we fucked, and it was a strangely quiet moment.

"Does it feel good?" I finally asked, my lips against her ear.

"Too good," she said. "But maybe on the bed? I can hardly stand."

I had to force myself to pull out of her, but together we rushed out of the shower and into my room without even pausing to dry ourselves off. She pushed me down, and I watched in awe as she straddled me with my cock in one hand.

"Is this what you want?" she asked, rubbing me against her again.

"Yes," I moaned, lifting my hips off the bed. "Fuck me, Kelly."

"Let me rephrase the question," she purred as she leaned down and kissed my mouth. I was so hard it hurt, but she held me there just inches away from her. "Do you want to fuck me, Daddy? Do you want to come inside your little girl?"

I grabbed her without a word. She screamed when I entered her, but then I was all the way inside her, and her eyes rolled back as she fucked me like she was on fire. I pulled her down onto me, still thrusting up, and then it was over.

"Oh fuck, I'm coming," I said, way sooner than I had expected.

"Do it," she pleaded. "Come inside me. I want to feel you, Daddy."

She collapsed onto me as I bit my lip and exploded within her. I could feel my balls tighten and the come move through my body until it filled the inside of her cunt. We kissed and moaned as I came, and her hands were on each side of my facing holding me still. Her hips rolled over me, and I almost couldn't stand it. Once I come my sensitivity is so high I can barely hold still, but she didn't stop moving, and I almost thought I might grow hard and come once again. She kissed me one last time before giving me a grin I had never seen before.

Without warning she lifted off me, moved up my body with her hand in my hair, and then pushed her cunt down onto my mouth.

"Oh, yes" she moaned, grinding her hips into my face, and all I could do was slip my tongue inside her, tasting my cum as it dripped from within her. "Just like that, Daddy, eat my pussy. Eat all your come right of me, Daddy. Just like that."

To my surprise I rolled her over with brute force, my mouth still against her, and I licked harder, sucked faster, and pushed two fingers inside her. I was filled with a hunger I had never felt, and her moaning and screaming didn't hurt. She clenched her legs around me as I fingered her, ate her, and swallowed everything. Her orgasm seemed to come from nowhere, and she nearly broke my neck as she squeezed me between her thighs. I could hardly breathe, but still I didn't stop. I would have climbed inside her and kept going if I could. It was messy, terrifying, and so insanely hot that I eventually found myself growing hard once more.

By the time she finally calmed down, I was inside her again and it started all over. I pinned her arms above her head and fucked her, not caring about anything other than coming once more. She egged me on, begging me to fuck her harder, and in the middle of it all I slapped her face.

"You're such a little bitch," I said. "You liked making me do that, didn't you? Well, now I'm going to fuck you again, and if you're not careful I'm going to fuck this tiny, little ass, too."

We had never talked about her ass, although I had worked a finger inside her on more than one occasion. I slapped it and grabbed it all the time, but not once did we discuss my cock inside it.

"Please, Daddy," she said, real fear suddenly crossing her face as she slipped back into her little place. "Not that. Please don't fuck my ass."

I fucked her harder and faster, picturing her on her knees with her ass in the air, and suddenly it was Jane and I was coming again. She is not supposed to be here! Fuck! Shit! Goddamn it motherfucker, this is bullshit! I'm fucking Kelly, I want her ass, and damn my stupid brain. I kissed her mouth, hoping it might bring me back, but even as I came the second time, my mind was stuck somewhere else and there was nothing to be done. Please don't let me say the wrong name.

"I love you, Babygirl," I finally moaned. "I love you so fucking much."

"I love you too, Daddy," she whispered, her pussy still tight around me as I moved down to kiss her neck and chin. I leaned up and looked down at her, blowing air over her sweaty body. I moved from her shoulder to her belly, covering her with my breath even as I struggled to catch it.

"Fuck that was a good idea," I said, when I finally rolled over next to her. She reached down and covered her pussy with one hand. "I can't believe you sat on my face though. I suppose I should have guessed when I met you."

"I'm full of good ideas," she whispered. "Also, your come. But yeah, you totally should have known. Besides, I've never been able to do that before. I mean not right after like that. It was so hot feeling you lick me right after you came. I think I was feeling bratty."

"It was bratty, and I may have to make you pay for it." I pulled her to me and slapped her lightly, watching her flinch beneath my hand.

"Another spanking?" she asked, her voice quiet once more.

"No, this time I think it should be something else. Something different."

"What are you going to do, Daddy?"

"You'll find out," I said, suddenly getting out of the bed and grabbing my towel. "But, for now, we need another shower before we go meet our friends."

She pouted at me, but a moment later we were back in the

shower washing my come and sweat off of our bodies. I had to think of something good, but making her wait for it was going to be just as much fun.

Chapter Eleven

"Hey, is Rachel coming?" Brent was sitting next to me at the bar. Kelly and I had staked out a corner near the front, and we held onto it until Jason and Brent showed up an hour later. We had started slowly, so it didn't take them long to catch up with us. He was looking around the bar with a slightly nervous twitch, and I wasn't sure if he was hoping she'd arrive or wouldn't.

"Why, you got another bitch coming, too?" Kelly asked.

"I like this girl, Thomas. I do. You should keep her. If she lets you. But seriously, is she coming?"

"She's got a good point, dude," I said. "Why do you ask?"

He looked around the bar again and tapped his fingers on the twisted wooden counter. He was practically dancing he was so nervous, and I hadn't seem him like that in years. In fact, I hadn't seen him like that since the sixth grade talent show. What the hell was going on with him? I finally reached out and grabbed his arm, trying to calm him down. I reached into my pocket and pulled out a joint. One of my regulars had given it to me as a tip, but I hadn't bothered to light it up yet. I was less than an occasional pot smoker, but it looked like Brent could use it.

"Want to go smoke?" I asked him.

"I'll watch out for Kelly," Jason said, leaning in against the bar next to her. He smiled, but it was about as offensive as a plain pizza. I grabbed Brent by the arm and pulled him outside into the warm night air. We crossed Avenue A and walked into the park. There were a few people sleeping under a benches and the occasional couple making out in dark corners, but it was generally quiet and there didn't appear to be any cops. Maybe it was early enough that no one cared.

We stopped beneath a tree in a dark corner against the fence, and I lit the joint, taking a small hit before passing it to Brent. It was skunky in just the right way. He took a huge drag and didn't bother to give it back. He never touched cigarettes, but the man would smoke a fucking ounce of weed if you let him.

"So, what's going on, El Macho. Give me the skinny."

"I can't talk about it. Seriously, I can't," he said.

"Because someone asked you not to, or you don't know what to say?"

"Yeah, that. I mean, it's not a big deal, but maybe it is. Fuck! I hate being stuck in this shit. I didn't ask for any of this. Rachel is confusing."

"Have you asked her out? Because apparently that's a thing. Like, you have to actually tell someone you want to date them. Otherwise they don't know. Trust me."

"It's not like that. I don't want to date her. Jane says I shouldn't tell you, but it's fucked up. I don't like having secrets."

I stole the joint back instantly and took another hit off it before lighting a cigarette. What the hell was he talking about?

"Since when do you talk to Jane?" I asked.

"What do you mean? I've been helping her plan the wedding. We talk all the time."

"How come I'm never invited?"

"She didn't want to bother you with Kelly and everything. But listen, it's not about Jane. It's Rachel. I did something stupid."

"What did you do Brent?" Stupid could mean a whole lot of things.

"I read her diary. It was open on her bedside table and when she was in the shower one morning I just read a few pages. I know

I shouldn't have, but I did, and I can't unread it now."

"You find out she's doing other guys or something?"

"I told you, I don't care about that. It's not about me. It's about Kelly."

My heart was suddenly pounding, and I wasn't sure what I was feeling. It was about Kelly? That didn't even make any sense. What could be going on with Kelly and what did it have to do with Rachel?

"I shouldn't have said anything." He paused for a long moment looking at the joint in his hand. It was nearly gone, but he stared at it all the same. "I think she's in love with her."

"Wait, who is in love with who?"

"Rachel. I think she's in love with Kelly. She wrote about walking in on you guys and eating Kelly's pussy, and then it just went on and on. Her life changed and she can't get her out of her head."

"Are you serious? After that one time? I heard you fucking her the next morning. Maybe she was just writing random shit. Come on, it's probably not a big deal."

"They're still fucking."

"What do you mean?"

"There were more entries," Brent said. "I read forward and Rachel and Kelly have hooked up two or three more times since then. Sometimes when you're at work and she's waiting for you, they just get naked and do whatever girls do. I'm sorry man, I didn't want to tell you."

"You're saying that Kelly, my Kelly, is fucking your girlfriend? And not telling me about it?"

"I told you. I think she's in love. And she's not my girlfriend." Brent took the last hit off the joint.

"Wait, you told Jane this? Does Jason know too?"

He looked down, his eyes now red from the weed and his

balance a little fuzzy. I leaned back against the fence and looked up at the night sky. Well, at least as much of it as I could see.

"I'm sorry," he said. "I should have told you sooner. I just read it yesterday though, I swear. But, when I realized all of us were going to be together, I had to say something. I was going to freak out if Kelly and Rachel sat there next to each pretending nothing was going on and everyone knew but you. Sorry, dude."

"This is fucked up," I said.

"Yeah."

"It's really hot though. I mean, watching the two of them was insane. Rachel's body is fucking killer."

"Oh my god. Those tits. She's like a less crazy version of Teeters. I can't picture them though. She's like a foot taller."

"What do I do?" I asked.

"Ask her? Nothing? I have no fucking clue, dude. I just couldn't wait any longer. But look, I think it's mostly Rachel. It was hard to tell what was in her head and what was real, but it's not just fun for her. I mean she had page after page about how much she loves that girl and it was a little creepy. Like Single White Female kinda creepy. Like she might possibly be stealing Kelly's panties and sleeping with them under her pillow."

"Kelly doesn't wear panties," I whispered.

"I guess that's good then," he said, trying not to laugh. I could feel the pot hitting me too, and I had to giggle as well no matter how fucked up it was. He looked at me and I tried to picture Rachel hoarding clippings of Kelly's hair or stealing her lipstick. It was all so absurd there was nothing else to do. We stood laughing for at least ten minutes before I finally grabbed him and started heading back to the bar.

"Well, fuck it, dude. There's nothing to do about it now but go back to Docs. I guess I'll find out one way or another!" I sounded more sure of myself than I felt.

We walked out of the park and back onto Avenue A and we were pleasantly high. I was annoyed, but strangely, I wasn't angry. When I thought back to our conversation, I even remembered Kelly telling me we were exclusive except for Rachel's pussy. I thought she was joking at the time, but maybe it's because I only heard what I wanted to hear.

When we walked into the bar, Jason was sitting in my seat with a tall boy of PBR, the jukebox was blasting "The Devil Went Down to Georgia," and Kelly and Rachel were dancing on top of the bar in their bras. I stood there, my mouth hanging open as the crowd hollered at them, but it was all I could do to keep from laughing.

"You tell him?" Jason whispered so loudly I couldn't miss it. Brent just nodded, but all six of our eyes were glued to the two hotties in tight jean shorts dancing on the bar. One of the bartenders finally climbed up with them, and as the song ended she made them kneel down as she poured shots of Southern Comfort into their mouths, splashing more onto the bar and patrons than down their throats. I reached a hand up and helped them down, one at time, while Jason handed them their shirts back. A few guys were yelling across the room to keep them off, but I gave them the finger as the girls got dressed.

"Holy shit, I haven't done that in ages," Rachel said, wrapping her arms around Kelly in a huge hug. "It was so much fun. We would have totally gotten tips you know."

The bartender handed us another round, and I took a big sip of my beer before pulling Kelly close and kissing her with more force than I might have. Was that a twinge of jealousy, or was I just stoned?

"That was so fucking hot," I whispered, kissing her cheek. "I like watching my little girl dancing on the bar with her pretty little friend."

"Daddy," she whined, pushing me back. "You'll mke me spill my drink."

"So, what are we celebrating today?" Jason asked. I turned around and he was holding up his big can of beer with a grin on his face.

"I think girls dancing on the bar," I said. "Definitely to hot girls dancing on the bar. Also, not having AIDS. Let's drink to that, too."

"Did you two get tested?" Rachel asked. "I mean, did you get results back?"

"We are squeaky clean," Kelly said, kissing her right on the mouth.

"Well, fucking cheers to that," Brent said.

We all drank to it, but I kept looking back and forth between the two girls wondering if I was missing something. Rachel and Brent stood close to each other, but it wasn't especially intimate. Every time Kelly said something funny Rachel laughed, and she touched her every chance she could get. Not once did I look at my roommate to see her watching anyone else, and Brent's suspicion made more and more sense as the night went on. I finally managed to pull Kelly aside for a few minutes, and I kissed her hard before whispering in her ear.

"I liked watching you on the bar." She was facing away from me, with her ass grinding against my cock.

"It was for you, Daddy," she whispered over her shoulder.

"I especially liked watching you with your pretty little friend," I said. One hand was on her stomach beneath her shirt, and I ran my fingertips along the inside of her jean shorts against her soft skin.

"She's pretty," she said, trying to hold still.

"Do you know what I'd like to see?" I asked. She simply shook her head, biting her lip at the same time that I slid my hand into her shorts. A small gasp escaped her, but I held her tightly, pushing a finger inside her. "I want to watch her kiss you here. I want to see her lick this pretty little pussy again after Daddy comes inside you. Would you like that, Babygirl? Would you like your little friend to eat this mess?"

I pulled my hand out and stuck two fingers between Kelly's lips without a word. I thought her knees might buckle she shook so hard in my arms, but she sucked my fingers and moaned as she pushed her ass against my hard cock. I didn't know what the hell I was doing, but I knew I had to do something.

"Yes," she finally moaned. "I want her to taste me. And you."

I didn't give her time to say anything else before I dragged her through the crowd towards the bathroom. The men's room at Docs is painfully small and never clean. But none of that mattered as I pushed her into the stall and closed the door behind me. I had her jeans around her knees in a second, and my cock was inside her once more before she could say a word. She bit her hand as she tried not to scream, and I bent her over further as I pushed into her, fucking her with my bare cock for the third time that day.

"When we get home, she's going to suck this little cunt," I growled. "She's going to eat this pussy, and you're going to sit on her face just like you did to me, do you understand?"

"Yes, Daddy," was all she could say. I fucked her faster, wanting to come more than anything else. And then there was a pounding on the door and the bouncer was yelling at us to get the fuck out of the stall. We struggled to pull our pants back up, and Kelly laughed as he dragged us out of the bathroom and back into the noise. He walked us all the way to the front door, and showed us out onto the street. We didn't even try to argue, and half a minute later, our three friends were there with us asking what the hell had happened.

"We were just fucking in the bathroom. I don't know what

the big deal is," Kelly said laughing.

"That's nasty," Brent said. "Have you seen that bathroom? What the fuck, guys? I was just about to order a round of car bombs and you have to go and get us kicked out."

"If you can't fuck in the bathroom of Docs, where can you fuck?" I said, shaking my head and adjusting my dick in my pants. I was still hard, and the entire situation was absurd.

"My bed?" Rachel, said looking at all us. "Or the floor. Or the couch if Martin isn't home. Hell, even if he is home it probably wouldn't matter. And there's always Princess's bed too. We can fuck anywhere."

Jason looked as us like we were on crack, and I wasn't sure what to say. Was Rachel really inviting all of us back home to fuck? And what did that mean? I loved Jason and Brent, and while Brent and I had definitely had a few threesomes, this was something else. This was more like an orgy, and I wasn't sure if I was up for it. Besides, the chances that Jason would actually go for it were slim to none, and it didn't seem right to send him home just because he didn't want to orgy with us. But, his quizzical look turned into a smile a second later.

"Sounds good to me," Jason said. I looked at him and he just shrugged.

"Great," Rachel said. "Let's go home, smoke some weed and get naked."

She was up the block without another word, and I grabbed Kelly and started after her. Brent and Jason were right behind me, but all of us were confused about what was actually going to happen.

"Kelly, what the hell? Is she serious?"

"I don't know, but it might be fun to find out. Are you worried?"

"No, it's fine," I said, taking her hand in mine. "It's just not what I expected."

"Well, what better way to celebrate, right? Besides, you've wanted to watch me get fucked for a long time now. And I think Rachel has some cleaning up to do."

I stopped long enough to light a cigarette and when I looked up Kelly had caught up to Rachel. What did she mean? Watch her get fucked? Was she serious? It was one thing to talk about it in bed, but this was something else. I was suddenly even more nervous. They looked like the odd couple with Rachel more than a head taller, but my eyes were glued to their asses, and I tried not to think too hard.

"Dude, are we really doing this?" Brent stepped up next to me as we walked up Avenue A. "I mean, like, all five of us?"

"Why not?" Jason said. "Your girlfriends are hot. Besides, if they're really having some secret lezzy thing going on, I want to watch."

"Guys, this is insane. Kelly is actually my girlfriend, no matter what's going on with Rachel and El Macho here. What the fuck?"

"Oh, come on," Brent said. "I've fucked your girlfriends before."

"That was once, dude, and look how it ended up. We broke up a month later, and she fucked with my head more than anyone. Seriously, I can't believe we're doing this."

"Thomas, do you really think anything is going to happen?" Jason was always the voice of reason. "We're just going back to your place to keep drinking. You're the one who got us kicked out of my new favorite bar. Let's just go home, open some beers and not worry about it. No one is going to fuck your girlfriend unless you tell them to."

"Great," I said, walking faster and dropping my cigarette onto the sidewalk. "Just fucking great."

Chapter Twelve

The first thing that happened when we walked in the door was Rachel took off her shirt. It was still covered in her erstwhile shot, and it so was hot in the apartment I couldn't really blame her. She was wearing a lacy black bra beneath it, and I had to agree there was a reason the guys at the bar were hollering. She was hot, and not just because of the weather. Kelly joined her a second later, her small breasts covered by pink cotton, and I smiled, knowing she had bought it a week earlier just for me. It was adorable.

The second thing that happened is that Brent got behind the bar and started mixing drinks. After lots of beer at Docs it was probably a bad idea, but that didn't make a difference. It felt like a night of bad ideas, and who was I to stop anything? He handed us all some whisky concoction he swore he hadn't invented, and surprisingly it didn't taste completely like ass. Jason put a record on Martin's old record player, and before I knew what was happening the girls were dancing around the living room while the three of us leaned against the bar watching.

At first they just swayed and shook, without paying much attention to anything, but the closer they got to each other, the more they whispered; that could only mean trouble. Kelly had to stand on her tip toes whenever Rachel wanted a kiss, but within minutes the two girls were grinding on each other like it was high school. They kept looking over their shoulders at us standing there with our jaws open, but not one of us moved.

"Okay, that's hot," Brent said. "Kelly is kinda tiny for me, but that's hot."

"They're both hot. And in their bras. For now." I jabbed Jason in the gut, and he just barely managed not to spill his drink. We watched them dance to one entire song before finally moving closer.

"Come here," Rachel said, her arm wrapped around my little girl. She was waving at us though, and we obeyed almost instantly. "Who wants to watch Thomas's girlfriend take off the rest of her clothes?"

All three of us looked back and forth, but my two best friends ended up staring at me. Fuck, what the hell was I supposed to do? It was suddenly up to me to ruin the party if I didn't feel like letting my friends watch Kelly strip? Fuck, fuck, fuck.

"I think it's pretty clear everyone wants to watch that," I finally said, giving up.

Rachel walked over to the turntable, pulled off the record Jason had put on, and suddenly we were listening to Prince, and Kelly was dancing once again. Rachel came back to the couch and pulled Jason and Brent down with her: one on each side. I sat by myself a few feet away, but not before I managed to dim the lights enough to make me more comfortable. Kelly swayed with her eyes closed, and for a while I wasn't sure if she even noticed we were there.

And then, without warning, she undid her bra, turned her back to us, and tossed it casually over her head. It landed on the coffee table, but no one noticed. Their eyes were all glued to the tiny dancer in the middle of the room who was turning around with just her hands covering her tits. I noticed Rachel's hands on my best friends' thighs, and I leaned back and tried to enjoy it.

When Kelly finally uncovered herself so she could slide her hands down her body to her hips, all of us cheered, and the room grew hot in an instant. The bulges in my friends' pants were becoming more apparent as Rachel stroked them, and I was having a similar trouble myself. Watching her dance was one thing, but she was also turned on. She danced slowly, her hips swaying, but I could tell in a heartbeat that she was loving it. When she stood directly in front of Rachel I moved closer until I was almost on Brent's lap.

Kelly stepped forward, taking my roommate's head in her hands and pulling her closer.

"Undo them with your teeth," she growled. Without a second's pause Rachel had her jeans undone and her zipper halfway down before Kelly stepped back and kept dancing. We were dead silent except for the music, and when she dropped her shorts to the floor I was practically coming in my pants. Her back was to us, and once again I was mesmerized by her ass as she bent over until all four of us had a clear view of her smooth pussy lips between her perfect thighs.

When I looked back to my friends I realized Rachel had managed to get their cocks out of their pants, and she had one in each hand. They were both as hard as Kelly's ass, and I didn't blame them. I almost pulled out my own cock, but I couldn't keep from looking at the dancing girl, along with the one on the couch jerking off two guys at once. When Kelly turned to face us I heard her gasp along with the rest of us. She noticed what was happening on the couch the same time everyone got a view of her naked body. I was stuck, unable to move as I watched, and too many things went through my head. I wanted everything and nothing at the same time, but I had a feeling I didn't have too many choices.

Rachel reached out a hand, waving Kelly towards her with one finger. She moved without thought until she was standing right in front of us. Brent and Jason just stared, her tiny body completely naked, smooth, and covered in light beads of sweat.

"Closer," Rachel said, her hand going back to Brent's cock. "Turn around," she commanded. Their legs were practically touching she was so close, and Kelly trembled as she turned.

"Open your legs," she said, and Kelly did it without pause. "Now bend over."

If I thought the view a moment before was too much, this was a whole new thing. Kelly's legs were open just wide enough that her pussy was exposed like never before. She was soaking wet, and I wasn't sure if it was all her or some of my come leftover from earlier in the day. I had to remind myself that only a half hour before I was inside her, because from where I was sitting, nothing felt real.

"Touch your pussy," Rachel said, and I heard both of my friends groan. Her hands moved faster and faster, and they struggled to sit still as she jerked them off. Again, without pausing, Kelly moved one hand between her legs and opened the lips of her cunt with two fingers. Moans escaped her lips almost instantly, and I finally had to pull my cock out of my jeans as I stared at her.

Rachel leaned in closer, her hands still moving, until my girlfriend was inches from her face. Kelly shoved her fingers deeper into her cunt, and suddenly Jason was moaning and biting his arm as he began to spurt all over Rachel's hand. She hardly seemed to notice as she kissed Kelly's ass cheeks, but still she didn't stop. Rachel finally leaned all the way in and licked her way from Kelly's asshole all the way down her pussy.

"Oh fuck," Brent said, his cock twitching, as he struggled to hold back. I wasn't far behind him, my fist now a blur, but I was determined to wait. Rachel might be able to get what she wanted, but I wasn't going to go without a fight.

I took a deep breath and made a decision. No one told Kelly what to do but me, and this had to stop. Besides, both girls still needed to be punished, and my mind was suddenly full of ideas. I stood up, still watching the scene in front of me, before I kissed Kelly's mouth as she moaned and pushed back against Rachel's lips.

"Turn around," I said, taking her by the shoulders. I didn't give her any time to think. She stood up, looking up at me with big eyes and it was done. I leaned in and whispered in her ear.

"You're going to turn around and face them, Babygirl, and you're going to do exactly as I tell you. It's time you showed everyone just how much of a slut you really are. I'm going to fuck you as they watch, and when I tell you to, you're going to lean down and suck Brent's cock. Do you understand?"

"Yes, Daddy," she whispered so quietly I almost didn't hear her. She was trembling as I held her, and the look in her eyes was unmistakable. When I turned her around, I saw Rachel had finally lost her bra. Jason was still staring at us, his cock hard even after he came. Brent was jerking himself off, his fist moving slowly up and down and I pushed Kelly closer to the couch.

"Are you ready?" I asked. She simply nodded her head as I pushed her down onto her knees, my body following behind her. Rachel watched us, and I was unsure if she was going to try to take control again. Instead she undid her own jean shorts, and as I positioned myself behind Kelly, she pulled them off, taking her panties with them. Once again I was staring at her pussy, wondering how the hell I had gotten into this.

Brent turned to look at her, and for a moment his hand stopped. He had seen her naked plenty of times, but suddenly she was spread eagle on the couch while all four of us watched. She just smiled as she slipped two fingers into her pussy.

"Now," I said, not waiting any longer. At almost exactly the same time Kelly leaned in to envelope Brent's cock, I started to fuck her. She moaned, he groaned, and then suddenly my sweet little girl had her mouth around his dick, her hand sliding up and down his shaft as I fucked her like there was no tomorrow.

Watching her was not what I expected. It was hot, and it did make me jealous, but it did something else as well. Maybe it was the way her mouth had to stretch around his girth, or maybe how she choked each time she tried to take him even halfway in, but for just a moment I felt disgust fill my whole body. I wanted to call her names, not because they turned me on, but because for at least a second, I believed them. She was a filthy slut, struggling to take a cock in her mouth as she was fucked from behind, and I hated them both. In fact I hated all of us. I hated Rachel and myself for making it happen, Jason for coming as he stared at my girlfriend's pussy, and Brent and Kelly for the noises coming out of their mouths.

I stared at Kelly's ass for a moment, suddenly wondering what she would do if I tried to force my cock into her, and when I looked up Rachel was rolling a condom down over Jason's dick. How was he still hard? She climbed onto his lap a few seconds later, and I had to close my eyes to keep it all away.

"Oh shit, Kelly," I heard Brent moan. "I'm gonna fucking blow."

She didn't stop though, and that made me angrier even as I got closer and closer to coming myself. Rachel was moaning like a teenager, and even Jason was telling her to fuck him harder. I leaned over Kelly, pushing as deeply inside her as I could go, and I watched Brent's come spill out of her mouth as she choked on him. I pulled her up by the hair, arching her back as I fucked her, and suddenly I was calling out and coming as well.

"Oh fuck," I screamed as I slammed into her. She put her head down, and somehow pushed back even harder onto me as she begged me to fill her.

"More," she moaned as she came. "I need more."

And then I was exploding, my eyes moving from Kelly's ass to Rachel's cunt getting fucked, and then back to Brent's come on my Babygirl's lips; I was lost. I came over and over again, and I didn't think I would stop. Her pussy was so tight, and the scene in front of me was too much to handle. I finally thrust into her one last time as she urged me on.

"Come in me, Daddy," she screamed. "Come in my little pussy."

When I finally fell back, my cock made a pop as it slipped out of her. Her lips were red and swollen, and even in the darkened room I could see my come leaking out of her used cunt. She rolled back onto me, and I wrapped my arms around her as she began to whisper I'm sorry over and over again into my neck. I didn't know if it was for calling me Daddy in front of our friends or for swallowing Brent's load, but it didn't matter. I held her and told her everything was alright. It was a lie, a terrible lie, but it didn't matter.

"Everything is going to be fine, Babygirl," I whispered. "You're almost done. It's almost over."

The three of us sat there, Brent on the couch, and us on the floor as Jason and Rachel moved faster and faster. It was strangely normal after a while, and I had to stop myself from laughing. They moved like anyone fucking, and their bodies were like everyone else's. Jason's balls were huge and squished between his legs, and whenever she sat up, I could see her asshole, surrounded by just the lightest touch of blonde hair.

"Fuck me," she kept moaning over and over again, and it felt like it went on forever. He finally pushed her down onto her back, her head on Brent's lap, before filling her again. One leg was on the floor in front of us, and the other up over his shoulder, giving us a good view of his cock sliding into her; Brent sat there perfectly still as his sometimes girlfriend got fucked on his lap.

"I'm so close," Jason said. "Fuck, I'm close."

Rachel reached a hand between her legs and rubbed her clit frantically, not wanting to be left behind. As he arched into her, she thrust up against him, begging him not to stop. When his shoulders began to tense and it looked like it was over, she started to scream as well. She reached up and took Brent's hands in hers as she lifted her hips off the couch.

"Come on me," she said. "Pull out and come on me."

Without another pause Jason tore the condom off his dick, tossed it over his shoulder, and grabbed his cock as he leaned close.

His hand was a blur, and all four of us watched as he exploded onto her stomach, her tits, and then at the last moment he laned back and some of his come landed on the lips to her pussy.

"Fuck!" she screamed, reaching one finger down and carefully wiping it up. Without hesitating though she brought it to her lips and sucked it off. "Be careful you asshole. Don't fucking jizz on my cunt."

He fell back onto the couch trying to apologize even as he finished jerking himself off. He was covered in sweat, and breathing fast enough to make him shake. She didn't move, but she did reach down and begin rubbing his come into her skin, making patterns over her tits and stomach.

"Fuck, I love being covered in come," she said.

"Good," I finally said. Kelly was still in my lap, but she was sitting up staring at everyone else in amazement. I looked around the room, and I instantly started laughing. "We are so fucking insane."

Brent started laughing as well, his voice deep and rich, and Rachel's head bounced up and down as his stomach moved. Jason was simply smiling on the couch, suddenly looking shy for the first time all night, and Rachel smiled at us, her own grin growing bigger by the second.

"Your girlfriend just totally blew your best friend," she said.

"She did," I said, knowing what came next. Just because we had all blown our loads, didn't mean this was over. One last person still needed payback, and she was going to get it while I still had the chance. "But, she has a present for you, Rachel. My little slut has something she wants to give you. Don't you, Babygirl?"

Kelly looked up at me for a moment as I pushed her forward, and suddenly a flash of recognition appeared on her face. Crawling slowly, she pulled herself up on the couch, kissing Rachel's arm as she did it. She kissed her neck, her lips, and finally her forehead.

"I do have a present," she whispered, her legs coming up as she straddled my roommate with a fierce determination. A second later she knelt over Rachel's face as Brent watched in amazement. She reached down with one hand, spread the lips of her pussy, and then sat down without a word.

To her credit, Rachel didn't pause. She didn't hesitate, argue, or make a sound other than a moan. She opened her mouth, stuck out her tongue, and seconds later she had her hands on Kelly's hips pulling her down as if she couldn't get enough.

"That's right," Kelly moaned. "Eat my pussy. Eat my sloppy, wet, come-soaked, pussy, you filthy slut."

Jason and Brent just stared at me, and I smiled as the girls began to moan and scream all over again. I lit a cigarette and leaned back as I watched. I still had no idea if they were actually fucking around behind my back, but it no longer mattered. I had never seen anything hotter in my life, with the possible exception of Kelly sucking Brent's cock a few minutes earlier.

Kelly started to come again in minutes, and for a while I didn't think Rachel would ever stop. The little girl shook and trembled over her mouth, and it was only once all her spasms stopped that she climbed back down onto the floor and into my waiting arms.

"Now we're insane," Rachel said. "Before we were just crazy. But now, I think we've officially moved to the next level."

"You guys are so weird. But that was like, so pretty to watch. I thought it was a dream, and I like my dreams, but then it was real and so beautiful. I love you all."

All five of us looked up at the new voice, shock appearing on our faces at exactly the same time. Katie was standing in the doorway to Martin's room in just a t-shirt, and she was smiling like it was the first day of spring. She swayed as she blew us all kisses, and before anyone could say a word, she said she loved us again and vanished into the bedroom, closing the door behind her.

Chapter Thirteen

Two days later I got an email from Talia. I didn't have a computer - I swear I was last - but I checked my Hotmail on Martin's on a regular basis in case some fucking technophile dropped me a note. As my luck would have it, I had exactly three emails. One from my father who turned out to be an early adopter, one from Nathan asking if I was coming back to Japan for his wedding, and one from Talia. She was coming to New York and she wanted to have dinner.

It was a shock in many ways that I wasn't ready for, but that I think I needed. For more than forty-eight hours I was a mess and not in a hot way. I was anxious, freaked out, and generally not in a good place. Kelly had slept over that night, Brent and Jason took a cab home, and Rachel passed out on her own without another word from our strange voyeur Katie. But, the next day we didn't talk about it. Sure, we talked around it, referenced it, and I tried hard to make it feel like a normal thing. The truth is that much of it was hot. I liked watching Kelly suck cock, and I especially liked watching her sit on Rachel's face. But, I never once mentioned Brent's snooping into the diary and it didn't come up otherwise. There was about as much transparency going on as a CIA press release.

Kelly went on like nothing strange had happened, and if she did mention it, it was only while we were fucking, and I played right along. Like I said, it turned me on to think about. It also made me into a complete nervous wreck. Kelly was lying to me, Jason was crazier than I ever expected, Brent probably wanted to fuck my girlfriend, and Rachel was a manipulative bitch who was trying to ruin my life. Like I said, I was a wreck. It didn't have to make sense to drive me to drink, and it didn't have to be realistic to freak me out.

But, suddenly there was Talia. Sweet, brilliant, beautiful Talia who was more grounded than all five of us put together. Talia who always knew what she wanted, always planned ahead, and took enough time to make sure she was moving in the right direction. She was a rock and a savior. She was the best of humanity all wrapped up into a perfect body, and that night my fantasies turned into something else completely. As I lay in bed, Talia's email printed out and placed on my night stand, I dreamed of love: easy, simple, beautiful love. I wanted to hold her and kiss her for hours. I wanted to ask permission, hear her say yes, and buy her flowers as we walked along the beach.

I got hard when I whispered I love you into her imaginary ear and it drove me to distraction. I pictured her next to me, drinking a glass of wine as we discussed our future, and all of it made sense. She had saved me once and she could do it again. Even when I pictured us making love it was tender and sweet. Her breasts heaved beneath me as we cried tears of joy and there was nothing messy about what we did. Soft skin, warm kisses, and gentle fingers kept me awake as I relished the joy of waiting for her arrival. In just a week she would be here. She'd be in New York, and everything would alright with the world. The craziness I had fallen into would vanish and love would prevail. True love would win in the end, and everything would be okay. Everything would be fine.

"Hey, handsome," Kelly said when she crawled into bed at two a.m., waking me up. She had been working late, and I was overjoyed to have the time to myself.

"Did I wake you up, Daddy?" she asked.

I felt a familiar twitch, but I was smart enough to suppress it. I wrapped my arms around her and kissed her gently on the cheek. There was no way I was going to let go of Talia when she was suddenly so close. Kelly couldn't do a think to bring me back to our fucked up place.

"Hi, Baby," I whispered. I closed my eyes again, rolled over, and pretended to sleep. She combed my hair with her fingers, and I swear I could hear her thinking. After six hours at the karaoke bar she was most likely pumped up, wide awake, and if I knew her at all, horny as all hell. Especially if her cute little gay couple had shown up again to remind her of what it was like to be with two men who liked to make out. I pretended to snore.

"Daddy?" she asked again. It was only then that I realized she wasn't naked. It was too hot for sheets, but when I opened my eyes and looked at her I nearly burst. She was wearing a simple white nighty that looked lost in time. It was practically sheer, with simple lace work around the edges, and it spoke of more innocence that I could handle. Kelly looked like the perfect little girl. This was completely not fair.

"Daddy, I can't sleep," she whispered. "I had a bad dream."

I kissed her forehead and held her, trying to keep the situation from escalating.

"It's okay," I mumbled, "Daddy's here." I felt my cock twitch when I said the words, but I fought it all the same. She wasn't going to win this easily.

"I dreamed you didn't love me any more." Her voice was so quiet I almost didn't hear her, but my heart broke in an instant and every thought of Talia vanished in a heartbeat.

I sat up, and leaned over to the table next to my bed. I found a lighter in the drawer and lit a candle that smelled of honeysuckle. I turned back to her, and she sat up as I wrapped my arms around her. I kissed her head and pulled her close, whispering in her ear.

"It was a just a dream. I promise, Babygirl, it was just a nightmare. Of course I love you."

'Do you promise?" she asked. "I know I've been bad, but I

don't want to be."

I cursed my hard-on under my breath, but there was nothing to be done. I held her closer, her ass rubbing against my cock through her simple shirt. Christ, why did she have to look so cute in that? I could barely make out her body through the thin fabric, but I found myself staring no matter how hard I tried not to.

"It's okay," I whispered again. And then I went one step further in spite of myself. "You can't help it. I know you try, but it's hard. You're such a pretty girl, and sometimes it's just too hard to resist. It's okay, Babygirl."

"I try to be good," she whispered, turning to face me. Without thinking I lifted her nightgown off over her head until her perfect little body was naked in front of me.

"You are good," I said, pulling her to me and kissing her again. "You're the best little girl ever."

And then she was on top of me, and I kissed her breasts as she cried against me. Without even trying she slipped me inside her, and we rocked there on the bed, hardly moving at all. She wrapped her legs around me, and I kissed her over and over again. I petted her hair, kissed her face, and whispered I love you into her ear like a record on repeat. Together we made love more slowly than we ever had before, and it was a completely new thing.

"I love you," I said again. "I love you no matter how bad you are."

It was the wrong thing to say if I wanted to stay where we were, but there was no helping it. I was still angry, and I was still jealous. I was still too many things to let it be.

"I tried, Daddy. I did, but his cock was there, and you told me to."

"I know, Babygirl," I whispered. "I know."

"Am I a slut, Daddy? Am I a terrible girl?"

"You're perfect," I said, rolling us over until she was beneath me. I was right back to that moment, and I was too hard to do anything about it. I pictured her on her hands and knees with Brent's cock in her mouth, and the question wouldn't go away. No matter how hard I tried, I couldn't not ask her.

"Did you like it, Babygirl? Did you like sucking Brent's cock?"

She was redder than the sea, and she looked down as she blushed, trying to avoid my eyes. I combed her hair and kissed her face, telling her it was okay. She could tell me.

"Yes," she whispered, burying her head into my neck even as I slid back inside her.

"Did you want more?" I asked, knowing that I couldn't go back. I had to know, and she would tell me the truth. Babygirl would tell me the truth, but so would Kelly. Whatever she said would be real. "Did you want to fuck him? Did you want that big, thick cock inside you?"

I felt like I was holding my breath between the time I asked her and she answered. At first her voice was so quiet I couldn't hear her, and I lifted her chin up until she was looking in my eyes. Her body was hot and sweaty beneath me, but even the sight of my cock inside her was too much. I asked her again and again, until finally I pulled out of her and held myself there, teasing her with just the head.

"Yes," said, crying louder and prettier than I had ever heard her before.

"Yes, what?" I asked, still teasing her.

"Yes, I wanted more?"

"Tell me what you wanted." I pushed barely inside her, and she moaned with a desire that she couldn't contain.

"I wanted to fuck him," she said, tears filling her eyes. "I wanted that big cock inside me, and I want to fuck him so badly. I wanted all of him Daddy, I'm so sorry. I'm such a whore. I'm such a dirty little girl, I'm sorry."

But, I was inside her and it didn't matter. I pictured her on the couch, but this time she crawled up onto his lap. This time Rachel held his cock in her hand as Kelly slid down around him, and I was coming before I could stop myself. He was fucking her and she was screaming and begging, and all I could remember was her telling me she wanted more. She said she needed more.

I watched, in my mind's eye, as he came inside her, his come spilling out from her pussy, even as he stretched her open wider than I had ever seen. Her moaning was louder, more powerful, and crazier than I thought possible, and it wasn't until I stopped coming that I regretted it all. It went from the most frenzied fantasy I could imagine to a stomach wrenching misery in just seconds.

Kelly looked up at me, her cheeks flushed, and her own spasms finally slowing down as well. She had come, and she had come hard. I was the one inside her, and I was the one fucking her, but none of that mattered. I knew what was going through her head, what she was wanting, needing, and craving, and it was almost too much. I had been down that path before, and I wasn't sure if I could do it again.

"I love you," I whispered. I kissed her lips and closed my eyes, wondering if maybe breathing would let me be. She kissed me back and there was so much love in her eyes that maybe it was okay. Maybe, even in our fantasy world, it was still about me.

"I love you too, Thomas," she whispered.

I sat back, unsure if I had heard her correctly. She told Daddy she loved him all the time, but Thomas? It was a first.

"Really?" I tried not to sound completely incredulous.

"Of course! Why do you think I do this? I mean, it's fun, but it's only fun because it's you. Because you love me, and I love you, and I know that if we go too far you'll pull me back. You're my rock, Thomas. You're solid and grounded and you keep me sane. Seriously, I couldn't do this with someone else. I'd go too far and shit would get bad. I'd do something I couldn't take back and no one would be happy. But, with you it's different. You're good for me."

I'm not sure if I was more surprised to hear that I was good for her or that I was stable in her mind. If I was her rock, she was in some serious trouble, because I was more likely to be the kind of rock that wrecked ships at night when they came too close to shore. I was the kind of rock that people smoked out of pipes, or possibly threw onto the sidewalks when it was snowing. At my best, I was the rock a kid might skip over calm waters.

"You think you'd be crazier than this?" It was hard for me to picture more. Sure, there were still plenty of things we had fantasized about, but after our little orgy, I thought we would be hard pressed to get more intense.

"We're just getting started, Thomas. I mean think of all the things we haven't done yet."

"Like what?" I rolled over next to her, and she slid a leg up onto my stomach as she played with my chest hair. She kissed my lips and rested her head against me.

"There's a lot of things. For example, you haven't fucked me up the ass yet."

"Are you serious? Is that on the list? I thought you didn't want me to do that."

"Thomas, when I say something like 'Daddy, please don't do x, y or z' it means do that. And if I say it scares me, then do it harder. You can totally fuck my ass. Do you want to?"

"Oh God, you have no idea. I can't even...."

"Good, so that's on the list. You've seen Rachel eat my pussy, but you've never watched me eat her pussy. So, that might be fun. Also, you've never really tied me up or blindfolded me. Just a few moments here and there. And you know what? We've never even figured out how old I am."

My cock twitched at her entire list, and once again I marveled how with her it was so simple. There had been times in my life when I struggled to get hard, but with Kelly it was like breathing, and I could feel myself swelling from her words alone.

"I don't know how old you are," I said honestly. "I think sometimes it changes. I mean when you're dirty, I always think of you as older, but when you climbed into bed with that adorable white shift on, then I'd say smaller."

"How old?" she asked, her hand moving down to my cock. Her fingers were gentle and curious, and I tried to think of an answer. At other times in my life I would have given an answer that was safe. At least close to safe, but she wanted the truth. What turned me on? It was all a game, right? Kelly was in fact a twenty-two-year-old woman, but in our minds she could be anything.

"When you're being dirty, then maybe you're fifteen?" I had no idea what she thought about age in our play, and I was terrified that whatever I said, she would be disgusted.

"Let's say I'm fourteen when I'm dirty. Like when you have me on my knees sucking your friend's cock, then I'm fourteen and a filthy little slut."

And then I was hard. She had to suppress a laugh, but she didn't stop stroking me. I sighed my relief, even as I wondered how far it would go.

"How about when I'm good? When I crawl into bed with Daddy because I can't sleep, and when you promise to show me how big girls kiss? How old am I then?"

I pulled her to me, kissing her mouth so gently it was almost chaste. I didn't give her my tongue or part her lips, but it was a kiss all the same. Suddenly I wanted to teach her everything.

"You are a big girl," I whispered. "You know just how Daddy likes to be touched."

"Am I doing it good?" she asked, looking down at her hand wrapped around me. "Is this how you like it?"

"It's perfect, Babygirl, it's perfect."

"The girls at school, the older ones in seventh grade, say that sometimes girls put it in their mouths. Is that true, Daddy?"

I moaned as she said it, and I instantly knew what she wanted me to say.

"It is true. Do you think you want to try that? Do you want to be like the older girls?"

"I'm scared," she whispered. "What if I do it wrong?"

I sat up just a little until she was closer to my cock, and she didn't once take her eyes off it. Her hand was still wrapped around me, and when she finally looked up, she was so sincere I almost got seriously creeped out. She was far too good at this.

"Just do what feels good to you. Open your lips and taste it. You don't have to try to do everything all at once."

Her lips were soft, gentle, and tentative. It was nothing like she had done before, and I was almost in pain. She opened them around me, swirling her tongue around the head of my cock, and I had to resist shoving her head down. I did finger her hair and guide her gently, but she was exploring just fine on her own. She took more and more of me, sucking the head into her mouth as her hand worked me slowly.

"Like that, Daddy?"

"Yes, Babygirl," I moaned. "Just like that. Just like that."

She squeezed me harder as she went back to sucking on me, and I had to say it. We had established the dirty self, but this one was still hanging there in the air, waving between extremes. I brushed her hair again as she sucked me harder, and I was close to coming once more.

"You're such a big girl," I whispered, hating myself even as the words left my mouth. "By the time you turn thirteen you'll know more than all of those silly girls."

And then she sucked me further into her mouth, her moan escaping around my cock, and it was over. She gagged as she took more of me, but the number had hit us both. Seconds later I was coming, and she didn't even try to swallow it all. Some of it she did, some she simply watched as it burst from my cock, and some dribbled down from her lips onto her chin, but no matter what happened she didn't stop smiling. In fact, her smile was so big it was contagious, and I started to laugh with release.

"Did I do that?" she asked, her voice still small. "I like it."

"Yes, Babygirl," I said, laughing as I pulled her up to me and kissed her firmly on the lips. "You made Daddy feel so good."

My come tasted salty and sweet on her lips, but I didn't care. I kissed her and held her, wrapping her up in my arms as I marvelled at how different it was to have a partner I actually communicated with.

"I think we're going to hell," she finally said, her smile never leaving her face.

"Just because you call me Daddy and pretend to be twelve?" I asked.

"And fourteen. I can't decide which one I like better. They're different, but good."

"Yeah, I guess we are going to hell. But, it's better than doing it for real. There are sick people out there, and we're just finding what turns us on in the privacy of our own home. Still, maybe we are fucked up." I don't know if I was trying to convince her or myself, but it was only half working. I was sick, and I was twisted. It was just a game, but what did it say about me that it turned me on? Why couldn't it have been feet or stockings? Why this?

"I didn't even get to finish my list. We got distracted by lessons," she was still smiling at me as I struggled against myself.

"I like lessons," I said, closing my eyes. "We may need more."

"Maybe if I'm really good you'll let me practice on someone else again." She stuck her tongue out at me, and I patted her ass with the hand that was beneath her.

"Only if you're good," I said. "If you're bad I might let him do something else to you. You need all sorts of practice."

"If we start this again I'm going to get turned on and we'll never sleep. It's bad enough that now I have to think about you tying me up, fuckng my ass, and making me eat Rachel's cunt. Not to mention other things…"

"Yeah, let's not get into other things." I leaned over and blew out the candle, and she pulled the light sheet up onto our bodies once more. As we lay there in the darkness I tried to forgive myself for letting it happen again. It was all just a game, but it was a dangerous game that was going to send me to dark places. Kelly nestled against me, but she may as well have been a million miles away.

I'm sorry, Talia. Please save me.

Chapter Fourteen

It's easy in the city to never spend time alone. And it's nearly impossible sometimes to spend time with any one person. Kelly and I did on a regular basis, but there are exceptions made for people in romantic relationships. No one invited themselves along if we had a dinner date, and if we vanished into my room they just rolled their eyes. But, with my other friends it was far more difficult. Jane was out of the question, and while I occasionally had a cup of coffee with Martin in the morning, that was about it.

When Jason and I made plans to meet up in Washington Square park one afternoon, I had to intentionally not invite anyone else along. It would have been easy to mention it to Rachel who was watching TV in the living room. And asking Kelly along would have been the most natural thing in the world, but I needed some time alone with my old friend, and I held onto those plans with an iron grip. Since he had moved in with Brent, I saw them both quite a bit. Even after our little orgy we still hung out, but not once did I see either of them unless we were all together.

It was a cloudy Saturday afternoon, but it was typically warm for late June. The mugginess in the air didn't especially bother me, and I took my time walking from my apartment over to where we planned to meet. There were a few performers in the park, a bunch of guys playing guitar, and of course the perpetual drum circle that just went on and on. People were sitting out on the lawn reading, sunbathing, and talking. I recognized a few of the acts along with some of the bums and the smoke smoke smoke guys.

"Yo, dude, over here."

Jason was sitting on the edge of the fountain as I approached. I sat down next to him and kicked off my flip flops letting my toes get wet.

"How's it going? Still surviving living with Brent?" I asked.

"Heh, most of the time. You surviving that girl you're sleeping with?"

"I don't know. Seriously, I don't actually know. I still can't believe we all did that. Dude, you fucked Rachel. On Brent's lap."

"I'm the fucking boss. It was insane. Kelly's the one who sucked his dick though."

"Yeah, don't remind me. This summer has been completely fucking crazy, Jay. It was only two months ago that I was driving home, trying to figure out what to do with my life. I thought maybe I'd go home. Seriously, I haven't seen my dad once since I got back. I'm half surprised he hasn't called me, but you know him. But, I didn't expect to be having orgies on the couch in my living room."

"It could be worse. It could have been on the floor. Rug burn and all that. But seriously, it's pretty fucking awesome. Brent and Rachel are still weird, but who cares? Everything with that girl is weird. I still can't believe I fucked her."

"You totally came on her."

This was exactly what I had been missing. We joked about everything, but it also meant that we talked about everything. Even with Brent, it was hard to have a conversation like this, but Jason and I just went there. Maybe it was because neither one of us was completely convinced it was real. Both of us always seemed somewhat surprised by the world.

"How's the bartending? Do you like pouring beers all night?"

"I like talking to people. Especially people I don't know very well, and I have a bunch of regulars now. They come in at the same time on the same days and generally drink the same things. The IPA guys drink IPAs and the Porter guys freak out every time we get something new. Even in this weather. But, I like it. It keeps me busy, and not thinking about Kelly all the time. Or Jane, for that matter."

"What the hell happened with you two? She comes up to our place all the time with her wedding shit, but she doesn't talk about you. It's not like she's avoiding it, but every time we suggest getting together she tells us she's busy and runs out. Please tell me you didn't do something stupid."

"Of course I did. But, it wasn't my fault. Seriously, I didn't know she was engaged until after. She came to my place and didn't say a goddamn word until three days later. Are you sure this guy is the right one? Have you met him?"

"He's nice. He's a doctor, so what's not to like? But, honestly? I don't know. He's not a bad guy, but she doesn't look like someone who's crazy in love. It's more like she's tired of all the bullshit and this is a good way out. Fuck, I'm so goddamn cynical. When did we get old?"

"Do you think I'm stupid for staying with Kelly?"

"What? Why would you say that? She's cute and smart, and she can sing like a fucking rockstar. So what if she likes to party hard and suck your friends' cocks?"

He was smirking at me with the same damn smirk he used whenever he said something true like it was a joke.

"And what about the whole Rachel thing? Do you think they really have some secret affair going on behind my back? I honestly don't care if they're fucking every day, I just don't want it to be secret. I don't like being lied to. Not after Claire."

"I don't know man. Rachel is hard to read, and she's not the most stable girl in the world. I don't think Kelly would do that though. She loves her Daddy."

"You heard that?" I asked, cringing at the word.

"We all heard that," he said. I pulled out a smoke and handed him one as well. I guess it said something that they hadn't been making constant fun of me since that night.

"She's so hot, and she makes me do terrible things. Wonderful, terrible things."

"Don't fuck it up."

"Jay, I just don't know if it's what I want. I mean, after Claire I think I've had enough kinky sex to last me a lifetime. Maybe Jane has the right idea. Maybe I should be looking for someone stable, normal, and a little less intense."

"Yeah, Thomas. What you need is someone less hot. Maybe controlling and jealous all the time? A girl who yells at you for smoking, doesn't like you working in the bar, and absolutely, under no circumstance, would let you watch her make out with another girl. That sounds much better.

"Listen, it's the summer. You just graduated college. This is what you're supposed to do. You should be having crazy amounts of hot sex with that little fuck machine, and you should be getting so drunk at Docs you do stupid shit. We should be singing the goddamn moose song every night until we get arrested, and then we should sing it in jail as well. We're not getting any younger."

I got up off the edge of the fountain, and he followed me without a word. We walked around the circle watching some of the musicians and jugglers, and he was right. Maybe. He sounded so reasonable, but each time I thought about it I wasn't so sure. And besides, he didn't know Talia was coming.

"I have to tell you something," he said, as we headed down the path.

"Uh-oh, that doesn't sound good." He was grinning though and shaking his head. It looked more like a secret he was dying to let out than anything bad. "What is it?" I asked.

"So, um, you remember when Katie came out in the middle of that thing?"

"When she watched you fuck Rachel on the couch, you mean?"

"Yeah, that. So, the next morning we met up for coffee. She left a note in my jacket pocket, and I met her at the Starbucks in Columbus Circle. Did you know she has her own apartment? I mean like she owns it. And it's insane."

"I didn't know that. She practically lives at our place, and I've never seen her without Martin."

"So, anyway, we met up for coffee and started talking, and it turns out we get along really well. We've always been friendly with each other, but this was different. We, um, we kinda made out."

"What the fuck, man? It's like my apartment is suddenly Grand Central for hooking up. Are you serious? Does Martin know?"

"She says that Martin is gay. Like Gay gay with a capital G. They're good friends and he has good weed, but it's not serious. She says he doesn't want to tell anyone because, quote, it's none of their fucking business."

"Martin is gay? Really? Huh, I guess that actually makes sense. Nevermind. Did you fuck her?" I asked. We had made it all the way to the west side of the park and almost to 6th Avenue. We weren't paying any attention at all to where we were going.

He shrugged with that sheepish grin again, and I wasn't sure if I wanted to slap him or high five him. I had lived with Katie for two months and we probably said ten words to each other. She was always lurking about in Martin's room or getting high on the couch watching TV in her underwear. And she did that a lot. The girl smoked more weed than anyone I had ever met. When she did talk it was normally along the lines of what she said the other night. Something odd. Something strange. Something incredibly high.

"I like her," was all he said as we crossed 6th Ave and walked down W. 4th St. "Hey, you want to stop by Jane's? She right here."

Jane answered the door in a bathrobe and music blasting behind her. She waved us in and poured us each a glass of wine. Well, she poured wine into coffee mugs and handed them to us without saying a word, and Jason and I simply walked in and sat down on her bed. There was nowhere else to sit.

"Where's Brent?" she asked.

"We were just in the neighborhood and wanted to say hi. He's not always with us." Jason looked at me and shrugged his shoulders.

"Yeah right, but seriously, why isn't he here too? I want to tell you guys something. All three of you."

"Jane, he's home," I said. "Or fucking Rachel. Or something, we haven't seen him all morning. What's up?"

"Fine," she said, moving us both to the side and sitting down between us on the bed. "You three are going to be my bridesmaids."

"Excuse me?" we both said at the same time.

"Look, you're my three best friends. And Sean's best friend's are girls. So rather than both of us try to pretend that we can scrounge up some new buddies of the same gender, we decided to just have our real friends there instead. He gets to have three girls for his groomsmen, and I get you three."

"Isn't it traditional to ask us?" Jason asked.

"Whatever, you'll say yes. Isn't this exciting? You get to be my wedding party. Which means you have to throw me a bachelorette party, and make sure I don't get so drunk I miss the wedding. Or sleep with a stripper. It's going to be awesome."

She wrapped her arms around both of us, pulling us in and kissing the tops of our heads. "I love you guys. And this is going to be the best wedding ever. But, I gotta get showered and go to work, so will you tell Brent for me, and then maybe next week we can meet up for drinks and talk wedding shit? Or just get drunk and celebrate. Whatever, it's going to be perfect!"

Before we could say anything, she jumped up, hung her bathrobe over the door, and climbed into the shower. She was whistling the whole time, and we finally let ourselves out, shaking our heads and wondering just what the fuck we had gotten ourselves into. It was bad enough she was marrying a guy we hardly knew, but now this? If she tried to put us in dresses I was going to freak out.

Jason walked me back across town to Saints where I had an afternoon shift. We bullshitted about the wedding, talked a little bit more about Katie, and smoked another couple of cigarettes. When I finally crawled behind the bar again, I realized that I hadn't said much of anything about my big concern. Talia was coming, and I was a sick, fucking bastard. I did stuff I couldn't tell him about, and that just made it worse. If I couldn't tell Jason the things Kelly and I did in bed, they must really be fucked up.

Chapter Fifteen

Talia called early in the morning, and I answered the phone in the kitchen completely naked.

"When did you get in?" I asked.

"Late last night. I'm in Midtown at the hotel with Maddy."

I had somehow missed the part of the email where she told me the reason for her trip. Talia was the chaperone for her little sister's college tour of New York, and they'd be here for a week visiting every school in the five boroughs.

"It's so good to hear your voice," I said. "I mean, email is nice and all, but it's good to hear you as well. The summer has been good, but a little crazy. I know, my life is always a little crazy, but Talia, it's been hard. I'm so glad you're here and… Hold on a sec."

Without a word Kelly walked into the kitchen, wearing just as much as I was, and before I could stop her she knelt, grabbed my cock, looked up at me with a smile, and started blowing me. I tried to shoo her away, but she just put her finger to her lips and went back to sucking. No matter how I tried, I was as hard as the plastic phone in my hand, and it was all I could do to keep standing.

"Is something wrong?" Talia asked, hearing me take a quick breath.

"It's nothing, someone just walked into the room," I said, trying to keep my voice normal. Fuck, this was going to be difficult. Talia would probably just laugh at me, but it was not how I wanted our reunion to go.

"So, when do you want to meet up?" I asked, hoping she might talk for a while. Kelly was on a mission, and it didn't help that I knew what she was doing. She wanted to make me come, and she wanted to do it quickly. There was no teasing, no taunting, and most importantly, no waiting. As I stood there, trying to pay attention to what Talia was saying, I felt a hand on my ass, and then a finger dangerously close. She took me all the way into her throat as she finally shoved her her finger up my ass, and it was over.

I held onto the counter with one hand as I just moaned uh-huh, and yeah sure, into the phone. I locked my knees, grabbed Kelly's head, and I exploded into her mouth like I hadn't come in days.

"Are you sure you're okay?"

"No, I'm fine," I mumbled. "I'm just a little hung over. I had to work late, but yeah, that sounds good. I'll meet you guys at your room this afternoon and we can go from there. So excited. Uh-huh. Love you, too."

I hung up the phone as Kelly looked up at me, her smile as big and joyful as ever.

"Fuck, Kelly that was so not fair."

"You left me alone," she pouted. "What was I supposed to do?"

I pulled her up and kissed her, before dragging her back into my bedroom hoping none of the other roommates had heard that. I was still shaking as she got into bed, and she was laughing at me even as she wiped her lips and kissed my face.

"Who was that?" she asked.

"Mr friend Talia from college. She's in town for a few days and wants to meet up."

"You're going to meet them in their room later, I heard. Who's them?"

"She's taking her little sister on a college tour, if you must know. They live out in Oregon, so I don't get to see her very often."

"Have you fucked her?"

"Kelly, what the hell is wrong with you? Do you think I've

fucked every woman I know?"

"Haven't you? I mean the second time I met you, you were balls deep in Jane, so I just assumed it was a normal thing. I thought you fucked all your friends. You know, Jason, Brent, Katie, the cat."

"You're fucking me with," I said, finally realizing she was just trying to get me defensive. She did it so easily these days that I was starting to worry. Either she was too good at it, or I was turning into a nervous wreck. It was possible that it was both.

"How old is her sister?" she asked, resting her head on my chest. I hardly noticed as I ran my fingers down her back to her ass, but she moaned when I pulled her too me, and she slid a leg up over my body.

"I don't know, seventeen or eighteen. College aged. Why?"

"I was just wondering if I should be worried. You're spending the afternoon with an old friend from college and her little sister. Is she cute?"

"Talia? She's pretty, but she's not like us. I mean, she's super smart, and nice, and all that, but she's normal. Or, better than normal. She's one of those people who've got all her shit together."

"I meant her sister," Kelly said. "Is her little sister cute?"

"I don't know. Sure. Why would you ask me that?"

"Because I know you. And while you may like this friend of yours, you're going to want to fuck her little sister."

"Kelly, I've only met her once and it was for two minutes back at school. Why would you say that?"

Her hand was on my cock once again, and she looked up into my eyes.

"You didn't answer the question. Is her little sister cute?"

"Yes," I said, remembering the quick glimpse I had of her when she visited a year ago. She was blonde and about the same size as Talia. Her hair was long and straight, and she had a smile that turned up on the left side.

"What's her name?"

"I think it's Maddy. Something like that. What's gotten into you?"

"I'm just thinking," she said, her hand still on my cock, squeezing me gently. "A cute little eighteen-year-old, who you're definitely not supposed to want? She's going to drive you crazy, and then some. She'll smile at you and tell you her older sister is so boring these days. She'll tell you she can't wait to get to college because older boys are so much cooler, and she'll get shy and look down, and you won't be able to keep your eyes off her. Maybe she'll lean in and you'll look down her shirt, or she'll try to climb into your lap when Talia's not looking.

"You'll fight it at first, but then something will happen."

"Kelly, this is insane. I'm not going to fuck Talia's little sister."

She looked at me, then looked back down to where her hand was wrapped around my once again hard cock. Without another word she climbed on top of me and slid me inside her. I was still amazed that we could do that. That we could just fuck any time we wanted. She felt so good, it was impossible to focus.

"It won't take long for her to tell you she wants you, and you won't be able to resist. She'll drop to the floor and pull out your cock, no matter how many times you tell her to stop."

"Kelly, don't do this," I said, pushing up into her and trying not to picture that blonde hair and awkward smile.

"Tell me you want her," she said, leaning down and kissing me as we fucked. "Call me Maddy and fuck me, just like you're going to fuck her later. You know you want it."

And then without thinking I rolled her onto her back, pulled out for just a second as I stared at her open pussy, and then I slammed back inside her, my eyes closed as I pictured the bed covered in long blonde hair.

"Oh fuck," I said, thrusting into her faster and harder.

"That's right, Thomas. Say it," she urged, her nails digging into my back. "Tell Maddy you want to fuck her tight little cunt."

"Oh god, Maddy," I finally whispered, anger mixing in with my arousal. "Oh, Maddy, you are so fucking tight."

"Yes, Thomas. Fuck me before my sister gets back. Fuck me so hard."

"You are so pretty," I said, kissing her eyes one at a time. I ran my hand down her face. "You're so pretty and sweet." I slowed down, moving inside her as if time was stopping. I didn't even think as the words left my mouth.

"You are so much sweeter than my girlfriend," I whispered. "So much prettier and tighter too."

Kelly's moans turned into whines, and as I kept talking they turned into sobs. She held me tightly as I fucked her, but still I didn't stop.

"She's such a whore, but you? You are a perfect, little girl, and I love you," I moaned, knowing that each word would push Kelly closer to the edge. "Oh fuck, Maddy, you are so perfect."

"Tell me more," she cried, clenching around me, even as her crying grew louder with each thrust.

"I don't know why I'm with her," I said, moving so painfully slowly it was dangerous. "She's nothing like you at all. You're pretty and smart, and so much better than her. Don't make me go back to her."

"I won't," she whispered into my ear, as I pushed as deeply inside her as I could go. "You can stay here forever. I'll love you for real, and I'll never leave you. It will just be us. Just you and me, fucking forever. Please, Thomas. Fuck me harder."

I started moving again, my eyes shut so tightly it hurt, and it was all too real. Maddy's body trembled beneath me. Maddy's breasts pressed against my chest, and Maddy's cunt clenched perfectly around me as we made love over and over again. Love and relief flooded my body as I arched my back, and I finally said it once more.

"I love you, Maddy, I love you so much more than her."

And then we were both coming, her through her tears, and mine in anger, want, and revenge. If she was going to push me she could take it as well. Kelly wanted to pull my strings, but I could pull back. No matter how far she wanted to take it, I could meet her there, and we'd see who gave in first.

"Holy shit that was so intense," she said when we finally stopped shaking. "I can't believe you did that!"

"It didn't upset you?" I asked, wiping the tears off her cheeks.

"Of course it upset me. That's what made it so hot. If you really do that I'm going to die."

I rolled over next to her and looked up at the canopy. For a moment, I was there. I was fucking Talia's sweet little sister, and every word that left my mouth had been true. I didn't even know the girl, but I suddenly realized that my afternoon might be a little bit more awkward than I expected. Oh, yes, it's nice to meet you again, Maddy. I've heard so much about you, and in fact, just this morning I fucked my girlfriend while pretending it was you. Welcome to New York.

I started laughing, as I looked up at the pink awning, and I couldn't stop. The entire thing was so absurd, so fucked up, and so hot, I couldn't help myself.

"What's so funny?"

"It's going to be a little strange seeing that girl this afternoon," I said. Kelly started laughing too, even as she cuddled up next to me again on the bed. We laughed for a while, as our breathing returned to normal, and I absentmindedly ran my fingers through her hair. Who was going to be my salvation now?

"Thomas?" Kelly finally said.

"Yeah?" I rolled over until I could look her in the eyes.

"Please don't really do it. I know I like to push, and tease, and it's fun to fantasize, but not this. Please don't fuck your friend's little sister."

"I won't," I said, pulling her to me. I kissed her again as I thought about it, and it was absurd. I had barely met the girl, and if Talia even thought I was flirting she would disown me. "I won't."

Talia met me in the lobby of the Algonquin, and I'm ashamed to admit that I was sad she was alone. I hugged her and kissed her face, holding her for probably way too long. She didn't seem to mind though, and she smiled and held my hands as we found a couch. Talia was as pretty as ever, her clothes perfectly put together, her hair impeccable, and it was all I could do not to kiss her more.

"It's so good to see you," I said.

"You, too. We got in super late. Otherwise, I would have called last night. Maddy was still wired from the flight, but I bought her a glass of wine and she passed out. I'm still a little jet-lagged, but looking forward to the week. We have an insane schedule. I thought I was bad, but Maddy is applying to every college in New York, and I don't know what to do with her. She's determined to come here. I guess we'll see how it goes. But, what's new with you? Are you doing better since graduation?"

"That's a big question," I said.

"Are you working?"

"I'm at a bar in the East Village. It's close to my apartment and super friendly. It's not like a club or anything, we serve craft beer and the patrons are mostly middle aged men who want to talk about hop profiles. It's just for now, but it's good. They like me, and I work hard."

"Well, it's not advertising, but it's a good start. How about the dating world?"

"I have a girlfriend."

"And? That's it? You have a girlfriend? Is she pretty, smart, and wonderful? Most importantly, does she love you? The actual you?"

"That's a whole lot of questions, Talia. Maybe we should wait until we have a drink in us, or at least take a walk. I'm not sure if the lobby of your hotel is the place to do it."

"We'll have time. It's a busy week, but I'm sure we can work it out."

I sighed a bit too loudly, but the truth was I didn't know where to begin. The last thing I wanted was to jump right back in to where we left off, with Talia having to pull me out of something because she was the only one who realized how bad it was. Kelly wasn't Claire, and I knew that, but in some ways it didn't matter. Yes, she loved me, and she didn't really make me do anything I didn't want to do, but it was complicated. How could I even begin to explain it?

"Oh, here's Maddy," Talia said, breaking me out of my head. I looked up, and walking towards us was a living nightmare. Her blonde hair was longer than the last time I saw her, and she looked more grown-up by far. The smile I remembered was even quirkier, and it was all I could do to stand up. Maddy was the prettiest girl I had ever seen in my life, and I was going to hell. I was going to a very deep and dark hell, and I was going to go with a smile on my lips.

"It's so good to see you," she said, throwing her arms around me, kissing my cheek, and hugging me. She was just an inch or two shorter than me, and she smelled like jasmine and cotton sheets. Her hair was silk against my skin and her arms were strong and assuring. When she finally let me go, I looked her up and down, as Talia put her arm around her.

"I'm so glad you two get to actually meet for more than just a few minutes. I've told her so much about you."

"It's lovely to see you, too," I said, trying to keep my gaze on her face. Don't think about it, don't do it, and don't close your eyes. No matter what you do, don't close your eyes.

But, even in the half second it took to blink, I was there. The bed was warm, and blonde hair covered everything. Her body moved slowly beneath me as we made love, and my words echoed in my head. I love you, Maddy. I love you so much more than her.

Chapter Sixteen

A day later I was sitting in my living room with Brent, Jason and Katie, having a beer and smoking a bowl, when Rachel stormed in like a hurricane. She had a few with the rest of us earlier, but her cheeks were so red I thought she might explode. All four of us looked up, and we were all too terrified to speak. Even before she opened her mouth, we knew it was trouble. I just didn't know it was mine.

"You are fucking sick," she said, walking into the room. I looked at the others, but they were looking back at me. As if there was any doubt to whom she was talking. "You're disgusting, twisted, and crazy, and if you think I'm going to let you mess with my friend, you are so fucking wrong."

"Rachel, what's going on?" Brent hated conflict as much as I did, but he jumped into the middle of it instantly.

"Shut up, this isn't about you. This is about this fucking sick-ass pedophile on the couch next to you. Do you know what he does with Kelly? Do you guys have any fucking idea what sort of shit they do?"

"Rachel, what the hell is wrong with you?" Kelly was standing behind her in the door, and there were tears running down her face. "Stop it!"

"No, I'm not going to stop! Not after what you told me. He's a pervert and everyone should fucking know it." She pulled a book off the shelf next to her and threw it at me. It barely missed me, and she pulled another one off and threw that one, too. I was still sitting on the couch in shock as she screamed, and I had no fucking clue what to do.

"Do you guys know? Has he told you this shit? He likes to pretend that she's twelve, and he makes her call him Daddy. What the fuck is wrong with you?"

Another book flew in my direction, and this time I had to put my hands up to keep it from hitting me in the face.

"You should be in jail, you fucking freak!"

"Stop it, stop it, stop it!" Kelly was on the floor now behind her friend, and she sobbed as she grabbed a hold of her leg. Her whole body trembled as she tried to pull her back, but Rachel just stood there yelling and screaming, ignoring the sobs behind her.

It was finally Brent who moved. It was Brent who walked calmly across the carpet, grabbed Rachel by the hand and tried to drag her back into her room. She struggled and yelled, but he didn't once raise his voice.

"Let's sit down and you can tell me," he said. "You can tell me all about it, and then we'll figure out what to do."

I was next to Kelly a second later, and Jason and Katie just stared as us, unsure of what to do at all. I wrapped my arms around her, and simply held her there, both of us on the floor against the wall, and I didn't let go. "It's okay," I whispered to her, "it's okay."

"You might want to go," I finally said, looking up at my old friend. Jason was standing, looking helpless, but I waved him away, not wanting to deal with his questions at all. He finally took Katie by the hand and they opened the door to the hallway and vanished into the stairwell.

"I'm sorry," Kelly said, her sobs moving from her head to her chest. I held her and kissed her and told her none of it mattered.

Everything was fine. Everything would be okay. I could hear Brent and Rachel in the back room, but her voice had finally returned to normal, and I couldn't make out the words.

I eventually managed to get Kelly up, and I walked her to the couch. She looked up for the first time in a daze and pointed to my room instead. I closed the door behind us and then the door to the kitchen as well. I lit a candle, wrapped a blanket around her, and handed her a lit cigarette. I tried not to smoke in my room, but this didn't count.

She sat on the bed, taking long drags as I held her and she shook. She kept apologizing, although I still didn't know what for. It was clear that Rachel knew more than I liked, but just because she had the nerve to talk to her friends, didn't mean I had any reason to be mad. By the time she finished smoking she had mostly stopped crying, and she hugged me one more time before crawling across the bed and leaning against the back wall. I crawled back with her, and resisted every urge I had to say a word. The last thing she needed was my questions.

"I've been messing around with Rachel when you're not here." Her voice was quiet, and she said it through her sniffles. She didn't look at me, and I didn't say anything. Part of me was glad that she was telling me, although I didn't like the truth of what I was hearing.

"I know when we got together it was sort of a joke, but after that first time when she walked in on us, it just sort of happened. It's usually just a kiss at the bar or something. She'll grab my ass or whisper something dirty in my ear, and for a long time I thought I was going to tell you any day. I'd tell you and it would be hot, and we'd have something else to talk about. But, the longer it went on, the more I didn't say anything.

"The first time we got really drunk and a little high, and she started talking all three of us again. She told me how much she wanted to go down on me, and I just didn't say no. I know I should have, but I was wasted and I kept telling myself how turned on you'd be if you could see us.

"But you couldn't see us, and I didn't tell you, and I'm so sorry. I don't have any good excuses."

She finally looked up at me, and I knew instantly she was hoping for a sign. Was I going to leave her right then or would I forgive her? I pulled her to me and kissed her forehead, unsure of myself as well. I didn't want to leave her, no matter how guilty I felt about what we did. The fact that Rachel had said everything to me that I had already thought didn't help. Maybe I was sick. Maybe I did deserve to be in jail.

"How many times?" I asked, as if that was a good question. For some reason it felt important though. If she was hooking up with Rachel every time I walked out of the room it was different than a few drunk nights of groping.

"It's only been a couple of times. Mostly just kissing, but a few times we had sex. She would tell me that it was okay, that she knew me first, and that you would like it anyway. I'm so sorry, Thomas. Maybe I really am a big whore."

"You're perfect," I said, trying to convince myself, too. I was well aware of the fact that if this had been an affair with a guy I would be freaking out. But, I didn't care. Right then, I would have drunk a toast to double standards and then another. Rachel was difficult, but anyone else would have been worse.

"What happened tonight?"

She looked away again, and she nearly started crying once more. I grabbed the ashtray off the nightstand and both of us lit up another cigarette and took long drags before speaking.

"She's been weird. It started right before our little orgy, but it's only gotten worse. Even though we were all there that night, it still felt like it was about me. You know? She made me take off my shirt before we started dancing. She made me dance and grind on her, and then she was the one who made me strip for you. Even when she was jerking off Jason and Brent, she was watching me, and it was almost like you weren't in the room. I don't know how to explain it, but I knew something was different.

"But, it was hot, and I was so relieved you were there that it didn't matter. When you finally stood up and kissed me I was almost myself again and it was good. I wanted you, because I always want you, but also I needed you to keep me safe. Which you always do.

"And after that, she wouldn't let it go. She kept telling me how much she loved watching me dance, and how she couldn't get the taste of my pussy out of her mind. I told her she was mostly tasting you, but she didn't care. That was hot, too, she said, and for a while I thought maybe it wasn't just about me. She started asking about you, and I thought that was good. I mean, I thought it was a good sign, god I'm so fucking stupid.

"I began telling her about some of the stuff we do, but just little bits here and there. She heard me yell Daddy, and she said it was hot. She wanted to hear more, and so I just told her. I didn't have anyone else to talk to, and sometimes I need to talk. Do you know what I mean? I love being with you and talking with you about it, but I needed to tell someone else, and she was so understanding. Sometimes she'd touch me as I talked about you, and it felt good. I don't know what's wrong with me."

"It's okay," I said, leaning back against the wall and taking a final drag off my smoke. "She has that effect. Even when she came in that first time we both said yes. We didn't really want to but we did. Hell, even Jason said yes to her. Jason who would normally never do that in a million years, fucked her on the couch because she told him to. She's persuasive."

Kelly smiled at me, but I could tell she thought I was being nice. I had seen her look a million ways, but guilty wasn't one of them. She was scared, and she felt terrible. Not angry, not frustrated, just terrified.

"Tonight was the worst. Everyone was over but she dragged me into her room anyway. We had all been drinking, as you know, but she had some coke and she took all of it. She was pacing the room and telling me she wanted to watch. I had never seen her like that before. When she got down on her knees I was afraid, and she grabbed me and kissed me so hard. She held me there, telling me she wanted to watch me get fucked by my Daddy, and I just kept on nodding and telling her we could do it. I promised her, but she wanted to know more. She wanted to know how often, what you called me, and how old I was. She kept asking what you made me do, but I didn't realize what was happening. I thought she just wanted to fuck me, but she was getting mad.

"When I finally told her she was scaring me, she flipped. She said you were the one who was scary, and I had to leave you. She tried to get me to go with her and just leave you guys in the living room. She said we could sneak off and no one would know.

"I told her she was crazy and that's when she started yelling. She told me she had to do something, and before I could say a word, she was standing in the living room saying those things, and I'm so sorry, Thomas. I'm so fucking sorry."

"It's not your fault," I said. "It is definitely not your fault. Brent told me she was obsessed with you, but I didn't say anything. I thought maybe it was a joke. No one blames you, especially not me. We all know that she's obsessed. We know."

Kelly moved the ashtray aside and crawled back into my lap, wrapping my arms around her waist like the very first night we met. I kissed the top of her head as we sat there, and she wiped her eyes, trying to keep herself from crying again.

"You're not going to leave me?" she asked, looking back at

me. Her eyes, her pretty blue eyes, were red and swollen and it nearly broke my heart.

"No," I said. "I would never leave you. I love you, Kelly. I completely and utterly love you."

"I love you, too," she said, holding me tighter.

After a while we undressed and climbed under the covers. I left the candle burning and we whispered to each other in the near darkness. We whispered sweet things and mundane things. I talked about the bar and Talia's tour of the city with her sister. She talked about work and the crazy woman who would only sing Michael Jackson. We spooned, and cuddled, laughing as often as anything else, and it was the perfect antidote.

Around midnight, we heard the door slam and we both sat up, suddenly remembering that Brent and Rachel had been just one room away the entire time. A few seconds later, there was a knock on the door and a deep whisper asking if he could come in. We both breathed a sigh of relief when we realized it wasn't her.

Brent sat down on the bed and we didn't bother to pull up the covers. He had already seen Kelly more than naked, so a few bare breasts and red eyes wasn't going to make a difference.

"She's going over to her brother's in Brooklyn," he said.

"Oh," Kelly said, looking down at her lap. I didn't even know she had a brother, but I was just as glad that she was no longer in the apartment.

"She said she's sorry if that helps. I think she meant it, too. How long has she been blowing so much coke?"

"I don't know," Kelly said. "I've only seen her do it a few times. But maybe she does it more?"

"It's not a big deal," he said. "I mean it is, but it's other things as well. She thinks she's in love with you, but she sounded pretty confused about it. Half the time she was talking about how you have everything so perfect, and the other half was about how lonely she is. She went back and forth between wanting to be you, and wanting to go out with you. Definitely confusing."

"How are you doing?" I asked, suddenly realizing that it wasn't just about us.

"Well, it wasn't the most fun I've ever had," he said with his big laugh. "But, whatever."

"Yeah, but she's kind of your girlfriend," Kelly said, looking concerned.

"We haven't done anything since the orgy, and even before then it was never serious. I like her, but she didn't let me get too close. She cancelled almost every time we had plans, and when we did sleep together it was after a drunk night with you guys. I'm an afterthought, and that's okay with me."

"When is she coming back?" Kelly asked.

"I don't know," he said. "I don't know much about her brother, so I'm not sure if he's going to give her more booze and get her riled up or take her to the hospital. I tried to stop her, but it honestly felt like the best idea. She talked about moving, though. She said she knew she fucked everything up and that it wasn't fair."

Kelly held her hands in front of her, fidgeting like mad. She had twisted the sheet into knots, and she was sweating and shaking.

"You know what?" I said, getting out of the bed and finding my shorts on the floor. "Why don't we sleep at your place, Kell? Maybe a change of scenery will help."

She nodded with a brief smile, and Brent even turned away when she crawled naked out of bed to find her clothes. We both dressed in silence as he sat there, but I couldn't think of anything else to do. If we stayed home every bump in the night would cause us to panic, and every car that went by would pull us wide awake.

"I'll walk with you," Brent said as I packed a small bag. No point in not having enough things for a few days just in case.

The night was warm, but there was a nice summer breeze blowing down 10th St. and I took a deep breath as we headed west. Kelly walked between us, and didn't say a word. It wasn't until we were nearly to her apartment that I realized she was holding both of our hands. Her knuckles were white she gripped us so hard, and not once did it occur to me to be jealous.

Chapter Seventeen

"Will you stay?"

I think it took both of us by surprise, and Brent looked at me with a shrug.

"It's not like that," Kelly continued. "I'm just scared, and you two are the only ones who know what happened. It's not just tonight either. It's been getting worse for weeks, and I've been holding it in. I'd just feel better with both of you here."

"Yeah, if you don't mind," Brent said, looking at me again. For some reason, it didn't bother me at all. I didn't have a flashback to her sucking his dick, and I didn't instantly wonder what would happen. He was my oldest friend, and it felt strangely normal.

Kelly grabbed some whisky from the cabinet in the kitchen and brought it back to her room. She put on a CD, turned the volume down, and lit a candle. She had the air conditioner blasting, and it was joyfully cool. We all drank right out of the bottle, since the chance of finding clean glasses in Kelly's place was slim to none. We stripped again, this time just to our underthings. Kelly put on a pair of my boxers that I had left weeks earlier, and didn't bother with a shirt. We all climbed down onto the bed, still passing the bottle back and forth.

"Did he tell you he's going to be a bridesmaid?" Brent asked, as we settled ourselves against the wall. "Actually, all of us. We're going to look so damn pretty." His laugh was contagious and we drank it in.

"He did tell me that. I think you'll all look lovely in pink. Maybe I can help you go shoe shopping. It's an important part of any bridesmaid outfits."

"She's putting us in tuxes. We're all going to wear red and green because it's fucking Christmas. Although not the tuxes, that would be ridiculous. Just the ties and cumberbunds." I was trying to picture us as I said it, and I still couldn't believe we had all agreed.

"Cumberbunds," Kelly said, rolling the word on her tongue. "Cumber bund. It's a silly word. I like silly words."

"Are you drunk again?" Brent asked, grabbing the bottle from her.

"I weigh a hundred pounds, you big jerk. Plus, whisky is good. Especially after tonight, whisky is good."

I took it from him next and it burned all the way down. There's nothing like drinking whisky straight out of the bottle to make you feel classy. Especially when you're sitting on a mattress on the floor with a topless girl listening to Tom Waits. We were the definition of class.

"Kelly, I don't know if I've ever told you this, but you have great tits." Brent was looking at her and grinning, and she simply smiled back.

"And I thought I was too small. What was her name? I thought El Macho preferred girls with big teeters."

"You fucker!" he screamed, nearly tackling me on her bed. "I can't believe you fucking told her that story." He pinned me to the mattress until we were both laughing so hard we couldn't stop. He finally sat back up, and pulled the bottle from her hand once more.

"I need more of this if she's going to start calling me El Macho. You both suck."

"I think it's a cute name," she said, leaning in and touching his nose with her index finger. "El. Macho. It's manly. And cute. It's both and I like it. It's better than Teeters. Who calls a girl Teeters?"

"Careful or I'll pin you too," he said, still laughing and shaking his head. She leaned back into my arms, and I covered her with my hands. I cupped both breasts and he stared at us, and I stuck out my tongue.

"They're fucking perfect," I said. "They are like the Platonic ideal of titties. When God made the world, he took an extra couple days just to make these titties, and when he looked down, he saw that it was good."

She kissed me hard without a word, and then raised the bottle of Jack up to my lips just as Tom started singing "I Wish I Was in New Orleans." We swayed to the music as I handed the bottle back to Brent, and everything was turning out just fine.

"I'll hoist a few tall cold ones," he sang, polishing off the rest of the bottle before slumping back against the wall. "Fuck, I'm drunk too. What the hell did you put in that whisky?"

"It's Jack, baby," Kelly mumbled. "Jack will get you every time."

****

When we woke up, Kelly was smooshed between us on the bed. The air conditioner was still going, and the room was so cold we were cuddling for warmth. Brent's face was nestled in her hair and she had one leg between my own, her knee touching my incredibly erect penis. Her eyes were open and she quietly raised a finger to her lips. I frowned at her, but she smiled as I leaned in closer.

"He's hard, too," she mouthed silently. I was suddenly far more awake than just a few seconds before.

"Is he sleeping?" I asked, in a thin whisper. She nodded her head and wiggled her ass ever so slightly. He snorted and moved just a bit, and her eyes opened wide in mock surprise.

"I like it," she whispered again, before leaning in and kissing me on the nose. It was sweet and tender, and nothing about the situation felt like it should. I was lying in bed with my girlfriend, my best friend was hard against her ass, and everything was perfectly fine. My stomach was not doing somersaults like it did back at my apartment, and my jealousy was hardly moving at all.

"Are you wet?" I asked. She opened her eyes wide again and then winked at me. Very slowly she moved a hand down her body before sliding it inside her boxers. She closed her eyes for the briefest of moments before pulling her hand back up and smiling. I opened my mouth when she offered me her fingers, and the taste of her pussy was as familiar as her kiss.

"Slut," I whispered, still smiling at her.

"Whore," she said back.

"Take them off," I told her, my eyebrow raised in a challenge. She looked worried for a moment, but then grinned once again defiantly. I watched as she reached down and ever so slowly began to work the boxers off her hips. Each time Brent moved, she froze, but he snored or grunted and she continued the journey down her thighs, over her knees, until they were around just one ankle.

She wiggled again, this time pushing back against him a little harder, and I was instantly curious how far she would go. I slid my own boxers down as well, until both of us were naked on the bed, the blanket now gone too. She closed her eyes and bit her lip, and I knew just what she was thinking.

"Oh god, Kelly," Brent moaned, and suddenly I bit my tongue and didn't move. She held still, and I wasn't sure if it was just a dream.

"Don't stop, you feel so good," he groaned, and then slipped back into snoring. His hips had moved though, and the look on Kelly's face was suddenly different. There was no faking that expression. I looked down at her pussy and ever so slowly she opened her thighs. When her leg was finally high enough, his cock poked between them until it was nestled against the smooth lips of her cunt. She reached down, opening her legs a little wider, and I held my breath as she touched him, pressing his cock until it parted her skin. She was soaking wet, and his head came out from between her thighs as she closed her legs gently.

His cock was big, and I knew this. I had seen it a million times before, but looking at it pressed against my little girl's pussy was a different thing. She held him there, and I knew instantly that she wanted it. Her hand was shaking, her pussy was soaking, and if I hadn't been there, he would have been inside her an hour ago. For a moment I wondered if she would try it, even as he slept. Did she have the nerve to fuck my best friend? Just like that?

"Okay, if we're going to fuck that's one thing, but this is too much."

She jumped up, rolled over, and pulled away from him with a squawk. He turned onto his back, laughing so hard I thought he might burst, and I wasn't sure if I was angry or relieved.

"Did you really think I was sleeping? Are you serious? I could hear you fucking talking, and no one can sleep through Kelly wiggling her ass like that. Oh my god, I thought you two were going to have heart attacks. Holy shit."

He was still hard as he laughed, and now it was my turn to press against Kelly's ass.

"How long were you going to wait?" she asked him.

"I was hoping until you were riding me like a cowgirl, and I was shooting my load inside you. But, seriously, how far were you going to go? I was like right in there, and if you hadn't shifted like that I would have been seriously right in there."

Kelly leaned back and kissed me. She shoved her tongue into my mouth, pulled on my hair and kissed me so hard I almost fucked her right there. Brent was still on his back, but he stopped laughing, and simply watched as she rolled onto her back between us. Without thinking his hand slid to his cock, and the moment hung in the air like time had stopped. I could smell her pussy, and the room was warmer than it had been just a few seconds before.

"Maybe we should try it again," she said quietly. "But this time, without the laughing."

"Are you serious?" he asked. I wasn't sure if it was to me or her, but it didn't matter.

"She's always serious," I answered.

When she turned back to me I felt that familiar twitch of jealousy and excitement. We had talked about it so many times, and now there was only one thing that was important. She had whispered stories in my ear, and promised me I could watch, but after all those nights of fantasizing, of hearing her beg me to let her do it, it was finally going to happen. I was going to watch her get fucked.

He turned on his side once more, and she was sandwiched between us. She kissed me, this time slowly and sweetly as she adjusted her ass, and it was all I could do to keep looking into her eyes. One of her hands reached out and touched me, pulling me towards her even as she leaned in. She kissed me again, and out of the corner of my eye I saw her raise her leg.

Brent was breathing quickly, but instead of looking at me, or the back of Kelly's head, he was looking down. He was looking at her ass and her cunt. He was looking at his cock, positioned right against the lips to her pussy, and he know that within seconds he would be inside her.

I bit my lip and closed my eyes as my whole body tensed up. I felt dizzy and lightheaded, and I listened to every sound from her mouth, knowing that I would know. When something changed, I would hear it .

"Look at me," she whispered, her hand on my chin. "Do you want this? Do you want him to fuck me?" She was so quiet I almost didn't hear her, and all I could do was nod in response.

Kelly reached one hand between her legs, but she never looked away. Her lips parted, and I could hear Brent grunting as he focused. The muscles in her arm tightened, her ass shifted, and suddenly her eyes opened wide. Her mouth opened in a silent scream, and I knew it was done. I kissed her once, but I couldn't resist any longer. I leaned back, my hand on my cock as I watched, and then I finally looked down. After all this time, I had to see it.

Her thighs were open, wider this time, and her lips were bright red. I stared in awe as I saw her stretched around Brent's thick cock, only half of him inside her. She closed her eyes and started to moan, her hips moving so slowly as she pushed down. Inch by inch he opened her, stretched her, and filled her, as she bit her lip and began to moan his name. I lifted her leg higher, hearing her scream, and I leaned in closer. He was moaning too, as he struggled not to move, letting her take as much as she could.

It felt like hours before finally he filled her all the way, and she moaned sounds I had never heard. Her body shook, the vein in his cock pulsed, but they held still for an eternity, him buried inside her. His cock inside my Babygirl. It was hard enough to watch, but the listening was something else completely. She grew louder and louder, even as they held still, and I was in awe. She was coming and they had barely started.

"Fuck, it feels good. It's so fucking big, but…"

"Is it okay?" he asked, speaking for the first time.

She nodded her head as she tried moving, and I couldn't look away. There was another man inside my little girl, and she was coming just from him entering her. She was clenching around him, moaning for him, and I knew everything was about to change.

"Say it, Babygirl." My voice was a whisper, but she looked at me, her face clouded with lust. "Tell him what you want. It's okay. You've already sucked his cock, so say it."

It took a moment for it to register on her face, but then it was done.

"Fuck me," she moaned. It was quiet at first, but it grew louder in seconds, and her simple request was instantly the sweet sound of her begging. "Fuck me, Brent. Please, fuck me hard. Do it, please, I need it."

And then he began to move, as I lay there jerking off while I watched. At first he slid in and out of her, once pulling all the way out until she begged him to put it back in, but then they fucked. There's no other way to describe it, and I was in heaven. He slammed into her cunt, and she pushed against him. He thrust into her, and the screaming and moaning must have woken the neighborhood.

"You are so tight," he screamed as he fucked my little girlfriend, and I was amazed. Not at their bodies, and not even at the size of his cock. I was in awe at how easily they moved, how loudly they begged, and how sweetly they fucked. When I kissed her mouth, Kelly smiled at me, and I was back to being myself, the jealousy completely overtaken by my want. I moved up on the bed, pulling a pillow behind my back, and I took her by the hair and forced her eyes to look up at me.

Brent rolled her over onto her knees, her whimper only lasting the few seconds he wasn't inside her, and then he fucked her again. I lowered her mouth to my cock and she swallowed me without a moment's wait. She grabbed me, sucked me into her mouth, and pushed back onto him.

"I love you so much," she whispered, looking into my eyes.

And then she was back around me, deepthroating me, and gagging each time he pushed her onto me. The world was a blur.

"Do you like getting fucked?" I asked, even though I knew she couldn't answer. "Do you like having his big cock inside you? Do you like fucking Daddy's friend?"

She started to come again, all of us having already lost count, and her body shook with screams of joy and release. She shook and trembled, her hands still on me even as she bucked her hips against him. I could see her orgasm move through her, and the expression on her face went from complete adoration to unfettered lust. She was prettier than I had ever seen her before.

"Guys, I'm gonna come soon," Brent said. He looked at me for the first time and shrugged his shoulders like we were just having a chat. I thought for a moment, then pulled her forward and threw her down on her back. I knelt above her and jerked off as she opened her legs wide.

"Keep fucking me," she moaned, and he was back inside her without a word. I watched them fuck, my eyes moving from her face to her pussy, and when I reached down and rubbed her clit she screamed my name. He started to shake and looked at me once more, as if asking me the question that I knew was on all our minds.

"Come on her," I said. "Come on her stomach."

He pulled out a second later, and somehow, maybe because we had been friends forever, we started to come at the same time – him between her legs, leaning forward – and me onto her lips, her chin, and her neck. Our fists were blurs as we pumped and jerked, and all three of us were making noises that were new. I watched his come land on her stomach, and even then I had an ounce of regret. It was beautiful and sexy, but no matter what the danger, there was a part of me that had longed to see him come inside her.

I pushed the thought away as I watched her open her lips around me, licking the come off my cock as her own body continued to spasm on the bed. She held me in her hand, even as she rubbed his come into her skin with the other, and by the time I kissed her mouth I was in love all over again. The mess on her body was perfect, and even her red and swollen pussy was a piece of art. Everything about the scene was a dream, and I never wanted to wake up.

I fell down next to her, even as Brent collapsed on her far side, and all of us lay there enjoying the cold air for the first time all morning.

"Holy shit."

"Fuck."

"I can't believe we did that."

We went around in a circle, each expressing the same sentiment over and over again, until there was nothing left to say. We were exhausted, covered in sweat and come, and it was a bright new morning. Brent kissed her cheek and it was only then that I realized they had never had a real kiss at all. She had sucked his cock, and now she had fucked him until they both came colors, and yet, not once had they kissed.

"You can kiss her," I said, smiling at them both. "Or you can kiss him. Either way."

When their lips touched it was more intimate than anything that had happened since we crawled into bed. They kissed slowly and warmly, and I stared at them for a long time until I began to feel like maybe I didn't belong. Finally, Kelly looked up and pulled me in for a kiss, too. It wasn't until then that I realized his hand had been on my head the entire time. Even while he was kissing her, he was holding me, and every doubt I had was gone.

"Come here," he said, not giving me a moment to think. His

lips were strong and his face scratchy. But, we kissed all the same, the first one in fifteen years, and it was absolutely the most normal thing in the entire world.

Chapter Eighteen

Two things happened that week: Rachel moved out of our apartment, and I didn't sleep with Maddy. Maybe that's just one thing, but in my mind, it was at least four. Not fucking Maddy wasn't especially difficult; in fact, I barely saw her the whole week she was there, but that didn't mean I didn't think about it. I don't know if it was my morning with Brent and Kelly, but, my fantasies continued moving towards women I hardly knew who told me pretty things that were far less complicated. It was sex on location, and they moved from island escapes to fancy hotel rooms. It was often Maddy in my dreams, but even then, she was less than real. She was ephemeral, mysterious, and perfect.

My time with Talia was also underwhelming. Unlike that last month of college, we didn't spend most every day together, and we didn't stay up until three in the morning watching the Indiana stars. We met for coffee while her sister shopped, and our conversations were easy and gentle. I'm not sure if she was coddling me or if that was simply how she normally behaved, but it was difficult to feel like I was making a connection.

The last evening they were in town she invited me up to the hotel room. Maddy was watching television in the other room of the suite, and we sat on the couch and drank a bottle of expensive wine I had never heard of. It was light and fruity without being overly sweet, and it went down surprisingly easy. I knew nothing of wine, but Talia drank it like it was nectar, and I followed along as best as I could. Towards the end of the bottle, she looked at me with that friendly smile I had missed so much, and I leaned in closer.

"I'm so glad you're here," I said, placing my hand on her knee. She covered it with her own and not a hint of worry crossed her face.

"Me too. It's good to see you, Thomas. You seem so much happier than last time. I'm sorry about the note. I didn't want to wake you, and you looked so peaceful sleeping. I hope you weren't offended."

"I loved your note, Talia. It was sweet and it was perfect. As for happier, I'm not sure. Life is still confusing, and while I love Kelly, I'm not sure how much better she is for me than Claire."

"Come on, she sounds wonderful. You like her, I can tell, and so what if she's challenging you? You need to be challenged, remember? It's part of who you are."

I had only told her so much. In fact, I had told her almost nothing. She knew I had a girlfriend named Kelly, and she knew our relationship was on the kinkier side of the spectrum. From what I knew of Talia though, it's possible she thought that meant sometimes Kelly was on top. Unsurprisingly, I didn't want to break her of that notion. If Talia had sweet notions of sex it was even better. It made her more perfect in my eyes, not less.

"I guess so, but it's difficult," I insisted.

"It's always difficult. That's part of what makes life so wonderful. We do things we love and they're hard. When we accomplish them we feel good, and then hopefully, we get to do them again. Maybe they get easier, but some things don't, and then we get old and die. It's not the best system in the universe, but it's what we have, and we should embrace it."

"Yes, oh wise one," I said, my hand never leaving her leg. She laughed and shook her head, but just then Maddy came into the room. Without even looking in our direction, she opened the door to the bathroom.

"I'm taking a shower before bed," she said, and I heard the fan switch on. Talia didn't look away from me, her hand still on mine, and her eyes full of love and kindness. I struggled not to look up, but out of the corner of my eye I watched her little sister undress through the slightly open door. She hung her clothes on the hook, one piece at a time, turned on the water, and then for just a second, I got a glimpse of her naked body as she climbed into the shower. Without a sound, she reached out and closed the door behind her.

"You don't have to figure it all out, you know." Talia either hadn't noticed, or hadn't thought it worth paying attention to, but my heart was slamming into my rib cage, and I was nearly in shock. There's no way she didn't know what she had done.

"I know," I said forcing my attention back to the beautiful woman in front of me. "But I have to say, it's easier when you're here. Are you sure you don't want to move to New York? You can watch out for Maddy, get a nice job, buy an apartment..."

"Thomas, don't be silly. Maddy can look out for herself, and I love my life in Oregon. It's quiet and slow, and all the traffic and smoke here would drive me crazy. I haven't biked in five days and already I can tell I'm getting cranky. I love you, and it would be great to see you more, but New York is not for me. Come visit me sometime in Portland and I'll take you to the breweries. You can even deduct it as a business expense now. You'll love it."

Without a word I leaned in and kissed her. At least I tried to. I put a hand on her head, pulled her to me, and opened my mouth against hers. For just a moment I felt her lips on my own, and her breath in my mouth, but then it was gone. She pulled away almost instantly, but even then she wasn't angry. Her frown spoke only of disappointment, and once again I felt like a child.

"Thomas, you have a girlfriend," she whispered. She looked

down for a moment, and I swear I saw an ounce of regret. Just a second of doubt, but it was enough. It had to be.

"I know, but it doesn't matter. You said you loved me, and you know I love you. It's just a kiss," I said again, leaning towards her. She put her hand on my chest and turned away, leaving no doubt this time. Leaning back I took another sip of wine and sighed, trying not to sound dramatic. She was right, of course. Talia didn't want me if it meant I was cheating. She would only take me whole. If at all.

"I do love you, but not like that," she said. "It's been good to see you, but not like that. But, listen, before you go I have a present for you. It's nothing special, but maybe you and Kelly can have it one night when you're celebrating something good. Hold on a moment."

I got up with her as she walked to the other room, but she held out a hand and I stood there waiting by the bed. She went through her bags, and just when I thought she had found it, the bathroom opened and Maddy walked out in a towel. Her hair was wet, and the towel came just below her waist. I struggled to keep my eyes on her face once more. She looked at me, smiled, and then stepped closer. With a hand on my shoulder she leaned in and whispered in my ear.

"She has a boyfriend, too, you know. Did she tell you that?"

And then she was in the other room, the towel still clinging to her body. Talia stood up and walked back towards me, but just as she reached the door Maddy turned and stared right into my eyes. She reached down to the towel around her chest, and just as she opened it and dropped it to the floor, her sister closed the door. I was jerked back to the present and the fully clothed woman in front of me with a small bag with a bottle of wine inside. It was stuffed with tissue paper, and tied up with a ribbon.

"Don't mind her, she's just pushing boundaries," Talia said as she handed it to me. "It's from a vineyard near where I grew up. They make delicious Pinot Noirs, and I think you'll love it. It's better than the one we had this evening."

"Thank you," I said, leaning in and hugging her, this time not even kissing her cheek. "Thank you for everything. For the wine, for your friendship, for everything."

She smiled again, and I wondered where she had learned to do that. It was almost as if she couldn't decide if she wanted to pat me on the head or kiss me, but either way I felt small, young, and completely unfit for life.

"Bye, Maddy," I called through the door. "It was great to see you again."

"See you soon, Thomas," she called back.

I kissed Talia's cheek at the door and she hugged me for a long time. When I finally turned to leave, she gave me one last squeeze of the hand.

"Thomas," she said. "Take care of yourself. You deserve to be happy."

And then I was on the street, the cabs were honking, and god how I hate midtown. It was too bright, too loud, and so full of tourists I wanted to scream. I thought about taking the train, and I even thought about taking a cab. I was sure the valet at the hotel would grab me one in a second, but I needed to be outside. Without another thought, I stuck the bottle of wine between my knees, pulled out a cigarette, lit it, and started my long walk downtown.

I've spent a lot of nights walking with old friends when we were too drunk to make any other decisions. In many ways this felt the same, although the wine wasn't truly the culprit. Everything ran through my head at once, my thoughts bouncing from Brent to Rachel, over to Talia, back to Jane, and always Kelly again. I was happy, I did love Kelly, but no matter how hard I tried, the guilt and the anxiety wouldn't leave me alone. The morning with her and Brent had been the hottest moment of my life, but mixed in with the turn-on was the ever growing fear that I was fucking everything up: my relationship, my friendship, my life. It was all going to hell because I couldn't say no to anything.

I lit another cigarette off the one in my mouth as I walked down Broadway, and I tried to let it all go. Jason was right, as always. It was summer, I was young, and the world was my oyster. I had a hot girlfriend who let me do anything in the world with her, and I had no reason to complain. My crazy roommate moved out, Talia had come and gone, and at the end of the day I didn't fuck her sister. I laughed as I thought about it, and it was difficult to stop. Out of all the things that happened to me, I was suddenly proud of the fact that I didn't have sex with someone. It was insane, absurd, and so full of ego to be ridiculous, but still it was the truth.

I didn't fuck Maddy, I said again, my steps getting lighter. I. Did not. Fuck. Maddy. I sang it as I walked, and I clung to it like a life raft. Maybe there were other things I didn't do that I could feel good about. Let's see, I also didn't fuck Jane up the ass. That was good! I didn't let Brent come in Kelly's pussy no matter how badly I wanted to watch that, and throughout all the craziness at our apartment, I never once touched Rachel. I didn't kiss her, fuck her, or even squeeze one of those teeters, no matter how close to my face she got.

It suddenly occurred to me that maybe my place of employment was incredibly apt. I was a fucking saint, and I should be happy about it. In fact, the number of people in New York that I hadn't fucked was gigantic. It was so large it was unfathomable. It was brilliantly large, and getting bigger every day.

By the time I passed Union Square I was on my fourth cigarette, and I was nearly skipping. I was so happy in fact, that I decided I would go home, climb into bed with Kelly, and finally fuck her up the ass until she promised Daddy that she would never cheat again. It was a good plan, a solid plan, and a nice plan. I was a saint, and there was nothing wrong with a little ass fucking between friends.

By the time I got home, I was covered in sweat, nearly hacking up a lung, and as happy as could be. I turned the corner to my block, took a deep breath, and smiled. The East Village was quiet, the cabs were gone, and there wasn't one fucking tourist within a six block radius. It wasn't until I got to my building that I noticed someone sitting on my stoop, and it wasn't until I dropped my cigarette that I realized it was Jane.

It wasn't until she looked up at me that I realized she was crying.

Chapter Nineteen

I sat down next to Jane and didn't say a word. I was getting good at not instantly blurting out the first thing that came to mind, and this felt like a perfect time to practice. She wasn't crying as hard as I first thought, but her eyes were red and she was definitely not a happy girl. Her cigarette was bent in her mouth like she had crushed it pulling it out of the pack, and her normal boots had been replaced by something light and comfortable. She was wearing linen pants and a button down shirt that was loose enough to let the wind blow through it.

"I have a bump," she said. I waited for more, but maybe this was a time to ask questions.

"What do you mean?"

"I mean I have a fucking bump on my vulva. It's small and it doesn't hurt, but I don't like it. It's not red or an open sore, but it's bumpy. Like a bump."

"Oh fuck," I said.

"Yeah."

"Have you had it looked at yet?" She shook her head, and suddenly I wondered why she wasn't talking to her fiancé instead. He was a fucking doctor, not me. Beside, we had only done it once, and I had been tested! Yes, I suddenly remembered that obvious fact, and I smiled in spite of myself.

"I was tested not long ago. I don't have anything. Not sure if that helps."

"Thomas, you're the only one."

"What? What do you mean, surely you've having sex with your fiancé. You told me you were having sex with him."

"That's not what I'm saying. Of course I've had sex, but that was the only time I've ever had sex without a condom. I've done it once in my whole fucking life and it was with you, on your bed, the night I got engaged to someone else. Brilliant isn't it? Do you have a smoke? I broke mine."

I handed her a Lucky and she lit it. I didn't join her, because after that walk I didn't want to ever smoke again. I was still trying to catch my breath and it wasn't a good sign.

"You're serious? I mean, you're telling me the truth?" I said.

"Of course I am, don't be stupid."

"Just once. And it was with me?"

"Look, we don't have to fucking analyze me right now. That's not why I'm here. Sean and I are waiting until we're married to stop using protection because the pill fucks me up."

"Wait, you're not on the pill either? Jane, we totally…"

"Thomas, I just said this isn't about you. Or me, or my fucking messed up head. It's about the fucking bump on my pussy, and the fact that I can't tell him about it because as far as he knows, our wedding night will be the first time I've ever had sex without a condom. It's supposed to be special. No one waits that long to have sex, but we thought this was a good substitute."

"And you haven't told him…"

"Shut up. Seriously, how many times do I have to tell you? All I want is for you to come with me to the doctor."

"Now?" I asked. "It's eight p.m. on a Tuesday night. Where are we gonna go?"

"I don't know. We could go to the emergency room. Or I could call my gyno and we could go tomorrow. I just have to find out what the fuck is going on before he finds out and leaves me."

"He's not going to leave you, Jane. I told you: I got tested, and this has to be something else. Maybe it's not related."

"They can't test for everything. There are plenty of things that don't show up," she said, smoking furiously.

"I know, but there's no point in getting worried until we know something. And even if it is something, you can get things from oral sex, too. You've done that before?"

She shrugged as she smoked on my stoop and my mind was slowly crumbling. I had only gotten tested a few weeks after fucking Jane. What if she gave me something? Fuck, I'm so selfish, what the hell is wrong with me? It's not about me, it's not about me.

"What do you want to do?" I asked.

"Smoke and cry on your stoop."

"We're definitely good at that. I think you and I have been smoking and crying since we were sixteen. Jesus, Jane, I'm sorry. I do think everything will be fine, but I'm sorry. I'll go with you wherever you like, even if you want to go now. We can go to the emergency room and see if they'll take you."

"That's stupid," she said. "There are people with real problems, and they don't need an overly emotional white girl with a minor skin irritation taking up space. But, will you come tomorrow? If she can see me, will you come then?"

"Of course," I said, wrapping my arm around her.

We sat there for a while, and in the middle of it all I realized I had missed her. Our one little visit with Jason had been short, and while we talked a few times about the wedding, we hadn't had a real conversation since just after she got engaged. There I was, sitting on the step with my old friend crying, scared that her life was falling apart, and I was just happy to see her. Still going to hell. Definitely still going to hell.

"I'm going home now, but I'll call you in the morning. Are you working?"

I shook my head. Wednesdays were my day off, and I had been looking forward to lying around in bed, fucking Kelly, and generally moping about the state of my life. With Talia gone, Rachel moved out, and Jason and Katie sneaking off to have their still secret affair, I deserved some moping.

"Just let me know when, and I'll be there." I tried to sound as sincere as I felt, and she nodded her agreement.

"Hey, Thomas," she said, standing on the sidewalk looking up at me. "Don't tell Kelly, okay? I don't want to make her worried."

I nodded again and she turned down my block without so much as a hug. She slouched like she always did, but even in those loose linen pants her ass looked amazing. I closed my eyes for just one second and pictured it again, before hitting myself in the face and turning back to the door. Don't be an asshole, Thomas. Just don't.

Kelly was lying in my bed when I walked in. Rachel's room was strangely empty, and the apartment felt almost eerie. For the first month we had parties all the time, but with Rachel gone and Martin's day job taking up so much time, it had slowed down. Even Katie was often away now, and I wondered if she was happy with Jason.

"Hey handsome," she said when I walked in. "I was just thinking about you. Well, you and your friend."

"That sounds much better than what I was thinking about."

"What's that?" she asked, sitting up, her pretty little white shift clinging to her body in all the right places.

"For some reason, I can't remember at all," I said, pulling off my shirt and sitting down on the bed. "It must be the incredibly sexy little girl in front of me thinking dirty things."

"I didn't say they were dirty things." She blushed and looked down. "Did you say goodbye to Talia? And her little sister?"

"I did. They're going to fly home early in the morning. It was nice to see them. You know…"

I stopped, suddenly unsure if Kelly wanted to hear about my evening at all.

"What?" she asked, climbing over the sheet and closer to me. She rolled over onto her back until she was resting her head on my lap and she blinked her eyes at me. Her shirt rode up just enough so I could see her pussy beneath the hemline.

"Well, it turns out that Talia's little sister is something of a naughty girl."

"You didn't!" She was sincerely alarmed.

"I didn't do anything, Babygirl. Don't you worry. But she on the other hand… Can you believe that she left the door open just enough for me to watched her get undressed and get into the shower? What kind of girl does that?"

"A naughty one," she said, rolling over and snuggling against me. "I don't like it. I don't like you looking at other girls. You're not supposed to look at anyone but me."

"Is that how it goes? I'm only supposed to have eyes for you?"

"That's right," she said, sticking her thumb into her mouth. This was her bratty side, her little side, and her teasing side all rolled up into one, and it meant trouble. I was already growing hard, and she was just getting started. I gave one last thought to Jane on my stoop and then shoved it away. I could worry about her in the morning.

"And how about you? If I can only look at you, can you look at other boys? Do you still get to look at men?"

"Of course," she said. "I can look at boys, but you can only look at me." She rolled onto her back once more, and pulled her shirt up higher until she was sure I was, in fact, just looking at her. I reached down and slipped my fingers between her thighs, feeling how wet she was already.

"Were you touching yourself?" I asked, pushing them into her without warning.

"No," she gasped, shaking her head.

"Are you lying to me?" She was going to keep pushing, and I was going to have to do something serious. "Tell me what you were thinking about, or Daddy is going to get very angry. Do you understand?" I pulled my hand away from her and grabbed her wrists, holding them down in front of her face. She pouted, as she struggled for a moment, but finally she closed her eyes and stopped moving.

"I was thinking about you, Daddy, I swear. I was just thinking about you."

"Just about me?" I asked, pulling her to a sitting position. I tossed her easily over my knee, grabbing the bottom of the white cotton and lifting it up onto her back. She wiggled and squirmed, but finally answered me.

"I was thinking about you and your friend," she said, somewhere between defiant and terrified.

"I thought that might be the case." Without warning my hand came down on her ass in a quick slap. I followed it with three more, each time listening to her cry out. "What have I said about touching yourself when I'm not here?" She knew exactly what she was supposed to say, but I wondered if she would. I had rarely seen her like this and it was so wonderful it completely wiped my mind clear of everything else.

"That you like watching, and I should do it all the time?" She was asking for more.

The slaps didn't stop for at least a minute, and her ass was the color of blood. She wiggled and screamed each time, but she didn't stop teasing and she barely cried out.

"Were you thinking about him, or me?" I asked, suddenly slowing down and touching her so lightly she jumped. "When you touched yourself, who were you picturing inside you?"

"Don't make me say," she whimpered. I slowly opened her legs wider, and traced my fingers over the lips of her cunt. Her moans were delicious, but I wanted to hear her scream. I touched her pussy with all five fingers, then raised my hand quickly enough that she could tell. She cried out, her whole body tightening as I brought it back down again, touching her gently.

"I'm not asking again," I said, raising my hand once more. "And this time, I'll hit you for real."

I slapped her ass hard, just to show her that I wasn't kidding, and she cried out each time. I only stayed in one spot for a few slaps, but still it brought a flush to her entire body. Each time I spanked her she screamed at me, unwilling to ask me to stop.

"Naughty girls get spankings, and if they don't answer their Daddies, they get worse."

She bit her lip and looked at me, and I knew then that she wanted to be punished more than anything else. My hand came down on her pussy lips, and this time it was not lightly. The cry from her mouth was loud and piercing, and I had raised it again, this time coming down on the inside of her thighs, both of them in quick succession.

"It was him," she said, tears flowing from her eyes as she cried out. "I was thinking of him fucking me while I sucked your cock. Please, Daddy. Don't do it again."

She was truly in pain now, and it was all I could do not to take her into my arms and hold her, but there was more that needed to happen. It didn't have to be my palm on her skin, but there was definitely more.

When I stood her up in front of me, her eyes were swollen and her cheeks were red. She wiped her face, but through everything I could tell she wasn't done either.

"Take off your dress," I whispered. She didn't argue this time. Like a good girl, she folded it and placed it on the foot of the bed before coming back to stand in front of me. She had her arms at her side like she had been taught, and she was so pretty I wanted to scream.

"Turn around," I said.

Her ass was crimson and beautiful, and her thighs were on fire. She trembled as she stood, and finally I wrapped my arms around her and brought her back to the bed. Her expression was shy as I lay her down onto her stomach, and she flinched when I traced her bruises with my fingertips.

I undressed quickly as she lay still, and I watched her body rise and fall with each breath. I opened the drawer silently and put a bottle of lube onto the bedside table. I flipped open the cap, then crawled in next to her, running my hands over her shoulders, back, ass, and thighs.

"Did you like fucking Daddy's friend?" I asked, my mouth now against her ear.

"Yes," she said.

"Did you like his big cock?"

"Yes, Daddy."

My hand moved between her legs, and she was still so wet that she coated my fingers instantly. I pushed three of them inside her, opening her wide as she tried to hold still. I was uncertain for a moment, but the sight of her ass compelled me, and I pulled her closer, my cock now hard against her.

"Do you want to fuck him again?" I asked, my own mind wondering how much I wanted to hear the answer. Again she struggled, mumbling into her arm until I pushed my fingers further inside her, thrusting them in and out of her as her voice turned to moans.

"Yes, Daddy. I'm sorry. I'm know it's wrong, but I want it."

As she talked, I turned her head so she was facing away from me me and pulled her ass up. I grabbed the lube off the table, coated my fingers that had already been soaked by her cunt, and kissed her head.

"Do you want him to fuck you right here?" I asked, making her wonder for just an instant what I meant. "Do you want him on Daddy's bed?"

"Yes," she moaned, her ass now lifting up as I moved her, and her legs opening on her own as if she was looking for my hand again.

"Do you know what I'm going to do?" I asked, not letting her answer. "Right now, right here?" I pressed my fingers against her asshole and she gasped in mixed horror and excitement. She moaned and squirmed as I pushed one finger into her, finding her impossibly tight. Fuck, this might be more difficult than I thought. I leaned over her, my weight now against her body as I pushed the finger deeper inside her, and then I said it aloud.

"You've been terrible, do you know that? You've been a dirty little slut, and that means only one thing. Do you know what happens to sluts? Do you know what Daddy does with girls like you?"

She shook her head as I pushed into her, adding another finger covered thickly with lube.

"I'm going to fuck your ass, Babygirl. Daddy is going to fuck your ass, so that no matter what happens, you remember that you're mine. Do you understand?"

"Yes, Daddy," she moaned over and over again, finally holding still when I pulled my fingers out.

"Are you ready?" I asked her. "Are you ready for Daddy to fuck you here?" The head of my cock was against her, and there was no way it was going to fit.

"I don't know," she whimpered as I pressed harder, spreading her cheeks with my free hand as I held myself there. For a long while, it felt like she was holding her breath as I struggled to line her up beneath me. I pulled her hips off the bed, opened her thighs, and pushed again. Finally, I poured more lube onto my hand, coated my cock, and tried it one more time.

"Oh fuck," she moaned when suddenly the head broke through, entering her for the first time. I didn't move as I held her, but it was all I could do to stay still.

"Breathe, Babygirl," I whispered. "Just relax, and breathe."

She took one deep breath, and I pushed in further, watching in amazement as my cock began to vanish inside her tiny body. Her moans grew deeper as I entered her, and her sobs mixed with cries of pleasure.

"Oh god, your ass is amazing. Babygirl, your ass is so tight." When I looked down again I was all the way inside her and we stayed there, unmoving for what felt like ages.

"Are you ready?" I finally asked her, my hands moving to her hips.

"Yes, Daddy," she moaned.

"Do you want it?" I asked, needing to hear her say it as much as it turned me on.

"Yes, Daddy. Please do it."

"Do what?" I asked, sliding slowly out of her.

"Please," she said, gasping for breath. "Please fuck my ass, Daddy."

I started slowly, still worried I might hurt her, but within minute she was pushing back against me and I fucked her. I was buried inside the prettiest ass in New York, and she was begging me to do it harder. I moved from watching our bodies to kissing the back of her neck, but I fucked her faster and harder with each groan.

"Daddy," she suddenly screamed, as if something strange was happening to her. She looked back at me as I thrust, and she bit her lip as she pushed onto my cock. "Oh fuck, Daddy, I'm coming. I don't know how, but I'm coming. Oh god, don't stop. Keep fucking my ass, please."

She shook harder than ever before, and I didn't once let up. I was close to coming as well, but it didn't matter. Her ass was was clenching around me, she was screaming, moaning and begging, and I didn't want to stop. I wanted to come for hours, and then fuck her once more. I wanted to hold her, and then fuck her again, and her ass was mine.

"Come for me," I told her, as if she had a choice. "Come for Daddy."

As soon as the words left my mouth, I was coming too, and it was over. She encouraged me with everything she had, and it was the most intense orgasm I've ever felt. Her tiny body shook as she came, and her ass was so tight it was painful. None of it mattered though. After everything we had done, we were finally back to something that was just us. It was something I didn't want to share. It was mine. Her ass was mine.

I exploded inside her, filling her over and over again, my eyes glued to her body, wanting everything. I collapsed against her, twitching within her, and she was hot to the touch. She cried and laughed as I shot my last bit of come inside her, and I was right behind her. I kissed her neck, her shoulders, and her cheek as I marvelled that any of it was possible.

I held her for a long time when we were done. Each of us was panting and sweating by the time our bodies returned to anything resembling normal, and we had smiles on our faces that wouldn't leave.

"You are such a good girl," I whispered into her blushing ear. "Such a good girl." She snuggled into me, and I kissed her hair as she held my hand. I finally got up and went to the kitchen for a glass of water. She was sitting up when I returned, and her smile was shy and joyful all at the same time.

"Holy shit, that was intense," she said.

"Have you ever done that before?" I asked, unsure once again if I wanted to know the answer.

"Not with someone as big as you. And just once. It hurt and it wasn't nice. He didn't know what to do."

"You liked it?"

"Oh god yes. I had no idea it would be like that, and I definitely didn't know I could come like that. Although I'm starting to think you could make me come just by whispering in my ear. You know all the right things to say."

"I didn't think it would fit. But then it did, and I can't even begin to describe it. I love you, and I definitely love your ass."

We lay on our backs for a long time looking at the dumb fucking canopy, and finally she got up with me and we went to the shower. I soaped up my cock, and we washed each other sweetly and tenderly. Her thighs and cheeks were still tender from my spanking, and I kissed them and caressed them beneath the warm water. We kissed in silence and let out long sighs of relief as we let the shower cleanse us.

"I love you," I said. "I know I've said it before, maybe too often, but I want to be clear. I'm in love with you, Kelly, and it's the best feeling in the world."

She kissed me without a word, wrapping her arms around my neck, and when she looked up again there were tears in her eyes.

"I love you too, Thomas. Madly, constantly, and without reason or rhyme. I will do anything for you, and I promise that no matter what happens, I am yours. Completely."

That night our bed never felt so good. I pulled the sheets up over our naked bodies and we stared into each other's eyes like we had just met. My whole body was alive, and my heart pounded in my chest as I struggled to understand how so much love could fit inside me. When she kissed me I wanted to cry, and when I wrapped my arms around her she sighed and laughed, happier than I had ever seen her.

It was only in the middle of the night, when I woke to pee, that the rest of my life came back. It was only at three in the morning, as I stood there in the bathroom, the apartment quiet behind me, that I remembered Jane.

Chapter Twenty

We still had stars in our eyes the next morning and it was disgusting. We smiled too much, laughed at stupid things, and rolled around in bed for over an hour without even fucking. We showered again, drank coffee by the window, and by the time she left to go home and do laundry, we were practically making ourselves sick.

"I'm going to beat you later," I said as we stood by the door.

"I'll strip for your friends and suck their cocks."

"I'll tie you to the bed and make you watch me fuck someone cuter."

"You wouldn't," she said, real shock in her voice.

"I might let you help."

She stood on her toes and tried to look intimidating, but it was a failed effort. I kissed her nose as she scrunched it up, and she put her hands on her hips.

"I'll fuck Brent, and this time I won't let you watch."

It was my turn to look horrified, but I scooped her up into

my arms and kissed her.

"You'll fuck whomever I tell you to, and you won't whine about it, do you understand? And if you're a bad girl again, last night will feel like a vacation."

"Yes, Daddy," she whispered as I put her down. She looked up with a smile, and I patted her ass when she turned to go down the stairs.

"See you tonight? Maybe we can get Jason and Katie out. And of course, we should invite Brent along. Docs?"

"Sounds like a plan," I said, waving her off and walking back into my apartment. Just as I closed the door and locked it the phone began to ring. Fuck.

Jane had managed to get an appointment in an hour, and so I was suddenly grabbing my things, combing my hair and running out the door. The plan was for me to meet her at her apartment, and then we'd hop in a cab to the doctor. I was nervous as I walked, but mostly I was concerned. I was more worried about Jane than anyone else, and for the first time all summer I suddenly realized I was worried about her marriage. Not that she was doing it, but that somehow this might mess it up. She was happier than I had ever seen her, and the last thing in the world I wanted was for that to end. If anyone deserved to be happy, it was Jane.

She was quiet when I met her, but she smiled assuringly as we walked over to Seventh Ave. and grabbed a taxi. Her doctor was in the Financial District, of all places, and it was like a whole new world. My life existed almost completely between 14th St. and Houston. On occasion I'd go as far south as Delancy, but this was a different city altogether

We rode in silence, looking out the windows as the scenery changed, and by the time we arrived at the address, she was holding my hand and trembling. I walked her in, pressed the button for the elevator, and together we entered the waiting room. She signed in and the receptionist smiled at us warmly before asking us to take a seat. The room was full of babies. Not real babies, but posters, articles, magazines, and pamphlets. If they thought we were there about a kid, they were in for a rude awakening.

"It's going to be fine," I said.

"You don't know that. It might be terrible. Maybe it's going to fall off."

"Your pussy is not going to fall off. It's going to be fine. I promise."

She laughed, but hit me all the same. There was only so much humor could help.

We waited for over half an hour before the nurse finally came out and waved Jane in. I stood for a moment but she told me to wait, and all I could do was sit. I paced back and forth, I tried to read, and for the first time in my life I wished I had a cell phone. Right, because who would I call about this? Who the hell would pick up the phone and make it all better?

A full hour later, Jane walked out of the room and she was not smiling. I'm not sure what I expected, but I was sure everything would be fine. It had to be. I hugged her without thinking and she hugged me back. Without a word she dragged me out to the elevator, back to the street, and then into another cab. She stared out the window, and I couldn't bring myself to say anything. What the hell was going on?

It was only when we turned onto 6th Ave. that she spoke.

"Well, you don't have to worry about anything. It's not contagious." I breathed a sigh of relief, but it didn't explain her mood. That was good news right? She turned and faced me, taking my hand in hers. "I am happy, I know I don't look it, but I am. I was so terrified it was something you gave me, or worse, something I gave you, that I didn't think about anything else. And I'm glad it's not you. You were right, you don't have anything. At least not this."

"What is it?" I asked, squeezing her hand tightly.

"She thinks it's cancer."

"What?" I said, before I could catch myself. I managed to lower my voice before speaking again. "Are you serious? Is she sure?"

"She has to run a test. It's a cyst, but she doesn't like the way it looks. A lot of times it's nothing, but this one doesn't look good. Fuck, I knew it didn't look good. What the hell am I going to tell Sean? What am I going to tell anyone?"

"Jane, we don't know yet."

"She sounded like she knew. It wasn't one of those times when the doctor tells you something just to be safe. She was scared, and I could tell."

"When do you find out?"

"Not soon enough," she said.

The cab pulled up to her apartment, and I paid the driver before we climbed out on her side. We walked up to her stoop, through the front door, and up the five flights of stairs until we got to her door. She opened it without a word, poured herself a huge glass of wine, and climbed into her bed with a blanket over her knees. She pulled a Marlboro out of her brand new pack and lit it with her Zippo.

"Is smoking a good idea?" I asked.

"It's not that kind of cancer," she said between drags. I poured myself a glass too, and plopped down next to her. She handed me the pack, and I took one without thinking. My lungs still hurt from the day before, but fuck it. This was a shit day.

"You know what's fucked up?" she asked, lighting another cigarette off the one in her mouth. I got up and refilled her wine glass. It was only eleven thirty in the morning, but it didn't matter.

"Everything?" I asked.

"Aside from everything. What's fucked up is that I'm happy

for the first time in my life. Seriously, you know me. I'm not happy. Ever. Sometimes I have a good night, but this is different. I love Sean, I'm excited to marry him, actually excited, not fake excited, and now this. It's like as soon as something good comes along I get a big fuck you from the powers that be.

"What if I die before my wedding? Seriously, what if it's deadly and by the time it's December, I'm fucking dead. That would suck. You guys would look ridiculous up there in your Christmas tuxes waiting for me to show up. Sean would be like, 'Where is she?' and you'd have to tell them. It's going to be your job, Thomas, just because it always is. It's going to be your job to tell them I'm dead. I'm sorry, but there's nothing else to be done."

"Can I leave a message on their answering machines? Maybe send a postcard? 'I'm sorry to inform you the bride won't be in attendance today due to her death. She sends her regards. In lieu of flowers, donation may be made to the Pussy Cancer Association of New York.'"

She laughed between drags, and I almost spilled my wine. It was absurd, but maybe we needed some crazy for a while.

"How come there is no pussy cancer group?" She asked. "If I have it I'm going to start one. I suppose we can't march or anything. Maybe it could be a drink-a-thon. Or a smoke-a-thon. That would go over well. Give me five dollars for every cigarette I smoke and together we can find the cure. Jesus Christ, what am I going to do?"

She looked up at me and a second later I had my arms around her. I held her as she started to cry once more, and her sobs were deep and long, moving through her body like a tide. When she finally let go, it was only to lean back and light another smoke. She smiled and took a sip of wine, and both of us sat there shaking our heads.

"Tell me something stupid. Anything to get my mind off it.

Something about Kelly or college or anything. Tell me something dirty or something crazy."

"I don't know, Jane. It doesn't seem like the time for a dirty story."

"I'm serious. Make it nasty. Anything to get my mind off this for just a second. I don't need a vacation, just a break."

"Jason is banging Katie, I'm not sure how dirty that is though."

"He told me that last month, try again." I was a little shocked, and mildly hurt that he had told her before me, but I guess it wasn't that important.

"It turns out my girlfriend was cheating on me with Rachel, and now she's gone home so she can get treatment for a cocaine addiction we didn't know she had. How's that for a juicy story?"

"Eh, I don't know. Were they fucking a lot? Did you walk in on them pissing on each other? Come on, work with me Thomas."

"Well, I did watch Rachel eat her out. On the couch in my living room. That was pretty intense."

"That sounds normal. No offense, but not that dirty."

"Well, I had just come in her a second earlier. And it was dripping all over her face, and onto the floor and couch. It was everywhere, and Rachel just lapped it up."

"Huh," she said, nodding her head. "That's actually not bad. Did it really happen? Or are you just making it up?"

"Swear to Buddha. Or whoever you're listening to these days. Right there on my couch as I sat on the floor and watched. Ask Jason. He was there."

"Wait, was that the night he fucked Rachel? The first time he knew he had a crush on Katie?"

"He told you that? Jesus, it's like he tells you everything."

"Of course he fucking tells me everything. What, do you think that because you're a guy, you're the only one who gets the truth? I bet he tells me shit you've never heard."

It was my turn to nod and drink my wine.

"Did that help?" I asked.

"A little. It's nice to know that your life is fucked up, too. I mean, at least I'm getting married to the man I love, then having lots and lots of babies. Assuming I don't die first."

"I'm madly in love with Kelly," I said. It came out as a whisper, but it was there all the same.

"Really? I thought it was just a summer fling for you, but that's good. She seems sweet. Even if she does like face sitting."

"She's crazy, and brilliant, and she gets me to do ridiculous things. I don't know that I would do any of it without her, but I'm glad that we do it together. It's like I can't say anything to her that would make her freak out, and I don't know how to handle it. It's amazing and terrifying at the same time. She loves me and she trusts me, and she's going to kill me - sorry, didn't mean to mention death again."

"It's fine. I'm used to it already. But, it's good. I mean, you and Kelly. I like seeing you happy."

I hugged her again and for a long while we simply lay on her bed not talking at all. We held hands, smoked, and drank our wine, but there was just nothing left to say. I tried to make her laugh on occasion and she pinched me and slapped me as we rolled about, but beneath it all was worry and fear, which we only survived through affection.

When I finally left, her promising me she was okay, I felt marginally better. I was worried, she was scared, but it was going to be fine. She was going to tell Sean, so she wouldn't be alone. It was scary, and it was going to be a difficult time, but it would all be fine.

It wasn't until I was halfway across town that I realized I hadn't once thought about her ass.

"I'm a saint," I said walking through the park. "I am a goddamned saint."

Chapter Twenty-One

Doc Holidays was dead, but what was worse was someone was playing Garth Brooks on the jukebox. I have had plenty of nights singing about my friends in low places, and I have no regrets, but if that is the only Garth song you know then you should count yourself lucky. While the few patrons that were there did sing along, it didn't help. Kelly was sitting at a table with Brent when I walked in, and for a moment that old friend jealousy poked his head in and gave me a kiss on the lips. I shook it off, which was made easier by the grin she gave me and the fact that she climbed over the back of the booth, jumped into my arms, kissed me, and told me that she loved me. Just a little, but it helped.

Jason and Katie were sitting across from them, and they looked as surprised as the rest of the crowd by the pint-sized girl climbing over things. We walked to the bar, said our hellos to Joanna behind it, and took a shot of Jameson before ordering a round of beers for the table. Kelly still fit perfectly under my arm, and while I was not in the most joyous of moods, I was happy to be there. The only thing that made it difficult, was that once again, I promised Jane I wouldn't tell a soul. Which meant any melancholy on my part would have be dealt with swiftly. No questions and no lies. It was easy as pie. Or Kelly.

"Hello, handsome," Brent said as I slid in next to him on the bench. Kelly was next, so the three of us scrunched up as best as we could on the seat made for two. He slid his arm around me as we passed out the beers, and I pinched his cheek like his grandma used to do. We had hung out exactly twice since the morning I watched him fuck my girlfriend, and neither time was it weird. Of course, neither time did we mention it either, but maybe that was how it went.

"What's up, El Macho? You have a good day pushing papers?" He growled something under his breath, but we all toasted nonetheless.

"Do you guys want to go somewhere else?" I said. "I mean, I fucking hate Garth Brooks, and it's kinda dead in here. Plus, I hear there is a thing going on at Jupiter. I know I hate clubs, but Martin told me it was cool. And kinda dirty. I have no idea what that means, but it might be fun."

"If Martin says it's dirty, then it's probably like, crazy." Katie was looking at her fingers as she talked, and once again I wasn't sure if she was high or just talked like that all of the time. "He took me to a party once where there was a guy on the floor tied up by all four legs. I mean like his arms and legs. And that was fine, like I don't mind seeing an old man tied up, but there were three naked girls standing over him and they were peeing everywhere. Like totally everywhere. On his face, and his body, the floor, my shoes, it was just piss. I don't like piss."

"Okay, let's not go to that party," I said, "but this didn't sound like that. It just sounded kinda fun. Also, he put our names on the list."

"That's always good," Katie said. "When, like, he actually does it."

"I like parties," Kelly said. "We haven't had one in a long time, and it might be fun. All we do is get drunk at shitty bars, and fuck. It's like all day long we just fuck, fuck, fuck." She waved her hands as she talked, making gestures I didn't even recognize, but the rest of the table was laughing, so I did to.

"I could go to a party. Especially if there are naked people. Are there naked people?" Brent asked.

I looked at Brent, and grinned. "I'm sure there will be naked people. In fact, you can count on it."

He hugged me and kissed my head as we all stood up, and

before I knew it we were chugging our beers like we were in sixth grade. He crushed his empty can onto the table, and I crinkled mine in my hand. Jason and Katie just slammed theirs down, but Kelly didn't even bother to try. She was way too cool to chug a fucking beer at Doc Holidays. That's my girl.

By the time we got to Jupiter, the beer and the shot had kicked in, but I was still in a funky mood. The bouncer gave us a dirty look, but sure enough all five of us were on the list. He checked Kelly's ID twice, but finally waved us in, grunting about Wednesday nights. We ducked through the entryway, walked past the closed up coat check, and into the main room of the bar. I grabbed Brent by the arm, waved my hand out and showed him the promised land.

The club was empty. There were a few people standing around in leather pants, and a woman in the far corner was topless except for purple stars covering her nipples. All of them were older than us by at least fifteen years, and we stood there realizing we were suddenly the center of attention.

"Well, she's almost naked," I said to Brent.

"Yeah, so's Kelly. At least she's not old enough to be my mom."

"Hey, don't make fun of your mom," Jason interjected. "She'd look good in that. In fact, I think I've seen pictures." Katie just giggled, but Brent punched him in the arm as we looked around the empty bar. The music was so loud it was nearly impossible to hear anything, and the lights were flashing overhead.

"What time is it?" I yelled to Jason, who was the only one of us who ever bothered to wear a watch.

"It's ten," he said. "Almost."

Two minutes later we were back on the street, looking up and down the block wondering what the fuck to do with ourselves. Kelly was leaning against me, and Jason and Katie looked like they might be ready to either pass out, or go make out in the corner.

"This sucks," Brent said. "It's not even ten on a Wednesday night and we have nothing to do. What the fuck is wrong with us? It's like we're thirty or something."

"Maybe we should just go home. Call it a night. I don't know, it's been a shitty day and maybe it's just not meant to be." They all looked at me, but I just shrugged my shoulders. A night home meant a night in bed with Kelly and that wasn't anything to complain about.

"Fine, where are you two going?" Brent looked at Jason and Katie.

"We're going back to our place. I mean, that was the plan." Jason was always the considerate roommate.

"Okay, let's go home then. Docs was lame, Jupiter is empty, and everywhere else down here is fucking dead. I wish you guys still had parties."

I looked at Brent and shrugged once again. It was a good point, but there wasn't much to be done about it. At least not on a Wednesday night at ten p.m. We had fun at our place, and it was a good location, but what the hell could we do about it?

"I could like, totally call Martin." Once again, Katie surprised me by talking at all.

"What would that do?" Brent asked.

"He could have like twenty people at the apartment in a half hour. Probably some coke, a case of beer, and a stripper or two. If you want."

I looked at her leaning on Jason's arm and he just smiled at me and nodded. I had no idea if she was telling the truth, although I didn't doubt that Martin could do it. Martin could throw a party in a blizzard and half the city would turn out. Unless it was at Jupiter, of course.

"Call him," Brent said. "I don't want to fucking go home." He looked over at us when he said it and for the first time in years I saw him blush. He was looking to get laid, and he thought his best chance was with us. Well, fuck him if he thought I was going to let him bang my girlfriend anytime he wanted. Just because we did it once, didn't mean it was going to happen again.

An hour later our apartment was full of people I hardly knew. Katie had called Martin, he had called Zen, and suddenly there was a party in our place and the music was jumping. The fucking cargo pants girl was behind the bar, Zen's boyfriend Spider was packing a giant bong, and Kelly was sitting on my lap watching people come and go like it was the most normal thing in the world.

"I'm sad it wasn't a sex party," she said. "I mean at Jupiter. I've never been to one, but I thought it might be interesting. Would you take me?"

"Never," I said, kissing her nose. "You're way too cute to bring to a party like that. There would be a line just to talk to you."

"Whatever, if that was true you'd love it. You would be hard as a rock watching me, and there's nothing you could do about it."

"Are you looking for a spanking?" I asked her, squeezing her leg and pulling her down for a kiss.

"What I want is a sex party. It's not just about me, Thomas. I want to watch, too. I'm just curious. Look around the room and picture it. What would it be like if everyone was just fucking. Even Zen and her shaved head over there. Imagine her sucking cock while she's getting fucked from behind. And that guy? I can see him getting fucked by a girl with a strapon while sucking some guy's cock. It would be so much fun."

"If Rachel was here she could get this crowd naked in a second." I shut my mouth the second I said it, but it was too late to take back. It was true, but that didn't mean we needed to think about it.

"Sometimes I miss her," Kelly said. I tried to hide my surprise, but it was nearly impossible. "I know she was crazy, but she did make stuff happen. And also, she was really good at eating pussy."

"I think I would freak out if she walked in. I haven't seen her since that night, and I don't know if I could handle it. I was so fucking mad."

"Don't think about that," she whispered. "Think about her on the couch, right here, sucking my pussy after you came in it. Think about that instead."

"Do you need me to find you another girl? Is that what this is about? Do you miss having someone else to play with?"

She just shrugged, and we sat back watching the crowd once more. I couldn't tell if she was upset, or just lonely, but whatever it was she needed something. She needed a shock or a kick, because otherwise she was going to shut down. I had learned in the last few months that a bored Kelly was a dangerous Kelly.

"What if we set the mood?" I whispered.

"What do you mean?"

I turned her around on my lap so she was facing me, and I kissed her slowly. I nibbled her chin, sucked her lip, and bit her nose. She wrapped her arms around me and kissed me back, and for a moment the whole party vanished. It was a warm sweet kiss, but that's not what the party needed.

"Jason, could you dim the lights?" I asked. He reached over and turned down the dimmer without saying a word. He was talking with Katie in the corner and it was perfect.

"Do you really want to see what might happen?" I asked, my attention squarely back on Kelly. "How far will you go?"

"I'll do anything," she whispered, looking nervously over her shoulder. "You know that. I'll do anything."

I kissed her again, this time my hands sliding under her shirt and cupping her breasts. Her skin was soft, and her sighs turned to moans within seconds. I kissed her chin and then her neck even as I pulled her down onto my lap. She wrapped her arms tighter around me and her hips were moving like they had a mind of their own. A few people whispered, and someone giggled, but within minutes the music was slower, the air was thicker, and no one was laughing.

When we finally looked up there was another couple making out on the couch next to us and everyone was quiet. I could hear voices in the other rooms, but in the darkness of the living room it was like the world had changed. I wondered if it would actually work, and if so, what it would take. A couple kissing on the couch was normal, but what if we went further? What if we did more?

"Are you ready?" I asked.

"For what?" Kelly replied, trying to kiss me again.

"For this," I said, pulling her shirt off over her head. She gasped, but didn't stop me. I dropped it to the floor behind her and moved my kisses down to her breasts, sucking her left nipple into my mouth and running my tongue over it. I licked it and sucked it as her moans grew louder and the whispers around us were frantic.

Without waiting for anything at all she reached down and undid my jeans, her hand pressing hard against my cock as we kissed. The couple next to us were lying down, and I could see hands beneath clothing, and skin slowly starting to appear. I moaned when Kelly pulled out my cock, but the mood in the room had changed in an instant. When she slipped down onto the floor, taking me in her hand and drawing me into her mouth, we suddenly had at least six people standing around us watching. She sucked me into her throat and suddenly people were losing clothes all around us.

"Fuck it," I head from the couch next to us, and a pair of black lace panties landed on the pillow beside me. I looked over as Kelly sucked my cock to watch some guy I didn't know open his partner's legs and bury his mouth against her beneath her skirt.

Her moans were far louder than my own, but it hardly seemed to matter. As he sucked her pussy, she moved closer and closer to me on the couch, until her head was nearly against my thigh, and it was only then that she looked up at me, her eyes glazed over in pleasure. I smiled at her, as I pulled Kelly up, undoing her shorts in a heartbeat.

"I want to fuck you," I whispered, pulling them down around her knees. "Right here. While they watch."

"Anything," she said. "I'll do anything you want."

The girl next to me watched intently as Kelly sat back down on me, and her eyes were glued to my cock as one small hand guided it inside her shaved cunt.

"Holy shit that's hot," the girl moaned, pulling the guy's head harder between her thighs.

When I looked back there were a couple of guys standing around the couch, adjusting themselves through their pants and watching us fuck. When the pussy eater next to me slid up and started fucking his date, I realized the party had officially changed. I looked around the room to see people kissing, undressing, and groping. Even the bartender had lost her tanktop.

"Can I watch?" asked the closest guy to us. Kelly looked up, and without a word she reached out one hand and grabbed a hold of his cock through his pants. She unbuttoned his jeans without even looking at him, and a second later she was jerking off a stranger as she fucked me; she was moaning louder than ever.

"Do it," I said to her, knowing she probably would anyway. "You know you're going to, you little slut. Just do it."

He groaned as she leaned in and took him into her mouth, but he didn't complain. Her fingers were wrapped around him, jerking him off as she blew him, and I slammed into her, leaning forward to suck on her tits. I felt a hand on my thigh as the girl next to me arched her back and lifted her hips up, taking her partner deeper inside her.

It felt like just seconds later that Kelly was swallowing his come before he was instantly replaced by another random cock in her hand. The night shifted almost instantly from my doing to something else, and I could feel the panic rise in my chest in a second. The first guy had been hot, but it was all spiraling out of control, and I wasn't sure how far it would go. It wasn't about me at all.

Did I not get a say in this? I watched her take the second guy into her mouth, and it was like she was on autopilot. I didn't recognize him, but his stupid fucking mustache looked ridiculous on his face. Who the hell was this guy? She didn't stop fucking me, but the cock in her mouth was far more important. The few people still watching us were making comments left and right, and I heard the phrases "cock-slut," "whore," and "tiny, little bitch" more than once.

"You are so fucking filthy," I said, suddenly unable to feel her around me as tightly as just a moment before. She was soaking wet, and my cock slid effortlessly in and out of her.

"Do you want to see him fuck me?" she asked. Her eyes were glazed over, and she pressed a condom into his hand before I could say a word. She stood up, my cock slipping out of her, and suddenly he slid into her cunt as she groaned and pleaded. He slammed into her, pushing her closer to me, and I grabbed her by the hair and held her tightly. It was only the second time I had seen her fuck another man, but I didn't like it.

"More," she said, as he fucked her harder and faster, and that was it. I was suddenly losing my erection, and I had no idea what was going on. She kept moving, unaware for a few moments, but then she looked at me and frowned. I arched my back and screamed out, my hand on my dick, hoping that maybe other people in the room would think I had come.

"Are you okay? What do you need?" He was still fucking her, and I had to look away. Fuck, I had to get away. This wasn't what I had signed up for.

"A break, okay? I just need a fucking break from watching you suck every cock that lands in front of your face. Christ, you really are a slut."

I got up, leaving her naked on the couch, with a strange man standing behind her jerking off his cock. I stormed back to my room like a grownup, threw out the couple on my bed, and slammed the door behind me. I lay down, buttoning up my jeans, and stared up at the canopy wondering what the hell I was doing. It had been hot at first. Watching her get more and more turned on, and then seeing her blow the first guy was intense. But then the talk, the visuals, and everything else came crashing home. It wasn't about me. It wasn't even about us. It was just about her getting fucked, and I should have known it all along.

"Fuck!" I screamed, laying there as I wondered how long it would be before she came to see if I was okay. Maybe she wouldn't. Maybe she'd stay there on the couch, naked as a baby, sucking dick until her mouth was exhausted and then she'd move to fucking them all. For all I knew, she would fuck the whole damn party, and while just hours ago that might have turned me on, all I felt now was disgust.

Chapter Twenty-Two

It was nearly an hour before Kelly came to bed. Just long enough for me to have imagined the worst. She must have fucked Brent, and probably a few other guys as well, and I bet she was so tired she was going to climb into bed and pass out. What the hell was I thinking? I should have known all along. But, when she climbed in beneath the covers I was surprised to see she had her clothes on. Maybe she didn't want me to see what they did to her body. She didn't hug me, or try to reach out, instead she simply lay there looking at me in the dim light of the room.

"Are you okay?" she finally asked.

"I don't know," I said, and it was the most truth I could handle. "Who else did you fuck after I left? You were out there long enough."

"That's not fair," she said. I looked at her and she wasn't smiling. She wasn't laughing, but she didn't look scared or guilty either. Mostly she looked concerned.

"What does that mean? Come on, I left you naked on the couch after you just fucked a stranger with a horrible mustache. It's not like I didn't expect you to enjoy yourself after I left."

"Really? That's what you expected? You stormed out of the party, slammed the door behind you, and you expected me to just start fucking more people? Maybe climb into bed later and tell you all about it? Thomas, do you think I'm an idiot?"

"You didn't do anything?"

"I put my clothes on and sat on the couch talking to Brent. You were clearly upset, and I thought you wanted to be alone. The rest of the party kept happening, but it definitely slowed down after you left. I think people didn't know what had happened. There's only a few people still here."

"Did Brent leave?" She nodded and I finally rolled over and faced her. She touched my cheek and I tried a smile to see how it felt. "I was sure he was just trying to fuck you again. I thought that's why he wanted this party."

"It didn't come up," she whispered.

"You really didn't hook up with anyone else?"

"No," she said.

"I'm sorry I ran out, I just didn't know what else to do. It was all just too much and my head sort of exploded. Why did you fuck that guy? I mean, it was hot having sex in front of people, but we never talked about that. Do you even know him?"

"I've met him a few times. He's a friend of Zen's. He's not bad, but Thomas, I fucked him for the same reason I blew the first guy. I thought you wanted me to."

"What? Why would you think that?"

"Maybe because you told me to? Something like, tell him what you want, Babygirl, I know you need it? Thomas, I didn't give a shit about either of them. I wasn't doing it because I suddenly needed more dick than the city had to offer. I was doing it because I thought it turned you on. I was doing it because I thought you wanted me to. It's only hot when you tell me what to do."

"You're serious," I said, sitting up on my elbow and trying to make out her features in the darkness. She nodded again, and I felt a mixture of relief and guilt slide through me. If she was doing it for me, then what the fuck was I doing? It did turn me on, at least at first, but then it all changed. Then it was more about her getting something, no matter what I wanted.

"I didn't tell him to fuck you. You asked me, but I didn't even have time to say anything before he was doing it."

"I know," she whispered, crawling closer to me and taking my hands in her own. She kissed my knuckles and said it again. "I'm sorry."

"Fuck, Kelly, I don't know what to say. I honestly thought you were out there this last hour getting the shit fucked out of you by Brent. He was so obvious all night, and I think that made me not want to do it. It was hot the other day, but I was in control. The thought of you two alone out there was more than I could handle."

"Can I ask you something. I don't want to pry, but what happened with you two and Claire? He talks about it like it was just some fun and games, but every time it comes up, you shut down. It's like two different things happened even though you were both there."

I turned onto my back again and rubbed my eyes. It wasn't a story I told anyone. Not even Brent, and I wasn't sure I could handle it right then. But she was right, it was all connected. Everything is connected.

"It's complicated. Sort of. I don't know, it's hard to talk about."

"You don't have to, but it might help. I feel like I'm missing something."

"You are. So is he, though." I sighed and took a deep breath. "Are you sure nothing happened after I left?"

"Thomas, I promise you. I didn't even kiss anyone. Not even that cute girl on the couch next to you. If you don't know me that well by now, then we need to talk about that, too. Do you trust me?"

I sat up, and ran my fingers through my hair. I crossed my leg and leaned over to light a candle.

"I trust you completely," I said. "You're going to think I'm an idiot, but I guess that's okay. You know me pretty well by now."

"You bet your ass I do."

"So, Brent came to visit for a week after hearing story after story about Claire. He knew she was crazy, horny, and that we did kinky shit. He knew I tied her up, slapped her around, and that she was always pushing for more.

"When he got there, it was clear they got along. They both like vodka and running, and they listened to the same music. It was fun, because my best friend got to meet my girlfriend, and everything was peachy. We got drunk and while we joked about sex, we never talked about it. I mean, not for real. Claire and I didn't talk like we do. We didn't have honest conversation unless she was drunk, and then they were forgotten in the morning.

"So, one afternoon I came back from class and they were fucking in our bed. I stood in the doorway watching him thrust into her, and before I could yell, scream, or break something she waved a finger at me and winked. She had that challenge look in her eye, and I just stopped. Brent looked over his shoulder, but she whispered in his ear and he just smiled at me.

"Without another word I stripped and climbed in, too. She sucked my cock to get me hard and then I fucked her while he watched. We took turns between her mouth and her pussy, and we probably fucked for an hour before we were done. He kept high fiving me, and I kept telling myself it was fine. She could push, and I could take it. I refused to give in and get angry.

"As we lay there exhausted, I heard her whisper to him again, telling him that she was right. I had wanted to watch, and didn't I do just what she said? Didn't I love it?"

Kelly didn't say a word, but she shook her head and reached out to me as I talked. I let her hold my hands, not realizing that I was getting closer and closer to breaking down. When she climbed into my arms I started crying, and she simply held me and told me it was okay.

"I don't know why I did it. I should have stopped them, but I couldn't. I just kept telling myself it was fine, and then later I couldn't say a word. He would have been so hard on himself if he thought I didn't know. If even for a second he thought I hadn't arranged it with her, he would never forgive himself. He's the most loyal friend in the world, and I never told him. She fucking lied to him, and there wasn't a damn thing I could do."

"Do you want a drink?" She asked. "Or a smoke?"

"Both would be good, but I don't want you to leave. Just stay here."

"Of course," she said as we lay down together. I wrapped her up in a hug and held her as I cried some more, and each time my cheeks were wet she wiped them with her sleeve.

"I would never do that," she said. "I would never lie to you, and I will never fuck anyone without you telling me to. Actually, I won't fuck anyone at all. It's just us, baby. It can just be us. Some fantasies are better left fantasies."

"Are you serious? You'd do that? Not even Brent?"

"I already told you. It's only fun if you make me do it. I don't want anyone else."

"Maybe we can slow down a little. I feel like all summer we've been pushing harder and harder, making ourselves do dumber shit just to see how far we can go. I think if we push any harder I might break. Is that okay? Can we slow down?"

"Of course."

"And maybe sometimes we can just have sex? Just you and me. Just Kelly and Thomas without Daddy or anything else. Just sweet, normal, beautiful sex."

"Whenever you want. I told you before. I love you, Thomas. I like our games, but we don't need them. At least not all the time."

After a while, laughter started mixing in with my tears, and I realized how closely related they are. I had started my morning taking Jane to the doctor, got drunk by noon, and ended up watching Kelly get fucked once again. It's no wonder I was crying. There was so much happening all at once, and who could handle it all?

We made love later that evening and it was tender and sweet. I didn't call her anything other than Kelly, and we didn't mention anyone else. It took me longer to get hard, but she played with me and kissed me, whispering sweet things into my ear, and not once did she make me feel bad about it. When I was finally inside her I started to cry again, but we simply rocked there on the bed, our bodies joined perfectly together as the city vanished around us.

****

As the weeks passed, our lives began to once again feel normal.

August came with more heat and humidity, and the whole city slowed down, including us. We spent more time drinking in our apartment, and Kelly and I took cold showers almost every day. I visited her at the karaoke bar and she came into Saints with lunch and a kiss. We lay in bed naked for hours without fucking, but even when we did, it was just us. She rarely called me Daddy, and while I occasionally still took her over my lap, her ass pink from my slaps, it was a quiet thing. Always at the end we held one another and whispered sweet words of love.

Our new roommate was an actress named Stephanie, and she was moved in two weeks after Rachel had left. We only talked to two or three people before offering her the room, but Martin was convinced she was the perfect fit. She was out as often as we were, but she was perfectly content with us having parties. It was good to have someone in the room again, and I got to know her slowly over coffee in the mornings.

Jane was in and out of the doctor's all summer after they had confirmed her cancer, but once she told Sean there was less and less I could do. The tests were confusing, different doctors said different things, but the wedding planning went on, and the three amigos did the best we could to be good bridesmaids. When Jane was too tired to do much of anything, we brought her coffee and wine, and even Kelly came with me for visits. It took them time to warm up to each other, and while they would never be best friends, they got along. We helped her with the invitations, we called caterers and rental houses, and before our eyes we saw it all unfolding. It was going to be a beautiful wedding, cancer be damned, and even when she broke down crying we were there to hold her up.

Brent and I didn't talk about what had happened with Kelly, but the tension I kept expecting never appeared. They got along perfectly, and if they still flirted on occasion it was always sweet and good-natured. I trusted them completely, and my memories of Claire were pushed back into the depths of my mind. Kelly and I only talked about Brent on occasion, but as summer moved along, a few of our fantasies did return. Maybe it was distance, or maybe we had simply not buried them deep enough, but still we kept them safe in the confines of our relationship. If on occasion I asked her if she had enjoyed him sliding inside her, and if she occasionally teased me for getting turned on when I watched, then that was just the way it was. We were grownups, and we knew the difference between fantasy and reality. We knew it all too well.

A big part of me felt like I was finally growing up. I even called Talia to let her know how happy I was, and while I couldn't fill her in on the details, my heart swelled with gratitude. Kelly and I were normal once again, and that was just fine with me. It was perfectly fine, and nothing could be better. Everything we had done in the spring had simply been us pushing boundaries, getting to know one another, and letting go of our pasts. But now it was us. It was Kelly and Thomas, two people learning to love each other until it felt easy. It was healthy, strong, and normal.

It wasn't until September arrived that anyone thought to mention New Year's. We all knew it was coming, and the news was full of Y2K almost twenty-four hours a day, but it was still a distant thing. The summer was so hot that even planning a Christmas wedding felt absurd, and it wasn't until the first chilly day of rain that we realized we needed a plan.

"We could rent a house in the woods, load it up with shotguns, bottled water, and jugs of wine, and keep ourselves warm by burning furniture." Brent had been coming up with suggestions for the last hour, and I'm sure the tallboys of PBR we were drinking at Doc's didn't help.

"Why don't we just find a party in the city?" Jason said. "I'm sure Martin will know of something. I'd rather be here if the world ends. Besides, we're going to be exhausted after Jane's wedding. The last thing we're going to want to do is drive up north to be ax-murdered."

"Jason, we're not going to get ax-murdered," Brent said. "We are the ax-murderers, remember? We're the ones with the guns, the wine, and the naked women. It will be epic."

"Why don't you have a party?" We all looked at Kelly who just shrugged her shoulders. "Seriously, Thomas's place is perfect, we can fit the right number of people, and no one has to go anywhere. I feel like every year I plan on doing something amazing and it just sucks. I get all dressed up and someone cries, someone is throwing up in a cab, and no one is happy. Just have a party and it will be perfect. You can get a keg of awesome beer from the bar, we'll put on music, and end the fucking century with our friends. Isn't that the point? Especially if the world is going to end."

I looked out the window onto 9th St. and watched the rain falling on the sidewalk. All summer long I had stared out that window, watching people sweat and curse as they stumbled through the heat. I was so tired of being hot, but fall always did things to my head. I slowed down and thought too much. I over analyzed and didn't want to leave the house. For my entire life, it meant the beginning of school, but suddenly, I was looking at the same thing as always. My job was the same, my apartment was, too, and even Kelly was the same. And it wasn't just the fall. It was the rest of my life. My crazy summer was over.

"Thomas, are you listening?" Kelly tapped me on the shoulder and brought me back to the table. I shook my head, trying to shake my thoughts away.

"Yeah, I'm here. A party at my place. Sounds like a good idea."

"Dude, are you okay?" Brent looked at me with an expression that meant trouble. "Do you need cheering up? Maybe tequila?"

"Oh god no, not that again. The last time we did tequila

shots, Kelly danced on the bar, and I puked in the urinal."

"I like watching Kelly dance on the bar," Jason said. Everyone else nodded, but there was no way I was getting talked into that. Especially not on a Tuesday night in the rain. No way.

Two minutes later Brent camed back with five shots of tequila though, and just like that I was licking my hand, shooting it back and sucking the lime out of Kelly's mouth. She didn't let me go and I held her for a moment, forgetting where we were. Everyone screamed as they slammed their glasses down on the table, and they kept screaming as we kept on kissing. Maybe it was a good idea.

"So, party at your place. New Year's. Y2K, bitches, it's going to be awesome. I mean, seriously, if the world ends, I want to be with you," Brent said. "I want to be with my best friends, and Katie too."

"Hey," she said, sticking her tongue out at him. "Fuck you, dude."

"I'm just kidding. I love you Katie. Anyone who can put up Jason for as long as you have must be a fucking saint." She crossed her arms over her chest, but finally smiled once more.

After three more shots of tequila, I was solidly drunk. We split up and made our way back to the apartment, Kelly hiding under my umbrella as we walked. It was just chilly enough that holding her close felt good again, and we splashed in the puddles as we swayed. Maybe a party was a good idea. Maybe New Year's would be nice this time. Maybe everything would be nice this time.

When I got home there was a message on the answering machine, and as Kelly stripped off her wet clothes in the bedroom I poured myself a glass of water and listened to it. I nearly spat it out when I heard Talia's voice. Maddy was coming to New York in a week and she wondered if possibly I might be able to put her up.

She had gotten into school starting in January, and she had a pre-enrollment event she needed to attend. Call me back! she said in her cheerful voice, and I hit delete before heading back to my room.

"What was that?"

"It was Talia. She wants to know if Maddy can stay with us while she's visiting next week."

"Does she know you? I mean, has she actually met you? Who would put their little sister in the same room with you, let alone ask her to stay?"

"Fuck you, Kelly. I'm a perfectly respectable person," I said falling over onto the bed. I kicked my shoes off and struggled with my shirt, the tequila clearly having its intended effects. Kelly helped me with my jeans, and a minute later we were both snuggled underneath a thick blanket wearing nothing at all.

"Are you going to say yes? Do we get a little blonde pet for the weekend?"

"Nothing is going to happen. She's Talia's sister, and of course I'll say yes. But we'll be good."

"I just thought it might cheer you up."

I rolled over and looked at her. "I don't need cheering up. I'm fine."

"You alway say you're fine, but you're not. Look, you've been acting strange since August, and it wasn't just the heat like you said. Things are good, but maybe they're too good. Maybe you needs things less good for you to be happy."

"What's that supposed to mean? I'm perfectly fucking happy."

"When was the last time you spanked me? When was the last time you called me a whore or even a brat? Come on, we both know you've been down. There's nothing wrong with it, I'm just saying maybe slowing things down wasn't what you needed. Maybe you need to be challenged instead."

"You sound like Talia," I said. I pulled her closer and her body was still cold from the rain.

"Where will she sleep, the poor thing," Kelly began. "I mean, there's only one bed here. You know what? Maybe she should just stay here with us. I'm sure we could fit her. I'm small."

"Now you're just trying to rile me up."

"I'm trying to get you to do anything. Thomas, you didn't stop talking about that girl for weeks, and now nothing? Have you been broken?"

"Wouldn't you be jealous if she was here?" I asked, finally letting myself actually think about it. I had pictured Maddy in my bed more than enough times, but Kelly was right. It had been a long time since I thought about her. The images came flooding back in a heartbeat though, and when I remembered her undressing in the bathroom of the hotel, I felt a familiar twitch.

"I thought that might get you going," Kelly whispered, grabbing hold of my cock. "Of course it would make me jealous, but maybe that's okay. After all, you've watched me fuck someone else. Maybe it's my turn to watch. Maybe it's my turn to hold my breath as I watch you slide this cock into someone else. Would you like that? Do you want me to watch you fuck her? I'll hold her legs open for you, spreading her pussy so you can do it."

I was inside her a second later and it all came flooding back. I pinned her arms above her head and fucked her harder than I had in weeks, picturing Maddy below me. I thought of Kelly licking her as we fucked, and I pictured the tears in her eyes. I could make Kelly watch, tied to the chair, or maybe I'd do it closer, holding her just inches away as I slid into Maddy's tight cunt.

"We'll do it right here," I said. "I'll put her on her knees above your head so you can watch me slide inside her – your mouth right below her cunt – as I fill her over and over again. You'll beg and plead, but I'll fuck only her all weekend, until you can't contain yourself. Maybe I won't even let you come. Just watch, for hours and hours until you're ready to explode, and you beg me for any release at all."

"Oh god," she moaned, as her orgasm ripped through her body. She clenched around me and screamed my name loudly, and it was the first time in weeks she had come like that. It was almost like waking from a dream, and it pushed me on. I kissed her mouth as she came, and I pulled her hair, fucking her faster, but by the time she was done shaking, I was still hard.

"That was amazing," she whispered, wrapping her arms around my neck. "I like this girl already. You haven't fucked me like that in weeks."

"I'm not done fucking you," I said, still moving slowly inside her.

"I like that too. You can fuck me all night if you want to. You can do anything."

"I can fuck this ass again?" I asked, squeezing her hard with one hand.

"Yes."

"And this mouth?" I asked, shoving three fingers between her lips. She nodded and moaned her consent. I started moving faster again, wondering what it would take to make me come. My mind was suddenly flitting through every fantasy I ever had, wondering which one would turn me on the most, and it was nearly overwhelming. After so long of not letting it in, the flood gate was suddenly opening, and I couldn't stop it.

"Tell me about fucking Brent," I finally said. Of course I had to pick the one thing that upset me the most. I had to pick my biggest fear to find my biggest turn-on. She moaned as she clenched around me, and I could tell it was different. "Tell me what it felt like to have him inside you as I watched. Tell me how hard he made you come."

I didn't need her to say a word because my mind was back

in that place, and I could picture it all. The look of lust in her eyes, the way his cock filled her, and her moans of pleasure as they fucked on her bed. I was right there again, more turned-on than I had been in ages, and I knew it wasn't enough. Kelly was right. I needed to be pushed. I needed something harder.

"I want to watch you again," I whispered. She tried to catch her breath, but only a gasp escaped her lips. We hadn't been there in forever, and she knew as well as I did that this was different. "I want to hold you and watch you; I want to listen to you. I want to hear you come as he fucks you again."

"Are you sure, Daddy?" She asked, and I was lost.

"Yes, Babygirl. But there's more."

"What do you mean?" she asked, lifting up to me, needing me deeper inside her.

"Remember when he fucked you last time?" I asked, the image clear in my mind. "Remember when he said he had to come?"

"Oh god," she said, another orgasm moving up from her toes and filling her as we writhed on the bed, our bodies coated in sweat. "I remember, Daddy."

"Where did I tell him to come? Where did Daddy tell him to come?"

"On my stomach," she said, her eyes opened wide as she wondered what I would say next.

"Where did you want him to come?" I asked. She instantly shut them again, and I knew. I fucked her faster, my jealousy and excitement filling me in equal parts. "Tell me."

"Please, I can't. Don't make me say it, Thomas."

And it was done. After an entire summer of trying to bring my life back to a normal place it was over. She didn't say Daddy. She said my name, and instantly we were talking about real life. I was asking her, Kelly, a serious question, and both of us knew the answer.

"Tell me, Kelly," I said, pulling all the way out of her. I rubbed the head of my cock against her lips, but held myself steady. I was dizzy and afraid, but I didn't care. I needed to hear her say it.

"Inside me," she moaned as I filled her once more. "I wanted him to come inside me, Thomas."

And then there were no words left. I kissed her, fucked her, and I slapped her face over and over again as she came so loudly I was sure we woke up our roommates. Each time I hit her, she clenched around me, and I pictured it all in vivid detail. I saw his cock inside her, but this time instead of pulling out he just didn't. I watched them fuck in my mind's eye, and when his body tensed, his balls tightened, he stayed just where he was, filling her cunt with his come as she begged him never to stop.

"Next time he fucks you," I moaned, just seconds away from coming, "next time he fucks you I want to see it. I want to watch him shoot his load inside you, filling you up as he comes. I want to watch him pull out and come on your open pussy, and I want to see it inside you. I want to hear you beg and scream and I want to taste it…"

And then I was coming too, and I was filling her. I buried my face against in her hair, I thrust into her and held myself there, exploding again and again as I moaned out my release. When I finally slowed down, stopped moving, and looked her in the eyes, there was no regret. There was no shame, and no fear at all. I pulled out of her, eliciting another gasp, and both of us stared at her cunt, wet with my come.

"Just like that," I said, kissing her again. "It will be just like that."

"Oh god, that was intense. I can't remember the last time you slapped me. Or any of it."

"It was okay?"

"It was better than okay, it felt like us again. Like you and me: sick, twisted, and more fun than anything else in the world."

I was playing with her cunt, my mind still stuck in memory and dream. I ran my fingers through her wet folds, and stared at the strands of white that dripped off my hand. There was nothing sick about it. It was the most natural thing in the world, but we ran from it with everything we had. We were sweaty, sticky, and we smelled like sex. Good, real, sex.

"Did you really want it? I mean at the time, was that what was running through your head?" I wasn't as turned on as a moment before, but my curiosity felt natural.

"I think so. It's hard to remember what I wanted. I was so lost and unable to believe it was happening at all that I wasn't thinking straight. Mostly I just didn't want it to stop, but I didn't like it when he pulled out. I know that. What about you? Did you think it at the time?"

"Yes," I said without pause. "Just for a second, and then I thought better of it. When he told me he was going to come, I almost did it. I almost told him to come inside you."

"I'm glad you didn't."

"Would you have stopped him?"

"No, but that's why. I couldn't have stopped it, and part of me wouldn't have wanted to, but when you told him what to do, I came even harder. You were keeping me safe, and I loved that. No matter what one part of my mind wanted, it was better that way. I knew you were there to protect me. At least a little."

We had never talked about that side of it before. It had been dumb, but for some reason not one of us, Brent included, had talked about the fact that it wasn't safe. Maybe we thought pulling out was fine, or maybe we just wanted it to be true.

"If I do fuck him again, we probably shouldn't do that," she said shyly. I wasn't sure if she was testing me again, but it didn't matter. She brushed my hair from my face and kissed me, but she was serious and I knew it. "It would be so hot, don't get me wrong, but maybe it's best if it's just a fantasy, okay? I like having fantasies we don't do. Even if we want to."

"So, you want him to come inside you, but you don't want him to?"

She nodded, and it made sense. I had enough fantasies like that to last a lifetime. Maddy was the first one that came to mind, and this was a close second. Or maybe a first. They were hot to think about, and I'd be lying if there wasn't a part of my that wanted it to happen. But the thinking part of my brain jumped in and let reason take over. Some thing are better left as fantasy. That's just the way it is.

Chapter Twenty-Three

A week later I invited Brent for a beer. I don't know what got into me, but something about the combination of sex I was having with Kelly again, and the honesty with which we were talking about it, made me think it might be time for me to tell him the truth. I was nervous, anxious, and completely unsure if it was a good idea, but once I had made up my mind, there was no way I could back out.

He came downtown, like he always did, and we met at a quiet bar close to Cooper Union. All I had told him was we should get a beer without the rest of the gang, and I had no idea what he thought that meant. Maybe it was about Kelly, maybe about Jane, hell, maybe he thought we just needed to catch up.

He did not expect it to be about Claire.

"I didn't tell you this so you would feel bad. In fact, maybe it's the opposite," I said.

He didn't take it well at all. He was angry, embarrassed and ashamed. He looked at me like he was going to cry, and it was not what I wanted.

"You really didn't tell her to do that?" he asked, obviously upset. "I mean, she was very clear that you had instructed her to do everything. She said you wanted to come home and find us in bed together because it would make you super turned-on, and you'd fuck her harder. Come on, you're messing with me."

"I'm not, but look, it doesn't matter. Claire liked to fuck with me. She pushed me to do things she thought I wanted. At least that's what she always said. I wasn't pissed at you. I knew just what had happened without her having to say a word, and I thought it was better to make a good situation out of a bad one. It was fun fucking her with you."

He was drinking a whisky rocks and biting his nails. Each time I said something new he raised an eyebrow and frowned at me as he shook his head.

"So, why are you telling me this?" he asked. "Oh fuck, please don't tell me that's what happened with Kelly."

"That's exactly not what happened with Kelly. Maybe that's why I'm saying it, hell, I don't know. I just needed to be honest about it because you're my friend and you can handle it. Also, we haven't talked about any of this. You've fucked two of my girlfriends now and we haven't said a word."

It was my turn to cross my arms, but I suddenly realized I had basically put him on the stand. Shit, none of this was what I meant. He was my friend, and I liked him fucking my girlfriends. Fuck.

"I don't know what there is to say. Honestly, it never would have occurred to me, because I would freak about if it was the other way around. I mean watching Kelly with Rachel was hot, but that's not the same thing. Everybody likes watching their girlfriend get it on with another girl and we weren't really dating.

I didn't ask any questions with Claire, because I knew it wasn't going to last. I mean, you told me you were going to break up with her, I just figured it didn't matter. Like you didn't care that much, and it was just some fun.

"But Kelly was different. When she and I were on the couch that first time, I almost stopped her. I didn't want it to be the same thing, but then you told her to. Right there in front of me. It wasn't her whispering in my ear while you were out of the room. Besides, Jason was fucking my girlfriend, and you were plowing yours. So I figured a little knob-job wouldn't hurt.

"But, then the next time…."

"That was a whole different thing," I said. Fuck, how do you talk about this? If it was some random girl, we would have high-fived and gone out drinking. We would have bragged about it to our friends, but because she was my girlfriend, it was a new thing. Guys weren't supposed to let their girls fuck other dudes. We weren't supposed to like it, and we definitely weren't supposed to stick our faces right there and watch.

"I don't know what to say," I began again. "You're my oldest friend, and I love you. The first time it was crazy, and I was a little jealous and turned-on, but then it was different. Spending that night with you two was sweet. We laughed and hung out like it was normal. It was normal, fuck, I don't know."

"I love hanging out with you two," Brent said. "I don't even feel like a third-wheel, and that's weird for me. That night was one of the best nights all summer, in spite of Rachel being a fucking bitch. It was just us, laughing and drinking and she was sitting there topless, and I didn't think a thing about it. It was just us. And it was good. But then the next morning…"

"We had talked about it before. I mean, Kelly and I talked about it. About her fucking you."

"Really? Like while you were in bed, or out for coffee?" He asked.

"A little bit of both. But, mostly in bed. Fuck, this is so weird." For some reason this was much harder than talking to Kelly about it, and I didn't know why. He was my friend, we should be able to talk about anything. "But the point is, we had already agreed that it was okay. That she should do it."

"Oh, so now I'm just a fucking piece of meat, huh? What the hell, man, you could have asked me, too, you know."

"She totally asked you. Your dick was between her legs and she said let's try it again. That's like asking." I was laughing, but mostly because it was so absurd. Of course we didn't ask him. Why would we ask him? It hadn't even occurred to us.

"Yeah, right. Like I could have said no then. Fuck, why do you have to date such hot girls, and why do you have to drag me into it? Seriously, man."

"Are you saying you didn't like fucking her?" He laughed, but still shook his head, and I wondered if there was something else. Something I was missing or something we were both missing. Also, he had a good point. Why did I bring him into it? Was it just that he had a big dick and I liked watching my girlfriends get fucked by someone bigger than me? I'm sure that made sense to someone, but not me. There had to be more to it. Something else was going on.

"I don't know," I said. "It feels easy with you. That morning was intense, but it wasn't hard. I mean we were, but you know what I mean. It was kinda sweet, dude. It was hot and messy, but it was still sweet. We weren't drunk at a party or baked out of our minds. We were all awake and knew just what we were doing."

"Do you want to hear something fucked up?" he asked. I nodded and he kept going. "At that party later? The one after Jupiter turned out to be so lame? I kinda freaked watching her with that dude. Like I have a right to be jealous, but it didn't matter. Watching you two was fine. She's your girlfriend, and that didn't bother me at all, but that fucking asshole with a mustache pissed me off. Crazy right?"

"I didn't like that dude either," I said laughing again. We ordered another round of drinks and, unsurprisingly, the whisky made the talking easier.

"There's something else we haven't talked about," he said, looking serious again.

"What's that?"

"I kissed you, dude! Like right after I fucked your girlfriend, we kissed, and you never fucking said a word about it."

"Are you hurt? You sound like you wanted me to ask you out or something."

"You never fucking talked about any of it again! What the hell was I supposed to do? I didn't know if things were good with you two, I sure as hell didn't know where we stand, and we fucking kissed! I don't kiss guys."

The other couple of patrons looked at us as he yelled, but he just gave them the finger without ever once looking up.

"It was a good kiss, my friend. For a dude kiss."

"Fuck you," he said.

"I'm being serious. I'm sorry we didn't talk, I just didn't know what to say. We totally used you. I mean, you got to fuck Kelly, but we never once asked you what you wanted. Hell, we didn't even send flowers."

"Maybe a card," he said. "Some chocolate would have been nice. At least a thank you would have been good. Fuckers."

"Next time I'll be sure to fix that."

"Next time?" he asked waving to the bartender. "Could we have two shots of Jameson?"

"I'm just saying," I said, trying to hide my blush.

"If there's a next time we're talking first. Like, for real. And you're not going to send me home at the end of the night either.

None of this, 'thanks for your dick, now go home.' I don't like it."

"You really are sensitive. I had no idea," I said.

"I love you guys. I already told you that."

"Yeah, we love you too, but…"

"No, I mean, I love you guys. Both of you. You're my oldest friend, but that morning was different. It was the best sex I've ever had. There, I said it. It was the best."

I stared at him as the bartender put the shots down, and I didn't know what to say. There's no way that could be true. He picked up hot girls all the time, and they loved it. Even he and Rachel probably had great sex. It was fun and sweet, and I'm sure it was hot, but the best? It was bullshit. We each took our shots, and I looked up at him one more time.

"You're serious. That was the best sex you've ever had?"

"Yeah, maybe I'm a freak. But having you there was nice. I mean, she's hot and wonderful, but it wasn't even all that much about me, and I knew it. It was you two and me, and it was all three of us. I was giving you both something that I think you wanted, and it felt important. I can't explain it."

"I think for me, too," I suddenly said. I tried to think back on the last year of my life, and I was amazed. I had some insane things happen, and some amazing sex. Hell, Claire and I had amazing sex before it got crazy. Maybe even after it got crazy, but Brent was right. That morning had been special. Watching Kelly get fucked turned me on, but it was more than that, too. He added something to our relationship that I didn't want to admit. It was bigger, and it was special.

"Whatever," he said, waving his hand at me as if he could brush me away.

"I mean it. I think about that morning all the time, and not just when I'm fucking my girlfriend. It was super hot, but it was sweet. Also, we came at the same time. When does that happen?

You and I totally came on her at exactly the same time. It was mindblowing."

"What do we do?" He was looking down into his beer, but it was a serious question. I wasn't used to serious Brent, but this was it. I had no idea how to answer him.

"Maybe get a drink sometime? Just the three of us? I don't know. I haven't talked to Kelly, other than the other night." I blushed as soon as I said it, and he didn't let it pass.

"What happened the other night? Come on, you can't mess with me."

"We just talked about doing it again. You know, with you."

"Are you serious? What did she say."

"She wants to. A lot."

"Fuck, now I'm getting turned on. I can't remember the last time the two us went out drinking and I got a raging hard-on. This is so gay."

I smiled at him, and he started laughing again with that deep rich sound I adored. Brent's laugh is infectious, and he can get a room going if he's not careful. We sat there for a while just chuckling, lost in our own thoughts.

"So, drinks?" I asked. "I'm not promising anything, but let's see what happens. We'll go to Docs or something, and if we feel like going back to my place, maybe we do. If it doesn't feel right, then no worries. We're still best friends."

"That sounds like a date. Well, other than being at Docs. Never go there on a date, dude."

It was my turn to shrug. It did sound kind of like a date, but after what had happened already it wasn't any crazier than anything else.

"We've already fucked, so we may as well try a date," I said.

Fifteen minutes later we hugged on the street as we said our goodbyes. I had no idea what I was going to say to Kelly, but I was strangely giddy as I walked home. It was good to be honest. It was good to talk. Most of all, I felt like not only did I have my best friend back, but something new was in the air. Something confusing. Something difficult. It might be fine. But it might not be. Fuck normal.

I smiled as I pulled a smoke from my pocket and lit it. The walk home was delicious and tasted only of opportunity.

Chapter Twenty-Four

When I walked into my room there were two girls sitting on my bed in their underwear. Kelly smiled at me with a wicked grin, and Maddy looked up with a wave. They were listening to Madonna, drinking red wine, and eating pretzels out of a bowl. I stood there, looking out into the living room, then back at them, but they didn't stop talking to each other.

"You don't have to know what your major is until at least next year. It took me forever to realize I wanted to study journalism. Seriously, I'm sure kids will be talking about it at the thing tomorrow, but there's no reason to feel bad for not knowing. In fact, I think it's better."

Maddy nodded as she listened, and I finally hung up my coat, poured myself a glass of wine, and sat down on the bed. I kicked off my shoes and leaned back against the wall.

"Offering college advice?" I asked.

"Your girlfriend is awesome. I can see why you didn't try harder to hook up with my sister."

"Maddy..." I started saying before I was cut off.

"I'm sure he tried plenty hard," Kelly added. "Although he might have been distracted by someone blonder."

"Okay, how long have you two been sitting here, and how

many bottles of wine have you had?" I had completely forgotten she was arriving tonight, but clearly Kelly had not. They looked like they had known each other for years, and I was so out of place I forgot it was my room.

"Two and two," Maddy said. Her bra and panties were matching pink and it was nearly too much for me. Even Kelly had put panties on, and they were sweet, innocent, and white; just like her.

"She means two hours and two bottles of wine. In case that wasn't clear."

"No, I got it," I said. The wine was delicious, and looking at the bottle I saw it was another Oregon vintage. "Did you bring this?"

Maddy nodded, and smiled at me with so many teeth I wanted to kiss her. "My parents say it's their favorite. At least for the fall. I usually drink beer, but you didn't have any."

"And how old is this young woman that you're sitting on my bed with, Kelly? Should she be drinking anything?"

"If you're going to be like that you can go sleep on the couch. Or with Martin. We are having a nice grown-up conversation as we sip this luscious Pinot Noir and eat artisanal pretzels."

"Those are Snyder," I said.

"Just like I said, dear. Now either put on something more comfortable and get drunk with us, or go bother someone else. We were perfectly happy having girl time before you arrived."

"How was your date with Brent?" Maddy asked me, and I nearly spit my wine out.

"Seriously, did you give her our whole life story since she arrived?"

"I learn quickly. Besides, it's only fair that I know who I'm staying with. Talia has only said sweet things, but my sister only ever says sweet things. It's annoying actually. I'm sure you're perfectly nice, but come on. She pats you on the head like a puppy.

She only does that to people who are interesting. People she's trying to fix."

I got up, and pulled my shirt off over my head. I was still giddy from my walk, and if there were two pretty girls on my bed, then who was I to complain? I stripped down to a pair of boxers that thankfully didn't have holes in them, and I sat down again, taking a handful of pretzels and stuffing them in my mouth.

"You should major in biology or something," I said. "And thank you, my date was fine. He's a good boy."

"That's much better," Kelly said, reaching out and squeezing my hand. "Aren't you more comfortable?"

We sat there for hours talking, laughing, and drinking the last bottle of wine Maddy brought. Apparently her folks thought that three bottles of expensive wine was the minimum you could offer someone putting up your daughter for a long weekend. It seemed reasonable, although it was probably best they didn't realize how happy I would have been just to have the girl in the same state with me. She hadn't changed since I saw her last, although the bra and panties were definitely cuter than the hotel towel.

We told her about our college experiences, although I'm sure both of us were heavy censors when it came to certain memories. Maddy had been forced to start late due to a fight with her parents about west coast schools, but she was overwhelmingly excited to be coming to New York. Kelly had already offered to show her the coolest bars and restaurants, and she peppered us with questions until it was nearly two in the morning.

"Is it sleep time?" Kelly asked when she saw me yawn for the third time. I nodded and all three of us plodded to the bathroom to brush our teeth and wash our faces. It was crowded and ridiculous, but neither of them would leave the other alone, and so I was stuck with it. We walked back to bed, I lit a candle, and Kelly turned out the lights.

"I can go sleep on the couch," I said. "Why don't you two take the bed?"

"Don't be stupid," Kelly said. "We can fit. Maddy and I are little." If the blonde girl noticed the look in Kelly's eye she ignored it, but I felt my heart beat faster, and I had to turn to make sure my boxers didn't suddenly become jumpy.

"Maddy, do you want the inside or the outside?" Kelly asked her like it was the most normal thing in the world, and I was too tired and tipsy to say a thing.

"Can I sleep in the middle? I get cold at night, and I don't want to fall off."

"Of course, dear," Kelly said, winking at me, and I had to stop myself from groaning out loud. She was trying to kill me and there was nothing I could do about it. I pulled back the comforter and sheets, and Kelly climbed in first, followed by Maddy, and then me. I turned away from them and faced the room, trying not to touch the eighteen-year-old girl next to me. Her skin was warm though, and each time she shifted I got a thigh or a foot against by body. She bumped me with a shoulder, and I could feel her ass against me as I struggled to get comfortable.

"Goodnight, Kelly," she whispered.

"Goodnight, dear," Kelly said and I heard a quick kiss followed by a giggle. I closed my eyes and pretended everything was fine. Everything was perfectly okay.

I lay there for hours, unable to sleep, even when the two girls in my bed were breathing deeply and lost to the world of the waking. Eventually I rolled over and tried to fit into the space left for me without getting too close, but Maddy pushed back against me as soon as I let her, and my arm fell around her body. I held my breath as I lay there, but I didn't sleep a wink for what felt like an eternity.

It must have been six in the morning when I awoke to a

subtle movement. I was more surprised that I had fallen asleep than anything, but when I opened my eyes Maddy's face was only inches from my own. She had one of Kelly's arms wrapped around her body, and somewhere in the night she had lost her bra. I could barely see her beneath the blankets, but her shoulders were bare, and Kelly's hand was clearly cupping one of her breasts.

I was wide awake once again, and my first thought was Talia was going to kill me. My second thought was, oh my god, I can see her tits. I'm not proud of either, but there you have it. My brilliant mind at work. Maddy made soft moans in her sleep, but I had no idea if Kelly was awake or not. I moved the blanket down, pulling my arm out from beneath it, until I could see more. Quietly, I pushed it down even further, and sure enough Maddy was sleeping next to me with Kelly's arm just barely covering her. Her breasts were larger than Kelly's, and I stared at them like an idiot for far too long.

When I finally looked up, Maddy's eyes were open and she was staring right at me. As much as I tried, I couldn't look away, and she was instantly aware at what I was looking. Our faces were nearly touching, and she reached up with one hand and pushed my hair behind my ear, leaving Kelly's arm draped across her body. She winked at me and then slowly rolled over onto her back, and then over again to face Kelly. A second later she pushed against me, and I struggled to keep my hardon from pressing into her ass. She was having none of it though, and soon I was positioned exactly as Kelly had been a moment before, my arms across Mady's bare breasts. This was getting ridiculous.

Kelly opened her eyes a moment later and the two girls stared at each other for a long time before anyone said a word.

"I think we're awake," Kelly said. "And someone lost a bra."

"It got itchy. I hate sleeping in my bra."

"Me, too," Kelly said, undoing hers and tossing it onto the

floor behind me.

"Are you two ready to get up?" I asked. "It's only six or so. We haven't been sleeping all that long."

Maddy rolled over again and looked back and forth between us. The blanket was now around her waist and her breasts fell easily to the sides of her chest, rising and falling with each breath. She reached out a hand and touched Kelly's cheek softly before doing the same thing to me.

"If you two don't do something with me soon I'm going to go crazy." It was barely a whisper, but it was clearly an invitation. She closed her eyes, leaned her head back, and I suddenly realized I had a fetish for perfect necks. It sloped up to her chin, down to her breasts, and out onto two strong shoulders. I wanted to kiss it and press my lips against her until spring came around again.

Kelly on the other hand didn't wait more than a few seconds. She nodded to me as she leaned in, and a second later her mouth opened around Maddy's left nipple. Her tongue was light as she circled it, but it wasn't until she reached over to me and pulled me closer that I let myself go. I opened my lips on her right nipple, and she arched her back even more and let out the most beautiful sigh in the world. I rolled closer to her, leaning up so I could get a better angle, and suddenly our fingers were in her hair as we sucked her nipples until they were almost painfully hard. They stood up straight, monuments to her arousal, and still we didn't stop.

Maddy began pushing the blanket down further, kicking it with her feet until her entire body was exposed, and there were six bare legs entwined. He skin was impossibly soft and my hand instantly found her stomach, her hips, and her thigh. She opened her legs wider, encouraging our exploration, and her moans of pleasure grew louder with each second. I kissed up to her neck, tasting her everywhere, before finally turning her to me and kissing her mouth for the first time. Her lips were full and warm and she kissed me back like I was a rich red wine.

She suddenly let out a squeal, and I looked down to see Kelly's hand had found it's way inside her pink panties. From what I could tell at least two fingers were deep inside her. Without pause, Maddy reached down and slid them off, opening her legs again to give Kelly better access.

"Take these off," she whispered to me, her fingers against my boxers. I didn't wait, and soon my cock was hard against her thigh, as she rubbed against me while we kissed once more. I moved to her neck when Kelly took over the kiss, and I stared at their lips and tongues as they explored one another. When I felt a hand on my cock I was only half surprised to discover it was Kelly's.

"I want you to feel something," Kelly whispered into Maddy's ear.

I watched in awe, as Kelly let go of me and reached up to to take Maddy's hand. They both leaned up and watched as Kelly placed her hand on me, before gently squeezing the blonde girl's fingers around my cock. She held me gently, as she rubbed me up and down, and this time the biggest sigh came from Kelly's mouth.

"Do you like that?" she asked her.

"Yes," came Maddy's reply. "What can I do with it?"

My eyes nearly rolled back in my head as they leaned over me, both of their hands touching me and caressing me.

"What do you want to do with it?"

They kissed again before Maddy had a chance to answer, and it was only then that I got a glimpse of her fully nude body. Her pussy was trimmed neatly and covered in light brown hair, and her lips were red and swollen. I groaned as I reached out and opened her, feeling her instantly spread her legs beneath my hand even as her own stayed on my cock.

"I want to suck it," she said, moaning into Kelly's mouth. "I want to suck his cock."

"Is that all you want, pretty girl? You just want him in your mouth?"

Maddy opened her eyes wider as I pushed my fingers inside her, marveling at how how soft her skin was. She rolled back to me, her hand now sliding quickly up and down the length of my cock, and I could feel Kelly's fingers push into her from behind. I brought my fingers up to my mouth and sucked them clean, closing my eyes as I tasted her for the first time.

"What else do you want?" Kelly sounded almost like she was going to come just from asking the question, and I wondered how far she would let it go. Maddy looked me right in the eyes, holding my gaze as she slowed down what she was doing with my cock. She pulled me closer, her grip tightening as she kissed me.

"I want to fuck him," she said, still looking at me. She was talking to Kelly, but I watched her lips form the words. "I want it inside me. Can I, Kelly? Can I have this?"

She pulled me to her, and rubbed the head of my cock into her her pubic hair, just above her swollen lips. I pulled her closer, my hand on her ass without even thinking, and suddenly Kelly was climbing over us and onto the floor. She fumbled with the drawer until she found a condom, then crawled back up onto the bed.

"Start here," Kelly whispered as she dragged Maddy down lower. She held the younger girl's hand once more before gently pushing her mouth towards me. Maddy looked me right in the eye before opening her lips and wrapping them around the head of my cock, closing along the ridge as I struggled not to scream. She sucked more of me into her mouth, her hand now tighter as she explored, alternating between licking my entire length and seeing how much she could take into her mouth. Kelly leaned in for a moment, and I watched as Maddy held me while my sweet girlfriend took me all the way into her throat, too, her eyes never leaving our new friend.

She coughed when she released me, then pushed Maddy back onto me as she moved down her body, kissing every inch of skin. I closed my eyes as I felt her begin to truly suck me, but a sudden gasp brought me back to see Kelly's tongue pushing into the folds of Maddy's cunt. She was on her side, still sucking me, but it was hard for her to focus as Kelly worked her fingers inside her, both of them moaning and groaning all three of our names.

"Fuck, you two are going to kill me. Don't stop, Maddy," I growled.

"He's wanted this for a long time," Kelly said, pausing for just a moment, and it only made Maddy suck harder. "He told me he wanted to fuck you the last time you were in New York, and I made him come as he told me."

"You two are so insane," Maddy said as my girlfriend reached up and handed her something. She looked up at me, her mouth still inches from my throbbing cock before she tore open the condom wrapped, pulled it out, and rolled it down over me.

"Now?" she asked, looking back at Kelly, who was still eat her pussy. "Can I fuck him now?"

Kelly climbed up next to me, only stopping to whisper in the other girl's ear, and then all of us watched Maddy sit up on the bed, kneeling over me with my cock in her hand. I was trembling and shaking as she moved closer, and even Kelly moaned as she watched. She reached out and replaced Maddy's hand on me, helping her as she pushed down around me.

"Oh god, Maddy," I moaned, my hands instantly going to her hips. She moved painfully slowly as I watched myself disappear inside her body, her cunt opening around me as she took me in. "Oh fuck, that feels good."

She leaned down and kissed me when I was fully inside her, and Kelly's hand stayed where it was, rubbing her clit as we slowly moved. Her eyes were big and green, and both of us just stared at each other in awe as we felt our joining. Each time she kissed me I pulled her to me, and it was almost too much.

"Fuck me," she said, wrapping her arms around me, and without another word I rolled her to her back, my cock never leaving her, and then raised myself up on my elbows. Her chest was heaving, her large breasts covered in sweat, and Kelly kissed her one more time.

"Fuck her," Kelly said. "Fuck this gorgeous little woman, and don't stop until you've come so hard you can't walk."

I didn't need any more encouragement than that. I began to move, faster and faster, pushing deeper inside her each time. I could feel her clenching around me as her moans grew louder, and I was in heaven. After too many nights of fantasizing about it, it was actually happening. I was fucking Talia's little sister and it was goddamn perfect. Kelly's hand was still between our bodies, touching us both as we fucked, and there was no way I was going to last.

"Oh, fuck," I said, leaning back and watching my cock move within her. "I'm going to come, Maddy. I'm going to come in your perfect little pussy."

And then suddenly Kelly leaned in and pressed her mouth to Maddy's clit, just as I pushed into her as far as I could go. The blonde girl screamed as she gripped my hands, and both of us began to shake.

"Oh god, don't stop. Either of you, don't stop. Please, just keep fucking me," Maddy screamed. Her head rolled back, her eyes opened wide, and her fingers dug into my palm as I pulled her down to me. Kelly kept on licking and sucking, her mouth and fingers on both of us as I finally felt myself explode inside the condom. Maddy kept on screaming and clenching, and I felt myself come again and again, my vision nearly going as I finally fell down against her panting chest.

Kelly kissed me instantly, once again letting me taste Maddy's amazing pussy. I tried to breathe, and Maddy kept saying "oh god" over and and over again. When I finally pulled out, my fingers around the base of the condom, holding it tightly, she whimpered in protest and then kissed me again.

I threw the condom into the garbage next to the bed, and pushed Maddy between us. Both Kelly and I rested our hands on her stomach as we kissed her, taking turns with her lips, neck, and tits. We didn't talk for a long time, and even when we did it was more moans of amazement than anything else.

"That was so perfect," Maddy finally said, pulling our fingers to her mouth and kissing them. "I've never come with someone inside me. Of course, I've never had someone suck my clit at the same time. Holy shit."

"How many guys have you been with?" Kelly asked.

"Counting Thomas? Two." She blushed bright red when she said it and looked down.

Both of us sat up on our elbows and looked down at her skeptically. "There's no way," I said.

"I've done other things. Lots of other things, but not like that. I mean, not with a cock in me. It just never really felt right."

"When was the other one?" Kelly asked, her head moving down to rest against Maddy's breasts."

"Last week," she whispered. "I wanted to get it out of the way before I came to New York."

"You're serious," I said. "You had sex for the first time last week, and now a threesome? Are you okay?"

"Why do you think I did it? I wanted to know something before I saw you, and my boyfriend had been pestering me all summer."

"Wait, you have a boyfriend?" Kelly asked.

Maddy nodded shyly, but there was nothing to say. Everything she had said already was too much for me to handle, but I found that I no longer cared. I had just fucked Talia's baby sister, the one thing I promised myself I wouldn't do. It was just six weeks ago that I was patting myself on the back for not doing just that. I looked back at the gorgeous naked women next to me and realized that maybe I needed to get my priorities straight. Or, to be clearer, it's possible I just had.

Chapter Twenty-Five

For the first time since I started working at Saints, Jane came in. Maddy had made her way over to NYU sometime after breakfast, and Kelly and I took a long nap before both of us had to go to work. She had picked up some freelance writing gigs, and was spending more and more time emailing than she was at the karaoke bar. I was washing glasses, cleaning the taps, and doing general house cleaning when Jane walked in, and I nearly dropped the pint I had just poured for the lone patron.

"Hello, handsome," she said, sitting down near the front window. I leaned over the bar and gave her a hug and a kiss.

"How are you doing?" The truth was she didn't look good. Her eyes were red, her face was pale, and she had lost weight in the last month. The treatments sounded like they were working, but it was slow going and taking a toll on her body. She smiled and shrugged, only sort of answering the question. There really wasn't much to say.

"You drinking, or just stopping by to say hello?"

"I'll have a beer, just pick one for me. I don't care what it is. I have to be at the coffee shop in an hour, but I figured I'd come say hi to you first. If you don't mind."

I walked over to the taps and poured her an amber ale from

Pennsylvania, then placed it on the bar in front of her. She eyed it cautiously, but took a long drink without making any expression at all.

"You know what doesn't feel sexy?" she asked. I shook my head, realizing there were probably a million things on that list for Jane right now.

"Cancer," she said. "Seriously, Sean has been amazing, but after going to the doctor three times a week with me, listening to me cry constantly, and still trying to plan a wedding, he's somehow not inspired to throw me down on the bed and fuck my brains out. It's like he's afraid I'll break or something."

"If you're just looking to get laid, you totally came to the right place. I can close up for a few, take you into the back…"

She laughed, and it was a good sound. It was a warm sound, and I felt relief flood my body. If she lost her sense of humor, I didn't know what I would do.

"I think even you would be hard pressed to find me attractive right now," she said.

"I'd fuck you in a heartbeat. Hell, I don't even need to close down. Just lean over the bar. Seriously, you look tired, but I don't care. You are still so fucking hot that I can barely stand it. I'd do you any day."

"It makes me feel a little better, I guess. I mean, if you stopped wanting me, I would probably give up all hope. I mean it. I haven't smiled this much all week."

She took a sip of her beer and looked out the window for a while. It was a cool fall day and people were finally wearing coats again. Sweaters, boots, and long pants were everywhere, and even a few of the leaves were turning.

"Are you guys really having a New Year's Party? Because if so, then I want in."

"I thought you'd still be on your honeymoon, but definitely,"

I said. "It's going to be epic, as Brent would say. When are you coming back?"

"If I'm not dead by then we're going to Aruba on the 26th and flying back to New York on the 31st. I want to come. No matter what happens, I want to spend Y2K with you guys. Sean promised me we could and it's important."

"Jane, you're not going to be dead. Even if you are, we'll stand you up in the corner and kiss you at midnight. But seriously, that would be amazing. I can't think of anything better than having the people I love the most there. Your wedding is going to be great, and then we can all recover in time to make a mess again New Year's Eve. And think on the bright side: maybe the world will end."

"That is cheerful. At least I wouldn't have to get prodded again, and getting laid would be the least of my worries."

I reached over the bar and hugged her, and she instantly began to cry into my shoulder. I held her there for a long time, awkward be damned, and she sobbed and sobbed as I kissed her head and brushed her hair with my fingers. When she finally sat back down she was smiling and she took a very long sip of her beer, polishing the last of it off.

"I feel so much better," she said, wiping her tears. "I suddenly realized this week that while I love Sean completely, I didn't want to end the year with a honeymoon. It's the start to our life together, but I want that to include you, too. All of you, but especially you."

"I'm glad, too," I said. "It wouldn't be same if you guys weren't there. I mean, who would I try to hit on when I drink too much champagne?"

"Right, I'm sure you'd have a tough time with that. But seriously, thank you. It makes it easier to get through everything. Even the wedding planning feels easier knowing I have another party to go to that doesn't require a fucking thing from me."

We hugged once more and she finally packed up her coat and purse. Just as she turned to go, I looked down at her ass once more, her tight jeans hiding almost nothing.

"Damn, Jane. I still want that ass," I said.

"I love you," she said, and then she ran out, wiping her eyes once more.

I spent the night talking beer with my regulars and the few beer tourists who came in, and I actually had a pretty good crowd. Images of Kelly and Maddy danced in my head, and I couldn't believe I still had two more nights with her in my apartment. It was unlikely I would survive, but I would die with a smile on my face.

It was only around one a.m. that I realized I hadn't even mentioned my talk with Brent. I had promised him a real date, although I didn't know what Kelly would think of that. When I thought about inviting him over while Maddy was still there I laughed, unsure if it was a brilliant idea or a terrible one. I had no idea how I felt about him and Kelly, other than the quick flashes of excitement and fear that showed up each time I pictured the three of us together again. On occasion, I had to hide my growing erection as I wondered what it would be like to do it once more, and by the time I left at two a.m. I was as excited and confused as ever.

The girls were sound asleep when I crawled into bed. They were also both naked, so I slid my boxers off and climbed in behind Kelly. I wrapped my arms around her and kissed her neck, listening to her sigh as she welcomed me home. She was warm, and the room smelled like they might have been having some fun without me. I wasn't sure if I was upset, but I didn't have long to think about it.

"You two are so pretty," Maddy whispered. "I like seeing you like that. It's so cute."

Kelly wiggled against me, and I put my hand on her hip, nestling my cock into the crack of her ass. She giggled as I got hard, and Maddy leaned up on her elbow and simply watched us. When Kelly moaned, I lifted her leg and slide my cock in between her thighs.

"God, I love seeing this," Maddy said. Her hand moved slowly between her legs, but she didn't reach out to either of us. "Can I watch?"

"Maddy," I said. "One of the nice things about this is that you can probably have whatever you want. All you have to do is ask. It was an amazing realization,when I learned that I could talk to Kelly, and if I actually asked for what I wanted, I usually got it. It's a revelation, I tell you." It was the truth, and I wish someone had told me when I was her age, because it would have saved me a lot of trouble.

"The most I usually get is 'hey, suck my dick' or maybe 'I wanna eat that pussy', but I'm not sure that counts. Guys don't want to talk in bed." Maddy was still touching herself, and I was rubbing my cock between the lips of Kelly's pussy without an ounce of hurry.

"Just ask for it," Kelly said. "I bet we'll say yes."

"Can I watch you fuck?" she whispered. "I've never really seen anyone up close before."

Kelly nodded as she opened her legs, and a second later I was inside her. We moved slowly, hardly making a sound as Maddy touched herself. It was strangely sweet and powerful, and I wasn't sure if I was more turned on by watching or by being watched. Whatever it was, I was happy. Tired, but happy. For a long time the three of us merely moaned and grinned, but Maddy's eyes were in fact glued to our bodies. She leaned in closely and stared at my cock sliding in and out of Kelly, and it was almost enough to push me over the edge.

"Do you want him again?" Kelly finally asked, reaching out and touching Maddy's cheek. Her hand had been moving faster and we could see her fingers pushing deeply into her cunt.

"You don't mind?" she asked. Kelly shook her head as she reached between my legs and pulled my cock out from within her.

"I like watching," she said. "I didn't know that I would, but god do I love watching him fuck you. I can come just thinking about it. I have come just thinking about it, and now I want to come watching it."

She pulled a condom out from under the pillow and without a sound she rolled it down over me. I sat up on the bed, unsure of where I was supposed to go, but Kelly spread her legs and pulled Maddy's head between them. I knelt behind Maddy, watching her open her mouth on my girlfriend, and then I was inside her again, and I was a happy boy. Her ass was up in the air as she knelt between Kelly's leg, and she felt amazing as I slid into her.

We moved slowly this time, all of the urgency from the morning gone, and it was dreamlike. I slid in and out of Maddy's pussy as she gently fingered and licked Kelly's. I stared at the dimples on the small of her back, and I had to resist everything that had to do with her ass. I watched our bodies move in slow motion, and everything about it was perfect.

Our moans were soft and sweet, and when I finally felt myself starting to come it nearly took me by surprise. She felt perfect around me, but as I moved faster and faster, it was suddenly a whole new thing.

"Oh god, you feel good," she moaned, looking back at me.

"You feel so delicious," I said, thrusting faster and harder than I had all night. "Oh god, Maddy, it's amazing. Your cunt is so good, I'm going to come."

"Do it," she moaned, her fingers still pushing in and out of Kelly. "Come in me," she moaned.

I thrust inside her as deeply as I could, and it was like nothing I had ever felt before. It was her whole body around me, and I couldn't hold back. I kissed her skin as I began to explode, and her moans grew louder with each spurt. Without a word, Kelly moved down her body as I came, until her mouth was right below us. When I pulled out, she sucked Maddy's swollen cunt like she was starving.

"Oh fuck," I said, suddenly looking down. Maddy was panting and moaning as Kelly's tongue pushed inside her, but I was staring at my cock in horror.

"Don't stop, I'm going to come again!" Maddy screamed as I watched Kelly lick her and suck her with more and more force.

"Kelly," I said, "Kelly, fuck, fuck, fuck."

She suddenly looked up, her head dropping to the bed between Maddy's knees.

"She tastes like you," she whispered as I stared at the broken condom. The ring was still around the base of my cock, but the top half was completely destroyed. My come was covering Kelly's lips, and I could still see some of it inside Maddy.

"What happened, why did you stop? Fuck, that felt so good. It was like you were…"

"The condom broke," Kelly said. She helped Maddy up gently, and both of them turned around until they were sitting next to each other. They looked at me, my cock now limp, and the latex sad and broken around it.

"I thought it felt too good," I said. "It felt too fucking good, I just thought it was you."

"Did you come in me? Oh my god, did you seriously come in me? What the fuck are we going to do? Oh Jesus, what are we going to do?"

Kelly wrapped her arms around the other girl, pulling her close, and telling her it was going to be fine.

"It's okay," she said. "It happens all the time. I promise. Are you on the pill?"

Maddy nodded, but still stared down between her legs and at me, as I unravelled the broken condom and took it off. I dropped it into the garbage, and I shook my head as I stared at them. It had felt too good, I knew it felt too good. Fuck, this was not supposed to happen. This is exactly why normal is better than fucking crazy. What the hell had we been thinking?

The two girls just hugged and rocked on the bed as Kelly tried to comfort her.

"We both got tested in June," she said. "It's all going to be fine. You're not pregnant and you won't catch anything. Just breathe and relax. It's going to be okay."

"Yeah, it'll be fine," Maddy said, repeating the words without seeming to believe them at all.

"Do you want me to go?" I asked, unsure if they were angry with me, and just as unsure about what I was feeling.

"No, just hold me, too. Hold me, but let's not do that again."

"Come with me first," Kelly said walking her out to the bathroom. I heard the water running and a few giggles that almost sounded like relief. I closed my eyes and tried to think of the worst possible scenario. It will be fine though, I said. Everything had to be fine.

They climbed back into bed a few moments later, and we pulled the blankets up around our bodies. I kissed Maddy again, telling her it would be okay, and she smiled and nodded her head. She held my hand tighter than she had that morning, but after an hour she finally began to breathe normally once again.

"Thank you," she finally said, kissing me lightly before closing her eyes. "For everything."

****

Maddy spent the next day back at NYU while Kelly and I ran

errands, did laundry, and generally tried to keep ourselves from worrying about the night before. We had slept in fits, but at some point in the night I found Maddy wrapped up in my arms. I felt my stomach clench even as my cock grew hard, but I pushed it away instantly. It was all I could manage not to leave them and go sleep on the couch. Even her smell reminded me of just how stupid I could be.

That night we talked and drank beer, but we did not undress or make out on the bed. It was tense and awkward, and by the time we fell asleep again I was mostly glad it was over. It wasn't until after we put Maddy in a cab at 5 a.m. the next morning that I felt some of the tension begin to leave me. Something had to change or I was going to lose it.

"What the fuck were we thinking?" I asked, as we walked back up the stairs to the apartment. We had called Talia the night before to let her know all was good, but I was sure she heard something in my voice no matter how hard I tried to hide it. Someone was going to find out.

"She'll be fine," Kelly said, yawning. "It really does happen, and while it's nice if you stop when you realize the condom is broken, I'm not all that worried."

"I didn't fucking do that on purpose," I said, the hair on the back of my neck suddenly rising. "Shit, what the hell is wrong with us? We were doing just fine until we decided it was somehow okay to fuck my friend's little sister."

"I was kidding," she said, climbing back into bed. "But don't get so weird about it. It happened, and now it's done. There's nothing to do about it. It's not like we planned it."

"Really?" I said angrily. "I definitely thought about it, and so did you. Hell, we fucked while talking about it. And when I got home from hanging with Brent and you two were in your underwear. You totally knew something was going to happen. Like hell we didn't plan that."

"Do you really think I had the nerve to plan anything? She was fun and easy to talk to, but all I did was get her tipsy and listen to Madonna. I was as surprised as you were. Okay, maybe a little less, but that's only because I can read women better than you. She was on a mission, that one. Didn't you hear her? She only fucked her boyfriend back home so she wouldn't be a virgin when she saw you again. I don't know what you did when she was here last time, but that girl wanted you, so don't fucking blame me. You've been begging for that for months."

"It was just a fucking fantasy, Kelly! We talk about a lot of shit, but it doesn't mean we have to do it. Fuck, I hope she's not pregnant." I put my hands to my head and tried to clear my mind. The whole weekend had been a bad idea. Hell, even saying yes to letting Maddy stay was probably a bad idea. What the fuck were we thinking?

"Do you think she'll say anything?" I finally asked.

"To Talia? Hell no. Did you hear how she talked about her? She's scared of her no matter how much she likes to tease. I think she'll be happy with it being her little secret."

It was a comforting thought, but I wasn't sure I believed it. I absolutely didn't want to think about Talia calling me up and screaming at me over the phone. In fact, thinking about anything else would be better. I pictured her yelling at me, as I tried to explain myself, but the truth is there wasn't any excuse. Kelly and I were sick and twisted, and we couldn't help ourselves. Maddy had crawled into bed and every ounce of restraint we had – which wasn't much to begin with – vanished in a second.

"You know, this is exactly what I said would happen," I said. "Everything was fine during August, and then you had to try to push me again. From Brent to Maddy you had to keep fucking pushing."

"Are you serious? You were fucking miserable! We've had better sex in the last few weeks than we had for a month. Just because one thing went wrong doesn't mean we're not doing the right thing. I'm not going back to that. I'm not going back to us pretending everything is fine when it's not."

"One little thing? I fucked Talia's little sister and the goddamn condom broke! That isn't one little thing. That's a huge fucking thing, and it wouldn't have happened if you hadn't gotten her drunk and naked on my bed. Hell, you were the one who brought it up the first time! You were the one who made me call you Maddy before I even saw the girl."

"And you were so damn hesitant," she screamed. "I seem to recall you fucked me so hard I almost couldn't walk. 'I love you, Maddy,' you whispered. 'I love you more than Kelly. You're so much prettier, and so much tighter.' What the fuck was I supposed to do with that?

"You're such a fucking asshole, you know that? Don't try to blame me after that. You wanted to fuck her, and if I had to play games with you in order to make it feel like my heart wasn't going to collapse, it's not my fault."

Kelly got up and began pacing in the room. She lit a cigarette, and didn't once look at me. She was angry, I was miserable, and nothing was fine at all. Maybe we were both fucked up, but I certainly wasn't going to take all the blame either.

"You were fine," I growled. "You wanted me to fuck her, don't give me that broken heart bullshit."

"Are you serious? Would you even know if I was fine? You know what would have been nice, Thomas? How about if I asked you if your friend's little sister was hot and you just said no. Or you told me she was too young and not your type. How about anything other than 'yes, baby, I want her so badly?'"

"Kelly, I didn't…"

She crumpled down onto the floor next to the bed with her hands in her face, and her tears burst from her eyes as she shook. I didn't know what to do, but sitting there watching wasn't going to cut it. I slipped down next to her and wrapped my arms around her.

"I really didn't know. I thought it turned you on. You've always liked watching me or hearing stories about me fucking other people. I just assumed it was your thing. Did it really make you jealous?"

"Of course, you dick. She's four years younger than me. She's tall, pretty, smart, and she has huge tits. I look like a little girl next to her and any day now I'm pretty sure you're going to want to date a grown-up."

I pulled her closer and kissed her hair. The thought of Kelly being jealous had never once occurred to me. From our very first meeting, it seemed like there was nothing I could do that wouldn't just turn her on.

"You know what's funny?" I asked, not waiting for her to answer. "I do like Maddy and she is pretty, but it was never like that. I mean, I honestly didn't think about her much until you brought it up. And then, I thought it turned you on. What's that you always say to me? I did it for you. You got so turned on when I said those thing, so I didn't stop. I hardly noticed if I wanted her. All I knew was that every word that came out of my mouth made you shake and come even harder."

She leaned in closer to me and I held her hand tightly. Her crying quieted down after a while, but we didn't talk for a long time. Both of us were lost in our heads, hoping to find some calm in the storm.

"Let's just go back to sleep," she said. "It's not even six in the morning and I don't have the energy to cry any more. Promise me you'll be here when I wake up?"

I climbed into bed next to her and wrapped her in my arms.

"I promise," I whispered.

It took us a long time to finally fall back asleep, and I had nightmares that all revolved around the same thing. Either someone in Maddy's family was calling me or Maddy was. I woke up in a sweat on occasion, and my body was tired and sore. When we did eventually crawl out of bed again it was just to shower and get ready for work. I was done talking, and I was done working through anything at all. We should have stayed normal and none of this would have happened.

Chapter Twenty-Six

We finally arranged a date with Brent, but over the next few days Kelly and I drifted even further apart than we had in August. Maddy felt like a breaking point, and for me it was a simple reminder of why we had slowed down in the first place. When we let ourselves go, stupid shit happened, and it was too much for me to handle. We were tired much of the time as the days grew shorter, and even when we tried to get in the mood we found nothing worked. I spanked her one morning, and I could see irritation flash across her face instead of excitement. She asked if Daddy needed help in the shower one night, and I actually told her I just wanted to go to bed.

It was as if all our fucking, fantasizing, and real life had simply pushed us beyond reason, and the simple things that used to turn us on where gone. We avoided talking about it, and when we did try to have sex we were out of sync; I lost my erection or she told me to stop right in the middle of something. We snapped at each other, grated on each other, and as our date with Brent grew closer, we spent our first few nights apart in ages. She simply didn't come home after work, and I didn't bother to call. I half-heartedly wondered if she was cheating on me, but even that didn't elicit much emotion. I threw myself into everything else for ten days, but then suddenly it was upon us.

We were supposed to meet up with him, have a nice dinner, and then bring him home. For the first few days it was clear what we intended, but as the week went on we kept putting off any real decisions at all, promising we'd leave it up to chance. We'd play it by ear and if sex happened, it did. Every time I thought about us fucking though, I pictured us getting carried away once more, and I didn't think I could do that. I couldn't go back.

Kelly met me at my place the night of our date. She didn't say anything about our missing nights, and I didn't ask. Along with not fucking, we also weren't doing a lot of talking.

"You ready?" she asked, leaning against the wall in my room.

"Should we just cancel? Come on, it's not like we're in the mood for a hot date. It's not even fair to Brent."

"No, I want to do it. Besides, even if it doesn't work with us, maybe he'll take me home. At least I know he wants me."

"Kelly, what the fuck is going on? Why are we like this?" I looked up at her, but I didn't know what else to say. Maybe we were done. Maybe all of the bullshit in the last few weeks meant it was over. She slid down to the floor and looked at me, just shaking her head. I couldn't tell if she was going to yell at me or start to cry. None of it made any sense, and for the first time in four months I felt almost completely alone.

"Maybe we broke ourselves," she said. "Seriously, maybe we did too much fucked up shit, and now it's over. We've done it all and that's all that it was. Is it possible our only connection was through fucked up sex? After banging Maddy there was simply nothing left to do."

"Are you trying to break up with me?" I slid down next to her and lit a cigarette. I hadn't had one in days, and I didn't care that we were still in my room. "Seriously, we were good. Even with all the crazy shit, hell, especially with the crazy shit. If we didn't lose it after any of that, why are we losing it now? It's like we're not in the same place. We're out of sync and there's no way to get back. All I want is for us to be fucking normal again."

She stole a drag from me and blew the smoke into the room, watching it swirl around in the light. When she handed it back, she took my hand in hers and held it for a long time.

"I don't like us normal, Thomas. It's not us. You may think it is, but it's not. We do fucked up shit, but we talk about it, and we do it well. It's not like we're out every day being assholes. It's not like we hurt anyone or screw anyone over. We're good people, and we don't need to fuck less for it to stay that way.

"I miss you. I didn't like these nights apart, but I just can't handle not knowing any more. I don't know what's was wrong or how to fix it, but I can't crawl into bed with you and wonder if you still want me. I'm not going to second guess you over everything, because it's driving me crazy. I haven't slept well, but it's been better than not knowing. It's been better than thinking you just don't want me anymore."

"I haven't slept either. I mean, I thought maybe you were with someone else."

She just shook her head before quietly resting it on my shoulder.

"He's going to hate us," she whispered. "He's expecting us to be all shiny, happy people and shit, but instead we're broken. It's cold out, we're grumpy, and I haven't even shaved my pussy in days."

I started to laugh, because it was absurd. If her biggest worry was that Brent would be offended by a little stubble, maybe we were okay. She looked at me, and started laughing as well. After everything we had been through, there had to be some way to salvage our relationship.

"I think if he gets that far, he'll forgive you for not shaving. I'm the one who likes to pretend you're a little girl, remember?"

"Almost. Do you still like that? I can't remember the last time I called you Daddy and it felt like it was true. Maybe right before Maddy came? But even then it was mostly us. It was Kelly and Thomas and that was fine, but Daddy is nice too."

"I don't know what happened," I said once again. "I think it got too real. It's all been so fucking intense all the time. We slowed down over the summer, but then suddenly Maddy was here and it was all about Daddy and Brent, and fucking Talia's sister. It's like we slipped right back without trying, and it was almost too much."

"Do you think we really are terrible? I mean, did we corrupt that girl? She's only four years younger than me, but did we still do something dumb?"

"I don't think we're terrible. I couldn't love a terrible person this much."

"You still love me?" she asked, looking up at me. I leaned in and kissed her, this time lingering long enough to taste her lips.

"Always," I said. "I just don't know what to do with it. If we let it all out, we go too far, but when we bottle it up, we go nowhere. I go back and forth between thinking we're saints and assholes, but I can't ever find the center." I finally crushed out my cigarette and took a deep breath. We had to fix it. We had to make it work, and it was possible that the answer was right in front of us. Maybe we just needed a little push in the right direction.

"We should go meet Brent," I said. "It's late and he's our friend. Even if we're grumpy he doesn't deserve to wait around for us. Besides, it's impossible to feel like an asshole with him in the room. Let's go."

"Yes, Daddy," she said, sticking her tongue out. And for the first time in two weeks I felt a twitch in my jeans.

Brent was in fact waiting, but by the time we arrived, we had at least partially worn off our horrible moods. We laughed as we walked and there were long moments when I stopped trying to figure it all out. Maybe when I was guilty I could just feel guilty. And maybe when I was turned on I could let that be as well. I slid my arm around Kelly as we walked in, and she held my hand until we found him sitting at the bar with a glass of scotch and that big, goofy grin we both loved.

"Hello, you gorgeous people," he said, giving us both a hug at the same time. He wrapped us up in his arms and kissed us each on the cheek, and I felt my whole body release. My shoulders dropped and my hands unclenched. The hostess showed us to our seat, and Brent's smile was so infectious we nearly fell out of our chairs laughing by the time the food arrived. He flirted with Kelly so effortlessly I almost didn't notice, but each time he complimented her or said something ridiculous, he looked at me and winked, letting me know I was in on the joke.

"I forgot how much I like you," Kelly said, leaning in and taking his hand. Dessert had just arrived and we had all ordered coffees and creme brule.

"You better like me," he said. "After all the shit we've been through. Plus, you know, the sex and stuff." He laughed again, and I took a big bite from the bowl in front of me. It was delicious, as was the coffee.

"I'm sorry about that," Kelly said. "Not about the sex, but about never talking. Or really doing anything about it. I'm even sorry about playing with you when I thought you were sleeping, that was fucked up."

"It was the old 'hard cock against the ass in your sleep trick'. It works almost every… Actually that never works," he said, laughing once more.

"It sure as hell worked on me. I can't remember the last time I was so turned on. You had both been so sweet to me after that shitty night before, and it felt right. It felt good and hot, and it was just what I needed."

"It was the best sex ever," I said. "I think for all three of us. God, I missed this. Just being together and talking, and not feeling like shit all the time. I forgot how much I liked seeing both of you happy. And I'm not talking about the sex this time. I just mean that you get along, and I like it. Almost as much as we get along," I said, pulling him towards me and kissing him firmly on the top of his head.

"Yeah, well after almost twenty years, we better fucking get along."

"Hey, Brent, can I ask you something?" Kelly had a serious look in her eye, and I wasn't sure where she was going to take it. "Do you think we're terrible people? I mean, like all the shit we've done, does it make us bad? Is there something wrong with us?"

"Are you serious? Why would you think that?"

"I don't know, man," I said. "We've just been wondering if we're not fucking everything up."

"You are two of the sweetest people I know. Seriously. I've never seen you push someone to do something they didn't want. Hell, it was often the other way around. Seriously, you are the most adorable couple ever."

"Even the Daddy shit?" Kelly asked. Brent just shrugged, and shook his head.

"None of that matters. You're good to people. I mean, you've been especially good to me. But seriously, you're fine."

"We were good to you," I chuckled. "I mean, that morning we were very giving."

"About that," Kelly said slowly. Brent and I both leaned in. "I know we never talked about this, and it's a little awkward now, but, um, have you been tested and stuff?"

"Me?" he asked, as if he was horrified by the question. "I get tested every six months, sometimes more. I would never have done that if I hadn't. With you guys I mean. Seriously, Thomas knows that. I assumed he told you. He told me when you guys went in June, so I figured it wasn't a big deal. Remember, we all drank a toast? Plus, I've only been with one other women in the last six month, and Rachel and I were super safe. She scared me."

"Are you serious?" I asked.

"Bro, you know this. Seriously, who takes better care of his dick than I do? I don't want my shit to fall off just because I'm stupid. Have you been scared this whole time? Why didn't you say anything?"

"I wasn't scared, I was just wondering," Kelly said. "I mean, Thomas didn't tell me, but I'm glad. It makes everything easier. Less scary. You know what I mean? Also it means that next time..." Kelly cut herself off before going any further and Brent leaned in closer.

"What about next time?" he asked. "Is there a next time?"

"Would you like there to be?" she asked.

"Of course. I mean, yes. Hell yes!"

"I think what she's really trying to say, is that next time, now that we know you're interested and clean, I won't tell you to pull out at the end."

"Holy shit, dude," Brent said, reaching down to his cock. "I'm so fucking hard right now, and I haven't even finished my coffee yet. You two are going to kill me. Are you serious?"

"Do you want to?" Kelly asked, pulling his hand up to her mouth and sucking two fingers between her lips. "Do you want to fuck me again? Tonight? Right now? Do you want to come in my tight little pussy, Brent?"

"Oh god, you have no idea," he whispered watching her lips

swirl around his fingertips. "I want you so badly right now I'm going to burst."

"Maybe we should get the check," I said. "I mean coffee is nice, but I think some little girl needs to be fucked, and she needs to be fucked right now by two men at the same time."

The whimper that came out of Kelly's mouth was tender, filthy, and sweet. Her whole body trembled, and the look in her eye was unmistakable. The three of us leaned in so closely all of our heads touched, and there was so much tension in the room you could cut it with a knife. The moment hung in the air as we each took deep breaths, and then it was done.

"Take me home," she whispered. "Now."

Brent and I threw money on the table and didn't even count it. It was more than enough, but there was no time for the check. There was no time for anything. We grabbed our coats, walked out the door, and turned towards my apartment without another word. My heart was pounding, but it felt good. It was the right kind of excitement.

As we got closer to the apartment, we began to walk faster, and by the time we were just half a block away, we began to run. Kelly burst forward, and we followed closely behind, staring at her ass in her tight blue jeans. She stopped, panting at the door before I opened it, and we practically stumbled up the stairs on top of one another. We threw our coats on the chairs in the kitchen, ran into my room, and within seconds, Kelly and Brent were kissing like he had just come back from the war.

I didn't bother with a candle. Hell, I didn't even turn off the lights. I stepped behind her, lifted up her hair, and kissed the back of her neck as I slid one hand down to her ass. She was moaning instantly, and she leaned back and kissed me between breaths. Brent had her shirt off a second later, and I undid her bra without pause. She kicked out of her jeans, falling onto the bed as each of us grabbed a leg and pulled. Our clothes came off just as quickly, and in less than a minute of returning home, Kelly was naked on my bed as we stood there looking down at her.

Brent and I were still catching our breath, but we watched her as she opened her legs and leaned back on the pillows.

"What do you think she wants?" he asked.

"I think she wants to be fucked. Hard."

Our hands were on our dicks already, although it's safe to say we didn't need much help. Her fingers slipped into her cunt, wet with her saliva, and she was practically fucking herself before we could move. I didn't wait a second longer, and she screamed out when I entered her. I lifted her knees up, spreading her legs wide as I watched Brent move to her mouth, leaning over until she wrapped her lips around his thick cock.

"Oh fuck," we both said, catching each other's eyes as the words slipped out. I pounded into her, not caring about anything other than fucking the woman I loved. I watched her choke on Brent's cock, sucking him deeper into her mouth each time I thrust into her. Her moans were primal and her body responded without thought.

After just a few minutes of fucking her I grabbed his shoulder and motioned for him to switch places with me. Even more than wanting to fuck her, I wanted to see it again. I watched him rub against her pussy as she pulled me towards her mouth with a moan, and then he was fucking her once more and she was coming for the first time that night. She let go of me just long enough to scream, and her hips bucked up off the bed as he slammed inside her, filling her all the way to the hilt.

"Fuck me, Brent," she moaned. "Fuck me with that big, gorgeous cock, and then come in me. Oh god, do it."

He slammed into her without stopping, and my hand was on my dick, jerking off into her mouth as much as she was blowing me.

"Let me get on top," she said, pulling Brent down. She leaned up and kissed him, their mouths and tongues full of want, and then he was on his back and she was guiding him back inside her. I moved behind her as she rode him, and watched his cock slide in and out of her pussy; it was a beautiful thing. My best friend and my girlfriend were fucking once more, and this time there was no question at all. There was no doubt, no fear, and nothing but pure lust in the room.

I climbed up behind her and lifted her ass, sliding my cock into her pussy the second he pulled out.

"Oh, fuck yes," she moaned, pushing back onto me as she kissed his mouth and wrapped her hand around his cock. I finally let her go once more, watching him fuck her again, and my body was pulled in so many places at once. I wanted everything, and I wanted it all at the same time. He fucked her as I worked my finger into her ass, and then I fucked her again, as she cried out my name. Back and forth, we continued, her body shaking as she came over and over again.

When I grabbed the lube out of the table, I heard her gasp, but she didn't hesitate to push back onto my fingers. I coated her insides, pushing them deep inside her ass and he never once stopped fucking her.

"Slow down," I said. "Just for a second. Just long enough for me to fuck this ass."

"Oh, fuck, I don't know if I can do it," she said. "Not both of you at once."

"You can," Brent said, kissing her as he held her head in her hands. "You can do anything because you are the hottest little girl in the whole fucking world."

I positioned myself against her, my cock also wet with the lube, and she closed her eyes and held her breath as I pushed against her asshole. She cried out when I finally entered her, and as I slid inside her, another orgasm ripped through her body.

"Holy shit," she cried. "Holy fucking shit, just stay there. Let me feel you both. Damn, that's intense. That is so fucking intense, I can't believe it."

We tried to hold still, but it was nearly impossible. I could feel Brent's cock through her body, and it was pulsing and trembling like he was ready to come. Each time I moved at all she screamed out again and bit his mouth with her kiss. After what felt like far too long she took a deep breath and pushed back onto us both.

"Okay," she said. "Do it. Fuck me, both of you. Fuck me ass and my cunt, and don't stop until you're coming."

"Oh fuck," we both said again, and then we started to move. I held her ass steady as I pushed into her, and his cock slid in and out of her, rubbing against my own. She gasped and begged, crying out with each thrust, but each yell only made us fuck her harder. Her ass was even tighter with Brent's cock filling her, and when he started to cry her name I knew it was almost over.

"I'm gonna fucking come," he said. "I'm gonna come so hard."

"Do it," she moaned. "Come inside me."

"Come in her," I said as well, my deepest fantasy finally on my doorstop. "Come inside that pussy, Brent. Fill our girlfriend with your fucking come and don't stop."

"Oh shit," he screamed, and I swear I could feel it. His cock pulsed and shivered, and I could feel it shooting out of him even as I started to come as well.

"Oh god, I'm coming too," I said. "Kelly, I'm coming in your fucking ass."

And then it was a blur of shaking bodies, screaming names, and pulsing cocks. In the middle of it all I think she fainted for a moment, but then her eyes opened again and she whimpered as we filled her. We were covered in sweat, and she was pressed between our bodies with more skin than was possible. Her ass clenched around me, and when Brent pulled out, I entered her deeper, the last of my orgasm exploding within her.

I finally pulled out, too, and she rolled off of Brent onto the bed next to him, and I couldn't resist. After all that time fantasizing about it, I had to know. I opened her thighs, amazed at how disgustingly beautiful it was, and I kissed her. I bit her thighs, I licked her pussy, and I shoved my tongue as far inside her as I could. She screamed again as Brent watched, but nothing mattered. I was eating her freshly fucked cunt, tasting his come, and I was practically hard again. My own come was dripping out of her ass, and the room smelled like we had been fucking for days. But, still I stayed there, my hands on her legs as I licked and sucked her pussy until she had one final orgasm that only slowed when I moved up her body and kissed her mouth again.

She lay between us for a long time after that, and none of us said a word. She touched herself gently, feeling her swollen skin, and soothing her belly with her fingertips.

"I don't think I can walk," she said.

"That means you've been properly fucked," Brent said. "It's true."

"Brent, there was nothing proper about that. Seriously, you two fucked me harder than I have ever been fucked. Hell, harder than I ever imaged, and that's saying a lot."

"Are you saying you liked it?" I asked, kissing her again.

"I love you. Both of you. I don't even have the words."

Our breathing slowed as we lay there, and I couldn't get the images out of my mind. I could still feel her ass around me, and the sight of them fucking was intoxicating, even to my mind's eye.

"I can't believe you still have that canopy," Brent said, his laughter filling the room once more. "Why haven't you taken that down?"

"It's pretty," I said. "Besides, I like how Kelly looks lying under it. It's fucking adorable."

"Yeah, I'm super adorable right now with your fucking come leaking out of every hole in my body. Picture perfect."

We lay there for a long time, catching our breath and kissing on the bed. I shared a kiss with Brent in the middle of it, and Kelly sighed and closed her eyes, leading to another. She lay beneath us as our scratchy faces touched, and his tongue was strong and invasive. When we finally pulled away, her fingers were in her pussy again and she was lost.

"Oh god, that was hot. Someone needs to fuck me again. Preferably while you two keep kissing."

And then we were back to tearing at her body, biting, clawing, and sucking every inch of her. We spent hours in bed, moving between laughter and coming so many times we lost count. Brent and I mostly kept to opposite sides of her, but he kissed me again while I was inside her, and she came just from watching. Late in the evening, when we were almost sleeping I watched as they struggled to fuck one last time. She was facing me on her side with her legs open, but his hands were on her shoulder and they couldn't manage to find the right angle.

"Please," she moaned, looking right into my eyes, and without thinking I reached down and wrapped my hand around his cock. It was surprisingly soft, and I held it tightly as I positioned him against her cunt, watching him once again sink inside her. They fucked for a long time as I watched, and when she came she kissed me and told me she loved me over and over.

We finally slept, her between us on the bed, and it was only in the early morning hours that I realized what I had said. I was just barely awake, and she was facing away, my arms wrapped around her body. Brent was on his back, his limp penis resting against his thigh, and I laughed to myself.

"Our girlfriend," I had said. "Fill our girlfriend."

Chapter Twenty-Seven

Brent didn't leave for three days. We all went to work, ran errands, ate food, and took showers, but each night he came home with us and the three of us fell back into bed with a hunger that wouldn't leave us. Sometimes it was tender and full of laughter, and at other times it was animal, instinctual, and without regard for anything but our desire and it's complete and utter fulfillment. He and I focused all of our energy on Kelly, and while it's impossible for two men in a situation like that not to touch, it wasn't about us. Even when she held our cocks together in her hands, moving her mouth back and forth between us, it was her. When he licked my come off her breasts or I held him steady, my hand wrapped around his dick as she lowered herself down onto him, it was still her.

My friendship with Brent changed, there is no doubt of that, but it's nearly impossible to describe. We had always been close, and the couple of times we had shared women before had been fun, but they were nothing at all compared to this. Even when we weren't in bed we were closer, and it wasn't strange for us to wander home at night, our arms around each other's shoulders as we drunkenly made our way down the street.

For the first time in my life, I had someone whom I could talk with about my relationship and he understood completely. They had become close over the summer, but in just a couple of days that friendship deepened until all three of us were finishing each other's sentences. In bed or out of it, we understood each other better than I thought possible, and those first few days still feel like a dream. We stumbled to work each day, exhausted from hours of making love, and we crawled back into bed at night knowing that just a few simple words would push us to exaltation.

And yet, in the middle of it all, my anxiety and worry didn't once return. Kelly and I were fucking again, but we had turned our fantasy into something real and it was perfect. It was messy and overwhelming, but it was safe in a way that I hadn't expected. Something about the three of us felt normal and natural, and no matter what we did to each other in bed, I was still happy when we left it.

When Brent finally returned to his own apartment it was to a long conversation with Jason that I'm sure he would have rather skipped. It was confusing to explain to ourselves, and so other people were nearly impossible. Jason listened as he always does, and his questions were practical ones. Was he moving out? Did this mean the three guys weren't hanging out any more? How often did Brent suck my dick and since when was he a big homo?

All considering, he took it fairly well, but Brent didn't really have answers. We invited Jason and Katie to go drinking, but you could feel the tension in the room, even though very little had changed. We still went to Docs, we still drank too many shots of tequila, and we still sang the moose song at two a.m. on our way home, but then we split off into twos and threes to discover how many degenerate things we could do with our bodies.

Katie hardly seemed to flinch though, and within a week she decided we were the cutest thing in the world. She found everything she could that came in three and suddenly there were cupcakes, books about kittens, billy goats, and pigs, alongside anything that had to do with a circus. They were always small, often just clippings or a postcard, but she seemed to get a strange pleasure out of discovering more things to leave for us. Stephanie and Martin were also easy-going, and if we happened to spend a lot of time together, they either didn't deign to notice, or else they simply minded their own business.

And then one night, two weeks into our new thing, I came

home to find Kelly alone in bed. Brent was out with some friends, and while it was late, she was awake and smiling at me like she had been waiting. I undressed, her eyes never leaving me as she lay on her back. When I climbed in next to her she rolled over and kissed me before whispering into my ear.

"I have a present for you," she purred. "Do you want it now?"

I was tired from working all night, but Kelly's presents were always good things. Besides, having just the two of us in bed was nice for a change. Brent had brought us back to a new normal, and it was the best I had felt in months. We had more space, but also, I had my Babygirl back, and I kissed her as I nodded my head, wondering what it was.

"Close your eyes," she said. I obeyed instantly and she pushed the blankets down as she moved over me. I felt her knees brush my arms as she straddled my body, and then lowered herself down to my mouth. Her pussy was impossibly smooth, every hair neatly shaven away until her skin was warm silk. With my eyes still closed I opened my mouth and kissed her, letting her hover just where she wanted me. I licked her gently, tracing the edges of her skin with my tongue, marveling as the contours of her lips.

"Are you ready?" she asked. I could only moan my assent before she opened herself with her fingers. For a moment I simply reveled in her, sticking my tongue deep within her, but I instantly realized it wasn't just her. She was wet, but she was more than wet. Her cunt was full of come, and we hadn't fucked since the night before.

"Do you like it?" she asked, opening wider around me. "Brent stopped by the karaoke bar an hour ago. He was going out, but he pulled me into one of the private rooms and fucked me so hard. It was over in minutes, but he came in me so much. Lick me clean. Suck me, Daddy, please."

I pushed her off me a second later and rolled her onto her back.

My heart was beating, and I didn't know what I was feeling. I was used to all of us fucking, but this was different. I pinned her arms above her head and slid inside her as she moaned underneath me.

"Since when do you fuck him without me?" I demanded, slapping her across the face without warning. "When does Daddy's little slut fuck him without telling me? How many times have you done that? How many times has Daddy's friend fucked you when I'm away?"

I didn't stop fucking her, but I was angry for real, and I had to hold myself back from hitting her harder.

"It was just tonight," she moaned, lifting her hips up to me, "It was just tonight, Daddy. We wanted to give you a present. It was just for you."

And then I stopped. I braced myself on my elbows as I looked down at her, and her eyes were open in surprise. I didn't pull out, but I didn't move either, and I wasn't sure what to do. Part of me wanted to come, and part of me wanted to leave and never come back. I had watched them fifty times in the last few weeks, but this was the first time that I wasn't there. As far as I knew, this was the first time they fucked without me.

"Did anyone see you?" I finally asked, slowly moving my hips once more. "Did anyone see my little girl getting fucked in the back room?"

She smiled again and looked down, her shy expression filling her face.

"No, Daddy, no one saw us. It was just him and me. It was just Uncle Brent fucking your little girl. I promise, it was just us."

"Did you know I'd be mad, Babygirl?" I asked, fucking her faster and faster.

"No, Daddy. I thought you'd like it. I thought you'd like him fucking me so I could bring you a present. It was all for you, Daddy."

"Did you come?" I asked, "In just a few minutes of fucking Uncle Brent, did you come?"

"Yes, Daddy," she moaned as I slammed into her, my balls beginning to tighten. "I came so hard, Daddy. I came so hard for him."

And then it was over, and I was filling her sloppy cunt with my own, and she wrapped her arms around me as told me she loved me. It was all for me, she said. It was all for me.

The second after I came, the feeling of hurt returned, and I rolled onto my back and raised my hands to my head, pushing back my hair and wiping away the sweat. I wasn't supposed to feel jealous any more. The three of us were perfect, and the nights we spent were better than anything I had ever imagined. I loved him, and I loved her, and fuck, this was hard.

"I don't like it," I finally said. "I don't want you to fuck him without me."

"Are you really jealous?" she asked, poking me in the ribs as she faced me. "You are! You're totally jealous. You were really fucking angry when you hit me. Come on, I fuck you all the time when he's not here, and one quickie in the karaoke booth and you're freaking out? I can't believe it."

"Kelly, you're my girlfriend! We're not allowed to fuck on our own."

"Oh, and what is he? He's just our toy again? He's just someone we play with when the two of us get bored of our little Daddy game? Is that it? Fuck you, you just came so goddamn hard."

"Fuck, Kelly! Give me a break. I didn't expect it, okay. I know it's more than that. He's a part of this too, and no, he's not just a toy. I love you both, but for some reason it never occurred to me that it might happen. And just because something turns me on, doesn't mean I like it. I think we've already covered that a few times."

She sat up, and pulled a cigarette from the pack on the table.

She lit one for me, too and placed the ashtray on the bed between us. We didn't smoke when Brent was around, but when he wasn't it was open season.

"I didn't think about it either," she said. "I mean, I really thought you'd love it. You love eating me out after he fucks me. He likes eating me after you fuck me. You both love eating my messy pussy and it didn't occur to me, honestly. I know it's different with him and you. We've been dating for six months, and I love you. But we haven't talked about what's going on with us all that much. I think it's been hard for him too. I think he liked having me to himself for a few minutes."

"I can't believe how jealous I am. Seriously, it's driving me crazy. I just didn't think about it, even though it makes all the sense in the world. Are you going to start staying with just him now?"

I couldn't handle that thought, and I took a long drag before blowing the smoke up into my pretty, pink canopy. She shook her head and reached out to take my hand.

"I don't know. We haven't talked about it. None of us, I mean. Not even Brent and I. It's not like we're sneaking around behind your back making plans. It just happened. He stopped in to say hi and not fucking felt absurd. We fuck all the time, so why would we not, just because you weren't there?"

"I get it. I do, and it makes total sense. I would have done the same thing, but it's hard for some reason. Maybe it was mostly the surprise. Honestly if you had told me you were going to come home later with Brent's load inside you, I probably would have been hard at work all day waiting for it. But, I didn't like the surprise. It felt to much like what happened with Claire."

"I didn't even think of that."

"You shouldn't have. It's totally different," I said. "But my brain is stupid and that's where it went. Listen, why don't we talk about it. I mean let's have a real conversation about what the hell is going on. I don't want to feel like I'm losing you, but I love what's happening. In some ways I feel closer to you now, even though he's so often between us."

"Mostly I'm the one in the middle," she said putting the ashtray back onto the table and climbing into my lap, her back against my chest. "I like the middle."

"Can we agree that you two won't fuck without me until we talk?"

"You'll let me do it later? I mean, if we talk, you're open to him and I being together sometimes without you?"

"I don't know. It feels hard, but we can talk. I'll promise that much."

"I can live with that," she said, pulling my hands up to her mouth and kissing my knuckles.

"I probably shouldn't say this. 'Cause you'll think I'm not upset, but I kinda liked the Uncle Brent thing. As soon as you said it I was ready to blow my load. Maybe it makes me feel better to be Daddy to his Uncle, but whatever it was, it was hot. Have you called him that to his face?"

"Oh god no. He's never said anything about the Daddy thing, although he does say I'm a pretty little girl sometime."

"Hmm, well maybe that's something else we have to talk about. You know: you, me, and Uncle Brent."

"You're going to turn me on again," she whispered, this time sucking my fingers into her mouth, licking them one at a time.

"Then maybe I'll just have to fuck you again," I said, kissing her neck.

"Yes, Daddy," she whispered, and then we were done talking.

Chapter Twenty-Eight

Jane and Sean decided to have their separate stag parties six weeks before the wedding. With Jane's illness, the planning overload, and everything else going on, they wanted a break more than anything. His friends were going to take him out to some strip clubs, get him nice and drunk, and generally make themselves a nuisance to the rest of the city's population. It was a grand tradition, and we all agreed that it should be honored. As for Jason, Brent and I, we decided to do the same thing. If Jane needed cheering up, what better way to do it than to get her drunk and watch naked women dance on stage?

She agreed to let us plan the whole thing, and between the three of us we made an impressive itinerary. We had a nice dinner lined up, drinks, three clubs of varying degrees of class, and then dessert and more drinks somewhere quiet and closer to home so we could end the night together without the smell of baby powder and champagne. It was a good plan, and while Kelly was sad that she couldn't come along, she understood. The four of us went back a long ways, and a night out was just what Jane needed.

The day of the party however, I got a phone call.

"I can't do it," Jane said, as soon as I answered the phone. "I'm sorry, Thomas, but I can't."

"You can't do what? Get married? Run a marathon? What are you talking about?"

"That party tonight, you moron. I can hardly get out of bed, and running around the city with you three would kill me. It's just a bad day, but as bad days go this one is worse. You guys should go without me. Go out and have fun, take some pictures, and then tell me about it. It will be almost the same, except you won't have to carry me home. Please, do this for me?"

"Jane, we're not going anywhere without you. Don't be silly. We can reschedule. You'll be better soon, and we can do it then."

"I'm being serious, Thomas, I want you guys to go. I need someone to be having fun while I'm not."

"I'm sure Sean will have fun enough. Or did he cancel?" It would be like him to cancel. He was a good fiance, and it was unlikely he would go out when she was feeling this bad.

"I didn't tell him," she admitted. "He looked worried, but I told him I just needed some rest and I'd be ready to go. I didn't want him to stay home because of me."

"I'll tell you what," I said. "Let me talk to the guys and we'll see what we want to do. Maybe we'll just come over and keep you company. I'll call you back, okay?"

"Fine," she said. "I love you, but don't do anything stupid."

"No promises," I said, before hanging up the phone.

Brent and Kelly were still lying naked in bed when I went back to the room, and they looked up at me with questioning faces. She was absentmindedly stroking his cock, and I leaned against the doorway and stared at them for a moment before saying anything. The last thing I wanted to do was ruin such a perfect picture.

"What is it?" Brent asked.

"Jane doesn't want to go. She says she doesn't feel good enough, but she lied to Sean so he's still going out. She wants us to have a party without her. I don't like it."

"Shit, that's not good," Brent said, sitting up. Kelly wrapped her arms around his waist as I sat down next to them. He reached out and took my hand, squeezing it gently in his own before finally getting up. Pacing back and forth in the room, he rubbed his head and scratched his three day beard. "We gotta do something. We're not going to let her get away with not having a bachelorette party, and we are most definitely not going out without her."

"I told her that. There's no way we can do it without Jane.

It's stupid."

He stopped in the middle of the room and looked as us with his hands raised. It was a ridiculous sight, a naked man smiling like a fool, but it was perfect. If anyone could solve this, it would be him.

"Kelly, can you get someone to cover for you tonight?" he asked. "I mean, can you get the night off? We need you."

"Probably, what do you have in mind?"

"And Jason and Katie, we need them, too. I know Jay was already planning to come, but how about Katie? Can we get her, too? Fuck, I wish Rachel wasn't still crazy. This would be right up her alley, but I think I got it. We can totally do this. Thomas, call Katie. Kelly, see if you can get out of work. Then we'll fuck one more time, and get things moving!"

He was practically screaming and waving at us to move, and it wasn't until I was on the phone with Jason that I realized the sneaky sex part in the middle of our schedule.

Six hours later all five of us were on our way across town to Jane's apartment. We had two large bags, stupid grins, and a plan that was either brilliant or insane. She buzzed us in, and we walked up her flight of stairs, the three boys in the front as the girls hung back behind us. Jane had finally agreed to let us come to her place, but she was still insisting that we then go out on our own.

We left the girls in the stairway, quietly ducking down so Jane wouldn't see them when she let us in, and with somber expressions we filed into her place, closed the door behind us, and pulled out twelve bottles of champagne. I lined them up in her small fridge before joining the rest of them. We opened one bottle, filled four glasses and sat around Jane on the floor.

She looked exhausted, skinny, and pale, but it didn't matter. We were there and we were going to celebrate one way or another.

"You guys didn't have to do this. I can probably have one glass before I throw up. What are we going to do with all that?" She tried to smile, but it came out as more of a smirk.

"We wouldn't miss this for the world," Jason said. "And you thought we would leave you. If you can't go out and party, then the least we can do is party with you here."

We raised our glasses and it was my turn to make a toast. I took a deep breath and gave it my best shot.

"To Jane: I've known you for way longer than either of us would like to remember, and I've loved you since about ten minutes after we met. Maybe ten minutes before if I count the time I spent staring at your ass across the room. But this isn't about your ass or your tight jeans. It isn't about our sordid history, or even the time you pushed me out of a moving car for throwing your cigarettes out the window.

"This is about you and Sean, who I have to say, is a lucky fucking man. You are brilliant, resilient, territorial, sarcastic, grumpy, hot, generous, funny, hot, but more than anything you are a better friend than any of us deserves to have. Even with your wedding plans, your doctors' visits, and your work schedule, you have always made time for us, always supported us, and always made us feel like real, honest human beings who were worthy of love.

"We adore you, we love you, and we are so fucking happy for you it makes us sick. So, here's to you, the best of us all, and here's to your marriage. Now let's get drunk and see some strippers!"

We raised our glasses and toasted as Jane tried to fight back tears, but seconds later Brent turned on the music as Jason shut off the lights and hit the switch to his portable disco ball. She laughed as she drank her champagne, but when I opened the door and Katie walked in, wearing fishnet stockings, and an incredibly ridiculous police uniform, her hand went to her mouth.

"You didn't," she said.

Just as Prince started singing, Katie started dancing, and it was beautiful. She stomped around the room in her trashy uniform, hitting us all with her baton as she frisked us up and down. In the middle of it, she lost her top, and we collapsed onto the bed next to Jane as she danced. Jane's mouth was still open in shock, and the laughter was contagious. By the time she was down to just her fishnets, panties, and bra, Jane was laughing as well. Katie walked over to Jason, reached into his pocket and made a mock gesture of surprise when she pulled out a joint. She cuffed his hands together and shook her finger before lighting the joint in her mouth. She took one long hit and then walked up to Jane.

With the joint still between her lips, she reached behind her and undid her bra, her tits bouncing into Jane's face. She stuck the joint into Jane's mouth before blowing her a kiss. She played peek-a-boo with her panties as she continued dancing, but by the time the song was done, I had more champagne out, Jane was seriously hitting the joint, and Katie was in just a pair of dark blue undies that said NYPD on the ass.

Brent smiled at me before skipping to the next song, and suddenly it was The Boss coming out of the stereo singing 'I'm on Fire'. Kelly sauntered into the apartment in the most adorable and ludicrous schoolgirl uniform we could find. It was plaid with white knee socks, and her shirt was tied around her midriff, with only one button done.

Jane laughed again, coughing on the bed as Kelly began her routine, and we hooted and hollered as I poured more drinks. She was far friendlier with Jane than Katie had been, and she pressed her breasts into her face as she undid the shirt. She left it wrapped around the bride's neck, leaving her pert tits bouncing as she turned and bent over, her tiny white thong covering almost nothing at all. We all leaned in to watch as she pretended to pull it down, but each time she turned back and put her fingers to her lips as Jane clapped.

"Do it," Jane finally yelled. "Take it fucking off!"

When she turned around again, all of us were shouting, and without hesitating Kelly slid the thong off her hips, down her knees, and then kicked it across the room. Her ass was directly in front of Jane's face who didn't stop cheering even as she reached out and grabbed Kelly's buttcheeks in both hands. We all laughed as she pressed into Jane's face, and then the skirt was gone, and Kelly was dancing in just her knee-high white socks; it was adorable and hot all at the same time.

"But wait!" I said, moving to the stereo as the song ended. "There's more!"

"No, please no," Jane said looking up at me. "No more, I can't handle any more!"

But with a flip of the switch, it was Kurt Cobain and Brent was in the middle of the room pulling off his jacket. His hips swirled like a young Elvis, and as the music played, he danced around the room, rubbing his body against each of us as Jane laughed so hard there were tears in her eyes. When he pulled off his shirt we all yelled, and then without pause he reached down, grabbed his pants around the waist, and yanked them off in one tug. They tore away down the sides, and he tossed them onto the bed as he stepped in front of Jane.

He reached out and grabbed her head, pulling her closer. All he was wearing was a very tacky thong with an elephant's trunk and ears hanging out of the front. His cock was stuffed into the trunk, and even soft, it spun around as he danced, shaking himself while Jane pretended to be shocked. He thrust his hips, his cock flopping about, and the five of us could hardly stand we were laughing so hard.

When the song finally ended he collapsed onto the bed next to her; she was clapping, laughing, and coughing, even as she took another hit off the joint.

"I cannot fucking believe you," she said, looking around the room. "Seriously, I feel so fucking awful, and then you come over, get me high, and give me the best bachelorette party I could imagine. This is so much better than going out.

"Brent, if I ever see your dick in an elephant trunk again I'm going to puke, but Kelly, you can dance for me any time. You too, Officer. Jesus, that was awesome."

Kelly put on a small robe and she was wrapped up in it drinking champagne while Katie simply lounged around in her underwear. She had unsurprisingly found another joint, which she passed easily between us all. Jane had tried to give hers back, and we insisted she smoke it all—on doctor's orders.

"They do give weed to cancer people, don't they," she said, holding the small roach that was left. "I can see why. I feel fucking better than I have in a week. I love you guys. Seriously, I love you all."

We spent the next two hours listening to music, drinking the bubbly, and telling stories about the last ten years. Jane and I had more embarrassing memories than anyone had a right to, and as soon as I said something about her, she was back at me with something I'd rather have forgotten. She got more and more tired as the night went on though, and while she looked happy for the first time in a while, it was clear around ten that the party was ending.

We cleaned up her apartment, taking the empty bottles with us, and making sure we had all the discarded clothes from the performance. We packed it all up as she climbed into bed, still a little stoned, but now mostly just sleepy. Each of us leaned down and kissed her in turn, and I was the last one to leave.

"Do you want someone to stay? Just to be here? I can sleep at the foot of the bed if you like. I won't even try to molest you."

"No, I'll be fine. Sean promised to be home by midnight, and he won't be a second late. Right now I just want to sleep and remember this. If I stay up or try to talk too much more I'll get cranky again, and I don't want to ruin a perfect thing. Go. Fuck your girlfriend – and your boyfriend for that matter – and have a good time. I love you and this was amazing. It was better than that. Now, go."

I kissed her once more before heading to the door, and when I finally got down to the street, I could hardly stand. I slipped down to her stoop as my friends stared at me, and before I knew what was happening there were tears streaming down my face, and I couldn't stop crying.

Chapter Twenty-Nine

Brent sat down next to me and Jason joined him on the other side. They wrapped their arms around me, but rather than me cheering up, they started crying as well and there was nothing to be done. We swayed as we let it out, and we rubbed each other's shoulders as the girls leaned against the fence smoking. It had hit me out of nowhere, and I realized that it was the first time I had really cried since Jane told us she was sick. She was so strong, so steady, and so amazing, but there was no getting around the fact that she was ill, and it was not going to be easy.

"She's going to be fine," Brent said.

"If she's not I'm going to kill her," Jason said.

"The last tests were good," Brent continued. "They think it's gone, maybe all of it. She's just going through a rough part right now. It's going to get better." I hugged Brent tighter as he said it because I needed to believe it was true. She had said the same thing earlier that week, but she had looked so small in bed that it was hard to believe.

"Maybe we should walk," I said after about ten minutes of crying on her stoop. "She'd murder us if she knew we were still here, and the last thing we need is Sean coming back and wondering what the hell happened. Let's walk. And maybe drink more. Do I need to drink more?"

"We always need to drink more," Brent said, helping me to my feet. Jason handed me a Lucky Strike as we picked up our bags, and he pulled out a silver Zippo and lit it for me. I inhaled deeply, completely aware of the irony of me smoking.

We walked over to Washington Square Park, but it was dark and empty. It was cold outside, and while we were bundled up, there was no getting over the chill. We walked close together, all five of us, as we stumbled through the East Village, and no one was surprised at all when we landed back at my apartment. We dropped off everything in my room, then crashed down on the couch.

"Do you guys want to go to Docs? Or just sit here? I don't know, we should do something." Jason was fidgeting, which meant he didn't know what to do.

Katie sat between Jason's knees on the floor, her head resting against him, while the three of us sat next to him, our legs entwined as Kelly stretched out across our laps. I was drained, and not just from the drinking. Second to Brent, Jane was my oldest friend, and it had been getting harder as each month passed.

"Maybe you three want to go to bed," Katie said. "We can head out if you're tired."

"I don't know," I said leaning back. "Maybe bed is a good idea. I'm not very good company right now."

"Why don't we get brunch tomorrow? It'll be good to do something easy," Jason asked, and it was a good idea. If we all spent too much time away from each other, it was just going to make it harder.

"I like brunch," Kelly said. "Let's do that. I'm tired, too. All that dancing makes a girl sleepy."

Ten minutes later the three of us were in my bedroom, spread out on the bed and looking at one another. Kelly was still in her schoolgirl uniform, and she looked adorable. It was trashy, but she somehow managed to pull it off and still make it look sweet. The pigtails didn't help. Brent and I stripped down to our boxers, but nothing felt especially sexy.

"It was a good party," I finally said. "I mean she liked it. And watching you dance was awesome. You, I don't know about," I said, looking at Brent and smiling.

"Yeah, I think I'd rather watch her too," he said, his hand resting on her bare thigh.

"I know I wasn't supposed to be there, but I'm glad I was. I mean, now that we're all together, or whatever, it feels even more important that I know your friends. She's awesome, and she totally grabbed my ass! I thought she was going to bite me for a second."

"It was definitely better than it would have been going out," I said. "We never would have found anyone half as cute as you."

"Plus, I got to see Katie's titties for the first time," Brent added.

"Pervert," Kelly said, punching him on the arm.

"You know when I was saying goodbye she told me to go home with my girlfriend. And boyfriend. She didn't even say it like a joke. Technically she told me to come home and fuck you both."

"I think that's super cute. You two should definitely be boyfriends. We've been fucking for like a month now. What else would you call it?" Kelly looked back and forth between us.

"Is this a relationship talk? Because I am a free bird. I am a lone wolf and a free-roaming chicken. No one can tie me down, and no one can hold me back, I'm…"

"You're a fucking idiot," I said to Brent. "And you're stuck with us. Not that we've tried to tell you what to do."

"That's a good point. For all you know, I've been fucking bitches left and right. Like all over town."

"Right," Kelly said. "If that was true, you'd never have the energy to do me so often."

I laughed along with them, but it was a valid point. The three of us were spending at least four nights a week together, and when Brent wasn't there we found that we missed him. The sex was different when we were alone, and while it was tender and sweet, the three of us were something else. It was fire and lightning. It was energy that we had little control over.

"Can we talk about that thing?" Kelly asked looking at me. I knew instantly what she meant, and I didn't have enough energy to say no. We had avoided having the talk with Brent about the two of them fucking on their own, and I had been happy to let it go. Kelly not so much. I finally just nodded, unsure if I could handle it in my emotional state, but recognizing it had gone too long already. Also, I needed to think about anything other than Jane.

Brent and Kelly had behaved, but it was mostly because he was here often enough that it hardly mattered. They didn't have time to be alone, and they hadn't had sex without me again since her surprise present after the karaoke bar.

"Kelly wants to know if she can fuck you when I'm not here," I said, looking down at my hands. There was no point in beating around the bush.

"Like that time in the karaoke bar? I was kind of wondering about that. We never talked about it, and I felt sort of bad. It's not like we weren't all doing it, but that was different. It was strange."

"Did you like it?" Kelly asked, as she slid her knees up under her arms. Brent and I instantly leaned in and looked up under her tiny skirt to her still bare skin. She had left the thong somewhere in Jane's apartment, and none of us had been able to find it.

"Yeah, I mean, it was awesome, but we never discussed it. I guess I was worried about upsetting you," he said, turning in my direction.

"It was hard for me," I said. "I'm selfish and I still think of Kelly as my girlfriend. But that's not really true is it? She's not mine. I mean, not only mine. She's our girlfriend."

Absentmindedly, Kelly undid her top and tossed it onto the floor. She rolled the socks down and tossed them off the bed as well. She looked cute in her tiny skirt, but we needed to keep talking, and this wasn't helping.

"Are you trying to distract me?" I asked. "I thought you wanted to have this conversation?"

"I'm just getting comfortable. You two were already looking up my skirt, so why bother? But yes, I do want to talk about it. Brent, I don't know what we have. I love being with you, and this month has been amazing. Hell, hanging out with you all summer has been amazing. You make me laugh nearly as much as you make me come."

"That's a pretty good reference," he said. "Can I put you on my resume?"

"I'm serious," she said. "It's been good, but I don't know what it is. Thomas and I have been together since May, and I love him. We do different things when you're not here, and I don't know what it would be like for us. I mean, just you and me."

"I don't know either, but if the karaoke room is any indicator, it wouldn't suck." He laughed and I looked at both of them, realizing that the decision had already been made. We were moving in one direction, and trying to push back against the tide would get me nowhere.

"I think I'm happiest when we're talking," I said. "If I know you two are going to meet up somewhere and fuck, then I'd like to know beforehand."

"Hey, I never know when you two are doing it." Brent was joking, but it was true.

"I know," I said. "And it's not fair, but I saw her first, so there."

"We can take it slowly," Kelly said. "I don't want to mess anything up, but I don't want to it get weird either. I guess I'd rather make a pact that we only fuck when it's all three of us than make someone feel left out. If we have to. Although if you two want to get it on while I'm out of the room, feel free."

"I could go for that," Brent said. "I mean, it's not like I'm losing out though. It would be more of an issue for you two. I do get a little jealous, but not really. I got into this knowing that you two were together. It's one of the things I love about what we do. Maybe we're all dating or something, but you two still feel like the thing. The couple."

We were going around in circles and there didn't seem to be an easy way out. Part of me wanted to take Kelly's offer, but I knew instantly that I'd miss my time alone with her. But could I live with them being on their own? Could I spend a night home by myself, knowing that just uptown Kelly was riding his cock? I was sure I could fetishize it, but that wasn't enough. It might turn me on for a while, but at the end of the night, I'd still be alone and she'd be somewhere else.

"Can we start slowly?" I said. "I can live with you two fucking when I'm not there. At least a little. But can you tell me, and can you come back to me? I don't care if it's both of you coming back here, but I'm not ready to spend the night alone. I know that's probably fucked up, but it's where I'm at. Maybe it will change or get easier, but that's what I can handle now."

"I can live with that," Brent said. "I'm happy to tell you I'm about to go fuck her during my lunch break. Besides, the thought of sending her home to you turns me on. And for some reason, I don't mind the being alone part. I need it sometimes. I know you two are doing your whole Daddy thing while I'm not here, and that's fine, too. Seriously, I think it's good."

"Kelly?" I asked. She nodded as she chewed on her lip.

"I think so. I mean, I don't want to push it. So what are the rules? I have to tell you, and then I have to come back home to you?"

"That's about it," I said.

"Okay, let's try it," she said, her shy smile suddenly looking mischievous. "Thomas? I'm going to fuck Brent. Right now. But then I'll come back to you."

My stomach dropped, but I wasn't sure what was going on. Were they going to leave me there? Were they going to go into the other room or maybe back to her place, just so they could fuck without me? After everything that had happened that night, I was going to lose my shit if that was their plan.

Instead, she got up and undid her skirt, dropping it to the floor next to her other things.

"Brent, do you want to join me on the floor? Thomas can stay on the bed."

I gulped again as he crawled down to her, but this I could most likely survive. I watched as he opened her legs and moved his mouth down to her pussy. She grabbed his hair as he ate her, and she moaned softly, looking up at me on occasion with a pretty grin. I was hard in an instant, but watching from so far away felt nearly impossible.

By the time he moved up, kissed her mouth and slid his cock inside her, I was nearly back in tears, but still I didn't move. I wasn't sure what I wanted, but it was like time froze around me and all I could do was watch. They moved slowly, and our normal frantic pace was gone, but that only made it harder. He was sweeter than I had ever seen before, and she looked into his eyes with so much love it was overwhelming. She moaned softly and opened her legs wider as he thrust inside her. Was that what it was like without me there? Were they tender and in love when I wasn't looking?

"Do you want to join us?" she finally asked me shyly. I nodded, my heart still in my throat, but they untangled their limbs and crawled back into the bed as I sighed my relief. She opened her mouth to mine in a second, and I pulled her to me, trying to hold back tears again. He pushed into her from behind, but all I cared about was that she was in my arms.

"We can take is slowly" she whispered as he fucked her. "I love you, Daddy, and I love him too, and we can take is slowly. Was it hard to watch? From so far away?"

"Yes," I mumbled, kissing her again as I reached down and touched them, letting his cock slide between my fingers.

"Maybe next time I'll make you wait in the living room and listen. Would that be harder?"

"Yes," I moaned, pulling her closer to me, my jealousy trigger instantly connecting to my cock. Brent reached out and guided me into her before moving up next to me.

"You can be mean," he said to her, watching her close her eyes as she fucked me slowly.

"I'm sorry, Daddy," she whispered into my ear. "I didn't mean to make you mad."

I pulled her down harder, and when she looked at Brent I suddenly knew she was going to say it. She was going to let it out, and there was no stopping her when she was like that.

"You fuck me so much harder when you get angry, though," she whispered, her face back to mine. "So much harder. Sometimes I have to make you mad just to get what I want."

I leaned her back, lifting her off the bed before I lay her down, and Brent followed me until he was next to us, watching us fuck faster and faster.

"You always fuck me better when I've been bad. Like that

time before," she said, her orgasm suddenly appearing on the horizon. "When I came home last time, and I told you I had fucked Uncle Brent. You fucked me so good then. Do it, Daddy, fuck me hard again."

I pounded into her, and Brent moved up until his cock was right over her face. His fist was frantic as he jerked off, and she stared at both of us, her eyes moving back and forth.

"Do it, Babygirl," I said. "Suck Uncle Brent's cock for Daddy. Show me how you like to suck his cock."

She started coming the second the words were out of my mouth, but she wrapped her lips around him and sucked him for all she was worth. He looked at me, his eyes glazed over in his own lust, and I fucked her faster and harder, needing to come more than anything else in the world. I needed to erase everything and forget about the rest, even if it was just for a moment. More than release I needed to lose myself. He moved from staying still to fucking her mouth, and she gagged and coughed even as she came, her body writhing beneath me as she shook.

"Oh fuck," he said. "Fuck, I'm going to come in your pretty little mouth. Suck Uncle Brent's dick. Swallow it."

She instantly started to come again, and she wrapped her hand around him, her eyes filled with love as we fucked her. I watched as he exploded inside her, his come dripping out of her mouth and down onto her chin, and it was just minutes later that I pulled out and came on her stomach and tits, my fist a blur as I pumped my come all over her body.

"You're such a good little girl," I moaned. "Daddy loves you so much."

I kissed her, tasting his come, even as he leaned down and licked her tits clean of mine. We lay on each side of her, kissing her body, biting her lips, and rubbing our come into her skin. She was panting and shaking, her body still spasming between us.

"Uncle Brent loves you, too," he said, and she shivered one more time as she looked into his eyes.

"My life just keeps getting better and better," she said, her laughter making her shake as much as her orgasm. "God, you two are going to spoil me. If you do that again I don't know what I'll do."

"I liked it," Brent said. "I don't mind you being little, but the whole Daddy thing never worked for me. But Uncle Brent? Uncle Brent can fuck the shit out of you and feel awesome about it."

I reached out and grabbed his hand and he smiled at me.

"It's good to know we're all sick and twisted," I said.

"So, it's kinda decided, right?" Kelly said. "I mean, we can stop pretending otherwise and just admit that we're all going out? I have two boyfriends, and everyone who doesn't like it can go fuck themselves."

"Not just two boyfriends" Brent and I both said at the same time.

"Yeah, you have a Daddy," I said.

"And also an Uncle," he added.

"Fuck, I'm a lucky girl."

Chapter Thirty

A few nights later the three of us were out for dinner, talking about New Year's. We had already made a guest list, and figured out what we were going to serve and how. We were slowly stocking the bar, and I was trying to keep the apartment as clean as possible. I even replaced a few lightbulbs and fixed some outlet covers that had broken over the years. I was truly going all out.

"I want to go out with a bang," Kelly said, sitting between us at Go, eating a big bowl of ramen.

"Of course. The party is going to be awesome, and we will

start the new millenium with the people we love the best," Brent smiled as he talked, and I realized that since we all started dating, he was happier than I had seem him in a long time. All of us were.

"That's not quite what I mean," Kelly said, looking down into her bowl of soup.

"Do you want a bigger party?" I asked.

"Um, sort of? Okay, what's the point of having two kinky boyfriends with twisted minds if I can't tell you shit? I don't know why this is hard, but I have a fantasy. My oldest fantasy for ever. Since I was a teenager."

"About New Year's?" Brent asked.

"It wasn't, but this year it makes sense. Like I said, I want to go out with a bang. A gang bang."

We looked at her, and for a brief second I thought she might be joking. And then I remembered it was Kelly and nothing was surprising. He looked at me and shrugged, and I suddenly pictured her on the floor of my room with eight guys standing around her in a circle.

"Are you thinking a large gang bang or a medium sized one?" I asked. "It's really a different thing, and if we have more than nine or ten guys there, we'll need a fluffer. Maybe two. It's a logistical nightmare." I was trying to be funny, but it sounded true. That was a lot of hard cocks to get in one room.

"I was thinking five or six," she said, looking down, her shy, blue eyes prettier than ever. "You two and a few others."

"You're serious," Brent said. "You really wanted to get fucked by a bunch of guys? On New Year's?"

"New Year's is just a bonus. But I can't think of a better time. Are you both freaked out? Did I pass a line there?"

"I just can't think of anyone who deserves a piece of you," he said, laughing and smiling. "But if you're serious, we can talk about it. Thomas?"

"You know neither Brent or I liked watching you fuck that guy with the mustache."

"We won't invite him." She stuck her tongue out at me, and I kept going.

"Good. No mustache guy. But, it's pretty hot in general. I mean, how many guys could you actually fuck? I've never seen you do more than two in one night, although you do two most nights now."

"Five seems like a good number," she said. "Ten is way too many, but three doesn't feel all that different. I mean, it would just be one more than normal."

"Do you want to know who they are?" Brent asked, putting his hand on her leg under the table. I moved over to the booth, sitting on her other side, and my hand was instantly on her thigh.

"I don't know," she whispered. "I don't want to it be scary people, but I don't have to know them."

"Do you want to know the details?" I asked, squeezing her harder. "Or should we just take it from here. Five guys. New Year's Eve. Kelly gets fucked really hard."

Her eyes were closed as she leaned back in her chair, and Brent grinned at me with the look that meant his mind was spinning. I nodded, because I suddenly realized I had ideas as well. If Kelly wanted to get fucked by five men, I definitely had ideas.

"I could come just thinking about it. Are you two seriously okay with this? I mean, you won't hate me after and think I'm a dirty slut?"

"You are a dirty slut," I said.

"But you're our dirty slut," Brent added, both our hands moving higher. "And we love you. Even if you want to get nailed by a bunch of guys."

"And you two," she said, nearly moaning out the words. "I need you both there. Holding me, fucking me, too, but mostly telling me it's alright. Telling me I deserve it, and I'm a dirty girl. Oh god, I think I might come. Tell me more."

She was clenching her thighs, and I couldn't resist. Telling her stories was something I was good at since the very beginning, and this one felt right.

"I'll leave you naked in my room before the party starts," I whispered. "You'll kneel on the floor, maybe with a blindfold around your head, and you'll wait, patiently, unsure of what will happen or when."

"Oh god, keep going." I loved the sound of her voice when she begged.

"We'll leave the lights on, so when all five of us walk in we can see you naked and ready to get fucked. No darkness for you. I want them to see your tiny, little body, and I want them to see how wet you are. How much you need it. Without warning I'll pull your hand up to someone's cock and you'll stroke it. Then you'll move to the next as we gather around you, until you are surrounded."

Kelly's knees clenched and her body shook as she bit her lip so as not to alarm the other patrons. I was tempted to cover her mouth with my hand, but instead I leaned in and kept going.

"And then you'll suck their cocks, our cocks, until we're hard. You'll suck all five of us until someone decides they've had enough. We'll throw you down you the floor, your legs open as they stare at you, touch you and grope you. Their hands on your breasts, in your pussy, pushing into your mouth before you feel the first hard cock opening you up."

"Oh fuck, I'm coming," she said, her head dropping forward as she bit her lip harder, and her orgasm moved through her whole body. "Oh fuck," she said again, trying not to make a sound. Brent looked like he was close as well, and I leaned back before taking a sip of my beer.

"Is that it?" she asked, when she finally opened her eyes.

"Well, I can't tell you the rest, it's a surprise. Besides, you already came. You'll have to wait until New Year's to see what happens."

"I'm going to be a wreck until then. Seriously, you two are going to have to fuck me constantly or I'm going to go do something stupid. That was so fucking hot."

She leaned in and kissed me before kissing Brent just as deeply. We were mostly used to the stares we got when she moved so easily between us, and we just smiled and waved when it got awkward. Her body was still trembling, and I was amazed that she could come with just her jeans and our hands between her legs.

"Let's go home," she said. "Now."

The apartment was quiet and we climbed the stairs with only one thing on our mind. We were going to fuck her until she didn't remember her name, and nothing was going to slow us down. I grabbed the mail at the bottom of the steps and carried it up, and by the time I got to the bedroom Kelly had pulled off her shirt and was kneeling in front of Brent.

"Come on," she said, "I can't wait."

"This is strange," I said, holding up an envelope. "We got a letter from Maddy."

"Lemme see!" she shouted, jumping up off the floor and ripping it out of my hands. Ignoring both of us she climbed onto the bed in just her jeans and a bra, and she tore the letter open like it was Christmas morning. I went to the bar and poured us each a whisky before coming back in and passing them out. Kelly took hers absentmindedly without looking up.

"That's the little, blonde girl you fucked?" Brent asked. "I so wish I was there for that. You couldn't have asked me out earlier? Come on man."

"Holy shit," came Kelly's voice from the bed. She looked up at me and her mouth was wide open.

"What is it?" I asked, sitting down next to her. She folded the letter and put it back on her lap. Brent sat down next to her, and we both waited for her to say something.

"So, you know how she said she had a boyfriend? The only other guy she fucked before you?"

"Kelly, what's this about?"

"What's going on?" Brent asked. "Is she pregnant or something? Didn't you wear a condom?"

"Of course," Kelly said. "Although it did break. Thomas was fucking her, but none of us realized. She said she was on the pill and we had been tested, so it wasn't a big deal. But that doesn't matter. She's fine, she just felt guilty."

"Kelly, what are you talking about? Guilty about what?"

"According to her she doesn't actually have that boyfriend at home. She told us she did so we wouldn't freak out."

"If she didn't have a boyfriend, then that means…" I was trying to process it.

"That was her totally first time. She was scared if we knew that we wouldn't do it. That we'd be too worried about her."

"Holy shit, you de-virginized your friend's little sister?" Brent said. "You are more badass than I thought. Holy shit, dude."

"Please tell me this is a joke, Kelly. Why is she telling us this?"

"She said she couldn't live with herself for lying, and she hopes that when she comes to school in January, we can still be friends. And that's it. That's the entire letter. Other than this one naked photo."

"Let me see that," Brent said, ripping it out of her hands. He held it up and just stared. "Are you serious? This is so unfair. You slept with this girl? You were her first?"

He handed me the picture, and there was our Maddy lying on her bed, naked as a jay bird. Her blonde hair was splayed out over the pillow as she smiled at the camera. One leg was rolled over so we could see was the curve of her ass, and her perfect breasts were stunning in the early morning sun. There was a lipstick mark on the bottom left corner and she had written the words, "I'm sorry" in black sharpie.

"Jesus," I said. "I can't decide if I'm upset that she lied to us or turned on. I can't believe that was her first time. She didn't bleed or anything."

"Not everyone bleeds the first time," Kelly said looking down shyly. "I didn't."

Brent and I leaned in closer and kissed her gently on the cheek. I reached behind her and undid her bra as he ran his fingers up her thigh. The picture was hot, and the realization that she had wanted me to be her first was insane, but all three of us were moving in the same direction.

"So, tell us more about your virginity," Brent whispered as he undid her jeans and slid his hand inside them. Kelly leaned in, looked back and forth between us, and then covered herself with her arms across her chest.

"I'm scared," she said in her little girl voice. "I'm scared, but I'm ready. I don't want to be a virgin any more. Will you help me?"

By the time she was naked, we were trembling as we struggled to slow down. So often we simply dove in, fucking and sucking one another until our bodies were weak with exhaustion, but this was a new game. We held her between us, the photo of Maddy lying on the pillow, as we whispered words of assurance.

"We'll be gentle, Babygirl," I said. "I promise we'll be gentle."

Chapter Thirty-One

It was just a few days later that it happened. In my mind everything was still theoretical, but clearly I was the only one.

Kelly and I had spent a night alone together, and we were getting dressed in the morning after taking our time with coffee and showers when she told me.

"I was thinking I might visit Brent at work this afternoon when you're at the bar," she said.

"Sounds nice of you," I said, completely missing the undertone of what she was trying to tell me. "You going to take him to lunch?"

"I was thinking we might stay in. He has his own office this week until they can clear up another space for him, so I thought it might be fun to visit. You know, just us two."

"Oh," I said, standing up with my sweater in my hands. "You mean, a visit with a capital V. Like you're going to stop by his office and fuck him."

"Is it okay? We talked about it and made up the rules, and this is it, right? I can go and fuck him and them come home to you. It's what we decided."

I sat down on the bed, unsure of what I could say. She was right. It was exactly what we decided, but I wasn't positive I loved the idea. Besides, fucking him in his office during the workday sounded somewhat dangerous. It also sounded like something we had never done. They had already fucked in the karaoke bar, but the only place the two of us had done it other than our beds was in the bathroom at Doc Holidays. And that was just until we got thrown out.

"You're right," I said. "You're telling me ahead of time, and it's totally what we said we'd do. It's fine. Go, and give him my love. Fuck his brains out and then come home so I can eat that pussy."

"Are you sure? You're not freaked out."

"Kelly, how many times have I watched you two fuck? Come on, it doesn't bother me any more. It's good. I like it. You should totally do it."

I don't know if I was more convincing to her or to myself, but she hugged me and kissed me while whispering thank you in my ear. She promised to come visit me at work later that afternoon and tell me all about it. It would just be an hour or two, and there was nothing to worry about at all. Not a thing.

When she walked out the door I crawled back into my room and lay down on the bed. I didn't like that it felt hard at all, but more importantly I didn't like where it sent my mind. The first thing that happened was that I suddenly had a desire to fly to Portland, throw Maddy down on her bed, and fuck her brains out until I felt better. It was a foolish fantasy, but after her letter and the picture, it was what I had. I unzipped my pants, pulled my cock out and tried to remember what she tasted like. I pictured her on her hands and knees on my bed, the same bed I was lying in, with my cock sliding in and out of her virgin cunt, and I was hard in seconds.

But my mind wouldn't stay still and before I knew what was happening it was Jane on her hands and knees begging me to fuck her ass. I groaned, the old fantasy coming back with as much force as ever. Within an hour or two Kelly would be downtown kneeling on the floor of Brent's office with his dick down her throat, so what was wrong with a little fantasy of my own?

And then was when I decided to call her.

I dragged the phone into my room and closed the door behind me, before dialing Jane's number. My cock was out once more and by the time she answered the phone I was already moving in a slow and steady motion.

"Hey, sexy," I said. "What are you up to?"

"I'm lying in bed trying not to die. What are you doing?"

"About the same. At least the bed part. Mostly I'm trying not to go crazy. What are you wearing?"

"Thomas, are you seriously trying to have phone sex with me?

What's going on?"

I sighed and let go of myself before sitting up. There was no point in talking to Jane if I wasn't going to be honest. Not that she ever gave me a choice.

"It's stupid. I don't even know why it's bothering me, but I feel like an idiot."

"Tell me," she said. I pictured her in bed, the same bed we had fucked on just months before, and I slid down again and pulled the blanket up over me.

"Kelly is going to visit Brent at the office today during his lunch break. I don't know why it bothers me after everything we've done, but they're totally going to fuck in his office. While I'm here. Or at work. Or anywhere other than with them. And I don't like it."

"Haven't you guys been together for months now? I assumed they did that all the time. Not at his office, but without you. Isn't that how it works?"

"No, it's not. Well, it hasn't been. She was my girlfriend and now she's our girlfriend, but mostly he just comes over here. He sleeps at home sometimes, but it's always the three of us. Or just me and Kelly. Like I said, it's stupid."

"So now it's just them, and you're jealous? That makes sense."

"Really? How does that make sense?"

"I don't know. If you're normally there it's one thing. But when you can't see it, you probably worry about all sorts of dumb shit. Does she love him more, is she different with you, and all the rest of it. When you're there it's still about you. Like it always is."

She was right, of course. It was about me. And I liked it that way. I brought him into our bed, I told her she could suck his cock, and I told them to fuck while I watched. It was all about me. Fuck. I reached a hand back down beneath my jeans and my mind moved back to Jane.

"It's better than them doing it behind my back, I guess. Like last time."

"What happened last time?" She asked.

"You don't want to know. Hell, maybe you do, but it was intense. She came home one night and just climbed on top of me. They had fucked in the karaoke bar earlier in the day, but they didn't tell me about it until afterwards."

"Did she sit on your face?" Jane asked, and I could hear her laughing.

"Maybe," I said. "But we hadn't talked about it. I mean, it had never come up and then she was suddenly making me eat her fucking pussy right after they fucked."

I was hard once again, and my hand started to move slowly as I listened to Jane breathing on the other end of the phone.

"Did you like it?" She asked, a hint of something warm slipping into her voice.

"Yes," I said quietly. "I mean, I was jealous, but it was hot, too. I didn't want it to be, but it was hot."

"And how about now, Thomas? When you think about him bending her over his desk and fucking her, do you get hard?"

"Oh fuck, Jane, I can't talk about this."

"Answer the question, Thomas. Does it make you hard?"

I finally slid my jeans off, and kicked them onto the floor. My mind was everywhere at once, and it moved from picturing them in his office, to imaging Jane on her bed touching herself as we talked.

"Of course. I'm so fucking hard, Jane, I can't even stand it."

Her breathing had grown loud and quick, and for a few moments neither of us said a word. I closed my eyes as I listened into the phone, and I could feel my body tightening as I jerked off slowly beneath the covers. The first time she moaned I growled back, both of us knowing exactly what was happening on the other end of the line.

"Do you fuck her up the ass?" she finally asked between breaths.

"Oh fuck, Jane, I can't believe you asked me that."

"Tell me, Thomas. Do you?"

"Oh god yes. I love her ass so fucking much. It's so tight and she comes so goddamn hard when I fuck her."

"Can I ask you something?" Her voice was ragged now, and I was close to coming.

"Anything," I said, gripping myself harder.

"When you're inside her? When you're fucking her ass. Do you ever wish it was me?"

"Oh god, Jane, you know I do. When she's kneeling on my bed, and I'm behind her, sometimes I can't help it. I remember you right here. Right here on this bed with your ass in the air and my cock inside you." I could hardly talk I was so close to coming.

"Keep going, Thomas. Please, I want to hear it."

"I think of you here, and I can feel you around me, Jane. Your perfect pussy around my cock as we fuck, and I hear you telling me to do it. To fuck your ass, but this time no one interrupts us. No one comes in, and instead I pull you to me and press my cock against you."

"Oh fuck, I'm so close. Don't stop," she moaned.

"And then I'm inside your, I'm in your ass, Jane, and you're coming and telling me to fuck you harder. My cock is in you and you come so loudly. You shake and tighten even more as I fill you, my cock exploding inside you. Oh fuck, I want you. I want your ass so badly."

"Fuck, fuck, Thomas. I wish you were here. I wish you were inside me right now. In my ass. I've never done it. I've never been fucked there, but I want it so fucking badly. Oh god, I'm coming. Oh fuck me."

And then we were simply moans of pleasure and release

without any words at all. I pushed the blanket down and watched as I jerked off faster and faster, all the time picturing Jane beneath me even while I listened to her come over the phone. Her moans were deep and loud, and it had been so long since I had hear her that I wanted to scream. But more than anything in the world, I wanted to see her. I wanted to watch her face as she came for me, and I wanted to kiss her lips.

I watched as my cock began to spasm and spurt, my come shooting up onto my stomach and chest. My whole body shook as I came, and it was completely delicious.

"Oh god," she sighed, as the last of her orgasm slipped from her body. She began to laugh between moans, and it was the prettiest sound in the world. "I can't believe we just fucking did that."

"At least it was safer than last time. God, Jane, I miss you."

"I miss you, too. Fuck, what the hell is wrong with us?"

"We were just having a nice phone conversation. It was just old friends catching up."

"Yeah right. It was fucked up, but my god it was nice. I haven't come in weeks. I didn't even know that I needed it until you started telling me about them. I don't know why, but I think there's a little part of me that's jealous about you three. I love Sean, but having two men in bed is a fantasy that doesn't seem like it should be allowed to actually happen. It's really not fair."

"It doesn't feel real to me either most of the time. Especially right now."

"Are you going to tell Kelly?" She asked.

"About our phone call? What is there to say? We just talked. Are you going to tell Sean?"

"About what? A phone call with my bridesmaid? Sometimes it's okay to have a few secrets. Besides, there's too much to explain. And it's none of their business."

"Are you going to be okay?" I asked finally.

"Yes. Are you? The whole Kelly and Brent thing isn't going to kill you?"

"I'll survive. And thank you, Jane. That was not what I expected when I called you."

"Of course it was. It was exactly what you expected. I could hear you jerking off when I answered the fucking phone. You forget that I know you, Thomas."

I sighed again, but this time with a smile. She did know me. And that was strangely comforting right then.

"Okay, I'll see you tomorrow for our next planning thing. It's three, right? At your place?" I asked her, slipping back into normal.

"Yes. All my bridesmaids will be here, I can't wait. Just don't think I'm going to let you touch me, Thomas. This was its own thing."

"I would never," I said. "But, thank you. And I love you."

"I love you, too."

****

Kelly came into the bar around 3 p.m. and it was dead. It was a cold winter afternoon and the only people in the bar were a couple of German tourists drinking overly-hopped IPAs. I climbed out from behind the bar and gave her a big hug and a kiss. She looked up at me with a question in her eyes that I answered with a smile.

"Did you have fun?" I asked. She nodded and sat down.

"His office is nice. It was a slow day, and no one seemed to notice that we closed the door for an hour."

"Where did he fuck you? Over his desk?"

"On the floor. And against the wall. And then again on the floor."

"Sounds like a busy hour."

"Are you okay? I mean, was it a hard day? I was worried."

"Kelly, I'm fine. I was nervous for a little this morning, but I got over it. I love you two so much, and I think it's hot. How long did we fantasize about the two of you fucking? And now it happens almost every day. It's amazing. And I'm fine. And this time I'm not lying about it either. I really am okay."

"Do you want to come to the bathroom with me for a minute? I have something you might like." She winked at me and I felt myself growing hard in an instant.

I looked around the empty bar with a grin, before following her to the back. I told my two customers I'd be right back, and we slipped into the bathroom and locked the door. Without a word she had her jeans undone and down around her knees. I knelt instantly and pushed her against the wall, my mouth opening her cunt as I fucked her with my tongue.

"He came in me twice," she said. "God, he fucked me so hard, Thomas. He fucked me so goddamn hard. He had one finger up my ass as he bent me over his desk, and he was so deep inside me. It was so hot. Please don't stop."

By the time I stood up again, my cock was out and she turned to face the wall.

"I feel like such a whore," she moaned, "but I need more. God, I need to be fucked again. Please."

It was less than three minutes later that we walked out of the bathroom zipping up our jeans. I had filled her as well, but I was still hard. All my jealousy had vanished when I slid my cock inside her, and her moans of pleasure where all that mattered. I kissed her once more before climbing back behind the bar, and neither of us stopped smiling.

"It's really okay, isn't it?" she said.

"It is."

"I might have been more worried than you were. I guess I

didn't want to fuck anything up by pushing too hard."

"Kelly, if you don't push me hard I get stupid, remember? August is what happens when you stop pushing me. I get bored and complacent, and I start thinking it's more romantic to get drunk on wine than to fuck your brains out in the bathroom of the bar."

"He was sweet, too, you know. He told me if it was going to difficult we shouldn't."

"I'm glad you did. It was going to happen one way or another, so I'm glad it was like this. It's better than the alternative. Besides, I still love going down on you afterwards. I don't know why, and I don't care any more. I love it, and I love you."

"I love you, too. And tonight all three of us can fuck once again. Just like normal people."

I kissed her one last time before she left, and I could smell her and taste her on my lips. I watched her ass as she walked out the door and smiled to myself. There had been a brief moment when I considered telling her about my phone call with Jane, but I pushed it away almost instantly. Some secrets are important.

Chapter Thirty-Two

Sean's parents gave the couple something of a dream for their wedding. It had started as a joke, but by summer's end the room had been booked and it quickly became a reality. Back in high school, Jane read that the Museum of Natural History rented out the great hall with the Blue Whale hanging from the ceiling for private events, and ever since then it was her dream location. It was decked out in greens, lights flashing everywhere, and from the skylights overhead to the fish tanks surrounding the space, it was gorgeous. The tables were set in red and green, and the whale hung in the center of the room, a giant reminder of just how small we are. None of us could believe they had done it, but we stared in awe, marvelling at everything around us.

The bridesmaids had a room to the side where we sat with Jane before the service, going over the last minute concerns and helping her get ready. She was looking better than she had in months, and it wasn't just the wedding. A week beforehand the doctors told her she was in the clear. They would need tests for at least a year to follow, but as far as they could tell, she had beaten the cancer, and it would only be downhill from then on. She moved between laughter and tears, and it was hard to imagine that just a year ago, none of it had even been a whisper on the horizon. Her old self was more present than ever as we sat in the dressing room watching her get her hair done. She was wearing black stockings, a garter, matching panties and bra, and nothing else. The hairdresser had looked at the three of us like we were crazy, but with Jane's assurance, she went to work without comment.

"Are you seriously wearing black underwear. On your wedding day? I mean come on, Jane. I know you used to be a baby goth, but is that necessary?" Brent was pacing back and forth, trying not to look at our nearly naked friend, and he was clearly concerned.

"Dude, have you seen me in white? Look at my skin, and try to picture me in white bridal lingerie. It's enough that I'm wearing a white dress, I have no desire to look like a corpse when I take it off. Besides, I look sexy for the first time in months. Come on, look at this, Brent. If you weren't so fucking in love with those two, you'd be all over me."

"Watch out," I said, "he might be all over you anyway."

"Yeah, you would know," she said, sticking her tongue out at me.

All three of us were in black tuxedos with red ties and green cumberbunds. We looked good: we were clean, shaven, and our hair had been managed by one of the best barbers in New York. Our shoes were brightly polished, our shirts pressed, and for a moment I wondered why we didn't wear tuxedos more often. We were three handsome men, and we were going to watch our friend get married to Doctor Perfect no matter what.

When the hairdresser finally left, the four of us sat around Jane for a final champagne toast. She was still in her lingerie, and while she was thin, the color was back in her face, and she was almost glowing.

"To Jane, the only bride I've ever seen in her underwear," Brent began. "You have been such a good friend, and if Sean deserves you then I'm a fucking turnip. But if it's not going to be one of us, I suppose it may as well be him. To both of you, with all my love."

We cheered, trying not to spill our drinks on our tuxes. All of us but Jane emptied our glasses before Jason refilled them again. It was his turn and he took his time. As the most serious of us all, we patiently waited on his words.

"Sometimes I don't know why you hang out with us. Especially in your underwear, and especially with those two in the room, but whatever temporary insanity struck you when you asked us to do this, I'm glad of it. It hasn't been an easy time. I can't imagine planning a wedding is ever easy, but with everything else you've been going through, I find myself being even more in awe of you. You are the strongest, most brilliant woman I know, and that's saying a lot.

"So, here's to a happy marriage, a healthy new year, and to a continued friendship if you'll have us. I love you, and I am so happy for you."

We clinked once more, all of us trying not to cry. Fucking weddings always drive me to drink, and this one was not going to be an exception.

"If you ruin my mascara, I'm going to get very upset," Jane said rubbing her eyes gently with her fingertips. "Maybe we don't need another one. I don't think I can deal with it."

"I was just going to say that I've never been to a wedding where I've slept with the bride before. I mean, I've slept with a few after their weddings, but this is a first."

I raised my glass, but they kept looking at me, as if that wasn't enough. What they hell did they want from me? There were no words to describe my happiness. There were no smart, witty, or sweet things I could say that would come close to capturing my emotions.

"That was the sweetest thing I could think of. I'm serious," I said. "Jane, I love you, I want you, and I'm so fucking disappointed that you're getting married, because now I'll never get to have sex with you again. I want to be happy, but seeing you here in your underwear is only reminding me again how fucking stupid I am."

"It's okay, Thomas," she said smiling. "I never would have married you no matter how many times you asked. Of course, you did miss out on this ass." She turned around and bent over, her stockings and garter framing her bottom perfectly, and all three of us groaned as we pretended to reach out and slap her.

"Well, that is some consolation I suppose," I continued. "As for the ass, I'll never forgive myself, and if you ever say that again I'm going to go insane and move into a cave in Central Park. But seriously, this wasn't supposed to be about how much I still want to fuck you. Um, make love to you."

"Finish the speech," Brent shouted, his hands around his mouth.

"Fine! Jane, you are the prettiest bride in the history of the world. You are going to make that man so happy he won't know what to do with himself, and if he ever so much as looks at you funny, I'm going to break his legs. I love you and wish you both the best."

I raised my glass and everyone sighed their relief as we leaned in. Then I couldn't resist.

"Also, I hope the whale doesn't fall on you before you kiss the groom."

We drank our third glass of champagne and hugged her again. We were careful not to mess with her hair, and she was careful not to let us get too close to her ass. It was a long while before we stepped back, and there were at least two or three of us that required tissues almost instantly. Jane vanished behind the folding screen, and we stood impatiently waiting for her to return in her dress.

"Thomas," she called out. "Come help me."

I winked at the other two, made an appropriately obscene gesture, and stepped behind the screen. She wrapped me in her arms instantly and kissed me on the mouth. I kissed her back, and before I knew what was happening her mouth was open and her tongue was pushing between my lips. The kiss didn't last long, but it was long enough to bring a flush to my cheeks. My hands moved instantly to her ass and she didn't move them.

"Thank you," she said. "For everything. For sleeping with me, for taking me to the doctor, and for being here no matter what. That last time together was stupid and crazy, and I wouldn't trade it for anything in all the world. And don't even get me started on that phone call. Maybe I'm crazy to be getting married. Maybe I should have married you, I don't know. But we're here, and I can't say thank you enough. I love you, and I'll always love you."

"I'll always love you too," I said. Her ass was soft and warm, and it was all I could do not to kiss her again. "But if we don't get you dressed they're going to have to pull me off you, Jane. Seriously, you look so gorgeous I can hardly stand it. Let me help you with the dress."

She stepped into and I held it up as she climbed in. It corseted up the back, and I helped her lace it up as she struggled with the neck, and made sure everything was lined up correctly. When I finally tied the back off I kissed her neck as I held her there for just a moment longer. As she turned around I stepped back and smiled, my eyes opened wide at the gorgeous sight in front of me. She was stunning and she was alive. Her cheeks were flushed, her lipsticked slightly smudged, and it was perfect.

"You look incredible. Seriously, he's going to want to do you right there at the altar. If we had more time, I'd bend you over right here."

I pushed the screen back, moving it out of the way as she stood with her hands folded in front of her, and Brent and Jason gasped as they stared at her in her white dress for the first time. She turned around for us and we clapped and hollered, each one of us telling her how hot she was.

"I don't think girl bridesmaids would have done this," she said. "I mean they would have ooh-ed and ah-ed, but there's something nice about being told you look fuckable in your wedding dress. Hopefully, Sean thinks the same thing."

"If he doesn't, we'll be right here," Brent said.

She twirled once more, and less than two minutes later a child came in telling us it was about to start. We moved in closely, smiled at her as we carefully avoided stepping on her dress, and then it was done. She stood at the door as the music played, and from where we were standing we could just see the groom and his three groomsmen – in long red dresses – walk up the aisle. Jane took a deep breath as her father stepped up next to her and took her arm.

The three bridesmaids stepped out in front of her, me in front, as we gave her one last squeeze. I took a deep breath, smiled one more time at the bride, and began the long walk down the aisle with Brent and Jason trailing behind.

Chapter Thirty-Three

New Year's Eve was cold, the wind blew hard, and New Yorkers bundled up in scarves and gloves as they huddled around Times Square to watch the ball drop. The news was still focused on the impending collapse of civilization due to the Y2K bug, but as far as we could tell, everything had already been fixed that needed to be fixed. Richard Branson promised his customers that he would be in the air on one of his planes when the clock turned, and the media swirled around it because there wasn't anything else to say. It was the end of the millenium, the end of the century, and for many of us, it was the end of our youth and the beginning of something we couldn't begin to grasp.

We vacuumed and cleaned the apartment, filled the bathtub with bottles of champagne and cold beer, and made the place as festive as we could. Martin took care of the music, brought his bartender friend in, and generally made sure it would be an event no one would forget. Brent and I spent much of the morning so excited we couldn't contain ourselves. We had demanded that Kelly not come over until two in the afternoon, and we knew that she would be driving herself crazy with anticipation. It was Brent who came up with the idea that we shouldn't let her come the night before, and she whimpered and begged like I had never seen. We had to struggle not to give in, but we held strong throughout the evening. When it became clear she was going to come if we touched her at all, we simply lay her down on her back, her hands tied above her head, as we jerked off over her naked body.

We were tempted to make her sleep that way, her tits covered in our come and her hands tied above her head, but in the end, we did relent, and we held her between us when we finally were all able to sleep.

I invited one of the other bartenders from Saints to come that afternoon. He had commented on how hot Kelly was almost every time she came in, and when I brought up the idea, his eyes nearly popped out of his head. He was handsome, although nearly ten years older than me, but somehow I suspected that the age wouldn't be a problem at all. If anything, Kelly would most likely love getting fucked by men in their thirties or even forties. Brent had two co-workers he promised he could trust, and while the idea of her fucking people I didn't know was hard to process, it was also so hot that I couldn't say no. It was mildly surprising how many people we had to ask before we found our three, but by one in the afternoon, there were five men in living room wearing their best suits.

All she knew was that she was to arrive at two, go directly into my room and close the door behind her. She was to undress completely, kneel on the floor, and make sure all of the lights were on. At first she begged us to let it be dark, but we held firm. She was going to get fucked in the light, and there would be nowhere to hide. Nowhere to pretend that she was doing something else.

The men were nervous as they stood waiting, but the photos Brent and I showed them definitely helped pass the time. We had posed her naked in the bed, on the floor, and on all fours with her fingers inside her cunt. By the time we heard the door open on the other side of the apartment, half of them were fully hard just from the pictures.

"So, you all know the deal. Brent and I are the only two who can fuck her without a condom. You can use her mouth without one, and you can come on her face, but don't come anywhere near her pussy. If she asks for something it's okay to do it, but if you're not sure, look at one of us and we'll either nod or shake our heads.

"This is supposed to be fun, and remember, it's been her biggest fantasy for a long time. She's going to love it, but don't forget that she's a real person. She's twenty-two years old, brilliant, and talented. This afternoon we may be using her as a fuck toy, but it doesn't make her less worthy of our respect."

I had gone over the speech with Brent, and I felt it was important. It was one thing to give her what she wanted, but I didn't want one of those guys to feel like he was getting something he deserved. They were getting a gift, and they had to know it.

I finally walked over to the bedroom door and knocked gently. I couldn't imagine what was going through her head, but after a few moments I heard her little voice telling me to come in.

When I opened the door I had to hold onto the frame to keep myself from falling. She was kneeling on the floor, a pillow beneath her, and she was breathing so quickly I thought she might pass out. I could already smell her excitement, and she looked so pretty it was nearly too much. I stepped into the room, and walked around her, the four other men filling in behind me as we formed a circle. She kept her head down as Brent closed the door, and even when he joined us, she still didn't look up.

"This is the slut who we're going to fuck," I said quietly. "You can use her mouth and her cunt. You can touch her, finger her, and eat her pussy if you want. She is here for us to use and to fuck."

She tried to hold in a whimper, but still it slipped out of her mouth as she raised her head ever so slightly. She had no idea who the other three men would be, and it made it that much more exciting.

"Oh, I almost forgot." I stared right at her as I talked. "You can also fuck her ass if you want. This little whore loves getting ass fucked."

The words that came out of her mouth were incomprehensible, but the meaning was clear. We had talked about it all before, and her fantasy was not a light one. She didn't want anyone to hold back. If she was going to do it, she was going all the way, and it made her more nervous than she could possibly explain.

We moved closer to her, each man looking at her little body on the floor, and when I was standing right behind her, I finally grabbed her by the hair and pulled her head back. There were sighs of praise from the men in the room as they got the first full glimpse of her naked body, and she looked up and around the room, fear and lust showing in her eyes in equal amount. As soon as my hand went to my suit pants, the other four men stepped closer, and before she could say a word there were five cocks only inches from her face.

"Are you sure you want this?" I asked, as the men stroked themselves, staring down at her open mouth. "This is the last chance to say no. Do you want these five men to fuck you? Is that what you want?"

"Yes," she said without pause. It was so quick I felt my stomach clench, but there was no going back. "Please, yes."

I held her hair as the man to my left instantly shoved his cock into her mouth. She reached up, grabbing two more in her hands, and then it was a blur of bodies as we all tried to get closer. Men reached down and felt her tits as we took turns letting her suck our cocks. They touched her hair, and one even reached down between her legs and shoved his fingers inside her when she leaned up to take me between her lips. Her hands were busy jerking us off as she switched between us, and I'm not sure who was more surprised by her vigor, she or I.

Brent and I caught each other's eyes as she knelt, blowing our co-workers, and it's a hard moment to describe. In that one look there was jealousy, fear, excitement, and overwhelming love. Our little girl was getting her mouth used by men we hardly knew, and she was nearly lost in her desire like nothing we had ever seen. There were moments when I wanted to hold her and tell her it was over, but my excitement overpowered me, and I was lost to desires I didn't know I had.

When Brent finally pulled her up, we watched the men attack her, pulling her in for kisses, their hands groping her body as she turned this way and that. I watched the bartender press his hard cock between her ass cheeks and she pushed back onto him without even knowing who it was. She was panting with desire, but for a moment I wasn't sure if I could handle what was next.

"Put her on the bed," Brent finally said, not giving me any more time to consider it. She was lifted, laid down on her back, and her legs were spread open by his two colleagues. We stood there for a moment, looking at the small girl panting like she was in heat, and her pussy was wet and obscene. She was almost unrecognizable. The look on her face was one of abject desire, and she was begging within seconds.

"Someone fuck me," she began. "Please, anyone, just fuck me."

She lay back, her hands between her legs as the other three men fumbled with condoms. There was cursing and swearing, but it was finally my friend from the bar, his cock nearly as thick as Brent's, who climbed between her legs and started to fuck her. I held my breath for just a moment, and then suddenly I had her by the hair, her mouth around me as Brent knelt on her other side. She moved between our two cocks, sucking us between moans, and the three of us watched as the men took turns. Within minutes each one had a chance with her, and she was crying and coming so hard her body looked like it was convulsing. She tried to focus on us, but it was impossible, and we simply held her as the last man fucked her hard.

Not one of the men took of his suit, and it was part of the plan that we loved the most. She was the only naked person in the room, and each of our rigid cocks stood out from our pants as we gathered around her. The man fucking her was wearing a grey pinstripe, and all we could see was his cock as he slammed in and out of her, fucking our little girl on my bed.

"Oh, shit, I'm gonna come," he said, leaning over her body and kissing her mouth with surprising tenderness. He pulled back and looked into her eyes as he tensed, and it was clear to everyone when he started. "You are so tight," he kept moaning, as he unloaded into the condom.

The second he was done, I lay down on my back and pulled her on top of me. If she was going to fuck everyone, I was going to have a front row seat. I slid my bare cock inside her, and she moaned out her pleasure as she kissed my face.

"You are such a pretty little girl," I said, pushing into her as she writhed above me. "We are going to fuck you so hard."

She kissed me once more before her head was pulled away and a hard cock shoved between her lips. I couldn't tell who it was, and suddenly I found that I didn't care. When she sat up and someone else took my place in her cunt, I simply held her tighter, listening to the sounds coming from her body. I took her back after just a few seconds, reclaiming my space in her pussy, when someone else moved up behind her.

"Can I fuck her ass?" he asked. "Seriously?"

I didn't have time to answer before Kelly pulled the cock from her mouth and screamed out.

"Do it. Fuck my ass. I don't even know who you are, but do it."

And then then someone else was working himself inside her ass for the first time since we started dating. I could feel him sliding in against me, and she screamed out as she pushed back onto us both; she was instantly coming again. She kept sucking on the dick in her mouth and bucking her hips, and she was completely full. We had talked about it so many times, but here she was with three men using her, and it was all I could do not to come.

Seconds later the guy in her mouth called out, and I watched as she swallowed his load without a second of hesitation. She licked him clean even as the guy in her ass began to scream as well. She pushed back onto us as he fucked her faster, but this time she gave out the command.

"Come on my back," she said. "Pull out and come on me. I want more."

A second later he was done, and I wrapped my arms around her as I listened to him jerking off behind her, his come finally splashing onto her back amid his groans of release. Without another moment's pause Brent pulled her off me, his own look of lust stronger than I had ever seen before.

"I want to fuck my little slut," he said, sliding into her cunt. "You are such a filthy little whore, and I love you."

The other three men had all come, but they still stood around the bed, their hands on their cock as they struggled to get hard again. The next half hour was a blur. Kelly came more times than any of us could count, and evey man there fucked her again. For one strange moment in the middle, Brent and I stood back as the three men used her on their own, and it's something I'll never forget. His friends were in her ass and cunt, and she was sucking my co-working as he fucked her mouth without holding back. She seemed completely unaware of who was who, and maybe it didn't matter. Kelly wanted to get lost, and she was so far gone in her need to be fucked, that the who was no longer important.

"It's kind of pretty," I said, as I put my arm around him.

"It's fucking hot," he said. "I'm never going to forget this."

"Neither will she. Or them. Or any of us. How many times does something like this actually happen?"

"Are you jealous?" he asked, suddenly looking up at me. "I mean, is it hard to watch?"

"I'm good for another minute, and then I need to fuck her again and call her my pretty little girl. Are we going to throw them out soon?"

He nodded as we watched, and before long they rolled her onto her back as they all pulled off their condoms. She lay there, looking up, her eyes glazed over, her pussy crimson and soaking wet, but they didn't stop. Each one of them stared at her as if she was the last women in the world as they jerked off faster and faster.

"Come on me," she moaned, "all of you. Come on me, and then let me get fucked again. Just one more time."

The plan had been fairly loose, but we let them know that once they all came on her body one last time, the party was over. We were going to stay, but they were to leave, and close the door behind them. There were no photos, no trophies, and once it was done, it was done. They could gossip all they wanted among themselves, but if they brought it up again with us, we would pretend it had never happened. Maybe it was caution, or maybe survival, but either way those were the rules and they felt important.

We took a step closer, our own cocks still sticking out from within our suit pants as the first man came, unloading onto her face and neck as she leaned up and sucked his cock clean. He knelt, panting as the other two leaned over further, one of them sliding his fingers into her wet pussy as he came on her tits. A few minutes later the third one came on her stomach, and by the time they were done she was a filthy mess. Her skin was bruised and covered in come, and her face was as red as her cunt. Her chest rose and fell with each breath, and without a sound I gripped Brent's hand in mine. Kelly had never looked prettier, and I had never been more in love.

When they filed out of the door, I went to my dresser and pulled out my old thirty-five millimeter camera. She lay there watching as I came back to the bed and slowly started taking pictures of her naked body.

"I want to remember this," I said. "I want to always remember our sweet little girl getting fucked by five men."

As I kept snapping, Brent moved between her legs, his cock in his hand. He teased her with the head, and she was moaning again in seconds. I leaned down and shot him just as he slid inside her, and she opened easily around his girth. He pulled off his jacket as they fucked, and his shirt and tie followed a second later. I kept taking pictures as he fucked her, and when he lay down on top of her, not caring at all about her come-soaked skin, I moved up to her face. Her lips were swollen, her eyes were red, and there was still come on her lips from one of the three men I didn't know. I clicked three more times before finally putting the camera down. I took off my own suit before leaning in and kissing her.

She licked her lips and then kissed me back, her neck arched as Brent moved inside her. I lay down next to her, my hand rubbing the come into her skin as the they fucked. and I kissed her cheek as I watched.

"Did you like getting fucked?" I asked.

"I'm still getting fucked," she said, her breath short as she arched up to meet him.

"Was it enough?" She looked at me for a moment and then looked down at Brent. Without a word, she pulled him from her and rolled over onto her knees above me. For a few seconds she simply stayed there, her head down as she tried to catch her breathe, but then she looked up at me and smiled.

"No," she whispered. "I need something else."

Brent looked at me and shrugged, before pulling off his pants and climbing behind her once more. She didn't respond at all when he slid back inside her cunt, but her eyes never once left mine. Kelly knelt over me as he fucked her like so many times before, but nothing was the same.

"What do you need, Babygirl?" I asked, leaning in closely so she could whisper it to me. "Tell Daddy what you want, you filthy little whore. Tell me, and maybe I'll let you have it."

"I want…" She could hardly speak, and I wasn't sure if it was out of fear or embarrassment.

"Tell Daddy," I said taking her chin in my hand and pulling her eyes back up to mine. "It's okay, Babygirl. Everything is okay, just tell me what you need."

"Uncle Brent," she whispered. "I want him to fuck me."

She closed her eyes as he moved faster inside her, and then finally she looked up once more, her eyes open wide as she blurted it out.

"I want Uncle Brent to fuck my ass."

I held her there for a long time, and all the movement on the bed stopped in a heartbeat. She didn't once break eye contact, and I tried my best not to make any expression at all. It was the one thing we had never done, the one thing she refused, and now she was ready. Now she needed it, and there was no one who could say no.

"Do it," I said, looking up at him. "Fuck her tight, little ass until you come. You won't get another chance."

"Are you sure?" he asked, and I realized the question wasn't to her at all. I nodded my head as he pulled out of her body. I leaned in and kissed her as she closed her eyes, her fists clenching the sheets in tight balls. Her lips were hot and her breath tasted of sex.

"Okay, Babygirl," I whispered. "Just breathe now. He's going to do it. Uncle Brent is going to fuck your ass as Daddy watches."

"Wait," she said, looking over her shoulder. "I want Brent. For this, I just want Brent."

"Do it," I said, nodding my head again. "Fuck Kelly's ass."

She screamed as he pushed against her, and I held her steady. There were no more words and I didn't care about anything. I was terrified and turned on, and it was a place I was more and more comfortable with every day. Her eyes opened wide as he moved behind her, but I couldn't see a thing.

"Is he inside you?" I asked. She simply nodded and bit her lip, and then she closed her eyes and pushed back onto him with a scream.

"Oh fuck," he yelled grabbing her hips, and then it was done. I reached my hand between her legs, touching her pussy before reaching up until I could feel him sliding inside her.

"Fuck her," I said. "Hard."

And then they were moving, and she was crying and coming for the millionth time that night. She arched her back as he pushed into her, and she didn't stop coming as he filled her over and over again. I was harder than I had been all day, and I moved down just enough to rub against the lips of her cunt.

"Let me feel you both," she said. He reached down and helped me, until suddenly we were both inside her once more, but this time I was looking into her eyes as he moved inside her ass. She was sobbing as she kissed me, and by the time Brent and I came there was nothing left in any of us. He filled her ass as I did the same with her cunt, and when we rolled her to her side, her body between us, she moved between laughing and crying.

"I love you," she said, her body still shaking. "I love you both so much. So, so much."

Brent kissed her hair, and I kissed her lips, before she turned and kissed him as well. We held her there between us, her body still sticky and sweaty, and it was done. We had fucked like never before, with too many orgasms to count, and it was over. It was New Year's Eve, our girlfriend has just fucked five men as we watched, and we were in love. We were all madly, madly in love.

"We love you, too," we said at the same time, before all three of us broke out into laughter.

Chapter Thirty-Four

We had wisely left enough time between the fucking and the party for us to take a long nap. The three other guys had only been there for two hours, and we fell asleep almost instantly once we were done. It wasn't until we awoke around nine that we realized we hadn't even bothered to shower, and the room smelled like people had been fucking for weeks. We crawled out of bed, made our way to the shower, and we held up Kelly's limp body as we washed off her come-soaked skin. She was sore and exhausted, but the nap had helped. New Year's Eve was going to be better than ever. Even in the shower she often looked up at us and broke out in a grin of thanks, completely unable to believe we had actually done it.

Brent and I put our suits back on, and Kelly put on a silver dress that came almost to the floor. She wore exactly nothing underneath it, and it clung to her body in all the right places. When we finally opened the door to the living room, it was half full and people were still coming in. Jason and Katie came to us instantly, hugging us and wishing us a happy New Year's, without knowing at all what had just happened. Martin and Stephanie were getting the bar finalized, and even Zen and Spider were dressed to the nines, drinking martinis out of real glasses.

"So, I think the world is not going to end," Jason said, as the five of us stood near the bar, nursing our drinks. "I've given it some thought, read a lot of articles, and I think it's a good bet. There's a slim possibility that I'm wrong, but we mostly likely won't know if I am."

"That's why we're having this party," Brent said. "If it does end, I want to be with you. With my oldest friends, my girlfriend, my boyfriend, all of you."

Jason still shook his head when we said it out loud, but Katie sighed as she looked at the three of us.

"You all look so beautiful. I didn't even know you guys owned suits."

"Thank you," Kelly said. "You look stunning as well."

Katie was wearing a skin tight black dress that I had never imagined on her. Her hair was tied up, and for the first time since I had known her, she wore dark red lipstick. Jason kissed her and held her close, and it was perfect.

"If we have to listen to that fucking Prince song one more time I'm going to lose my shit though," I said. "Martin promised he'd only play it once, but I am so tired of partying like it's anything. Let's just party like it's now. And us. I don't know. Let's just party."

The drinks kept flowing, and by eleven it was packed and everyone was dancing. Kelly was pressed between our bodies, and at one point Brent and I lifted her off the ground and held her between us as we danced, both of us kissing her pretty face. We drank more champagne than should be allowed, we smoked more weed than was healthy, but it wasn't until a half hour before midnight that we realized Jane wasn't there.

"Hey, Jason," I said, finally finding him in the kitchen looking for a beer. "Have you heard from Jane? I haven't seen her yet. Aren't they coming back from Aruba tonight?"

"Yeah, she should be here. I haven't heard anything, but she was planning on it. Maybe her flight was delayed?"

I kept looking around the apartment, going through all three rooms, saying hello to everyone I knew, and welcoming those I didn't, but as the time went by I got more and more frantic. I had promised her, and now she was nowhere to be found. We couldn't end the year like this. It wasn't allowed.

"Dude, where have you been?" Brent called out when he saw me in our bedroom. "We have like two minutes, and Kelly's going to freak if you're not here."

Sighing, I walked into the living room where Martin had turned on the giant television. The music was off and people were standing in small groups staring at the screen, watching the giant red ball slowly begin to descend in Times Square. Jason and Katie found us quickly, and the five of us stood there even as I fidgeted back and forth, looking constantly around the room. One minute left and still no sign of Jane. I gripped Kelly's hand hard while Brent held the other one as we watched, but it wasn't right.

"Did I miss it?" came a deep voice next to me. Jane pushed into our little circle between me and Jason. My arms were around her in a second, and I held her so tightly I thought she might break. When I finally put her down she smiled and sighed. "Sean's parking the car, but I ran up."

Her cheeks were red, and for the first time in her life she looked tan. I kissed her instantly, as we opened up the cirlce enough to welcome her. She gave me a grin, raised her eyebrow and took my free hand in her own. All around us people were counting down, and I finally let out my breath as I looked at all of my friends. We leaned in closer, our heads nearly touching as the entire city tensed up, ready to spring.

The year was ending, the century was turning, and the next thousand years had to better than the last. I'm sure there were some low points, but as far as I was concerned the next ten centuries were going to fucking rock. I leaned in and kissed Jane on the cheek before Brent and Kelly and I all pressed our faces together. There was nothing easy or pretty about a three way kiss, but we didn't care at all. The only thing that mattered was we were there.

The only thing that mattered was that we were together.

"Ten, nine, eight!"

Epilogue

Maddy lay on her bed staring at her packed bags on the floor. Her year had been crazy, she wasn't sure what to do with herself, but suddenly it was January and she was going to New York. She was getting away from home, from her parents, and from her wonderful, lovely, and controlling sister. She was going to be free, and she was going to be gone.

"Hey, honey, there's a letter for you."

"Thanks," she said, taking it without even looking up at her mother. When she saw the address she slammed her doors and climbed back into bed. She reached beneath the covers and slid her pajama bottoms off before pulling off her shirt. Completely naked, she rolled around in the warm sheets as ever so slowly she opened the envelope, her heart pounding in her chest as she looked inside. She pulled out the letter first and devoured the words. Three times she read it, her fingers moving between her legs on the second reading, and not looking to stop any time soon. When she finally put it down, she pulled out the four photos and held them up in the dim light in her room.

There was Kelly on her back, smiling into the camera with her legs spread wide and her breasts and face glistening with a familiar coat of white. The next one was Kelly on her knees with Brent inside her. She could see his thick cock opening Kelly's cunt, and it was the most obscene photo she had ever seen in her life. The third one was her mouth wrapped around Thomas's cock, his eyes looking straight into the camera, and she arched her back, pushing her fingers deeper inside her.

The last was photo was all three of them, naked and wrapped up in each other's arms. Their smiles were uncontrollable, and she grinned as she stared at it. She turned it over in her hand, and there on the back, in Kelly's careful script, it read, "We can't wait to see you!"

Maddy held the photos to her chest as she clenched her thighs around her hand. She closed her eyes, remembered everything in vivid detail, and seconds later she was moaning their names as she came over and over again.

Printed in Great Britain
by Amazon